LADY SUSAN
and
LOVE AND FRIENDSHIP

WORLD CLASSICS IN LARGE PRINT

British Authors Series

The aim of World Classics in Large Print is
to make the most enduring and popular works of
literature available in comfortable softcover editions
printed in clear, easy-to-read large type.

LADY SUSAN

and

LOVE AND FRIENDSHIP

and Other Early Works

Jane Austen

The LARGE PRINT
BOOK COMPANY

SANBORNVILLE, NEW HAMPSHIRE

Lady Susan was written in 1795 and
Love and Friendship and Other Early Works about 1790.
None of these writings were published
during Jane Austen's lifetime

Typeset in 16 point Adobe Caslon type

ISBN 978-1-59688-100-6

This edition of *Lady Susan* and *Love and Friendship
and Other Early Writings*
by Jane Austen
published in June 2007
by
The Large Print Book Company
P.O. Box 970
Sanbornville, NH 03872-0970

CONTENTS

LADY SUSAN

I. *Lady Susan Vernon to Mr. Vernon*

Langford, Dec.

MY DEAR BROTHER,—I can no longer refuse myself
the pleasure of profiting by your kind invitation when
we last parted of spending some weeks with you at
Churchhill, and, therefore, if quite convenient to you
and Mrs. Vernon to receive me at present, I shall hope
within a few days to be introduced to a sister whom I
have so long desired to be acquainted with. My kind
friends here are most affectionately urgent with me
to prolong my stay, but their hospitable and cheerful
dispositions lead them too much into society for my
present situation and state of mind; and I impatiently
look forward to the hour when I shall be admitted into
Your delightful retirement.

I long to be made known to your dear little children,
in whose hearts I shall be very eager to secure an interest. I shall soon have need for all my fortitude, as I
am on the point of separation from my own daughter.
The long illness of her dear father prevented my paying her that attention which duty and affection equally
dictated, and I have too much reason to fear that the
governess to whose care I consigned her was unequal
to the charge. I have therefore resolved on placing her

at one of the best private schools in town, where I shall have an opportunity of leaving her myself in my way to you. I am determined, you see, not to be denied admittance at Churchhill. It would indeed give me most painful sensations to know that it were not in your power to receive me.

Your most obliged and affectionate sister,
S. VERNON.

II. *Lady Susan Vernon to Mrs. Johnson*

Langford.

YOU WERE MISTAKEN, my dear Alicia, in supposing me fixed at this place for the rest of the winter: it grieves me to say how greatly you were mistaken, for I have seldom spent three months more agreeably than those which have just flown away. At present, nothing goes smoothly; the females of the family are united against me. You foretold how it would be when I first came to Langford, and Mainwaring is so uncommonly pleasing that I was not without apprehensions for myself. I remember saying to myself, as I drove to the house, "I like this man, pray Heaven no harm come of it!" But I was determined to be discreet, to bear in mind my being only four months a widow, and to be as quiet as possible: and I have been so, my dear creature; I have admitted no one's attentions but Mainwaring's. I have avoided all general flirtation whatever; I have distinguished no creature besides, of all the numbers resorting hither, except Sir James Martin, on whom I bestowed a little notice, in order to detach him from Miss Mainwaring; but, if the world could know my motive *there* they would honour me. I have been called an unkind mother, but it was the sacred impulse of maternal affection, it was the advantage of my daughter that led me on; and if that daughter were not the greatest simpleton on earth, I might have been rewarded for my exertions as I ought.

Sir James did make proposals to me for Frederica; but Frederica, who was born to be the torment of my life, chose to set herself so violently against the match that I thought it better to lay aside the scheme for the present. I have more than once repented that I did not marry him myself; and were he but one degree less contemptibly weak I certainly should: but I must own myself rather romantic in that respect, and that riches only will not satisfy me. The event of all this is very provoking: Sir James is gone, Maria highly incensed, and Mrs. Mainwaring insupportably jealous; so jealous, in short, and so enraged against me, that, in the fury of her temper, I should not be surprized at her appealing to her guardian, if she had the liberty of addressing him: but there your husband stands my friend; and the kindest, most amiable action of his life was his throwing her off for ever on her marriage. Keep up his resentment, therefore, I charge you. We are now in a sad state; no house was ever more altered; the whole party are at war, and Mainwaring scarcely dares speak to me. It is time for me to be gone; I have therefore determined on leaving them, and shall spend, I hope, a comfortable day with you in town within this week. If I am as little in favour with Mr. Johnson as ever, you must come to me at 10 Wigmore street; but I hope this may not be the case, for as Mr. Johnson, with all his faults, is a man to whom that great word "respectable" is always given, and I am known to be so intimate with his wife, his slighting me has an awkward look.

I take London in my way to that insupportable spot, a country village; for I am really going to Churchhill. Forgive me, my dear friend, it is my last resource. Were there another place in England open to me I would prefer it. Charles Vernon is my aversion; and I am afraid of his wife. At Churchhill, however, I must remain till I have something better in view. My young lady accompanies me to town, where I shall deposit her under the care of Miss Summers, in Wigmore street, till she becomes a little more reasonable. She will make good connections there, as the girls are all of the best families. The price is immense, and much beyond what I can ever attempt to pay.

Adieu, I will send you a line as soon as I arrive in town.

Yours ever,
S. VERNON.

III. *Mrs. Vernon to Lady De Courcy*

Churchhill.

MY DEAR MOTHER,—I am very sorry to tell you that it will not be in our power to keep our promise of spending our Christmas with you; and we are prevented that happiness by a circumstance which is not likely to make us any amends. Lady Susan, in a letter to her brother-in-law, has declared her intention of visiting us almost immediately; and as such a visit is in all probability merely an affair of convenience, it is impossible to conjecture its length. I was by no means prepared for such an event, nor can I now account for her ladyship's conduct; Langford appeared so exactly the place for her in every respect, as well from the elegant and expensive style of living there, as from her particular attachment to Mr. Mainwaring, that I was very far from expecting so speedy a distinction, though I always imagined from her increasing friendship for us since her husband's death that we should, at some future period, be obliged to receive her. Mr. Vernon, I think, was a great deal too kind to her when he was in Staffordshire; her behaviour to him, independent of her general character, has been so inexcusably artful and ungenerous since our marriage was first in agitation that no one less amiable and mild than himself could have overlooked it all; and though, as his brother's widow, and in narrow circumstances, it was proper to render her pecuniary assistance, I cannot help thinking his pressing invitation to her to visit us at Churchhill perfectly unnecessary. Disposed, however, as he always is to think the best of everyone, her display of grief, and professions of regret, and general resolutions of prudence, were sufficient to soften his heart and make him really confide in her sincerity; but, as for myself, I am still unconvinced, and plausibly as her ladyship has now written, I cannot make up my mind till I better understand her real meaning in coming to us. You may guess, therefore, my dear madam, with what feelings I look forward to her arrival. She will have occasion for all those attractive powers for which she is celebrated to gain any share of my regard; and I shall certainly endeavour to guard myself against their influence, if not accompanied by something more substantial. She expresses a most eager desire of being acquainted with me, and makes very gracious mention of my children but I am not quite weak enough to suppose a woman who has behaved with inattention, if not with unkindness, to her own child, should be attached to any of mine. Miss Vernon is to be placed at a school in London before her mother comes to us which I am glad of, for her sake and my own. It must be to her advantage to be separated from her mother, and a girl of sixteen who has received so wretched an education, could not be a very desirable companion here. Reginald has long wished, I know, to see the captivating Lady Susan, and we shall depend on his joining our party soon. I am glad to hear that my father continues so well; and am, with best love, &c.,

CATHERINE VERNON.

IV. *Mr. De Courcy to Mrs. Vernon*

Parklands.

MY DEAR SISTER,—I congratulate you and Mr. Vernon on being about to receive into your family the most accomplished coquette in England. As a very distinguished flirt I have always been taught to consider her, but it has lately fallen in my way to hear some particulars of her conduct at Langford: which prove that she does not confine herself to that sort of honest flirtation which satisfies most people, but aspires to the more delicious gratification of making a whole family miserable. By her behaviour to Mr. Mainwaring she gave jealousy and wretchedness to his wife, and by her attentions to a young man previously attached to Mr. Mainwaring's sister deprived an amiable girl of her lover.

I learnt all this from Mr. Smith, now in this neighbourhood (I have dined with him, at Hurst and Wilford), who is just come from Langford where he was a fortnight with her ladyship, and who is therefore well qualified to make the communication.

What a woman she must be! I long to see her, and shall certainly accept your kind invitation, that I may form some idea of those bewitching powers which can do so much—engaging at the same time, and in the same house, the affections of two men, who were neither of them at liberty to bestow them- -and all this without the charm of youth! I am glad to find Miss Vernon does not accompany her mother to Church-hill, as she has not even manners to recommend her; and, according to Mr. Smith's account, is equally dull and proud. Where pride and stupidity unite there can be no dissimulation worthy notice, and Miss Vernon shall be consigned to unrelenting contempt; but by all that I can gather Lady Susan possesses a degree of captivating deceit which it must be pleasing to witness and detect. I shall be with you very soon, and am ever,

Your affectionate brother,

R. DE COURCY.

V. *Lady Susan Vernon to Mrs. Johnson*

Churchhill.

I RECEIVED YOUR NOTE, my dear Alicia, just before I left town, and rejoice to be assured that Mr. Johnson suspected nothing of your engagement the evening before. It is undoubtedly better to deceive him entirely, and since he will be stubborn he must be tricked. I arrived here in safety, and have no reason to complain of my reception from Mr. Vernon; but I confess myself not equally satisfied with the behaviour of his lady. She is perfectly well-bred, indeed, and has the air of a woman of fashion, but her manners are not such as can persuade me of her being prepossessed in my favour. I wanted her to be delighted at seeing me. I was as amiable as possible on the occasion, but all in vain. She does not like me. To be sure when we consider that I *did* take some pains to prevent my brother-in-law's marrying her, this want of cordiality is not very surprizing, and yet it shows an illiberal and vindictive spirit to resent a project which influenced me six years ago, and which never succeeded at last.

I am sometimes disposed to repent that I did not let Charles buy Vernon Castle, when we were obliged to sell it; but it was a trying circumstance, especially as the sale took place exactly at the time of his marriage; and everybody ought to respect the delicacy of those feelings which could not endure that my husband's dignity should be lessened by his younger brother's having possession of the family estate. Could matters have been so arranged as to prevent the necessity of our leaving the castle, could we have lived with Charles and kept him single, I should have been very far from persuading my husband to dispose of it elsewhere; but Charles was on the point of marrying Miss De Courcy, and the event has justified me. Here are children in abundance, and what benefit could have accrued to me from his purchasing Vernon? My having prevented it may perhaps have given his wife an unfavourable impression, but where there is a disposition to dislike, a motive will never be wanting; and as to money matters it has not withheld him from being very useful to me. I really have a regard for him, he is so easily imposed upon! The house is a good one, the furniture fashionable, and everything announces plenty and elegance. Charles is very rich I am sure; when a man has once got his name in a banking-house he rolls in money; but they do not know what to do with it, keep very little company, and never go to London but on business. We shall be as stupid as possible. I mean to win my sister-in-law's heart through the children; I know all their names already, and am going to attach myself with the greatest sensibility to one in particular, a young Frederic, whom I take on my lap and sigh over for his dear uncle's sake.

Poor Mainwaring! I need not tell you how much I miss him, how perpetually he is in my thoughts. I found a dismal letter from him on my arrival here, full of complaints of his wife and sister, and lamentations on the cruelty of his fate. I passed off the letter as his wife's, to the Vernons, and when I write to him it must be under cover to you.

Ever yours,
S. VERNON.

VI. *Mrs. Vernon to Mr. De Courcy*

Churchhill.

WELL, MY DEAR REGINALD, I have seen this dangerous creature, and must give you some description of her, though I hope you will soon be able to form your own judgment she is really excessively pretty; however you may choose to question the allurements of a lady no longer young, I must, for my own part, declare that I have seldom seen so lovely a woman as Lady Susan. She is delicately fair, with fine grey eyes and dark eyelashes; and from her appearance one would not suppose her more than five and twenty, though she must in fact be ten years older, I was certainly not disposed to admire her, though always hearing she was beautiful; but I cannot help feeling that she possesses an uncommon union of symmetry, brilliancy, and grace. Her address to me was so gentle, frank, and even affectionate, that, if I had not known how much she has always disliked me for marrying Mr. Vernon, and that we had never met before, I should have imagined her an attached friend. One is apt, I believe, to connect assurance of manner with coquetry, and to expect that an impudent address will naturally attend an impudent mind; at least I was myself prepared for an improper degree of confidence in Lady Susan; but her countenance is absolutely sweet, and her voice and manner winningly mild. I am sorry it is so, for what is this but deceit? Unfortunately, one knows her too well. She is clever and agreeable, has all that knowledge of the world which makes conversation easy, and talks very well, with a happy command of language, which is too often used, I believe, to make black appear white. She has already almost persuaded me of her being warmly attached to her daughter, though I have been so long convinced to the contrary. She speaks of her with so much tenderness and anxiety, lamenting so bitterly the neglect of her education, which she represents however as wholly unavoidable, that I am forced to recollect how many successive springs her ladyship spent in town, while her daughter was left in Staffordshire to the care of servants, or a governess very little better, to prevent my believing what she says.

If her manners have so great an influence on my resentful heart, you may judge how much more strongly they operate on Mr. Vernon's generous temper. I wish I could be as well satisfied as he is, that it was really her choice to leave Langford for Churchhill; and if she had not stayed there for months before she discovered that her friend's manner of living did not suit her situation or feelings, I might have believed that concern for the loss of such a husband as Mr. Vernon, to whom her own behaviour was far from unexceptionable, might for a time make her wish for retirement. But I cannot forget the length of her visit to the Mainwarings, and when I reflect on the different mode of life which she led with them from that to which she must now submit, I can only suppose that the wish of establishing her reputation by following though late the path of propriety, occasioned her removal from a family where she must in reality have been particularly happy. Your friend Mr. Smith's story, however, cannot be quite correct, as she corresponds regularly with Mrs. Mainwaring. At any rate it must be exaggerated. It is scarcely possible that two men should be so grossly deceived by her at once.

Yours, &c.,
CATHERINE VERNON

VII. *Lady Susan Vernon to Mrs. Johnson*

Churchhill.

MY DEAR ALICIA,—You are very good in taking notice of Frederica, and I am grateful for it as a mark of your friendship; but as I cannot have any doubt of the warmth of your affection, I am far from exacting so heavy a sacrifice. She is a stupid girl, and has nothing to recommend her. I would not, therefore, on my account, have you encumber one moment of your precious time by sending for her to Edward Street, especially as every visit is so much deducted from the grand affair of education, which I really wish to have attended to while she remains at Miss Summers's. I want her to play and sing with some portion of taste and a good deal of assurance, as she has my hand and arm and a tolerable voice. I was so much indulged in my infant years that I was never obliged to attend to anything, and consequently am without the accomplishments which are now necessary to finish a pretty woman. Not that I am an advocate for the prevailing fashion of acquiring a perfect knowledge of all languages, arts, and sciences. It is throwing time away to be mistress of French, Italian, and German: music, singing, and drawing, &c., will gain a woman some applause, but will not add one lover to her list—grace and manner, after all, are of the greatest importance. I do not mean, therefore, that Frederica's acquirements should be more than superficial, and I flatter myself that she will not remain long enough at school to understand anything thoroughly. I hope to see her the wife of Sir James within a twelvemonth. You know on what I ground my hope, and it is certainly a good foundation, for school must be very humiliating to a girl of Frederica's age. And, by-the-by, you had better not invite her any more on that account, as I wish her to find her situation as unpleasant as possible. I am sure of Sir James at any time, and could make him renew his application by a line. I shall trouble you meanwhile to prevent his forming any other attachment when he comes to town. Ask him to your house occasionally, and talk to him of Frederica, that he may not forget her. Upon the whole, I commend my own conduct in this affair extremely, and regard it as a very happy instance of circumspection and tenderness. Some mothers would have insisted on their daughter's accepting so good an offer on the first overture; but I could not reconcile it to myself to force Frederica into a marriage from which her heart revolted, and instead of adopting so harsh a measure merely propose to make it her own choice, by rendering her thoroughly uncomfortable till she does accept him—but enough of this tiresome girl. You may well wonder how I contrive to pass my time here, and for the first week it was insufferably dull. Now, however, we begin to mend, our party is enlarged by Mrs. Vernon's brother, a handsome young man, who promises me some amusement. There is something about him which rather interests me, a sort of sauciness and familiarity which I shall teach him to correct. He is lively, and seems clever, and when I have inspired him with greater respect for me than his sister's kind offices have implanted, he may be an agreeable flirt. There is exquisite pleasure in subduing an insolent spirit, in making a person predetermined to dislike acknowledge one's superiority. I have disconcerted him already by my calm reserve, and it shall be my endeavour to humble the pride of these self important De Courcys still lower, to convince Mrs. Vernon that her sisterly cautions have been bestowed in vain, and to persuade Reginald that she has scandalously belied me. This project will serve at least to amuse me, and prevent my feeling so acutely this dreadful separation from you and all whom I love.

Yours ever,
S. VERNON.

VIII. *Mrs. Vernon to Lady De Courcy*

Churchhill.

MY DEAR MOTHER,—You must not expect Reginald back again for some time. He desires me to tell you that the present open weather induces him to accept Mr. Vernon's invitation to prolong his stay in Sussex, that they may have some hunting together. He means to send for his horses immediately, and it is impossible to say when you may see him in Kent. I will not disguise my sentiments on this change from you, my dear mother, though I think you had better not communicate them to my father, whose excessive anxiety about Reginald would subject him to an alarm which might seriously affect his health and spirits. Lady Susan has certainly contrived, in the space of a fortnight, to make my brother like her. In short, I am persuaded that his continuing here beyond the time originally fixed for his return is occasioned as much by a degree of fascination towards her, as by the wish of hunting with Mr. Vernon, and of course I cannot receive that pleasure from the length of his visit which my brother's company would otherwise give me. I am, indeed, provoked at the artifice of this unprincipled woman; what stronger proof of her dangerous abilities can be given than this perversion of Reginald's judgment, which when he entered the house was so decidedly against her! In his last letter he actually gave me some particulars of her behaviour at Langford, such as he received from a gentleman who knew her perfectly well, which, if true, must raise abhorrence against her, and which Reginald himself was entirely disposed to credit. His opinion of her, I am sure, was as low as of any woman in England;

and when he first came it was evident that he considered her as one entitled neither to delicacy nor respect, and that he felt she would be delighted with the attentions of any man inclined to flirt with her. Her behaviour, I confess, has been calculated to do away with such an idea; I have not detected the smallest impropriety in it—nothing of vanity, of pretension, of levity; and she is altogether so attractive that I should not wonder at his being delighted with her, had he known nothing of her previous to this personal acquaintance; but, against reason, against conviction, to be so well pleased with her, as I am sure he is, does really astonish me. His admiration was at first very strong, but no more than was natural, and I did not wonder at his being much struck by the gentleness and delicacy of her manners; but when he has mentioned her of late it has been in terms of more extraordinary praise; and yesterday he actually said that he could not be surprised at any effect produced on the heart of man by such loveliness and such abilities; and when I lamented, in reply, the badness of her disposition, he observed that whatever might have been her errors they were to be imputed to her neglected education and early marriage, and that she was altogether a wonderful woman. This tendency to excuse her conduct or to forget it, in the warmth of admiration, vexes me; and if I did not know that Reginald is too much at home at Churchhill to need an invitation for lengthening his visit, I should regret Mr. Vernon's giving him any. Lady Susan's intentions are of course those of absolute coquetry, or a desire of universal admiration; I cannot for a moment imagine that she has anything more serious in view; but it mortifies me to see a young man of Reginald's sense duped by her at all.

I am, &c.,
CATHERINE VERNON.

IX. *Mrs. Johnson to Lady S. Vernon*

Edward Street.

MY DEAREST FRIEND,—I congratulate you on Mr. De Courcy's arrival, and I advise you by all means to marry him; his father's estate is, we know, considerable, and I believe certainly entailed. Sir Reginald is very infirm, and not likely to stand in your way long. I hear the young man well spoken of; and though no one can really deserve you, my dearest Susan, Mr. De Courcy may be worth having. Mainwaring will storm of course, but you easily pacify him; besides, the most scrupulous point of honour could not require you to wait for *his* emancipation. I have seen Sir James; he came to town for a few days last week, and called several times in Edward Street. I talked to him about you and your daughter, and he is so far from having forgotten you, that I am sure he would marry either of you with pleasure. I gave him hopes of Frederica's relenting, and told him a great deal of her improvements. I scolded him for making love to Maria Mainwaring; he protested that he had been only in joke, and we both laughed heartily at her disappointment; and, in short, were very agreeable. He is as silly as ever.

Yours faithfully,
ALICIA.

X. *Lady Susan Vernon to Mrs. Johnson*

Churchhill.

I AM MUCH OBLIGED TO YOU, my dear Friend, for your advice respecting Mr. De Courcy, which I know was given with the full conviction of its expediency, though I am not quite determined on following it. I cannot easily resolve on anything so serious as marriage; especially as I am not at present in want of money, and might perhaps, till the old gentleman's death, be very little benefited by the match. It is true that I am vain enough to believe it within my reach. I have made him sensible of my power, and can now enjoy the pleasure of triumphing over a mind prepared to dislike me, and prejudiced against all my past actions. His sister, too, is, I hope, convinced how little the ungenerous representations of anyone to the disadvantage of another will avail when opposed by the immediate influence of intellect and manner. I see plainly that she is uneasy at my progress in the good opinion of her brother, and conclude that nothing will be wanting on her part to counteract me; but having once made him doubt the justice of her opinion of me, I think I may defy her. It has been delightful to me to watch his advances towards intimacy, especially to observe his altered manner in consequence of my repressing by the cool dignity of my deportment his insolent approach to direct familiarity. My conduct has been equally guarded from the first, and I never behaved less like a coquette in the whole course of my life, though perhaps my desire of dominion was never more decided. I have subdued him entirely by sentiment and serious conversation, and made him, I may venture to say, at least half in love with me, without the semblance of the most commonplace flirtation. Mrs. Vernon's consciousness of deserving every sort of revenge that it can be in my power to inflict for her ill-offices could alone enable her to perceive that I am actuated by any design in behaviour so gentle and unpretending. Let her think and act as she chooses, however. I have never yet found that the advice of a sister could prevent a young man's being in love if he chose. We are advancing now to some kind of confidence, and in short are likely to be engaged in a sort of platonic friendship. On my side you may be sure of its never being more, for if I were not attached to another person as much as I can be to anyone, I should make a point of not bestowing my affection on a man who had dared to think so meanly of me. Reginald has a good figure and is not unworthy the praise you have heard given him, but is still greatly inferior to our friend at Langford. He is less polished, less insinuating than Mainwaring, and is comparatively deficient in the power of saying those delightful things which put one in good humour with oneself and all the world. He is quite agreeable enough, however, to afford me amusement, and to make many of those hours pass very pleasantly which would otherwise be spent in endeavouring to overcome my sister-in-law's reserve, and listening to the insipid talk of her husband. Your account of Sir James is most satisfactory, and I mean to give Miss Frederica a hint of my intentions very soon.

Yours, &c.,
S. VERNON.

XI. *Mrs. Vernon to Lady De Courcy*

Churchhill

I REALLY GROW QUITE UNEASY, my dearest mother, about Reginald, from witnessing the very rapid increase of Lady Susan's influence. They are now on terms of the most particular friendship, frequently engaged in long conversations together; and she has contrived by the most artful coquetry to subdue his judgment to her own purposes. It is impossible to see the intimacy between them so very soon established without some alarm, though I can hardly suppose that Lady Susan's plans extend to marriage. I wish you could get Reginald home again on any plausible pretence; he is not at all disposed to leave us, and I have given him as many hints of my father's precarious state of health as common decency will allow me to do in my own house. Her power over him must now be boundless, as she has entirely effaced all his former ill-opinion, and persuaded him not merely to forget but to justify her conduct. Mr. Smith's account of her proceedings at Langford, where he accused her of having made Mr. Mainwaring and a young man engaged to Miss Mainwaring distractedly in love with her, which Reginald firmly believed when he came here, is now, he is persuaded, only a scandalous invention. He has told me so with a warmth of manner which spoke his regret at having believed the contrary himself. How sincerely do I grieve that she ever entered this house! I always looked forward to her coming with uneasiness; but very far was it from originating in anxiety for Reginald. I expected a most disagreeable companion for myself, but could not imagine that my brother would be in the smallest danger of being captivated by a woman with whose principles he was so well acquainted, and whose character he so heartily despised. If you can get him away it will be a good thing.

Yours, &c.,

CATHERINE VERNON.

XII. *Sir Reginald De Courcy to His Son*

Parklands.

I KNOW THAT YOUNG MEN IN GENERAL do not admit of any enquiry even from their nearest relations into affairs of the heart, but I hope, my dear Reginald, that you will be superior to such as allow nothing for a father's anxiety, and think themselves privileged to refuse him their confidence and slight his advice. You must be sensible that as an only son, and the representative of an ancient family, your conduct in life is most interesting to your connections; and in the very important concern of marriage especially, there is everything at stake—your own happiness, that of your parents, and the credit of your name. I do not suppose that you would deliberately form an absolute engagement of that nature without acquainting your mother and myself, or at least, without being convinced that we should approve of your choice; but I cannot help fearing that you may be drawn in, by the lady who has lately attached you, to a marriage which the whole of your family, far and near, must highly reprobate. Lady Susan's age is itself a material objection, but her want of character is one so much more serious, that the difference of even twelve years becomes in comparison of small amount. Were you not blinded by a sort of fascination, it would be ridiculous in me to repeat the instances of great misconduct on her side so very generally known.

Her neglect of her husband, her encouragement of other men, her extravagance and dissipation, were so gross and notorious that no one could be ignorant of them at the time, nor can now have forgotten them. To our family she has always been represented in softened colours by the benevolence of Mr. Charles Vernon, and yet, in spite of his generous endeavours to excuse her, we know that she did, from the most selfish motives, take all possible pains to prevent his marriage with Catherine.

My years and increasing infirmities make me very desirous of seeing you settled in the world. To the fortune of a wife, the goodness of my own will make me indifferent, but her family and character must be equally unexceptionable. When your choice is fixed so that no objection can be made to it, then I can promise you a ready and cheerful consent; but it is my duty to oppose a match which deep art only could render possible, and must in the end make wretched. It is possible her behaviour may arise only from vanity, or the wish of gaining the admiration of a man whom she must imagine to be particularly prejudiced against her; but it is more likely that she should aim at something further. She is poor, and may naturally seek an alliance which must be advantageous to herself; you know your own rights, and that it is out of my power to prevent your inheriting the family estate. My ability of distressing you during my life would be a species of revenge to which I could hardly stoop under any circumstances.

I honestly tell you my sentiments and intentions: I do not wish to work on your fears, but on your sense and affection. It would destroy every comfort of my life to know that you were married to Lady Susan Vernon; it would be the death of that honest pride with which I have hitherto considered my son; I should blush to see him, to hear of him, to think of him. I may perhaps do no good but that of relieving my own mind by this letter, but I felt it my duty to tell you that your partiality for Lady Susan is no secret to your friends, and to warn you against her. I should be glad to hear your reasons for disbelieving Mr. Smith's intelligence; you had no doubt of its authenticity a month ago. If you can give me your assurance of having no design beyond enjoying the conversation of a clever woman for a short period, and of yielding admiration only to her beauty and abilities, without being blinded by them to her faults, you will restore me to happiness; but, if you cannot do this, explain to me, at least, what has occasioned so great an alteration in your opinion of her.

I am, &c., &c,

REGINALD DE COURCY

XIII. *Lady De Courcy to Mrs. Vernon*

Parklands.

MY DEAR CATHERINE,—Unluckily I was confined to my room when your last letter came, by a cold which affected my eyes so much as to prevent my reading it myself, so I could not refuse your father when he offered to read it to me, by which means he became acquainted, to my great vexation, with all your fears about your brother. I had intended to write to Reginald myself as soon as my eyes would let me, to point out, as well as I could, the danger of an intimate acquaintance, with so artful a woman as Lady Susan, to a young man of his age, and high expectations. I meant, moreover, to have reminded him of our being quite alone now, and very much in need of him to keep up our spirits these long winter evenings. Whether it would have done any good can never be settled now, but I am excessively vexed that Sir Reginald should know anything of a matter which we foresaw would make him so uneasy. He caught all your fears the moment he had read your letter, and I am sure he has not had the business out of his head since. He wrote by the same post to Reginald a long letter full of it all, and particularly asking an explanation of what he may have heard from Lady Susan to contradict the late shocking reports. His answer came this morning, which I shall enclose to you, as I think you will like to see it. I wish it was more satisfactory; but it seems written with such a determination to think well of Lady Susan, that his assurances as to marriage, &c., do not set my heart at ease. I say all I can, however, to satisfy your father, and he is certainly less uneasy since Reginald's letter. How provoking it is, my dear Catherine, that this unwelcome guest of yours should not only prevent our meeting this Christmas, but be the occasion of so much vexation and trouble! Kiss the dear children for me.

Your affectionate mother,
C. DE COURCY.

XIV. *Mr. De Courcy to Sir Reginald*

Churchhill.

My dear Sir,—I have this moment received your letter, which has given me more astonishment than I ever felt before. I am to thank my sister, I suppose, for having represented me in such a light as to injure me in your opinion, and give you all this alarm. I know not why she should choose to make herself and her family uneasy by apprehending an event which no one but herself, I can affirm, would ever have thought possible. To impute such a design to Lady Susan would be taking from her every claim to that excellent understanding which her bitterest enemies have never denied her; and equally low must sink my pretensions to common sense if I am suspected of matrimonial views in my behaviour to her. Our difference of age must be an insuperable objection, and I entreat you, my dear father, to quiet your mind, and no longer harbour a suspicion which cannot he more injurious to your own peace than to our understandings. I can have no other view in remaining with Lady Susan, than to enjoy for a short time (as you have yourself expressed it) the conversation of a woman of high intellectual powers. If Mrs. Vernon would allow something to my affection for herself and her husband in the length of my visit, she would do more justice to us all; but my sister is unhappily prejudiced beyond the hope of conviction against Lady Susan. From an attachment to her husband, which in itself does honour to both, she cannot forgive the endeavours at preventing their union, which have been attributed to selfishness in Lady Susan; but in this case, as well as in many others, the world has most grossly injured that lady, by supposing the worst where the motives of her conduct have been doubtful. Lady Susan had heard something so materially to the disadvantage of my sister as to persuade her that the happiness of Mr. Vernon, to whom she was always much attached, would be wholly destroyed by the marriage. And this circumstance, while it explains the true motives of Lady Susan's conduct, and removes all the blame which has been so lavished on her, may also convince us how little the general report of anyone ought to be credited; since no character, however upright, can escape the malevolence of slander. If my sister, in the security of retirement, with as little opportunity as inclination to do evil, could not avoid censure, we must not rashly condemn those who, living in the world and surrounded with temptations, should be accused of errors which they are known to have the power of committing.

I blame myself severely for having so easily believed the slanderous tales invented by Charles Smith to the prejudice of Lady Susan, as I am now convinced how greatly they have traduced her. As to Mrs. Mainwaring's jealousy it was totally his own invention, and his account of her attaching Miss Mainwaring's lover was scarcely better founded. Sir James Martin had been drawn in by that young lady to pay her some attention; and as he is a man of fortune, it was easy to see *her* views extended to marriage. It is well known that Miss M. is absolutely on the catch for a husband, and no one therefore can pity her for losing, by the superior attractions of another woman, the chance of being able to make a worthy man completely wretched. Lady Susan was far from intending such a conquest, and on finding how warmly Miss Mainwaring resented her lover's defection, determined, in spite of Mr. and Mrs. Mainwaring's most urgent entreaties, to leave the family. I have reason to imagine she did receive serious proposals from Sir James, but her removing to Langford immediately on the discovery of his attachment, must acquit her on that article with any mind of common candour. You will, I am sure, my dear Sir, feel the truth of this, and will hereby learn to do justice to the character of a very injured woman. I know that Lady Susan in coming to Churchhill was governed only by the most honourable and amiable intentions; her prudence and economy are exemplary, her regard for Mr. Vernon equal even to *his* deserts; and her wish of obtaining my sister's good opinion merits a better return than it has received. As a mother she is unexceptionable; her solid affection for her child is shown by placing her in hands where her education will be properly attended to; but because she has not the blind and weak partiality of most mothers, she is accused of wanting maternal tenderness. Every person of sense, however, will know how to value and commend her well-directed affection, and will join me in wishing that Frederica Vernon may prove more worthy than she has yet done of her mother's tender care. I have now, my dear father, written my real sentiments of Lady Susan; you will know from this letter how highly I admire her abilities, and esteem her character; but if you are not equally convinced by my full and solemn assurance that your fears have been most idly created, you will deeply mortify and distress me.

I am, &c., &c.,

R. DE COURCY.

XV. *Mrs. Vernon to Lady De Courcy*

Churchhill

MY DEAR MOTHER,—I return you Reginald's letter, and rejoice with all my heart that my father is made easy by it: tell him so, with my congratulations; but, between ourselves, I must own it has only convinced ME of my brother's having no *present* intention of marrying Lady Susan, not that he is in no danger of doing so three months hence. He gives a very plausible account of her behaviour at Langford; I wish it may be true, but his intelligence must come from herself, and I am less disposed to believe it than to lament the degree of intimacy subsisting, between them implied by the discussion of such a subject. I am sorry to have incurred his displeasure, but can expect nothing better while he is so very eager in Lady Susan's justification. He is very severe against me indeed, and yet I hope I have not been hasty in my judgment of her. Poor woman! though I have reasons enough for my dislike, I cannot help pitying her at present, as she is in real distress, and with too much cause. She had this morning a letter from the lady with whom she has placed her daughter, to request that Miss Vernon might be immediately removed, as she had been detected in an attempt to run away. Why, or whither she intended to go, does not appear; but, as her situation seems to have been unexceptionable, it is a sad thing, and of course highly distressing to Lady Susan. Frederica must be as much as sixteen, and ought to know better; but from what her mother insinuates, I am afraid she is a perverse girl. She has been sadly neglected, however, and her mother ought to remember it. Mr. Vernon set off for

London as soon as she had determined what should be done. He is, if possible, to prevail on Miss Summers to let Frederica continue with her; and if he cannot succeed, to bring her to Churchhill for the present, till some other situation can be found for her. Her ladyship is comforting herself meanwhile by strolling along the shrubbery with Reginald, calling forth all his tender feelings, I suppose, on this distressing occasion. She has been talking a great deal about it to me. She talks vastly well; I am afraid of being ungenerous, or I should say, *too* well to feel so very deeply; but I will not look for her faults; she may be Reginald's wife! Heaven forbid it! but why should I be quicker-sighted than anyone else? Mr. Vernon declares that he never saw deeper distress than hers, on the receipt of the letter; and is his judgment inferior to mine? She was very unwilling that Frederica should be allowed to come to Churchhill, and justly enough, as it seems a sort of reward to behaviour deserving very differently; but it was impossible to take her anywhere else, and she is not to remain here long. "It will be absolutely necessary," said she, "as you, my dear sister, must be sensible, to treat my daughter with some severity while she is here; a most painful necessity, but I will *endeavour* to submit to it. I am afraid I have often been too indulgent, but my poor Frederica's temper could never bear opposition well: you must support and encourage me; you must urge the necessity of reproof if you see me too lenient." All this sounds very reasonable. Reginald is so incensed against the poor silly girl. Surely it is not to Lady Susan's credit that he should be so bitter against her daughter; his idea of her must be drawn from the mother's description. Well, whatever may be his fate, we have the comfort of knowing that we have done our utmost to save him. We must commit the event to a higher power.

Yours ever, &c.,
CATHERINE VERNON.

XVI. *Lady Susan to Mrs. Johnson*

Churchhill.

NEVER, MY DEAREST ALICIA, was I so provoked in my life as by a letter this morning from Miss Summers. That horrid girl of mine has been trying to run away. I had not a notion of her being such a little devil before, she seemed to have all the Vernon milkiness; but on receiving the letter in which I declared my intention about Sir James, she actually attempted to elope; at least, I cannot otherwise account for her doing it. She meant, I suppose, to go to the Clarkes in Staffordshire, for she has no other acquaintances. But she shall be punished, she shall have him. I have sent Charles to town to make matters up if he can, for I do not by any means want her here. If Miss Summers will not keep her, you must find me out another school, unless we can get her married immediately. Miss S. writes word that she could not get the young lady to assign any cause for her extraordinary conduct, which confirms me in my own previous explanation of it, Frederica is too shy, I think, and too much in awe of me to tell tales, but if the mildness of her uncle should get anything out of her, I am not afraid. I trust I shall be able to make my story as good as hers. If I am vain of anything, it is of my eloquence. Consideration and esteem as surely follow command of language as admiration waits on beauty, and here I have opportunity enough for the exercise of my talent, as the chief of my time is spent in conversation.

Reginald is never easy unless we are by ourselves, and when the weather is tolerable, we pace the shrubbery for hours together. I like him on the whole very well; he is clever and has a good deal to say, but he is sometimes impertinent and troublesome. There is a sort of ridiculous delicacy about him which requires the fullest explanation of whatever he may have heard to my disadvantage, and is never satisfied till he thinks he has ascertained the beginning and end of everything. This is one sort of love, but I confess it does not particularly recommend itself to me. I infinitely prefer the tender and liberal spirit of Mainwaring, which, impressed with the deepest conviction of my merit, is satisfied that whatever I do must be right; and look with a degree of contempt on the inquisitive and doubtful fancies of that heart which seems always debating on the reasonableness of its emotions. Mainwaring is indeed, beyond all compare, superior to Reginald—superior in everything but the power of being with me! Poor fellow! he is much distracted by jealousy, which I am not sorry for, as I know no better support of love. He has been teazing me to allow of his coming into this country, and lodging somewhere near *incog.*; but I forbade everything of the kind. Those women are inexcusable who forget what is due to themselves, and the opinion of the world.

Yours ever,

S. VERNON.

XVII. *Mrs. Vernon to Lady De Courcy*

Churchhill.

MY DEAR MOTHER,—Mr. Vernon returned on Thursday night, bringing his niece with him. Lady Susan had received a line from him by that day's post, informing her that Miss Summers had absolutely refused to allow of Miss Vernon's continuance in her academy; we were therefore prepared for her arrival, and expected them impatiently the whole evening. They came while we were at tea, and I never saw any creature look so frightened as Frederica when she entered the room. Lady Susan, who had been shedding tears before, and showing great agitation at the idea of the meeting, received her with perfect self-command, and without betraying the least tenderness of spirit. She hardly spoke to her, and on Frederica's bursting into tears as soon as we were seated, took her out of the room, and did not return for some time. When she did, her eyes looked very red and she was as much agitated as before. We saw no more of her daughter. Poor Reginald was beyond measure concerned to see his fair friend in such distress, and watched her with so much tender solicitude, that I, who occasionally caught her observing his countenance with exultation, was quite out of patience. This pathetic representation lasted the whole evening, and so ostentatious and artful a display has entirely convinced me that she did in fact feel nothing. I am more angry with her than ever since I have seen her daughter; the poor girl looks so unhappy that my heart aches for her. Lady Susan is surely too severe, for Frederica does not seem to have the sort of temper to make severity necessary. She looks perfectly timid, dejected, and penitent. She is very pretty, though not so handsome as her mother, nor at all like her. Her complexion is delicate, but neither so fair nor so blooming as Lady Susan's, and she has quite the Vernon cast of countenance, the oval face and mild dark eyes, and there is peculiar sweetness in her look when she speaks either to her uncle or me, for as we behave kindly to her we have of course engaged her gratitude.

Her mother has insinuated that her temper is intractable, but I never saw a face less indicative of any evil disposition than hers; and from what I can see of the behaviour of each to the other, the invariable severity of Lady Susan and the silent dejection of Frederica, I am led to believe as heretofore that the former has no real love for her daughter, and has never done her justice or treated her affectionately. I have not been able to have any conversation with my niece; she is shy, and I think I can see that some pains are taken to prevent her being much with me. Nothing satisfactory transpires as to her reason for running away. Her kind-hearted uncle, you may be sure, was too fearful of distressing her to ask many questions as they travelled. I wish it had been possible for me to fetch her instead of him. I think I should have discovered the truth in the course of a thirty-mile journey. The small pianoforte has been removed within these few days, at Lady Susan's request, into her dressing-room, and Frederica spends great part of the day there, practising as it is called; but I seldom hear any noise when I pass that way; what she does with herself there I do not know. There are plenty of books, but it is not every girl who has been running wild the first fifteen years of her life, that can or will read. Poor creature! the prospect from her window is not very instructive, for that room overlooks the lawn, you know, with the shrubbery on one side, where she may see her mother walking for an hour together in earnest conversation with Reginald. A girl of Frederica's age must be childish indeed, if such things do not strike her. Is it not inexcusable to give such an example to a daughter? Yet Reginald still thinks Lady Susan the best of mothers, and still condemns Frederica as a worthless girl! He is convinced that her attempt to run away proceeded from no justifiable cause, and had no provocation. I am sure I cannot say that it *had*, but while Miss Summers declares that Miss Vernon showed no signs of obstinacy or perverseness during her whole stay in Wigmore Street, till she was detected in this scheme, I cannot so readily credit what Lady Susan has made him, and wants to make me believe, that it was merely an impatience of restraint and a desire of escaping from the tuition of masters which brought on the plan of an elopement. O Reginald, how is your judgment enslaved! He scarcely dares even allow her to be handsome, and when I speak of her beauty, replies only that her eyes have no brilliancy! Sometimes he is sure she is deficient in understanding, and at others that her temper only is in fault. In short, when a person is always to deceive, it is impossible to be consistent. Lady Susan finds it necessary that Frederica should be to blame, and probably has sometimes judged it expedient to accuse her of ill-nature and sometimes to lament her want of sense. Reginald is only repeating after her ladyship.

I remain, &c., &c.,
CATHERINE VERNON.

XVIII. *From the Same to the Same*

Churchhill.

MY DEAR MOTHER,—I am very glad to find that my description of Frederica Vernon has interested you, for I do believe her truly deserving of your regard; and when I have communicated a notion which has recently struck me, your kind impressions in her favour will, I am sure, be heightened. I cannot help fancying that she is growing partial to my brother. I so very often see her eyes fixed on his face with a remarkable expression of pensive admiration. He is certainly very handsome; and yet more, there is an openness in his manner that must be highly prepossessing, and I am sure she feels it so. Thoughtful and pensive in general, her countenance always brightens into a smile when Reginald says anything amusing; and, let the subject be ever so serious that he may be conversing on, I am much mistaken if a syllable of his uttering escapes her. I want to make him sensible of all this, for we know the power of gratitude on such a heart as his; and could Frederica's artless affection detach him from her mother, we might bless the day which brought her to Churchhill. I think, my dear mother, you would not disapprove of her as a daughter. She is extremely young, to be sure, has had a wretched education, and a dreadful example of levity in her mother; but yet I can pronounce her disposition to be excellent, and her natural abilities very good. Though totally without accomplishments, she is by no means so ignorant as one might expect to find her, being fond of books and spending the chief of her time in reading. Her mother leaves her more to herself than she did, and I have her with me as much as possible, and have taken great pains to overcome her timidity. We are very good friends, and though she never opens her lips before her mother, she talks enough when alone with me to make it clear that, if properly treated by Lady Susan, she would always appear to much greater advantage. There cannot be a more gentle, affectionate heart; or more obliging manners, when acting without restraint; and her little cousins are all very fond of her.

Your affectionate daughter,
C. VERNON

XIX. *Lady Susan to Mrs. Johnson*

Churchhill.

YOU WILL BE EAGER, I know, to hear something further of Frederica, and perhaps may think me negligent for not writing before. She arrived with her uncle last Thursday fortnight, when, of course, I lost no time in demanding the cause of her behaviour; and soon found myself to have been perfectly right in attributing it to my own letter. The prospect of it frightened her so thoroughly, that, with a mixture of true girlish perverseness and folly, she resolved on getting out of the house and proceeding directly by the stage to her friends, the Clarkes; and had really got as far as the length of two streets in her journey when she was fortunately missed, pursued, and overtaken. Such was the first distinguished exploit of Miss Frederica Vernon; and, if we consider that it was achieved at the tender age of sixteen, we shall have room for the most flattering prognostics of her future renown. I am excessively provoked, however, at the parade of propriety which prevented Miss Summers from keeping the girl; and it seems so extraordinary a piece of nicety, considering my daughter's family connections, that I can only suppose the lady to be governed by the fear of never getting her money. Be that as it may, however, Frederica is returned on my hands; and, having nothing else to employ her, is busy in pursuing the plan of romance begun at Langford. She is actually falling in love with Reginald De Courcy! To disobey her mother by refusing an unexceptionable offer is not enough; her affections must also be given without her mother's approbation. I never saw a girl of her age bid fairer to be the sport of mankind. Her feelings are tolerably acute, and she is so charmingly artless in their display as to afford the most reasonable hope of her being ridiculous, and despised by every man who sees her.

Artlessness will never do in love matters; and that girl is born a simpleton who has it either by nature or affectation. I am not yet certain that Reginald sees what she is about, nor is it of much consequence. She is now an object of indifference to him, and she would be one of contempt were he to understand her emotions. Her beauty is much admired by the Vernons, but it has no effect on him. She is in high favour with her aunt altogether, because she is so little like myself, of course. She is exactly the companion for Mrs. Vernon, who dearly loves to be firm, and to have all the sense and all the wit of the conversation to herself: Frederica will never eclipse her. When she first came I was at some pains to prevent her seeing much of her aunt; but I have relaxed, as I believe I may depend on her observing the rules I have laid down for their discourse. But do not imagine that with all this lenity I have for a moment given up my plan of her marriage. No; I am unalterably fixed on this point, though I have not yet quite decided on the manner of bringing it about. I should not chuse to have the business brought on here, and canvassed by the wise heads of Mr. and Mrs. Vernon; and I cannot just now afford to go to town. Miss Frederica must therefore wait a little.

Yours ever,
S. VERNON.

XX. *Mrs. Vernon to Lady De Courcy*

Churchhill

WE HAVE A VERY UNEXPECTED GUEST with us at present, my dear Mother: he arrived yesterday. I heard a carriage at the door, as I was sitting with my children while they dined; and supposing I should be wanted, left the nursery soon afterwards, and was half-way downstairs, when Frederica, as pale as ashes, came running up, and rushed by me into her own room. I instantly followed, and asked her what was the matter. "Oh!" said she, "he is come—Sir James is come, and what shall I do?" This was no explanation; I begged her to tell me what she meant. At that moment we were interrupted by a knock at the door: it was Reginald, who came, by Lady Susan's direction, to call Frederica down. "It is Mr. De Courcy!" said she, colouring violently. "Mamma has sent for me; I must go." We all three went down together; and I saw my brother examining the terrified face of Frederica with surprize. In the breakfast-room we found Lady Susan, and a young man of gentlemanlike appearance, whom she introduced by the name of Sir James Martin—the very person, as you may remember, whom it was said she had been at pains to detach from Miss Mainwaring; but the conquest, it seems, was not designed for herself, or she has since transferred it to her daughter; for Sir James is now desperately in love with Frederica, and with full encouragement from mamma. The poor girl, however, I am sure, dislikes him; and though his person and address are very well, he appears, both to Mr. Vernon and me, a very weak young man. Frederica looked so shy, so confused, when we entered the room, that I felt for her exceedingly. Lady Susan behaved with great attention to her visitor; and yet I thought I could perceive that she had no particular pleasure in seeing him. Sir James talked a great deal, and made many civil excuses to me for the liberty he had taken in coming to Churchhill—mixing more frequent laughter with his discourse than the subject required—said many things over and over again, and told Lady Susan three times that he had seen Mrs. Johnson a few evenings before. He now and then addressed Frederica, but more frequently her mother. The poor girl sat all this time without opening her lips—her eyes cast down, and her colour varying every instant; while Reginald observed all that passed in perfect silence. At length Lady Susan, weary, I believe, of her situation, proposed walking; and we left the two gentlemen together, to put on our pelisses. As we went upstairs Lady Susan begged permission to attend me for a few moments in my dressing-room, as she was anxious to speak with me in private. I led her thither accordingly, and as soon as the door was closed, she said: "I was never more surprized in my life than by Sir James's arrival, and the suddenness of it requires some apology to you, my dear sister; though to *me*, as a mother, it is highly flattering. He is so extremely attached to my daughter that he could not exist longer without seeing her. Sir James is a young man of an amiable disposition and excellent character; a little too much of the rattle, perhaps, but a year or two will rectify *that:* and he is in other respects so very eligible a match for Frederica, that I have always observed his attachment with the greatest pleasure; and am persuaded that you and my brother will give the alliance your hearty approbation. I have never before mentioned the likelihood of its taking place to anyone, because I thought that whilst Frederica continued at school it had better not be known to exist; but now, as I am convinced that Frederica is too old ever to submit to school confinement, and have, therefore, begun to consider her union with Sir James as not very distant, I had intended within a few days to acquaint yourself and Mr. Vernon with the whole business. I am sure, my dear sister, you will excuse my remaining silent so long, and agree with me that such circumstances, while they continue from any cause in suspense, cannot be too cautiously concealed. When you have the happiness of bestowing your sweet little Catherine, some years hence, on a man who in connection and character is alike unexceptionable, you will know what I feel now; though, thank Heaven, you cannot have all my reasons for rejoicing in such an event. Catherine will be amply provided for, and not, like my Frederica, indebted to a fortunate establishment for the comforts of life." She concluded by demanding my congratulations. I gave them somewhat awkwardly, I believe; for, in fact, the sudden disclosure of so important a matter took from me the power of speaking with any clearness, She thanked me, however, most affectionately, for my kind concern in the welfare of herself and daughter; and then said: "I am not apt to deal in professions, my dear Mrs. Vernon, and I never had the convenient talent of affecting sensations foreign to my heart; and therefore I trust you will believe me when I declare, that much as I had heard in your praise before I knew you, I had no idea that I should ever love you as I now do; and I must further say that your friendship towards me is more particularly gratifying because I have reason to believe that some attempts were made to prejudice you against me. I only wish that they, whoever they are, to whom I am indebted for such kind intentions, could see the terms on which we now are together, and understand the real affection we feel for each other; but I will not detain you any longer. God bless you, for your goodness to me and my girl, and continue to you all your present happiness." What can one say of such a woman, my dear mother? Such earnestness such solemnity of expression! and yet I cannot help suspecting the truth of everything she says. As for Reginald, I believe he does not know what to make of the matter. When Sir James came, he appeared all astonishment and perplexity; the folly of the young man and the confusion of Frederica entirely engrossed him; and though a little private discourse with Lady Susan has since had its effect, he is still hurt, I am sure, at her allowing of such a man's attentions to her daughter. Sir James invited himself with great composure to remain here a few days—hoped we would not think it odd, was aware of its being very impertinent, but he took the liberty of a relation; and concluded by wishing, with a laugh, that he might be really one very soon. Even Lady Susan seemed a little disconcerted by this forwardness; in her heart I am persuaded she sincerely wished him gone. But something must be done for this poor girl, if her feelings are such as both I and her uncle believe them to be. She must not be sacrificed to policy or ambition, and she must not be left to suffer from the dread of it. The girl whose heart can distinguish Reginald De Courcy, deserves, however he may slight her, a better fate than to be Sir James Martin's wife. As soon as I can get her alone, I will discover the real truth; but she seems to wish to avoid me. I hope this does not proceed from anything wrong, and that I shall not find out I have thought too well of her. Her behaviour to Sir James certainly speaks the greatest consciousness and embarrassment, but I see nothing in it more like encouragement. Adieu, my dear mother.

Yours, &c.,

C. VERNON.

XXI. *Miss Vernon to Mr De Courcy*

SIR,—I hope you will excuse this liberty; I am forced upon it by the greatest distress, or I should be ashamed to trouble you. I am very miserable about Sir James Martin, and have no other way in the world of helping myself but by writing to you, for I am forbidden even speaking to my uncle and aunt on the subject; and this being the case, I am afraid my applying to you will appear no better than equivocation, and as if I attended to the letter and not the spirit of mamma's commands. But if you do not take my part and persuade her to break it off, I shall be half distracted, for I cannot bear him. No human being but *you* could have any chance of prevailing with her. If you will, therefore, have the unspeakably great kindness of taking my part with her, and persuading her to send Sir James away, I shall be more obliged to you than it is possible for me to express. I always disliked him from the first: it is not a sudden fancy, I assure you, sir; I always thought him silly and impertinent and disagreeable, and now he is grown worse than ever. I would rather work for my bread than marry him. I do not know how to apologize enough for this letter; I know it is taking so great a liberty. I am aware how dreadfully angry it will make mamma, but I remember the risk.

I am, Sir, your most humble servant,
F. S. V.

XXII. *Lady Susan to Mrs. Johnson*

Churchhill.

THIS IS INSUFFERABLE! My dearest friend, I was never so enraged before, and must relieve myself by writing to you, who I know will enter into all my feelings. Who should come on Tuesday but Sir James Martin! Guess my astonishment, and vexation—for, as you well know, I never wished him to be seen at Churchhill. What a pity that you should not have known his intentions! Not content with coming, he actually invited himself to remain here a few days. I could have poisoned him! I made the best of it, however, and told my story with great success to Mrs. Vernon, who, whatever might be her real sentiments, said nothing in opposition to mine. I made a point also of Frederica's behaving civilly to Sir James, and gave her to understand that I was absolutely determined on her marrying him. She said something of her misery, but that was all. I have for some time been more particularly resolved on the match from seeing the rapid increase of her affection for Reginald, and from not feeling secure that a knowledge of such affection might not in the end awaken a return. Contemptible as a regard founded only on compassion must make them both in my eyes, I felt by no means assured that such might not be the consequence. It is true that Reginald had not in any degree grown cool towards me; but yet he has lately mentioned Frederica spontaneously and unnecessarily, and once said something in praise of her person. *He* was all astonishment at the appearance of my visitor, and at first observed Sir James with an attention which I was pleased to see not unmixed with jealousy; but unluckily it was impossible for me really to torment him, as Sir James, though extremely gallant to me, very soon made the whole party understand that his heart was devoted to my daughter. I had no great difficulty in convincing De Courcy, when we were alone, that I was perfectly justified, all things considered, in desiring the match; and the whole business seemed most comfortably arranged. They could none of them help perceiving that Sir James was no Solomon; but I had positively forbidden Frederica complaining to Charles Vernon or his wife, and they had therefore no pretence for interference; though my impertinent sister, I believe, wanted only opportunity for doing so. Everything, however, was going on calmly and quietly; and, though I counted the hours of Sir James's stay, my mind was entirely satisfied with the posture of affairs. Guess, then, what I must feel at the sudden disturbance of all my schemes; and that, too, from a quarter where I had least reason to expect it. Reginald came this morning into my dressing-room with a very unusual solemnity of countenance, and after some preface informed me in so many words that he wished to reason with me on the impropriety and unkindness of allowing Sir James Martin to address my daughter contrary to her inclinations. I was all amazement. When I found that he was not to be laughed out of his design, I calmly begged an explanation, and desired to know by what he was impelled, and by whom commissioned, to reprimand me. He then told me, mixing in his speech a few insolent compliments and ill-timed expressions of tenderness, to which I listened with perfect indifference, that my daughter had acquainted him with some circumstances concerning herself, Sir James, and me which had given him great uneasiness. In short, I found that she had in the first place actually written to him to request his interference, and that, on receiving her letter, he had conversed with her on the subject of it, in order to understand the particulars, and to assure himself of her real wishes. I have not a doubt but that the girl took this opportunity of making downright love to him. I am convinced of it by the manner in which he spoke of her. Much good may such love do him! I shall ever despise the man who can be gratified by the passion which he never

wished to inspire, nor solicited the avowal of. I shall
always detest them both. He can have no true regard
for me, or he would not have listened to her; and *she*,
with her little rebellious heart and indelicate feelings,
to throw herself into the protection of a young man
with whom she has scarcely ever exchanged two words
before! I am equally confounded at *her* impudence and
his credulity. How dared he believe what she told him
in my disfavour! Ought he not to have felt assured
that I must have unanswerable motives for all that I
had done? Where was his reliance on my sense and
goodness then? Where the resentment which true
love would have dictated against the person defaming
me—that person, too, a chit, a child, without talent
or education, whom he had been always taught to
despise? I was calm for some time; but the greatest
degree of forbearance may be overcome, and I hope I
was afterwards sufficiently keen. He endeavoured, long
endeavoured, to soften my resentment; but that woman
is a fool indeed who, while insulted by accusation, can
be worked on by compliments. At length he left me,
as deeply provoked as myself; and he showed his anger
more. I was quite cool, but he gave way to the most
violent indignation; I may therefore expect it will the
sooner subside, and perhaps his may be vanished for
ever, while mine will be found still fresh and implacable.
He is now shut up in his apartment, whither I heard him
go on leaving mine. How unpleasant, one would think,
must be his reflections! but some people's feelings are
incomprehensible. I have not yet tranquillised myself
enough to see Frederica. *She* shall not soon forget the
occurrences of this day; she shall find that she has
poured forth her tender tale of love in vain, and exposed

herself for ever to the contempt of the whole world, and the severest resentment of her injured mother.

Your affectionate
S. VERNON.

XXIII. *Mrs. Vernon to Lady De Courcy*

Churchhill.

LET ME CONGRATULATE YOU, my dearest Mother! The affair which has given us so much anxiety is drawing to a happy conclusion. Our prospect is most delightful, and since matters have now taken so favourable a turn, I am quite sorry that I ever imparted my apprehensions to you; for the pleasure of learning that the danger is over is perhaps dearly purchased by all that you have previously suffered. I am so much agitated by delight that I can scarcely hold a pen; but am determined to send you a few short lines by James, that you may have some explanation of what must so greatly astonish you, as that Reginald should be returning to Parklands. I was sitting about half an hour ago with Sir James in the breakfast parlour, when my brother called me out of the room. I instantly saw that something was the matter; his complexion was raised, and he spoke with great emotion; you know his eager manner, my dear mother, when his mind is interested. "Catherine," said he, "I am going home to-day; I am sorry to leave you, but I must go: it is a great while since I have seen my father and mother. I am going to send James forward with my hunters immediately; if you have any letter, therefore, he can take it. I shall not be at home myself till Wednesday or Thursday, as I shall go through

London, where I have business; but before I leave you," he continued, speaking in a lower tone, and with still greater energy, "I must warn you of one thing—do not let Frederica Vernon be made unhappy by that Martin. He wants to marry her; her mother promotes the match, but she cannot endure the idea of it. Be assured that I speak from the fullest conviction of the truth of what I say; I Know that Frederica is made wretched by Sir James's continuing here. She is a sweet girl, and deserves a better fate. Send him away immediately; he is only a fool: but what her mother can mean, Heaven only knows! Good bye," he added, shaking my hand with earnestness; "I do not know when you will see me again; but remember what I tell you of Frederica; you *must* make it your business to see justice done her. She is an amiable girl, and has a very superior mind to what we have given her credit for." He then left me, and ran upstairs. I would not try to stop him, for I know what his feelings must be. The nature of mine, as I listened to him, I need not attempt to describe; for a minute or two I remained in the same spot, overpowered by wonder of a most agreeable sort indeed; yet it required some consideration to be tranquilly happy. In about ten minutes after my return to the parlour Lady Susan entered the room. I concluded, of course, that she and Reginald had been quarrelling; and looked with anxious curiosity for a confirmation of my belief in her face. Mistress of deceit, however, she appeared perfectly unconcerned, and after chatting on indifferent subjects for a short time, said to me, "I find from Wilson that we are going to lose Mr. De Courcy—is it true that he leaves Churchhill this morning?" I replied that it was. "He told us nothing of all this last night," said she, laughing, "or even this morning at breakfast; but perhaps he did not know it himself. Young men are often hasty in their resolutions, and not more sudden in forming than unsteady in keeping them. I should not be surprised if he were to change his mind at last, and not go." She soon afterwards left the room. I trust, however, my dear mother, that we have no reason to fear an alteration of his present plan; things have gone too far. They must have quarrelled, and about Frederica, too. Her calmness astonishes me. What delight will be yours in seeing him again; in seeing him still worthy your esteem, still capable of forming your happiness! When I next write I shall be able to tell you that Sir James is gone, Lady Susan vanquished, and Frederica at peace. We have much to do, but it shall be done. I am all impatience to hear how this astonishing change was effected. I finish as I began, with the warmest congratulations.

Yours ever, &c.,
CATH. VERNON.

XXIV. *From the Same to the Same*

Churchhill.

Little did I imagine, my dear Mother, when I sent off my last letter, that the delightful perturbation of spirits I was then in would undergo so speedy, so melancholy a reverse. I never can sufficiently regret that I wrote to you at all. Yet who could have foreseen what has happened? My dear mother, every hope which made me so happy only two hours ago has vanished. The quarrel between Lady Susan and Reginald is made up, and we are all as we were before. One point only is gained. Sir James Martin is dismissed. What are we now to look forward to? I am indeed disappointed; Reginald was all but gone, his horse was ordered and all but brought to the door; who would not have felt safe? For half an hour I was in momentary expectation of his departure. After I had sent off my letter to you, I went to Mr. Vernon, and sat with him in his room talking over the whole matter, and then determined to look for Frederica, whom I had not seen since breakfast. I met her on the stairs, and saw that she was crying. "My dear aunt," said she, "he is going—Mr. De Courcy is going, and it is all my fault. I am afraid you will be very angry with me. but indeed I had no idea it would end so." "My love," I replied, "do not think it necessary to apologize to me on that account. I shall feel myself under an obligation to anyone who is the means of sending my brother home, because," recollecting myself, "I know my father wants very much to see him. But what is it you have done to occasion all this?" She blushed deeply as she answered: "I was so unhappy about Sir James that I could not help—I have done something very wrong, I know; but you have not an idea of the misery I have been in: and mamma had ordered me never to speak to you or my uncle about it, and—" "You therefore spoke to my brother to engage his interference," said I, to save her the explanation. "No, but I wrote to him—I did indeed, I got up this morning before it was light, and was two hours about it; and when my letter was done I thought I never should have courage to give it. After breakfast however, as I was going to my room, I met him in the passage, and then, as I knew that everything must depend on that moment, I forced myself to give it. He was so good as to take it immediately. I dared not look at him, and ran away directly. I was in such a fright I could hardly breathe. My dear aunt, you do not know how miserable I have been." "Frederica" said I, "you ought to have told me all your distresses. You would have found in me a friend always ready to assist you. Do you think that your uncle or I should not have espoused your cause as warmly as my brother?" "Indeed, I did not doubt your kindness," said she, colouring again, "but I thought Mr. De Courcy could do anything with my mother; but I was mistaken: they have had a dreadful quarrel about it, and he is going away. Mamma will never forgive me, and I shall be worse off than ever." "No, you shall not," I replied; "in such a point as this your mother's prohibition ought not to have prevented your speaking to me on the subject. She has no right to make you unhappy, and she shall *not* do it. Your applying, however, to Reginald can be productive only of good to all parties. I believe it is best as it is. Depend upon it that you shall not be made unhappy any longer." At that moment how great was my astonishment at seeing Reginald come out of Lady Susan's dressing-room. My heart misgave me instantly. His confusion at seeing me was very evident. Frederica immediately disappeared. "Are you going?" I said; "you will find Mr. Vernon in his own room." "No, Catherine," he replied, "I am not going. Will you let me speak to you a moment?" We went into my room. "I find," he continued, his confusion increasing as he spoke, "that I have been acting with my usual foolish impetuosity. I have entirely misunderstood Lady Susan, and was on the point of leaving the house under a false impression of her conduct. There has been some very great mistake; we have been all mistaken, I fancy. Frederica does not know her mother. Lady Susan means nothing but her good, but she will not make a friend of her. Lady Susan does not always know, therefore, what will make her daughter happy. Besides, I could have no right to interfere. Miss Vernon was mistaken in applying to me. In short, Catherine, everything has gone wrong, but it is now all happily settled. Lady Susan, I believe, wishes to speak to you about it, if you are at leisure." "Certainly," I replied, deeply sighing at the recital of so lame a story. I made no comments, however, for words would have been vain.

Reginald was glad to get away, and I went to Lady Susan, curious, indeed, to hear her account of it. "Did I not tell you," said she with a smile, "that your brother would not leave us after all?" "You did, indeed," replied I very gravely; "but I flattered myself you would be mistaken." "I should not have hazarded such an opinion," returned she, "if it had not at that moment occurred to me that his resolution of going might be occasioned by a conversation in which we had been this morning engaged, and which had ended very much to his dissatisfaction, from our not rightly understanding each other's meaning. This idea struck me at the moment, and I instantly determined that an accidental dispute, in which I might probably be as much to blame as himself, should not deprive you of your brother. If you remember, I left the room almost immediately. I was resolved to lose no time in clearing up those mistakes as far as I could. The case was this—Frederica had set herself violently against marrying Sir James." "And can your ladyship wonder that she should?" cried I with some warmth; "Frederica has an excellent understanding, and Sir James has none." "I am at least very far from regretting it, my dear sister," said she; "on the contrary, I am grateful for so favourable a sign of my daughter's sense. Sir James is certainly below par (his boyish manners make him appear worse); and had Frederica possessed the penetration and the abilities which I could have wished in my daughter, or had I even known her to possess as much as she does, I should not have been anxious for the match." "It is odd that you should alone be ignorant of your daughter's sense!" "Frederica never does justice to herself; her manners are shy and childish, and besides she is afraid of me. During her poor father's life she was a spoilt child; the severity which it has since been necessary for me to show has alienated her affection; neither has she any of that brilliancy of intellect, that genius or vigour of mind which will force itself forward." "Say rather that she has been unfortunate in her education!" "Heaven knows, my dearest Mrs. Vernon, how fully I am aware of that; but I would wish to forget every circumstance that might throw blame on the memory of one whose name is sacred with me." Here she pretended to cry; I was out of patience with her. "But what," said I, "was your ladyship going to tell me about your disagreement with my brother?" "It originated in an action of my daughter's, which equally marks her want of judgment and the unfortunate dread of me I have been mentioning—she wrote to Mr. De Courcy." "I know she did; you had forbidden her speaking to Mr. Vernon or to me on the cause of her distress; what could she do, therefore, but apply to my brother?" "Good God!" she exclaimed, "what an opinion you must have of me! Can you possibly suppose that I was aware of her unhappiness! that it was my object to make my own child miserable, and that I had forbidden her speaking to you on the subject from a fear of your interrupting the diabolical scheme? Do you think me destitute of every honest, every natural feeling? Am I capable of consigning *her* to everlasting: misery whose welfare it is my first earthly duty to promote? The idea is horrible!" "What, then, was your intention when you insisted on her silence?" "Of what use, my dear sister, could be any application to you, however the affair might stand? Why should I subject you to entreaties which I refused to attend to myself? Neither for your sake nor for hers, nor for my own, could such a thing be desirable. When my own resolution was taken I could nor wish for the interference, however friendly, of another person. I was mistaken, it is true, but I believed myself right." "But what was this mistake to which your ladyship so often alludes! from whence arose so astonishing a misconception of your daughter's feelings! Did you not know that she disliked Sir James?" "I knew that he was not absolutely the man she would have chosen, but I was persuaded that her objections to him did not arise from any perception of his deficiency. You must not question me, however, my dear sister, too minutely on this point," continued she, taking me affectionately by the hand; "I honestly own that there is something to conceal. Frederica makes me very unhappy! Her applying to Mr. De Courcy hurt me particularly." "What is it you mean to infer," said I, "by this appearance of mystery? If you think your daughter at all attached to Reginald, her objecting to Sir James could not less deserve to be attended to than if the cause of her objecting had been a consciousness of his folly; and why should your ladyship, at any rate, quarrel with my brother for an inter-ference which, you must know, it is not in his nature to refuse when urged in such a manner?"

"His disposition, you know, is warm, and he came to expostulate with me; his compassion all alive for this ill-used girl, this heroine in distress! We misunderstood each other: he believed me more to blame than I really was; I considered his interference less excusable than I now find it. I have a real regard for him, and was beyond ex-pression mortified to find it, as I thought, so ill bestowed We were both warm, and of course both to blame. His resolution of leaving Churchhill is consistent with his general eagerness. When I understood his intention, however, and at the same time began to think that we had been perhaps equally mistaken in each other's mean-ing, I resolved to have an explanation before it was too late. For any member of your family I must always feel a degree of affection, and I own it would have sensibly hurt me if my acquaintance with Mr. De Courcy had ended so gloomily. I have now only to say further, that as I am convinced of Frederica's having a reasonable dislike to Sir James, I shall instantly inform him that he must give up all hope of her. I reproach myself for having even, though innocently, made her unhappy on that score. She shall have all the retribution in my power to make; if she value her own happiness as much as I do, if she judge wisely, and command herself as she ought, she may now be easy. Excuse me, my dearest sister, for thus trespassing on your time, but I owe it to my own character; and after this explanation I trust I am in no danger of sinking in your opinion." I could have said, "Not much, indeed!" but I left her almost in silence. It was the greatest stretch of forbearance I could practise. I could not have stopped myself had I begun. Her assurance! her deceit! but I will not allow myself to dwell on them; they will strike you sufficiently. My heart sickens within me. As soon as I was tolerably composed I returned to the parlour. Sir James's carriage was at the door, and he, merry as usual, soon afterwards took his leave. How easily does her lady-ship encourage or dismiss a lover! In spite of this release, Frederica still looks unhappy: still fearful, perhaps, of her mother's anger; and though dreading my brother's departure, jealous, it may be, of his staying. I see how closely she observes him and Lady Susan, poor girl! I have now no hope for her. There is not a chance of her affection being returned. He thinks very differently of her from what he used to do; he does her some justice, but his reconciliation with her mother precludes every dearer hope. Prepare, my dear mother, for the worst! The probability of their marrying is surely heightened! He is more securely hers than ever. When that wretched event takes place, Frederica must belong wholly to us. I am thankful that my last letter will precede this by so little, as every moment that you can be saved from feeling a joy which leads only to disappointment is of consequence.

Yours ever, &c.,
CATHERINE VERNON.

XXV. *Lady Susan to Mrs. Johnson*

Churchhill.

I CALL ON YOU, dear Alicia, for congratulations: I am my own self, gay and triumphant! When I wrote to you the other day I was, in truth, in high irritation, and with ample cause. Nay, I know not whether I ought to be quite tranquil now, for I have had more trouble in restoring peace than I ever intended to submit to—a spirit, too, resulting from a fancied sense of superior integrity, which is peculiarly insolent! I shall not easily forgive him, I assure you. He was actually on the point of leaving Churchhill! I had scarcely concluded my last, when Wilson brought me word of it. I found, therefore, that something must be done; for I did not choose to leave my character at the mercy of a man whose passions are so violent and so revengeful. It would have been trifling with my reputation to allow of his departing with such an impression in my disfavour; in this light, condescension was necessary. I sent Wilson to say that I desired to speak with him before he went; he came immediately. The angry emotions which had marked every feature when we last parted were partially subdued. He seemed astonished at the summons, and looked as if half wishing and half fearing to be softened by what I might say. If my countenance expressed what I aimed at, it was composed and dignified; and yet, with a degree of pensiveness which might convince him that I was not quite happy. "I beg your pardon, sir, for the liberty I have taken in sending for you," said I; "but as I have just learnt your intention of leaving this place to-day, I feel it my duty to entreat that you will not on my account shorten your visit here even an hour. I am perfectly aware that after what has passed between us it would ill suit the feelings of either to remain longer in the same house: so very great, so total a change from the intimacy of friendship must render any future intercourse the severest punishment; and your resolution of quitting Churchhill is undoubtedly in unison with our situation, and with those lively feelings which I know you to possess. But, at the same time, it is not for me to suffer such a sacrifice as it must be to leave relations to whom you are so much attached, and are so dear. My remaining here cannot give that pleasure to Mr. and Mrs. Vernon which your society must; and my visit has already perhaps been too long. My removal, therefore, which must, at any rate, take place soon, may, with perfect convenience, be hastened; and I make it my particular request that I may not in any way be instrumental in separating a family so affectionately attached to each other. Where I go is of no consequence to anyone; of very little to myself; but you are of importance to all your connections." Here I concluded, and I hope you will be satisfied with my speech. Its effect on Reginald justifies some portion of vanity, for it was no less favourable than instantaneous. Oh, how delightful it was to watch the variations of his countenance while I spoke! to see the struggle between returning tenderness and the remains of displeasure. There is something agreeable in feelings so easily worked on; not that I envy him their possession, nor would, for the world, have such myself; but they are very convenient when one wishes to influence the passions of another. And yet this Reginald, whom a very few words from me softened at once into the utmost submission, and rendered more tractable, more attached, more devoted than ever, would have left me in the first angry swelling of his proud heart without deigning to seek an explanation. Humbled as he now is, I cannot forgive him such an instance of pride, and am doubtful whether I ought not to punish him by dismissing him at once after this reconciliation, or by marrying and teazing him for ever.

But these measures are each too violent to be adopted without some deliberation; at present my thoughts are fluctuating between various schemes. I have many things to compass: I must punish Frederica, and pretty severely too, for her application to Reginald; I must punish him for receiving it so favourably, and for the rest of his conduct. I must torment my sister-in-law for the insolent triumph of her look and manner since Sir James has been dismissed; for, in reconciling Reginald to me, I was not able to save that ill-fated young man; and I must make myself amends for the humiliation to which I have stooped within these few days. To effect all this I have various plans. I have also an idea of being soon in town; and whatever may be my determination as to the rest, I shall probably put *that* project in execution; for London will be always the fairest field of action, however my views may be directed; and at any rate I shall there be rewarded by your society, and a little dissipation, for a ten weeks' penance at Churchhill. I believe I owe it to my character to complete the match between my daughter and Sir James after having so long intended it. Let me know your opinion on this point. Flexibility of mind, a disposition easily biassed by others, is an attribute which you know I am not very desirous of obtaining; nor has Frederica any claim to the indulgence of her notions at the expense of her mother's inclinations. Her idle love for Reginald, too! It is surely my duty to discourage such romantic nonsense. All things considered, therefore, it seems incumbent on me to take her to town and marry her immediately to Sir James. When my own will is effected contrary to his, I shall have some credit in being on good terms with Reginald, which at present, in fact, I have not;

for though he is still in my power, I have given up the very article by which our quarrel was produced, and at best the honour of victory is doubtful. Send me your opinion on all these matters, my dear Alicia, and let me know whether you can get lodgings to suit me within a short distance of you.

Your most attached
S. VERNON.

XXVI. *Mrs. Johnson to Lady Susan*

Edward Street.

I AM GRATIFIED by your reference, and this is my advice: that you come to town yourself, without loss of time, but that you leave Frederica behind. It would surely be much more to the purpose to get yourself well established by marrying Mr. De Courcy, than to irritate him and the rest of his family by making her marry Sir James. You should think more of yourself and less of your daughter. She is not of a disposition to do you credit in the world, and seems precisely in her proper place at Churchhill, with the Vernons. But you are fitted for society, and it is shameful to have you exiled from it. Leave Frederica, therefore, to punish herself for the plague she has given you, by indulging that romantic tender-heartedness which will always ensure her misery enough, and come to London as soon as you can. I have another reason for urging this: Mainwaring came to town last week, and has contrived, in spite of Mr. Johnson, to make opportunities of seeing me. He is absolutely miserable about you, and jealous to such a degree of De Courcy that it would be highly unadvisable for them to meet at present. And yet, if you do not allow him to see you here, I cannot answer for his not committing some great imprudence—such as going to Churchhill, for instance, which would be dreadful! Besides, if you take my advice, and resolve to marry De Courcy, it will be indispensably necessary to you to get Mainwaring out of the way; and you only can have influence enough to send him back to his wife. I have still another motive for your coming: Mr. Johnson leaves London next Tuesday; he is going for his health to Bath, where, if the waters are favourable to his constitution and my wishes, he will be laid up with the gout many weeks. During his absence we shall be able to chuse our own society, and to have true enjoyment. I would ask you to Edward Street, but that once he forced from me a kind of promise never to invite you to my house; nothing but my being in the utmost distress for money should have extorted it from me. I can get you, however, a nice drawing-room apartment in Upper Seymour Street, and we may be always together there or here; for I consider my promise to Mr. Johnson as comprehending only (at least in his absence) your not sleeping in the house. Poor Mainwaring gives me such histories of his wife's jealousy. Silly woman to expect constancy from so charming a man! but she always was silly—intolerably so in marrying him at all, she the heiress of a large fortune and he without a shilling: one title, I know, she might have had, besides baronets. Her folly in forming the connection was so great that, though Mr. Johnson was her guardian, and I do not in general share *his* feelings, I never can forgive her.

Adieu. Yours ever,
ALICIA.

XXVII. *Mrs. Vernon to Lady De Courcy*

Churchhill.

THIS LETTER, my dear Mother, will be brought you by Reginald. His long visit is about to be concluded at last, but I fear the separation takes place too late to do us any good. She is going to London to see her particular friend, Mrs. Johnson. It was at first her intention that Frederica should accompany her, for the benefit of masters, but we overruled her there. Frederica was wretched in the idea of going, and I could not bear to have her at the mercy of her mother; not all the masters in London could compensate for the ruin of her comfort. I should have feared, too, for her health, and for everything but her principles—there I believe she is not to be injured by her mother, or her mother's friends; but with those friends she must have mixed (a very bad set, I doubt not), or have been left in total solitude, and I can hardly tell which would have been worse for her. If she is with her mother, moreover, she must, alas! in all probability be with Reginald, and that would be the greatest evil of all. Here we shall in time be in peace, and our regular employments, our books and conversations, with exercise, the children, and every domestic pleasure in my power to procure her, will, I trust, gradually overcome this youthful attachment. I should not have a doubt of it were she slighted for any other woman in the world than her own mother. How long Lady Susan will be in town, or whether she returns here again, I know not. I could not be cordial in my invitation, but if she chuses to come no want of cordiality on my part will keep her away. I could not help asking Reginald if he intended being in London this winter, as soon as I found her ladyship's steps would be bent thither; and though he professed himself quite undetermined, there was something in his look and voice as he spoke which contradicted his words. I have done with lamentation; I look upon the event as so far decided that I resign myself to it in despair. If he leaves you soon for London everything will be concluded.

Your affectionate, &c.,
C. VERNON.

XXVIII. *Mrs. Johnson to Lady Susan*

Edward Street.

MY DEAREST FRIEND,—I write in the greatest distress; the most unfortunate event has just taken place. Mr. Johnson has hit on the most effectual manner of plaguing us all. He had heard, I imagine, by some means or other, that you were soon to be in London, and immediately contrived to have such an attack of the gout as must at least delay his journey to Bath, if not wholly prevent it. I am persuaded the gout is brought on or kept off at pleasure; it was the same when I wanted to join the Hamiltons to the Lakes; and three years ago, when I had a fancy for Bath, nothing could induce him to have a gouty symptom.

I am pleased to find that my letter had so much effect on you, and that De Courcy is certainly your own. Let me hear from you as soon as you arrive, and in particular tell me what you mean to do with Mainwaring. It is impossible to say when I shall be able to come to you; my confinement must be great. It is such an abominable trick to be ill here instead of at Bath that I can scarcely command myself at all. At Bath his old aunts would have nursed him, but here it all falls upon me; and he bears pain with such patience that I have not the common excuse for losing my temper.

Yours ever,
ALICIA.

XXIX. *Lady Susan Vernon to Mrs. Johnson*

Upper Seymour Street.

MY DEAR ALICIA,—There needed not this last fit of the gout to make me detest Mr. Johnson, but now the extent of my aversion is not to be estimated. To have you confined as nurse in his apartment! My dear Alicia, of what a mistake were you guilty in marrying a man of his age! just old enough to be formal, ungovernable, and to have the gout; too old to be agreeable, too young to die. I arrived last night about five, had scarcely swallowed my dinner when Mainwaring made his appearance. I will not dissemble what real pleasure his sight afforded me, nor how strongly I felt the contrast between his person and manners and those of Reginald, to the infinite disadvantage of the latter. For an hour or two I was even staggered in my resolution of marrying him, and though this was too idle and nonsensical an idea to remain long on my mind, I do not feel very eager for the conclusion of my marriage, nor look forward with much impatience to the time when Reginald, according to our agreement, is to be in town. I shall probably put off his arrival under some pretence or other. He must not come till Mainwaring is gone. I am still doubtful at times as to marrying; if the old man would die I might not hesitate, but a state of dependance on the caprice of Sir Reginald will not suit the freedom of my spirit; and if I resolve to wait for that event, I shall have excuse enough at present in having been scarcely ten months a widow. I have not given Mainwaring any hint of my intention, or allowed him to consider my acquaintance with Reginald as more than the commonest flirtation, and he is tolerably appeased. Adieu, till we meet; I am enchanted with my lodgings.

Yours ever,
S. VERNON.

XXX. *Lady Susan Vernon to Mr. De Courcy*

Upper Seymour Street.

I HAVE RECEIVED YOUR LETTER, and though I do not attempt to conceal that I am gratified by your impatience for the hour of meeting, I yet feel myself under the necessity of delaying that hour beyond the time originally fixed. Do not think me unkind for such an exercise of my power, nor accuse me of instability without first hearing my reasons. In the course of my journey from Churchhill I had ample leisure for reflection on the present state of our affairs, and every review has served to convince me that they require a delicacy and cautiousness of conduct to which we have hitherto been too little attentive. We have been hurried on by our feelings to a degree of precipitation which ill accords with the claims of our friends or the opinion of the world. We have been unguarded in forming this hasty engagement, but we must not complete the imprudence by ratifying it while there is so much reason to fear the connection would be opposed by those friends on whom you depend. It is not for us to blame any expectations on your father's side of your marrying to advantage; where possessions are so extensive as those of your family, the wish of increasing them, if not strictly reasonable, is too common to excite surprize or resentment. He has a right to require a woman of fortune in his daughter-in-law, and I am sometimes quarrelling with myself for suffering you to form a connection so imprudent; but the influence of reason is often acknowledged too late by those who feel like me. I have now been but a few months a widow, and, however little indebted to my husband's memory for any happiness derived from him during a union of some years, I cannot forget that the indelicacy of so early a second marriage must subject me to the censure of the world, and incur, what would be still more insupportable, the displeasure of Mr. Vernon. I might perhaps harden myself in time against the injustice of general reproach, but the loss of *his* valued esteem I am, as you well know, ill-fitted to endure; and when to this may be added the consciousness of having injured you with your family, how am I to support myself? With feelings so poignant as mine, the conviction of having divided the son from his parents would make me, even with you, the most miserable of beings. It will surely, therefore, be advisable to delay our union—to delay it till appearances are more promising—till affairs have taken a more favourable turn. To assist us In such a resolution I feel that absence will be necessary. We must not meet. Cruel as this sentence may appear, the necessity of pronouncing it, which can alone reconcile it to myself, will be evident to you when you have considered our situation in the light in which I have found myself imperiously obliged to place it. You may be—you must be—well assured that nothing but the strongest conviction of duty could induce me to wound my own feelings by urging a lengthened separation, and of insensibility to yours you will hardly suspect me. Again, therefore, I say that we ought not, we must not, yet meet. By a removal for some months from each other we shall tranquillise the sisterly fears of Mrs. Vernon, who, accustomed herself to the enjoyment of riches, considers fortune as necessary everywhere, and whose sensibilities are not of a nature to comprehend ours. Let me hear from you soon—very soon. Tell me that you submit to my arguments, and do not reproach me for using such. I cannot bear reproaches: my spirits are not so high as to need being repressed. I must endeavour to seek amusement, and fortunately many of my friends are in town; amongst them the Mainwarings; you know how sincerely I regard both husband and wife.

I am, very faithfully yours,
S. VERNON

XXXI. *Lady Susan to Mrs. Johnson*

Upper Seymour Street.

MY DEAR FRIEND,—That tormenting creature, Reginald, is here. My letter, which was intended to keep him longer in the country, has hastened him to town. Much as I wish him away, however, I cannot help being pleased with such a proof of attachment. He is devoted to me, heart and soul. He will carry this note himself, which is to serve as an introduction to you, with whom he longs to be acquainted. Allow him to spend the evening with you, that I may be in no danger of his returning here. I have told him that I am not quite well, and must be alone; and should he call again there might be confusion, for it is impossible to be sure of servants. Keep him, therefore, I entreat you, in Edward Street. You will not find him a heavy companion, and I allow you to flirt with him as much as you like. At the same time, do not forget my real interest; say all that you can to convince him that I shall be quite wretched if he remains here; you know my reasons—propriety, and so forth. I would urge them more myself, but that I am impatient to be rid of him, as Mainwaring comes within half an hour.

Adieu!

S VERNON

XXXII. *Mrs. Johnson to Lady Susan*

Edward Street.

MY DEAR CREATURE,—I am in agonies, and know not what to do. Mr. De Courcy arrived just when he should not. Mrs. Mainwaring had that instant entered the house, and forced herself into her guardian's presence, though I did not know a syllable of it till afterwards, for I was out when both she and Reginald came, or I should have sent him away at all events; but she was shut up with Mr. Johnson, while he waited in the drawing-room for me. She arrived yesterday in pursuit of her husband, but perhaps you know this already from himself. She came to this house to entreat my husband's interference, and before I could be aware of it, everything that you could wish to be concealed was known to him, and unluckily she had wormed out of Mainwaring's servant that he had visited you every day since your being in town, and had just watched him to your door herself! What could I do! Facts are such horrid things! All is by this time known to De Courcy, who is now alone with Mr. Johnson. Do not accuse me; indeed, it was impossible to prevent it. Mr. Johnson has for some time suspected De Courcy of intending to marry you, and would speak with him alone as soon as he knew him to be in the house. That detestable Mrs. Mainwaring, who, for your comfort, has fretted herself thinner and uglier than ever, is still here, and they have been all closeted together. What can be done? At any rate, I hope he will plague his wife more than ever. With anxious wishes,

Yours faithfully,
ALICIA.

XXXIII. *Lady Susan to Mrs. Johnson*

Upper Seymour Street.

THIS *ECLAIRCISSEMENT* is rather provoking. How unlucky that you should have been from home! I thought myself sure of you at seven! I am undismayed however. Do not torment yourself with fears on my account; depend on it, I can make my story good with Reginald. Mainwaring is just gone; he brought me the news of his wife's arrival. Silly woman, what does she expect by such manoeuvres? Yet I wish she had stayed quietly at Langford. Reginald will be a little enraged at first, but by to-morrow's dinner, everything will be well again.

Adieu!

S. V.

XXXIV. *Mr. De Courcy to Lady Susan*

—— Hotel

I WRITE ONLY to bid you farewell, the spell is removed; I see you as you are. Since we parted yesterday, I have received from indisputable authority such a history of you as must bring the most mortifying conviction of the imposition I have been under, and the absolute necessity of an immediate and eternal separation from you. You cannot doubt to what I allude. Langford! Langford! that word will be sufficient. I received my information in Mr. Johnson's house, from Mrs. Mainwaring herself. You know how I have loved you; you can intimately judge of my present feelings, but I am not so weak as to find indulgence in describing them to a woman who will glory in having excited their anguish, but whose affection they have never been able to gain.

R. DE COURCY.

XXXV. *LADY SUSAN TO MR. DE COURCY*

Upper Seymour Street.

I WILL NOT ATTEMPT to describe my astonishment in reading the note this moment received from you. I am bewildered in my endeavours to form some rational conjecture of what Mrs. Mainwaring can have told you to occasion so extraordinary a change in your sentiments. Have I not explained everything to you with respect to myself which could bear a doubtful meaning, and which the ill-nature of the world had interpreted to my discredit? What can you now have heard to stagger your esteem for me? Have I ever had a concealment from you? Reginald, you agitate me beyond expression, I cannot suppose that the old story of Mrs. Mainwaring's jealousy can be revived again, or at least be *listened* to again. Come to me immediately, and explain what is at present absolutely incomprehensible. Believe me the single word of Langford is not of such potent intelligence as to supersede the necessity of more. If we *are* to part, it will at least be handsome to take your personal leave—but I have little heart to jest; in truth, I am serious enough; for to be sunk, though but for an hour, in your esteem Is a humiliation to which I know not how to submit. I shall count every minute till your arrival.

S. V.

XXXVI. *Mr. De Courcy to Lady Susan*

—— Hotel.

WHY WOULD YOU write to me? Why do you require particulars? But, since it must be so, I am obliged to declare that all the accounts of your misconduct during the life, and since the death of Mr. Vernon, which had reached me, in common with the world in general, and gained my entire belief before I saw you, but which you, by the exertion of your perverted abilities, had made me resolved to disallow, have been unanswerably proved to me; nay more, I am assured that a connection, of which I had never before entertained a thought, has for some time existed, and still continues to exist, between you and the man whose family you robbed of its peace in return for the hospitality with which you were received into it; that you have corresponded with him ever since your leaving Langford; not with his wife, but with him, and that he now visits you every day. Can you, dare you deny it? and all this at the time when I was an encouraged, an accepted lover! From what have I not escaped! I have only to be grateful. Far from me be all complaint, every sigh of regret. My own folly had endangered me, my preservation I owe to the kindness, the integrity of another; but the unfortunate Mrs. Mainwaring, whose agonies while she related the past seemed to threaten her reason, how is *she* to be consoled! After such a discovery as this, you will scarcely affect further wonder at my meaning in bidding you adieu. My understanding is at length restored, and teaches no less to abhor the artifices which had subdued me than to despise myself for the weakness on which their strength was founded.

R. DE COURCY.

XXXVII. *Lady Susan to Mr. De Courcy*

Upper Seymour Street.

I AM SATISFIED, and will trouble you no more when these few lines are dismissed. The engagement which you were eager to form a fortnight ago is no longer compatible with your views, and I rejoice to find that the prudent advice of your parents has not been given in vain. Your restoration to peace will, I doubt not, speedily follow this act of filial obedience, and I flatter myself with the hope of surviving my share in this disappointment.

S. V.

XXXVIII. *Mrs. Johnson to Lady Susan Vernon*

Edward Street

I AM GRIEVED, though I cannot be astonished at your rupture with Mr. De Courcy; he has just informed Mr. Johnson of it by letter. He leaves London, he says, to-day. Be assured that I partake in all your feelings, and do not be angry if I say that our intercourse, even by letter, must soon be given up. It makes me miserable; but Mr. Johnson vows that if I persist in the connection, he will settle in the country for the rest of his life, and you know it is impossible to submit to such an extremity while any other alternative remains. You have heard of course that the Mainwarings are to part, and I am afraid Mrs. M. will come home to us again; but she is still so fond of her husband, and frets so much about him, that perhaps she may not live long. Miss Mainwaring is just come to town to be with her aunt, and they say that she declares she will have Sir James Martin before she leaves London again. If I were you, I would certainly get him myself. I had almost forgot to give you my opinion of Mr. De Courcy; I am really delighted with him; he is full as handsome, I think, as Mainwaring, and with such an open, good-humoured countenance, that one cannot help loving him at first sight. Mr. Johnson and he are the greatest friends in the world. Adieu, my dearest Susan, I wish matters did not go so perversely. That unlucky visit to Langford! but I dare say you did all for the best, and there is no defying destiny.

Your sincerely attached
ALICIA.

XXXIX. *Lady Susan to Mrs. Johnson*

Upper Seymour Street.

MY DEAR ALICIA,—I yield to the necessity which parts us. Under circumstances you could not act otherwise. Our friendship cannot be impaired by it, and in happier times, when your situation is as independent as mine, it will unite us again in the same intimacy as ever. For this I shall impatiently wait, and meanwhile can safely assure you that I never was more at ease, or better satisfied with myself and everything about me than at the present hour. Your husband I abhor, Reginald I despise, and I am secure of never seeing either again. Have I not reason to rejoice? Mainwaring is more devoted to me than ever; and were we at liberty, I doubt if I could resist even matrimony offered by *him*. This event, if his wife live with you, it may be in your power to hasten. The violence of her feelings, which must wear her out, may be easily kept in irritation. I rely on your friendship for this. I am now satisfied that I never could have brought myself to marry Reginald, and am equally determined that Frederica never shall. To-morrow, I shall fetch her from Churchhill, and let Maria Mainwaring tremble for the consequence.

Frederica shall be Sir James's wife before she quits my house, and she may whimper, and the Vernons may storm, I regard them not. I am tired of submitting my will to the caprices of others; of resigning my own judgment in deference to those to whom I owe no duty, and for whom I feel no respect. I have given up too much, have been too easily worked on, but Frederica shall now feel the difference. Adieu, dearest of friends; may the next gouty attack be more favourable! and may you always regard me as unalterably yours,

S. VERNON

XL. *Lady De Courcy to Mrs. Vernon*

MY DEAR CATHERINE,—I have charming news for you, and if I had not sent off my letter this morning you might have been spared the vexation of knowing of Reginald's being gone to London, for he is returned. Reginald is returned, not to ask our consent to his marrying Lady Susan, but to tell us they are parted for ever. He has been only an hour in the house, and I have not been able to learn particulars, for he is so very low that I have not the heart to ask questions, but I hope we shall soon know all. This is the most joyful hour he has ever given us since the day of his birth. Nothing is wanting but to have you here, and it is our particular wish and entreaty that you would come to us as soon as you can. You have owed us a visit many long weeks; I hope nothing will make it inconvenient to Mr. Vernon; and pray bring all my grand-children; and your dear niece is included, of course; I long to see her. It has been a sad, heavy winter hitherto, without Reginald, and seeing nobody from Churchhill. I never found the season so dreary before; but this happy meeting will make us young again. Frederica runs much in my thoughts, and when Reginald has recovered his usual good spirits (as I trust he soon will) we will try to rob him of his heart once more, and I am full of hopes of seeing their hands joined at no great distance.

Your affectionate mother,
C. De Courcy

XLI. *Mrs. Vernon to Lady De Courcy*

Churchhill.

My dear Mother,—Your letter has surprized me beyond measure! Can it be true that they are really separated—and for ever? I should be overjoyed if I dared depend on it, but after all that I have seen how can one be secure? And Reginald really with you! My surprize is the greater because on Wednesday, the very day of his coming to Parklands, we had a most unexpected and unwelcome visit from Lady Susan, looking all cheerfulness and good-humour, and seeming more as if she were to marry him when she got to London than as if parted from him for ever. She stayed nearly two hours, was as affectionate and agreeable as ever, and not a syllable, not a hint was dropped, of any disagreement or coolness between them. I asked her whether she had seen my brother since his arrival in town; not, as you may suppose, with any doubt of the fact, but merely to see how she looked. She immediately answered, without any embarrassment, that he had been kind enough to call on her on Monday; but she believed he had already returned home, which I was very far from crediting. Your kind invitation is accepted by us with pleasure, and on Thursday next we and our little ones will be with you. Pray heaven, Reginald may not be in town again by that time! I wish we could bring dear Frederica too, but I am sorry to say that her mother's errand hither was to fetch her away; and, miserable as it made the poor girl, it was impossible to detain her. I was thoroughly unwilling to let her go, and so was her uncle; and all that could be urged we did urge; but Lady Susan declared that as she was now about to fix herself in London for several months, she could not be easy if her daughter were not with her for masters, &c. Her manner, to be sure, was very kind and proper, and Mr. Vernon believes that Frederica will now be treated with affection. I wish I could think so too. The poor girl's heart was almost broke at taking leave of us. I charged her to write to me very often, and to remember that if she were in any distress we should be always her friends. I took care to see her alone, that I might say all this, and I hope made her a little more comfortable; but I shall not be easy till I can go to town and judge of her situation myself. I wish there were a better prospect than now appears of the match which the conclusion of your letter declares your expectations of. At present, it is not very likely

    Yours ever, &c.,
    C. VERNON

CONCLUSION

THIS CORRESPONDENCE, by a meeting between some of the parties, and a separation between the others, could not, to the great detriment of the Post Office revenue, be continued any longer. Very little assistance to the State could be derived from the epistolary intercourse of Mrs. Vernon and her niece; for the former soon perceived, by the style of Frederica's letters, that they were written under her mother's inspection! and therefore, deferring all particular enquiry till she could make it personally in London, ceased writing minutely or often. Having learnt enough, in the meanwhile, from her open-hearted brother, of what had passed between him and Lady Susan to sink the latter lower than ever in her opinion, she was proportionably more anxious to get Frederica removed from such a mother, and placed under her own care; and, though with little hope of success, was resolved to leave nothing unattempted that might offer a chance of obtaining her sister-in-law's consent to it. Her anxiety on the subject made her press for an early visit to London; and Mr. Vernon, who, as it must already have appeared, lived only to do whatever he was desired, soon found some accommodating business to call him thither. With a heart full of the matter, Mrs. Vernon waited on Lady Susan shortly after her arrival in town, and was met with such an easy and cheerful affection, as made her almost turn from her with horror. No remembrance of Reginald, no consciousness of guilt, gave one look of embarrassment; she was in excellent spirits, and seemed eager to show at once by ever possible attention to her brother and sister her sense of their kindness, and her pleasure in their society. Frederica was no more altered than Lady Susan; the same restrained manners, the same timid look in the presence of her mother as heretofore, assured her aunt of her situation being uncomfortable, and confirmed her in the plan of altering it. No unkindness, however, on the part of Lady Susan appeared. Persecution on the subject of Sir James was entirely at an end; his name merely mentioned to say that he was not in London; and indeed, in all her conversation, she was solicitous only for the welfare and improvement of her daughter, acknowledging, in terms of grateful delight, that Frederica was now growing every day more and more what a parent could desire. Mrs. Vernon, surprized and incredulous, knew not what to suspect, and, without any change in her own views, only feared greater difficulty in accomplishing them. The first hope of anything better was derived from Lady Susan's asking her whether she thought Frederica looked quite as well as she had done at Churchhill, as she must confess herself to have sometimes an anxious doubt of London's perfectly agreeing with her. Mrs. Vernon, encouraging the doubt, directly proposed her niece's returning with them into the country. Lady Susan was unable to express her sense of such kindness, yet knew not, from a variety of reasons, how to part with her daughter; and as, though her own plans were not yet wholly fixed, she trusted it would ere long be in her power to take Frederica into the country herself, concluded by declining entirely to profit by such unexampled attention. Mrs. Vernon persevered, however, in the offer of it, and though Lady Susan continued to resist, her resistance in the course of a few days seemed somewhat less formidable. The lucky alarm of an influenza decided what might not have been decided quite so soon. Lady Susan's maternal fears were then too much awakened for her to think of anything but Frederica's removal from the risk of infection; above all disorders in the world she most dreaded the influenza for her daughter's constitution!

Frederica returned to Churchhill with her uncle and aunt; and three weeks afterwards, Lady Susan announced her being married to Sir James Martin. Mrs. Vernon was then convinced of what she had only suspected before, that she might have spared herself all the trouble of urging a removal which Lady Susan had doubtless resolved on from the first. Frederica's visit was nominally for six weeks, but her mother, though inviting her to return in one or two affectionate letters, was very ready to oblige the whole party by consenting to a prolongation of her stay, and in the course of two months ceased to write of her absence, and in the course of two or more to write to her at all. Frederica was therefore fixed in the family of her uncle and aunt till such time as Reginald De Courcy could be talked, flattered, and finessed into an affection for her which, allowing leisure for the conquest of his attachment to her mother, for his abjuring all future attachments, and detesting the sex, might be reasonably looked for in the course of a twelvemonth. Three months might have done it in general, but Reginald's feelings were no less lasting than lively. Whether Lady Susan was or was not happy in her second choice, I do not see how it can ever be ascertained; for who would take her assurance of it on either side of the question? The world must judge from probabilities; she had nothing against her but her husband, and her conscience. Sir

James may seem to have drawn a harder lot than mere folly merited; I leave him, therefore, to all the pity that anybody can give him. For myself, I confess that I can pity only Miss Mainwaring; who, coming to town, and putting herself to an expense in clothes which impoverished her for two years, on purpose to secure him, was defrauded of her due by a woman ten years older than herself.

LOVE AND FRIENDSHIP

To Madame La Comtesse De Feuillide
This Novel Is Inscribed By Her Obliged
Humble Servant The Author.

"Deceived in Friendship and Betrayed in Love."

LETTER THE FIRST
From ISABEL to LAURA

HOW OFTEN, in answer to my repeated entreaties that you would give my Daughter a regular detail of the Misfortunes and Adventures of your Life, have you said "No, my friend never will I comply with your request till I may be no longer in Danger of again experiencing such dreadful ones."

Surely that time is now at hand. You are this day 55. If a woman may ever be said to be in safety from the determined Perseverance of disagreeable Lovers and the cruel Persecutions of obstinate Fathers, surely it must be at such a time of Life.

ISABEL

LETTER 2ND
LAURA to ISABEL

ALTHO' I CANNOT AGREE with you in supposing that I shall never again be exposed to Misfortunes as unmerited as those I have already experienced, yet to avoid the imputation of Obstinacy or ill-nature, I will gratify the curiosity of your daughter; and may the fortitude with which I have suffered the many afflictions of my past Life, prove to her a useful lesson for the support of those which may befall her in her own.

LAURA

LETTER 3RD
LAURA to MARIANNE

AS THE DAUGHTER of my most intimate friend I think you entitled to that knowledge of my unhappy story, which your Mother has so often solicited me to give you.

My Father was a native of Ireland and an inhabitant of Wales; my Mother was the natural Daughter of a Scotch Peer by an italian Opera-girl—I was born in Spain and received my Education at a Convent in France.

When I had reached my eighteenth Year I was recalled by my Parents to my paternal roof in Wales. Our mansion was situated in one of the most romantic parts of the Vale of Uske. Tho' my Charms are now considerably softened and somewhat impaired by the Misfortunes I have undergone, I was once beautiful. But lovely as I was the Graces of my Person were the least of my Perfections. Of every accomplishment accustomary to my sex, I was Mistress. When in the Convent, my progress had always exceeded my instructions, my Acquirements had been wonderfull for my age, and I had shortly surpassed my Masters.

In my Mind, every Virtue that could adorn it was centered; it was the Rendez-vous of every good Quality and of every noble sentiment.

A sensibility too tremblingly alive to every affliction of my Friends, my Acquaintance and particularly to every affliction of my own, was my only fault, if a fault it could be called. Alas! how altered now! Tho' indeed my own Misfortunes do not make less impression on me than they ever did, yet now I never feel for those of an other. My accomplishments too, begin to fade—I can neither sing so well nor Dance so gracefully as I once did—and I have entirely forgot the Minuet dela Coeur.

Adeiu.

LAURA.

LETTER 4TH
LAURA to MARIANNE

OUR NEIGHBOURHOOD was small, for it consisted only of your Mother. She may probably have already told you that being left by her Parents in indigent Circumstances she had retired into Wales on eoconomical motives. There it was our friendship first commenced. Isobel was then one and twenty. Tho' pleasing both in her Person and Manners (between ourselves) she never possessed the hundredth part of my Beauty or Accomplishments. Isabel had seen the World. She had passed 2 Years at one of the first Boarding-schools in London; had spent a fortnight in Bath and had supped one night in Southampton.

"Beware my Laura (she would often say) Beware of the insipid Vanities and idle Dissipations of the Metropolis of England; Beware of the unmeaning Luxuries of Bath and of the stinking fish of Southampton."

"Alas! (exclaimed I) how am I to avoid those evils I shall never be exposed to? What probability is there of my ever tasting the Dissipations of London, the Luxuries of Bath, or the stinking Fish of Southampton? I who am doomed to waste my Days of Youth and Beauty in an humble Cottage in the Vale of Uske."

Ah! little did I then think I was ordained so soon to quit that humble Cottage for the Deceitfull Pleasures of the World. Adeiu.

LAURA

LETTER 5TH
LAURA to MARIANNE

ONE EVENING in December as my Father, my Mother and myself, were arranged in social converse round our Fireside, we were on a sudden greatly astonished, by hearing a violent knocking on the outward door of our rustic Cot.

My Father started—"What noise is that," (said he.) "It sounds like a loud rapping at the door"—(replied my Mother.) "It does indeed." (cried I.) "I am of your opinion; (said my Father) it certainly does appear to proceed from some uncommon violence exerted against our unoffending door." "Yes (exclaimed I) I cannot help thinking it must be somebody who knocks for admittance."

"That is another point (replied he;) We must not pretend to determine on what motive the person may knock—tho' that someone does rap at the door, I am partly convinced."

Here, a 2d tremendous rap interrupted my Father in his speech, and somewhat alarmed my Mother and me.

"Had we better not go and see who it is? (said she) the servants are out." "I think we had." (replied I.) "Certainly, (added my Father) by all means." "Shall we go now?" (said my Mother,) "The sooner the better." (answered he.) "Oh! let no time be lost" (cried I.)

A third more violent Rap than ever again assaulted our ears. "I am certain there is somebody knocking at the Door." (said my Mother.) "I think there must," (replied my Father) "I fancy the servants are returned; (said I) I think I hear Mary going to the Door." "I'm glad of it (cried my Father) for I long to know who it is."

I was right in my conjecture; for Mary instantly entering the Room, informed us that a young Gentleman and his Servant were at the door, who had lost their way, were very cold and begged leave to warm themselves by our fire.

"Won't you admit them?" (said I.) "You have no objection, my Dear?" (said my Father.) "None in the World." (replied my Mother.)

Mary, without waiting for any further commands immediately left the room and quickly returned introducing the most beauteous and amiable Youth, I had ever beheld. The servant she kept to herself.

My natural sensibility had already been greatly affected by the sufferings of the unfortunate stranger and no sooner did I first behold him, than I felt that on him the happiness or Misery of my future Life must depend. Adeiu.

LAURA

LETTER 6TH
LAURA to MARIANNE

THE NOBLE YOUTH informed us that his name was Lindsay—for particular reasons however I shall conceal it under that of Talbot. He told us that he was the son of an English Baronet, that his Mother had been for many years no more and that he had a Sister of the middle size. "My Father (he continued) is a mean and mercenary wretch—it is only to such particular friends as this Dear Party that I would thus betray his failings. Your Virtues my amiable Polydore (addressing himself to my father) yours Dear Claudia and yours my Charming Laura call on me to repose in you, my confidence." We bowed. "My Father seduced by the false glare of Fortune and the Deluding Pomp of Title, insisted on my giving my hand to Lady Dorothea. No never exclaimed I. Lady Dorothea is lovely and Engaging; I prefer no woman to her; but know Sir, that I scorn to marry her in compliance with your Wishes. No! Never shall it be said that I obliged my Father."

We all admired the noble Manliness of his reply. He continued.

"Sir Edward was surprised; he had perhaps little expected to meet with so spirited an opposition to his will. "Where, Edward in the name of wonder (said he) did you pick up this unmeaning gibberish? You have been studying Novels I suspect." I scorned to answer: it would have been beneath my dignity. I mounted my Horse and followed by my faithful William set forth for my Aunts."

"My Father's house is situated in Bedfordshire, my

Aunt's in Middlesex, and tho' I flatter myself with being a tolerable proficient in Geography, I know not how it happened, but I found myself entering this beautifull Vale which I find is in South Wales, when I had expected to have reached my Aunts."

"After having wandered some time on the Banks of the Uske without knowing which way to go, I began to lament my cruel Destiny in the bitterest and most pathetic Manner. It was now perfectly dark, not a single star was there to direct my steps, and I know not what might have befallen me had I not at length discerned thro' the solemn Gloom that surrounded me a distant light, which as I approached it, I discovered to be the cheerful blaze of your fire. Impelled by the combination of Misfortunes under which I laboured, namely Fear, Cold and Hunger I hesitated not to ask admittance which at length I have gained; and now my Adorable Laura (continued he taking my Hand) when may I hope to receive that reward of all the painful sufferings I have undergone during the course of my attachment to you, to which I have ever aspired. Oh! when will you reward me with Yourself?"

"This instant, Dear and Amiable Edward." (replied I.). We were immediately united by my Father, who tho' he had never taken orders had been bred to the Church. Adeiu

Laura

LETTER 7TH
LAURA to MARIANNE

WE REMAINED but a few days after our Marriage, in the Vale of Uske. After taking an affecting Farewell of my Father, my Mother and my Isabel, I accompanied Edward to his Aunt's in Middlesex. Philippa received us both with every expression of affectionate Love. My arrival was indeed a most agreable surprise to her as she had not only been totally ignorant of my Marriage with her Nephew, but had never even had the slightest idea of there being such a person in the World.

Augusta, the sister of Edward was on a visit to her when we arrived. I found her exactly what her Brother had described her to be—of the middle size. She received me with equal surprise though not with equal Cordiality, as Philippa. There was a disagreable coldness and Forbidding Reserve in her reception of me which was equally distressing and Unexpected. None of that interesting Sensibility or amiable simpathy in her manners and Address to me when we first met which should have distinguished our introduction to each other. Her Language was neither warm, nor affectionate, her expressions of regard were neither animated nor cordial; her arms were not opened to receive me to her Heart, tho' my own were extended to press her to mine.

A short Conversation between Augusta and her Brother, which I accidentally overheard encreased my dislike to her, and convinced me that her Heart was no more formed for the soft ties of Love than for the endearing intercourse of Friendship.

"But do you think that my Father will ever be reconciled to this imprudent connection?" (said Augusta.)

"Augusta (replied the noble Youth) I thought you had a better opinion of me, than to imagine I would so abjectly degrade myself as to consider my Father's Concurrence in any of my affairs, either of Consequence or concern to me. Tell me Augusta with sincerity; did you ever know me consult his inclinations or follow his Advice in the least trifling Particular since the age of fifteen?"

"Edward (replied she) you are surely too diffident in your own praise. Since you were fifteen only! My Dear Brother since you were five years old, I entirely acquit you of ever having willingly contributed to the satisfaction of your Father. But still I am not without apprehensions of your being shortly obliged to degrade yourself in your own eyes by seeking a support for your wife in the Generosity of Sir Edward."

"Never, never Augusta will I so demean myself. (said Edward). Support! What support will Laura want which she can receive from him?"

"Only those very insignificant ones of Victuals and Drink." (answered she.)

"Victuals and Drink! (replied my Husband in a most nobly contemptuous Manner) and dost thou then imagine that there is no other support for an exalted mind (such as is my Laura's) than the mean and indelicate employment of Eating and Drinking?"

"None that I know of, so efficacious." (returned Augusta).

"And did you then never feel the pleasing Pangs of Love, Augusta? (replied my Edward). Does it appear impossible to your vile and corrupted Palate, to exist on Love? Can you not conceive the Luxury of living in every distress that Poverty can inflict, with the object of your tenderest affection?"

"You are too ridiculous (said Augusta) to argue with; perhaps however you may in time be convinced that ..."

Here I was prevented from hearing the remainder

of her speech, by the appearance of a very Handsome young Woman, who was ushured into the Room at the Door of which I had been listening. On hearing her announced by the Name of "Lady Dorothea," I instantly quitted my Post and followed her into the Parlour, for I well remembered that she was the Lady, proposed as a Wife for my Edward by the Cruel and Unrelenting Baronet.

Altho' Lady Dorothea's visit was nominally to Philippa and Augusta, yet I have some reason to imagine that (acquainted with the Marriage and arrival of Edward) to see me was a principal motive to it.

I soon perceived that tho' Lovely and Elegant in her Person and tho' Easy and Polite in her Address, she was of that inferior order of Beings with regard to Delicate Feeling, tender Sentiments, and refined Sensibility, of which Augusta was one.

She staid but half an hour and neither in the Course of her Visit, confided to me any of her secret thoughts, nor requested me to confide in her, any of Mine. You will easily imagine therefore my Dear Marianne that I could not feel any ardent affection or very sincere Attachment for Lady Dorothea. Adeiu.

LAURA

LETTER 8th
LAURA to MARIANNE, in continuation

LADY DOROTHEA had not left us long before another visitor as unexpected a one as her Ladyship, was announced. It was Sir Edward, who informed by Augusta of her Brother's marriage, came doubtless to reproach him for having dared to unite himself to me without his Knowledge. But Edward foreseeing his design, approached him with heroic fortitude as soon as he entered the Room, and addressed him in the following Manner. "Sir Edward, I know the motive of your Journey here—You come with the base Design of reproaching me for having entered into an indissoluble engagement with my Laura without your Consent. But Sir, I glory in the Act—. It is my greatest boast that I have incurred the displeasure of my Father!"

So saying, he took my hand and whilst Sir Edward, Philippa, and Augusta were doubtless reflecting with admiration on his undaunted Bravery, led me from the Parlour to his Father's Carriage which yet remained at the Door and in which we were instantly conveyed from the pursuit of Sir Edward.

The Postilions had at first received orders only to take the London road; as soon as we had sufficiently reflected However, we ordered them to Drive to M——. the seat of Edward's most particular friend, which was but a few miles distant.

At M——. we arrived in a few hours; and on sending in our names were immediately admitted to Sophia, the Wife of Edward's friend. After having been deprived during the course of 3 weeks of a real friend (for such I term your Mother) imagine my transports at beholding one, most truly worthy of the Name. Sophia was rather above the middle size; most elegantly formed. A soft languor spread over her lovely features, but increased their Beauty—. It was the Charectarestic of her Mind—. She was all sensibility and Feeling. We flew into each others arms and after having exchanged vows of mutual Friendship for the rest of our Lives, instantly unfolded to each other the most inward secrets of our Hearts—. We were interrupted in the delightfull Employment by the entrance of Augustus, (Edward's friend) who was just returned from a solitary ramble.

Never did I see such an affecting Scene as was the meeting of Edward and Augustus.

"My Life! my Soul!" (exclaimed the former) "My adorable angel!" (replied the latter) as they flew into each other's arms. It was too pathetic for the feelings of Sophia and myself—We fainted alternately on a sofa. Adeiu

Laura

LETTER 9TH
LAURA to MARIANNE

Towards the close of the day we received the following Letter from Philippa.

"Sir Edward is greatly incensed by your abrupt departure; he has taken back Augusta to Bedfordshire. Much as I wish to enjoy again your charming society, I cannot determine to snatch you from that, of such dear and deserving Friends—When your Visit to them is terminated, I trust you will return to the arms of your" "Philippa."

We returned a suitable answer to this affectionate Note and after thanking her for her kind invitation assured her that we would certainly avail ourselves of it, whenever we might have no other place to go to. Tho' certainly nothing could to any reasonable Being, have appeared more satisfactory, than so gratefull a reply to her invitation, yet I know not how it was, but she was certainly capricious enough to be displeased with our behaviour and in a few weeks after, either to revenge our

Conduct, or releive her own solitude, married a young and illiterate Fortune-hunter. This imprudent step (tho' we were sensible that it would probably deprive us of that fortune which Philippa had ever taught us to expect) could not on our own accounts, excite from our exalted minds a single sigh; yet fearfull lest it might prove a source of endless misery to the deluded Bride, our trembling Sensibility was greatly affected when we were first informed of the Event. The affectionate Entreaties of Augustus and Sophia that we would for ever consider their House as our Home, easily prevailed on us to determine never more to leave them, In the society of my Edward and this Amiable Pair, I passed the happiest moments of my Life; Our time was most delightfully spent, in mutual Protestations of Friendship, and in vows of unalterable Love, in which we were secure from being interrupted, by intruding and disagreable Visitors, as Augustus and Sophia had on their first Entrance in the Neighbourhood, taken due care to inform the surrounding Families, that as their happiness centered wholly in themselves, they wished for no other society. But alas! my Dear Marianne such Happiness as I then enjoyed was too perfect to be lasting. A most severe and unexpected Blow at once destroyed every sensation of Pleasure. Convinced as you must be from what I have already told you concerning Augustus and Sophia, that there never were a happier Couple, I need not I imagine, inform you that their union had been contrary to the inclinations of their Cruel and Mercenery Parents; who had vainly endeavoured with obstinate Perseverance to force them into a Marriage with those whom they had ever abhorred; but with a Heroic Fortitude worthy to be related and admired, they had both, constantly refused to submit to such despotic Power.

After having so nobly disentangled themselves from the shackles of Parental Authority, by a Clandestine Marriage, they were determined never to forfeit the good opinion they had gained in the World, in so doing, by accepting any proposals of reconciliation that might be offered them by their Fathers—to this farther tryal of their noble independance however they never were exposed.

They had been married but a few months when our visit to them commenced during which time they had been amply supported by a considerable sum of money which Augustus had gracefully purloined from his unworthy father's Escritoire, a few days before his union with Sophia.

By our arrival their Expenses were considerably encreased tho' their means for supplying them were then nearly exhausted. But they, Exalted Creatures! scorned to reflect a moment on their pecuniary Distresses and would have blushed at the idea of paying their Debts.—Alas! what was their Reward for such disinterested Behaviour! The beautifull Augustus was arrested and we were all undone. Such perfidious Treachery in the merciless perpetrators of the Deed will shock your gentle nature Dearest Marianne as much as it then affected the Delicate sensibility of Edward, Sophia, your Laura, and of Augustus himself. To compleat such unparalelled Barbarity we were informed that an Execution in the House would shortly take place. Ah! what could we do but what we did! We sighed and fainted on the sofa. Adeiu.

LAURA

LETTER 10TH
LAURA to MARIANNE, in continuation

WHEN WE WERE somewhat recovered from the over-powering Effusions of our grief, Edward desired that we would consider what was the most prudent step to be taken in our unhappy situation while he repaired to his imprisoned friend to lament over his misfortunes. We promised that we would, and he set forwards on his journey to Town. During his absence we faithfully complied with his Desire and after the most mature Deliberation, at length agreed that the best thing we could do was to leave the House; of which we every moment expected the officers of Justice to take possession. We waited therefore with the greatest impatience, for the return of Edward in order to impart to him the result of our Deliberations. But no Edward appeared. In vain did we count the tedious moments of his absence—in vain did we weep—in vain even did we sigh—no Edward returned—. This was too cruel, too unexpected a Blow to our Gentle Sensibility—we could not support it—we could only faint. At length collecting all the Resolution I was Mistress of, I arose and after packing up some necessary apparel for Sophia and myself, I dragged her to a Carriage I had ordered and we instantly set out for London. As the Habitation of Augustus was within twelve miles of Town, it was not long e'er we arrived there, and no sooner had we entered Holboun than letting down one of the Front Glasses I enquired of every decent-looking Person that we passed "If they had seen my Edward?"

But as we drove too rapidly to allow them to answer my repeated Enquiries, I gained little, or indeed, no information concerning him. "Where am I to drive?" said the Postilion. "To Newgate Gentle Youth (replied I), to see Augustus." "Oh! no, no, (exclaimed Sophia) I cannot go to Newgate; I shall not be able to support the sight of my Augustus in so cruel a confinement—my feelings are sufficiently shocked by the recital, of his Distress, but to behold it will overpower my Sensibility." As I perfectly agreed with her in the Justice of her Sentiments the Postilion was instantly directed to return into the Country. You may perhaps have been somewhat surprised my Dearest Marianne, that in the Distress I then endured, destitute of any support, and unprovided with any Habitation, I should never once have remembered my Father and Mother or my paternal Cottage in the Vale of Uske. To account for this seeming forgetfullness I must inform you of a trifling circumstance concerning them which I have as yet never mentioned. The death of my Parents a few weeks after my Departure, is the circumstance I allude to. By their decease I became the lawfull Inheritress of their House and Fortune. But alas! the House had never been their own and their Fortune had only been an Annuity on their own Lives. Such is the Depravity of the World! To your Mother I should have returned with Pleasure, should have been happy to have introduced to her, my charming Sophia and should with Cheerfullness have passed the remainder of my Life in their dear Society in the Vale of Uske, had not one obstacle to the execution of so agreable a scheme, intervened; which was the Marriage and Removal of your Mother to a distant part of Ireland. Adeiu.

LAURA

LETTER 11TH
LAURA to MARIANNE, in continuation

"I HAVE A RELATION in Scotland (said Sophia to me as we left London) who I am certain would not hesitate in receiving me." "Shall I order the Boy to drive there?" said I—but instantly recollecting myself, exclaimed, "Alas I fear it will be too long a Journey for the Horses." Unwilling however to act only from my own inadequate Knowledge of the Strength and Abilities of Horses, I consulted the Postilion, who was entirely of my Opinion concerning the Affair. We therefore determined to change Horses at the next Town and to travel Post the remainder of the Journey —. When we arrived at the last Inn we were to stop at, which was but a few miles from the House of Sophia's Relation, unwilling to intrude our Society on him unexpected and unthought of, we wrote a very elegant and well penned Note to him containing an account of our Destitute and melancholy Situation, and of our intention to spend some months with him in Scotland. As soon as we had dispatched this Letter, we immediately prepared to follow it in person and were stepping into the Carriage for that Purpose when our attention was attracted by the Entrance of a coroneted Coach and 4 into the Inn-yard. A Gentleman considerably advanced in years descended from it. At his first Appearance my Sensibility was wonderfully affected and e'er I had gazed at him a 2d time, an instinctive sympathy whispered to my Heart, that he was my Grandfather. Convinced that I could not be mistaken in my conjecture I instantly sprang from the Carriage I had just entered, and following the Venerable Stranger into the Room he had been shewn to, I threw myself on my knees before him and besought him to acknowledge me as his Grand Child. He started, and having attentively examined my features, raised me from the Ground and throwing his Grand-fatherly arms around my Neck, exclaimed, "Acknowledge thee! Yes dear resemblance of my Laurina and Laurina's Daughter, sweet image of my Claudia and my Claudia's Mother, I do acknowledge thee as the Daughter of the one and the Grandaughter of the other." While he was thus tenderly embracing me, Sophia astonished at my precipitate Departure, entered the Room in search of me. No sooner had she caught the eye of the venerable Peer, than he exclaimed with every mark of Astonishment —"Another Grandaughter! Yes, yes, I see you are the Daughter of my Laurina's eldest Girl; your resemblance to the beauteous Matilda sufficiently proclaims it. "Oh!" replied Sophia, "when I first beheld you the instinct of Nature whispered me that we were in some degree related—But whether Grandfathers, or Grandmothers, I could not pretend to determine." He folded her in his arms, and whilst they were tenderly embracing, the Door of the Apartment opened and a most beautifull young Man appeared. On perceiving him Lord St. Clair started and retreating back a few paces, with uplifted Hands, said, "Another Grand-child! What an unexpected Happiness is this! to discover in the space of 3 minutes, as many of my Descendants! This I am certain is Philander the son of my Laurina's 3d girl the amiable Bertha; there wants now but the presence of Gustavus to compleat the Union of my Laurina's Grand- Children."

"And here he is; (said a Gracefull Youth who that instant entered the room) here is the Gustavus you desire to see. I am the son of Agatha your Laurina's 4th and youngest Daughter," "I see you are indeed; replied Lord St. Clair—But tell me (continued he looking fearfully towards the Door) tell me, have I any other Grand-children in the House." "None my Lord." "Then I will provide for you all without farther delay—Here are 4 Banknotes of £50 each—Take them and remember I have done the Duty of a Grandfather." He instantly left the Room and immediately afterwards the House. Adeiu.

LAURA

LETTER 12TH
LAURA, in continuation

YOU MAY IMAGINE how greatly we were surprised by the sudden departure of Lord St Clair. "Ignoble Grand-sire!" exclaimed Sophia. "Unworthy Grandfather!" said I, and instantly fainted in each other's arms. How long we remained in this situation I know not; but when we recovered we found ourselves alone, without either Gustavus, Philander, or the Banknotes. As we were deploring our unhappy fate, the Door of the Apart-ment opened and "Macdonald" was announced. He was Sophia's cousin. The haste with which he came to our releif so soon after the receipt of our Note, spoke so greatly in his favour that I hesitated not to pronounce him at first sight, a tender and simpathetic Friend. Alas! he little deserved the name—for though he told us that he was much concerned at our Misfortunes, yet by his own account it appeared that the perusal of them, had neither drawn from him a single sigh, nor induced him to bestow one curse on our vindictive stars—. He told

Sophia that his Daughter depended on her returning with him to Macdonald-Hall, and that as his Cousin's friend he should be happy to see me there also. To Macdonald-Hall, therefore we went, and were received with great kindness by Janetta the Daughter of Macdonald, and the Mistress of the Mansion. Janetta was then only fifteen; naturally well disposed, endowed with a susceptible Heart, and a simpathetic Disposition, she might, had these amiable qualities been properly encouraged, have been an ornament to human Nature; but unfortunately her Father possessed not a soul sufficiently exalted to admire so promising a Disposition, and had endeavoured by every means on his power to prevent it encreasing with her Years. He had actually so far extinguished the natural noble Sensibility of her Heart, as to prevail on her to accept an offer from a young Man of his Recommendation. They were to be married in a few months, and Graham, was in the House when we arrived. *We* soon saw through his character. He was just such a Man as one might have expected to be the choice of Macdonald. They said he was Sensible, well-informed, and Agreable; we did not pretend to Judge of such trifles, but as we were convinced he had no soul, that he had never read the sorrows of Werter, and that his Hair bore not the least resemblance to auburn, we were certain that Janetta could feel no affection for him, or at least that she ought to feel none. The very circumstance of his being her father's choice too, was so much in his disfavour, that had he been deserving her, in every other respect yet *that* of itself ought to have been a sufficient reason in the Eyes of Janetta for rejecting him. These considerations we were determined to represent to her in their proper light and doubted not of meeting with the desired success from one naturally so well disposed; whose errors in the affair had only arisen from a want of proper confidence in her own opinion, and a suitable contempt of her father's. We found her indeed all that our warmest wishes could have hoped for; we had no difficulty to convince her that it was impossible she could love Graham, or that it was her Duty to disobey her Father; the only thing at which she rather seemed to hesitate was our assertion that she must be attached to some other Person. For some time, she persevered in declaring that she knew no other young man for whom she had the the smallest Affection; but upon explaining the impossibility of such a thing she said that she beleived she *did like* Captain M'Kenrie better than any one she knew besides. This confession satisfied us and after having enumerated the good Qualities of M'Kenrie and assured her that she was violently in love with him, we desired to know whether he had ever in any wise declared his affection to her.

"So far from having ever declared it, I have no reason to imagine that he has ever felt any for me." said Janetta. "That he certainly adores you (replied Sophia) there can be no doubt—. The Attachment must be reciprocal. Did he never gaze on you with admiration—tenderly press your hand—drop an involantary tear— and leave the room abruptly?" "Never (replied she) that I remember—he has always left the room indeed when his visit has been ended, but has never gone away particularly abruptly or without making a bow." Indeed my Love (said I) you must be mistaken—for it is absolutely impossible that he should ever have left you but with Confusion, Despair, and Precipitation. Consider but for a moment Janetta, and you must be convinced how absurd it is to suppose that he could ever make a Bow, or behave like any other Person." Having settled this Point to our satisfaction, the next we took into consideration was, to determine in what manner we should inform M'Kenrie of the favourable Opinion Janetta entertained of him. . . . We at length agreed to acquaint him with it by an anonymous Letter which Sophia drew up in the following manner.

"Oh! happy Lover of the beautifull Janetta, oh! amiable Possessor of *her* Heart whose hand is destined to another, why do you thus delay a confession of your attachment to the amiable Object of it? Oh! consider that a few weeks will at once put an end to every flattering Hope that you may now entertain, by uniting the unfortunate Victim of her father's Cruelty to the execrable and detested Graham."

"Alas! why do you thus so cruelly connive at the projected Misery of her and of yourself by delaying to communicate that scheme which had doubtless long possessed your imagination? A secret Union will at once secure the felicity of both."

The amiable M'Kenrie, whose modesty as he afterwards assured us had been the only reason of his having so long concealed the violence of his affection for Janetta, on receiving this Billet flew on the wings of Love to Macdonald-Hall, and so powerfully pleaded his Attachment to her who inspired it, that after a few more private interveiws, Sophia and I experienced the satisfaction of seeing them depart for Gretna-Green, which they chose for the celebration of their Nuptials, in preference to any other place although it was at a considerable distance from Macdonald-Hall. Adeiu

LAURA.

LETTER 13TH
LAURA, in continuation

THEY HAD BEEN GONE nearly a couple of Hours, before either Macdonald or Graham had entertained any suspicion of the affair. And they might not even then have suspected it, but for the following little Accident. Sophia happening one day to open a private Drawer in Macdonald's Library with one of her own keys, discovered that it was the Place where he kept his Papers of consequence and amongst them some bank notes of considerable amount. This discovery she imparted to me; and having agreed together that it would be a proper treatment of so vile a Wretch as Macdonald to deprive him of money, perhaps dishonestly gained, it was determined that the next time we should either of us happen to go that way, we would take one or more of the Bank notes from the drawer. This well meant Plan we had often successfully put in Execution; but alas! on the very day of Janetta's Escape, as Sophia was majestically removing the 5th Bank-note from the Drawer to her own purse, she was suddenly most impertinently interrupted in her employment by the entrance of Macdonald himself, in a most abrupt and precipitate Manner. Sophia (who though naturally all winning sweetness could when occasions demanded it call forth the Dignity of her sex) instantly put on a most forbidding look, and darting an angry frown on the undaunted culprit, demanded in a haughty tone of voice "Wherefore her retirement was thus insolently broken in on?" The unblushing Macdonald, without even endeavouring to exculpate himself from the crime he was charged with, meanly endeavoured to reproach Sophia with ignobly defrauding him of his money . . . The dignity of Sophia was wounded; "Wretch (exclaimed she, hastily replacing the Bank-note in the Drawer) how darest thou to accuse me of an Act, of which the bare idea makes me blush?" The base wretch was still unconvinced and continued to upbraid the justly-offended Sophia in such opprobious Language, that at length he so greatly provoked the gentle sweetness of her Nature, as to induce her to revenge herself on him by informing him of Janetta's Elopement, and of the active Part we had both taken in the affair. At this period of their Quarrel I entered the Library and was as you may imagine equally offended as Sophia at the ill-grounded accusations of the malevolent and contemptible Macdonald. "Base Miscreant! (cried I) how canst thou thus undauntedly endeavour to sully the spotless reputation of such bright Excellence? Why dost thou not suspect *my* innocence as soon?" "Be satisfied Madam (replied he) I *do* suspect it, and therefore must desire that you will both leave this House in less than half an hour."

"We shall go willingly; (answered Sophia) our hearts have long detested thee, and nothing but our friendship for thy Daughter could have induced us to remain so long beneath thy roof."

"Your Friendship for my Daughter has indeed been most powerfully exerted by throwing her into the arms of an unprincipled Fortune- hunter." (replied he)

"Yes, (exclaimed I) amidst every misfortune, it will afford us some consolation to reflect that by this one act of Friendship to Janetta, we have amply discharged every obligation that we have received from her father."

"It must indeed be a most gratefull reflection, to your exalted minds." (said he.)

As soon as we had packed up our wardrobe and valuables, we left Macdonald Hall, and after having walked about a mile and a half we sate down by the side of a clear limpid stream to refresh our exhausted limbs. The place was suited to meditation. A grove of full-grown Elms sheltered us from the East—. A Bed of full- grown Nettles from the West—. Before us ran the murmuring brook and behind us ran the turn-pike road. We were in a mood for contemplation and in a Disposition to enjoy so beautifull a spot. A mutual silence which had for some time reigned between us, was at length broke by my exclaiming—"What a lovely scene! Alas why are not Edward and Augustus here to enjoy its Beauties with us?"

"Ah! my beloved Laura (cried Sophia) for pity's sake forbear recalling to my remembrance the unhappy situation of my imprisoned Husband. Alas, what would I not give to learn the fate of my Augustus! to know if he is still in Newgate, or if he is yet hung. But never shall I be able so far to conquer my tender sensibility as to enquire after him. Oh! do not I beseech you ever let me again hear you repeat his beloved name—. It affects me too deeply —. I cannot bear to hear him mentioned it wounds my feelings."

"Excuse me my Sophia for having thus unwillingly offended you—" replied I—and then changing the conversation, desired her to admire the noble Grandeur of the Elms which sheltered us from the Eastern Zephyr. "Alas! my Laura (returned she) avoid so melancholy a subject, I intreat you. Do not again wound my Sensibility by observations on those elms. They remind me of Augustus. He was like them, tall, magestic—he possessed that noble grandeur which you admire in them."

I was silent, fearfull lest I might any more unwillingly distress her by fixing on any other subject of conversation which might again remind her of Augustus.

"Why do you not speak my Laura? (said she after a short pause) "I cannot support this silence you must not leave me to my own reflections; they ever recur to Augustus."

"What a beautifull sky! (said I) How charmingly is the azure varied by those delicate streaks of white!"

"Oh! my Laura (replied she hastily withdrawing her Eyes from a momentary glance at the sky) do not thus distress me by calling my Attention to an object which so cruelly reminds me of my Augustus's blue sattin waistcoat striped in white! In pity to your unhappy friend avoid a subject so distressing." What could I do? The feelings of Sophia were at that time so exquisite, and the tenderness she felt for Augustus so poignant that I had not power to start any other topic, justly fearing that it might in some unforseen manner again awaken all her sensibility by directing her thoughts to her Husband. Yet to be silent would be cruel; she had intreated me to talk.

From this Dilemma I was most fortunately releived by an accident truly apropos; it was the lucky overturning of a Gentleman's Phaeton, on the road which ran murmuring behind us. It was a most fortunate accident as it diverted the attention of Sophia from the melancholy reflections which she had been before indulging. We instantly quitted our seats and ran to the rescue of those who but a few moments before had been in so elevated a situation as a fashionably high Phaeton, but who were now laid low and sprawling in the Dust. "What an ample subject for reflection on the uncertain Enjoyments of this World, would not that Phaeton and the Life of Cardinal Wolsey afford a thinking Mind!" said I to Sophia as we were hastening to the field of Action.

She had not time to answer me, for every thought was now engaged by the horrid spectacle before us. Two Gentlemen most elegantly attired but weltering in their blood was what first struck our Eyes—we approached—they were Edward and Augustus—. Yes dearest Marianne they were our Husbands. Sophia shreiked and fainted on the ground—I screamed and instantly ran mad—. We remained thus mutually deprived of our senses, some minutes, and on regaining them were deprived of them again. For an Hour and a Quarter did we continue in this unfortunate situation—Sophia fainting every moment and I running mad as often. At length a groan from the hapless Edward (who alone retained any share of life) restored us to ourselves. Had we indeed before imagined that either of them lived, we should have been more sparing of our Greif—but as we had supposed when we first beheld them that they were no more, we knew that nothing could remain to be done but what we were about. No sooner did we therefore hear my Edward's groan than postponing our lamentations for the present, we hastily ran to the Dear Youth and kneeling on each side of him implored him not to die—. "Laura (said He fixing his now languid Eyes on me) I fear I have been overturned."

I was overjoyed to find him yet sensible.

"Oh! tell me Edward (said I) tell me I beseech you before you die, what has befallen you since that unhappy Day in which Augustus was arrested and we were separated—"

"I will" (said he) and instantly fetching a deep sigh, Expired —. Sophia immediately sank again into a swoon—. *My* greif was more audible. My Voice faltered, My Eyes assumed a vacant stare, my face became as pale as Death, and my senses were considerably impaired—.

"Talk not to me of Phaetons (said I, raving in a frantic, incoherent manner)—Give me a violin—. I'll play to him and sooth him in his melancholy Hours—Beware ye gentle Nymphs of Cupid's Thunderbolts, avoid the piercing shafts of Jupiter—Look at that grove of Firs—I see a Leg of Mutton—They told me Edward was not Dead; but they deceived me—they took him for a cucumber —" Thus I continued wildly exclaiming on my Edward's Death—. For two Hours did I rave thus madly and should not then have left off, as I was not in the least fatigued, had not Sophia who was just recovered from her swoon, intreated me to consider that Night was now approaching and that the Damps began to fall. "And whither shall we go (said I) to shelter us from either?" "To that white Cottage." (replied she pointing to a neat Building which rose up amidst the grove of Elms and which I had not before observed—) I agreed and we instantly walked to it—we knocked at the door—it was opened by an old woman; on being requested to afford us a Night's Lodging, she informed us that her House was but small, that she had only two Bedrooms, but that However we should be wellcome to one of them. We were satisfied and followed the good woman into the House where we were greatly cheered by the sight of a comfortable fire—. She was a widow and had only one Daughter, who was then just seventeen—One of the best of ages; but alas! she was very plain and her name was Bridget. . . . . Nothing therfore could be expected from her—she could not be supposed to possess either exalted Ideas, Delicate Feelings or refined Sensibilities—. She was nothing more than a mere good-tempered, civil and obliging young woman; as such we could scarcely dislike here—she was only an Object of Contempt —. Adeiu

LAURA.

LETTER 14TH
LAURA, in continuation

ARM YOURSELF my amiable young Friend with all the philosophy you are Mistress of; summon up all the fortitude you possess, for alas! in the perusal of the following Pages your sensibility will be most severely tried. Ah! what were the misfortunes I had before experienced and which I have already related to you, to the one I am now going to inform you of. The Death of my Father and my Mother and my Husband though almost more than my gentle Nature could support, were trifles in comparison to the misfortune I am now proceeding to relate. The morning after our arrival at the Cottage, Sophia complained of a violent pain in her delicate limbs, accompanied with a disagreable Headake She attributed it to a cold caught by her continued faintings in the open air as the Dew was falling the Evening before. This I feared was but too probably the case; since how could it be otherwise accounted for that I should have escaped the same indisposition, but by supposing that the bodily Exertions I had undergone in my repeated fits of frenzy had so effectually circulated and warmed my Blood as to make me proof against the chilling Damps of Night, whereas, Sophia lying totally inactive on the ground must have been exposed to all their severity. I was most seriously alarmed by her illness which trifling as it may appear to you, a certain instinctive sensibility whispered me, would in the End be fatal to her.

Alas! my fears were but too fully justified; she grew gradually worse—and I daily became more alarmed for her. At length she was obliged to confine herself solely to the Bed allotted us by our worthy Landlady—. Her disorder turned to a galloping Consumption and in a few days carried her off. Amidst all my Lamentations for her (and violent you may suppose they were) I yet received some consolation in the reflection of my having paid every attention to her, that could be offered, in her illness. I had wept over her every Day—had bathed her sweet face with my tears and had pressed her fair Hands continually in mine—. "My beloved Laura (said she to me a few Hours before she died) take warning from my unhappy End and avoid the imprudent conduct which had occasioned it. . . Beware of fainting-fits. . . Though at the time they may be refreshing and agreable yet beleive me they will in the end, if too often repeated and at improper seasons, prove destructive to your Constitution. . . My fate will teach you this. . I die a Martyr to my greif for the loss of Augustus. . One fatal swoon has cost me my Life. . Beware of swoons Dear Laura. . . . A frenzy fit is not one quarter so pernicious; it is an exercise to the Body and if not too violent, is I dare say conducive to Health in its consequences—Run mad as often as you chuse; but do not faint—"

These were the last words she ever addressed to me. . It was her dieing Advice to her afflicted Laura, who has ever most faithfully adhered to it.

After having attended my lamented friend to her Early Grave, I immediately (tho' late at night) left the detested Village in which she died, and near which had expired my Husband and Augustus. I had not walked many yards from it before I was overtaken by a stage-coach, in which I instantly took a place, determined to proceed in it to Edinburgh, where I hoped to find some kind some pitying Friend who would receive and comfort me in my afflictions.

It was so dark when I entered the Coach that I could not distinguish the Number of my Fellow-travellers; I could only perceive that they were many. Regardless however of anything concerning them, I gave myself up to my own sad Reflections. A general silence prevailed—A silence, which was by nothing interrupted but by the loud and repeated snores of one of the Party.

"What an illiterate villain must that man be! (thought I to myself) What a total want of delicate refinement must he have, who can thus shock our senses by such a brutal noise! He must I am certain be capable of every bad action! There is no crime too black for such a Character!" Thus reasoned I within myself, and doubtless such were the reflections of my fellow travellers.

At length, returning Day enabled me to behold the unprincipled Scoundrel who had so violently disturbed my feelings. It was Sir Edward the father of my Deceased Husband. By his side sate Augusta, and on the same seat with me were your Mother and Lady Dorothea. Imagine my surprise at finding myself thus seated amongst my old Acquaintance. Great as was my astonishment, it was yet increased, when on looking out of Windows, I beheld the Husband of Philippa, with Philippa by his side, on the Coachbox and when on looking behind I beheld, Philander and Gustavus in the Basket. "Oh! Heavens, (exclaimed I) is it possible that I should so unexpectedly be surrounded by my nearest Relations and Connections?" These words roused the rest of the Party, and every eye was directed to the corner in which I sat. "Oh! my Isabel (continued I throwing myself across Lady Dorothea into her arms) receive once more to your Bosom the unfortunate Laura. Alas! when we last parted in the Vale of Usk, I was happy in being united to the best of Edwards; I had then a Father and a Mother, and had never known misfortunes—But now deprived of every friend but you—"

"What! (interrupted Augusta) is my Brother dead then? Tell us I intreat you what is become of him?" "Yes, cold and insensible Nymph, (replied I) that luckless swain your Brother, is no more, and you may now glory in being the Heiress of Sir Edward's fortune."

Although I had always despised her from the Day I had overheard her conversation with my Edward, yet in civility I complied with hers and Sir Edward's intreaties that I would inform them of the whole melancholy affair. They were greatly shocked—even the obdurate Heart of Sir Edward and the insensible one of Augusta, were touched with sorrow, by the unhappy tale. At the request of your Mother I related to them every other misfortune which had befallen me since we parted. Of the imprisonment of Augustus and the absence of Edward—of our arrival in Scotland—of our unexpected Meeting with our Grand-father and our cousins—of our visit to Macdonald-Hall—of the singular service we there performed towards Janetta—of her Fathers ingratitude for it . . of his inhuman Behaviour, unaccountable suspicions, and barbarous treatment of us, in obliging us to leave the House . . of our lamentations on the loss of Edward and Augustus and finally of the melancholy Death of my beloved Companion.

Pity and surprise were strongly depictured in your Mother's countenance, during the whole of my narration, but I am sorry to say, that to the eternal reproach of her sensibility, the latter infinitely predominated. Nay, faultless as my conduct had certainly been during the whole course of my late misfortunes and adventures, she pretended to find fault with my behaviour in many of the situations in which I had been placed. As I was sensible myself, that I had always behaved in a manner which reflected Honour on my Feelings and Refinement, I paid little attention to what she said, and desired her to satisfy my Curiosity by informing me how she came there, instead of wounding my spotless reputation with unjustifiable Reproaches. As soon as she had complyed with my wishes in this particular and had given me an accurate detail of every thing that had befallen her since our separation (the particulars of which if you are not already acquainted with, your Mother will give you) I applied to Augusta for the same information respecting herself, Sir Edward and Lady Dorothea.

She told me that having a considerable taste for the Beauties of Nature, her curiosity to behold the delightful scenes it exhibited in that part of the World had been so much raised by Gilpin's Tour to the Highlands, that she had prevailed on her Father to undertake a Tour to Scotland and had persuaded Lady Dorothea to accompany them. That they had arrived at Edinburgh a few Days before and from thence had made daily Excursions into the Country around in the Stage Coach they were then in, from one of which Excursions they were at that time returning. My next enquiries were concerning Philippa and her Husband, the latter of whom I learned having spent all her fortune, had recourse for subsistence to the talent in which, he had always most excelled, namely, Driving, and that having sold every thing which belonged to them except their Coach, had converted it into a Stage and in order to be removed from any of his former Acquaintance, had driven it to Edinburgh from whence he went to Sterling every other Day. That Philippa still retaining her affection for her ungratefull Husband, had followed him to Scotland and generally accompanied him in his little Excursions to Sterling. "It has only been to throw a little money into their Pockets (continued Augusta) that my Father has always travelled in their Coach to veiw the beauties of the Country since our arrival in Scotland —for it would certainly have been much more agreable to us, to visit the Highlands in a Postchaise than merely to travel from Edinburgh to Sterling and from Sterling to Edinburgh every other Day in a crowded and uncomfortable Stage." I perfectly agreed with her in her sentiments on the affair, and secretly blamed Sir Edward for thus sacrificing his Daughter's Pleasure for the sake of a ridiculous old woman whose folly in marrying so young a man ought to be punished. His Behaviour however was entirely of a peice with his general Character; for what could be expected from a man who possessed not the smallest atom of Sensibility, who scarcely knew the meaning of simpathy, and who actually snored—. Adeiu LAURA.

LETTER 15TH
LAURA, in continuation.

WHEN WE ARRIVED at the town where we were to Breakfast, I was determined to speak with Philander and Gustavus, and to that purpose as soon as I left the Carriage, I went to the Basket and tenderly enquired after their Health, expressing my fears of the uneasiness of their situation. At first they seemed rather confused at my appearance dreading no doubt that I might call them to account for the money which our Grandfather had left me and which they had unjustly deprived me of, but finding that I mentioned nothing of the Matter, they desired me to step into the Basket as we might there converse with greater ease. Accordingly I entered and whilst the rest of the party were devouring green tea and buttered toast, we feasted ourselves in a more refined and sentimental Manner by a confidential Conversation. I informed them of every thing which had befallen me during the course of my life, and at my request they related to me every incident of theirs.

"We are the sons as you already know, of the two youngest Daughters which Lord St Clair had by Laurina an italian opera girl. Our mothers could neither of them exactly ascertain who were our Father, though it is generally beleived that Philander, is the son of one Philip Jones a Bricklayer and that my Father was one Gregory Staves a Staymaker of Edinburgh. This is however of little consequence for as our Mothers were certainly never married to either of them it reflects no Dishonour on our Blood, which is of a most ancient and unpolluted kind. Bertha (the Mother of Philander) and Agatha (my own Mother) always lived together. They were neither of them very rich; their united fortunes had originally amounted to nine thousand Pounds, but as they had always lived on the principal of it, when we were fifteen it was diminished to nine Hundred. This nine Hundred they always kept in a Drawer in one of the Tables which stood in our common sitting Parlour, for the convenience of having it always at Hand. Whether it was from this circumstance, of its being easily taken, or from a wish of being independant, or from an excess of sensibility (for which we were always remarkable) I cannot now determine, but certain it is that when we had reached our 15th year, we took the nine Hundred Pounds and ran away. Having obtained this prize we were determined to manage it with eoconomy and not to spend it either with folly or Extravagance. To this purpose we therefore divided it into nine parcels, one of which we devoted to Victuals, the 2d to Drink, the 3d to Housekeeping, the 4th to Carriages, the 5th to Horses, the 6th to Servants, the 7th to Amusements, the 8th to Cloathes and the 9th to Silver Buckles. Having thus arranged our Expences for two months (for we expected to make the nine Hundred Pounds last as long) we hastened to London and had the good luck to spend it in 7 weeks and a Day which was 6 Days sooner than we had intended.

As soon as we had thus happily disencumbered ourselves from the weight of so much money, we began
to think of returning to our Mothers, but accidentally
hearing that they were both starved to Death, we gave
over the design and determined to engage ourselves to
some strolling Company of Players, as we had always a
turn for the Stage. Accordingly we offered our services
to one and were accepted; our Company was indeed
rather small, as it consisted only of the Manager his
wife and ourselves, but there were fewer to pay and
the only inconvenience attending it was the Scarcity of
Plays which for want of People to fill the Characters,
we could perform. We did not mind trifles however—.
One of our most admired Performances was *Macbeth*,
in which we were truly great. The Manager always
played *Banquo* himself, his Wife my *Lady Macbeth*. I
did the *three witches* and Philander acted *all the rest*. To
say the truth this tragedy was not only the Best, but
the only Play that we ever performed; and after having
acted it all over England, and Wales, we came to Scotland to exhibit it over the remainder of Great Britain.
We happened to be quartered in that very Town, where
you came and met your Grandfather—. We were in the
Inn-yard when his Carriage entered and perceiving by
the arms to whom it belonged, and knowing that Lord
St Clair was our Grandfather, we agreed to endeavour
to get something from him by discovering the Relationship—. You know how well it succeeded—. Having obtained the two Hundred Pounds, we instantly
left the Town, leaving our Manager and his Wife to
act *Macbeth* by themselves, and took the road to Sterling, where we spent our little fortune with great *eclat*.
We are now returning to Edinburgh in order to get

some preferment in the Acting way; and such my Dear Cousin is our History."

I thanked the amiable Youth for his entertaining narration, and after expressing my wishes for their Welfare and Happiness, left them in their little Habitation and returned to my other Friends who impatiently expected me.

My adventures are now drawing to a close my dearest Marianne; at least for the present.

When we arrived at Edinburgh Sir Edward told me that as the Widow of his son, he desired I would accept from his Hands of four Hundred a year. I graciously promised that I would, but could not help observing that the unsimpathetic Baronet offered it more on account of my being the Widow of Edward than in being the refined and amiable Laura.

I took up my Residence in a Romantic Village in the Highlands of Scotland where I have ever since continued, and where I can uninterrupted by unmeaning Visits, indulge in a melancholy solitude, my unceasing Lamentations for the Death of my Father, my Mother, my Husband and my Friend.

Augusta has been for several years united to Graham the Man of all others most suited to her; she became acquainted with him during her stay in Scotland.

Sir Edward in hopes of gaining an Heir to his Title and Estate, at the same time married Lady Dorothea—. His wishes have been answered.

Philander and Gustavus, after having raised their reputation by their Performances in the Theatrical Line at Edinburgh, removed to Covent Garden, where they still exhibit under the assumed names of *Luvis* and *Quick*.

Philippa has long paid the Debt of Nature, Her Husband however still continues to drive the Stage-Coach from Edinburgh to Sterling:— Adeiu my Dearest Marianne.

LAURA.

Finis
June 13th 1790.

*

AN UNFINISHED NOVEL IN LETTERS

To HENRY THOMAS AUSTEN Esqre.
Sir
I am now availing myself of the Liberty you have frequently honoured me with of dedicating one of my Novels to you. That it is unfinished, I greive; yet fear that from me, it will always remain so; that as far as it is carried, it should be so trifling and so unworthy of you, is another concern to your obliged humble Servant
THE AUTHOR

Messrs Demand and Co—please to pay Jane Austen Spinster the sum of one hundred guineas on account of your Humble Servant.
H. T. AUSTEN
£105. 0. 0.

LESLEY CASTLE

Lesley Castle   Janry 3rd—1792.

My Brother has just left us. "Matilda (said he at parting) you and Margaret will I am certain take all the care of my dear little one, that she might have received from an indulgent, and affectionate and amiable Mother." Tears rolled down his cheeks as he spoke these words—the remembrance of her, who had so wantonly disgraced the Maternal character and so openly violated the conjugal Duties, prevented his adding anything farther; he embraced his sweet Child and after saluting Matilda and Me hastily broke from us and seating himself in his Chaise, pursued the road to Aberdeen. Never was there a better young Man! Ah! how little did he deserve the misfortunes he has experienced in the Marriage state. So good a Husband to so bad a Wife! for you know my dear Charlotte that the Worthless Louisa left him, her Child and reputation a few weeks ago in company with Danvers and dishonour. Never was there a sweeter face, a finer form, or a less amiable Heart than Louisa owned! Her child already possesses the personal Charms of her unhappy Mother! May she inherit from her Father all his mental ones! Lesley is at present but five and twenty, and has already given himself up to melancholy and Despair; what a difference between him and his Father! Sir George is 57 and still remains the Beau, the flighty stripling, the gay Lad, and sprightly Youngster, that his Son was really about five years back, and that *he* has affected to appear ever since my remembrance. While our father is fluttering about the streets of London, gay, dissipated, and Thoughtless at the age of 57, Matilda and I continue secluded from Mankind in our old and Mouldering Castle, which is situated two miles from Perth on a bold projecting Rock, and commands an extensive veiw of the Town and its delightful Environs. But tho' retired from almost all the World, (for we visit no one but the M'Leods, The M'Kenzies, the M'Phersons, the M'Cartneys, the M'donalds, The M'kinnons, the M'lellans, the M'kays, the Macbeths and the Macduffs) we are neither dull nor unhappy; on the contrary there never were two more lively, more agreable or more witty girls, than we are; not an hour in the Day hangs heavy on our Hands. We read, we work, we walk, and when fatigued with these Employments releive our spirits, either by a lively song, a graceful Dance, or by some smart bon-mot, and witty repartee. We are handsome my dear Charlotte, very handsome and the greatest of our Perfections is, that we are entirely insensible of them ourselves. But why do I thus dwell on myself! Let me rather repeat the praise of our dear little Neice the innocent Louisa, who is at present sweetly smiling in a gentle Nap, as she reposes on the sofa. The dear Creature is just turned of two years old; as handsome as tho' 2 and 20, as sensible as tho' 2 and 30, and as prudent as tho' 2 and 40. To convince you of this, I must inform you that she has a very fine complexion and very pretty features, that she already knows the two first letters in the Alphabet, and that she never tears her frocks—. If I have not now convinced you of her Beauty, Sense and Prudence, I have nothing more to urge in support of my assertion, and you will therefore have no way of deciding the Affair but by coming to Lesley-Castle, and by a personal acquaintance with Louisa, determine for yourself. Ah! my dear Friend, how happy should I be to see you within these venerable Walls! It is now four years since my removal from School has separated me from you; that two such tender Hearts, so closely linked together by the ties of simpathy and Friendship, should be so widely removed from each other, is vastly moving. I live in Perthshire, You in Sussex. We might meet in London, were my Father disposed to carry me there, and were your Mother to be there at the same time. We might meet at Bath, at Tunbridge, or anywhere else indeed, could we but be at the same place together. We have only to hope that such a period may arrive. My Father does not return to us till Autumn; my Brother will leave Scotland in a few Days; he is impatient to travel. Mistaken Youth! He vainly flatters himself that change of Air will heal the Wounds of a broken Heart! You will join with me I am certain my dear Charlotte, in prayers for the recovery of the unhappy Lesley's peace of Mind, which must ever be essential to that of your sincere friend

    M. Lesley.

LETTER THE SECOND is from Miss *C. Lutterell* to Miss *M. Lesley* in answer.

Glenford Febry 12

I have a thousand excuses to beg for having so long delayed thanking you my dear Peggy for your agreable Letter, which beleive me I should not have deferred doing, had not every moment of my time during the last five weeks been so fully employed in the necessary arrangements for my sisters wedding, as to allow me no time to devote either to you or myself. And now what provokes me more than anything else is that the Match is broke off, and all my Labour thrown away. Imagine how great the Dissapointment must be to me, when you consider that after having laboured both by Night and by Day, in order to get the Wedding dinner ready by the time appointed, after having roasted Beef, Broiled Mutton, and Stewed Soup enough to last the new-married Couple through the Honey-moon, I had the mortification of finding that I had been Roasting, Broiling and Stewing both the Meat and Myself to no purpose. Indeed my dear Friend, I never remember suffering any vexation equal to what I experienced on last Monday when my sister came running to me in the store-room with her face as White as a Whipt syllabub, and told me that Hervey had been thrown from his Horse, had fractured his Scull and was pronounced by his surgeon to be in the most emminent Danger. "Good God! (said I) you dont say so? Why what in the name of Heaven will become of all the Victuals! We shall never be able to eat it while it is good. However, we'll call in the Surgeon to help us. I shall be able to manage the Sir-loin myself, my Mother will eat the soup, and You and the Doctor must finish the rest." Here I was interrupted, by seeing my poor Sister fall down to appearance Lifeless upon one of the Chests, where we keep our Table linen. I immediately called my Mother and the Maids, and at last we brought her to herself again; as soon as ever she was sensible, she expressed a determination of going instantly to Henry, and was so wildly bent on this Scheme, that we had the greatest Difficulty in the World to prevent her putting it in execution; at last however more by Force than Entreaty we prevailed on her to go into her room; we laid her upon the Bed, and she continued for some Hours in the most dreadful Convulsions. My Mother and I continued in the room with her, and when any intervals of tolerable Composure in Eloisa would allow us, we joined in heartfelt lamentations on the dreadful Waste in our provisions which this Event must occasion, and in concerting some plan for getting rid of them. We agreed that the best thing we could do was to begin eating them immediately, and accordingly we ordered up the cold Ham and Fowls, and instantly began our Devouring Plan on them with great Alacrity. We would have persuaded Eloisa to have taken a Wing of a Chicken, but she would not be persuaded. She was however much quieter than she had been; the convulsions she had before suffered having given way to an almost perfect Insensibility. We endeavoured to rouse her by every means in our power, but to no purpose. I talked to her of Henry. "Dear Eloisa (said I) there's no occasion for your crying so much about such a trifle. (for I was willing to make light of it in order to comfort her) I beg you would not mind it—You see it does not vex me in the least; though perhaps I may suffer most from it after all; for I shall not only be obliged to eat up all the Victuals I have dressed already, but must if Henry should recover (which however is not very likely) dress as much for you again; or should he die (as I suppose he will) I shall still have to prepare a Dinner for you whenever you marry any one else. So you see that tho' perhaps for the present it may afflict you to think of Henry's sufferings, Yet I dare say he'll die soon, and then his pain will be over and you will be easy, whereas my Trouble will last much longer for work as hard as I may, I am certain that the pantry cannot be cleared in less than a fortnight." Thus I did all in my power to console her, but without any effect, and at last as I saw that she did not seem to listen to me, I said no more, but leaving her with my Mother I took down the remains of The Ham and Chicken, and sent William to ask how Henry did. He was not expected to live many Hours; he died the same day. We took all possible care to break the melancholy Event to Eloisa in the tenderest manner; yet in spite of every precaution, her sufferings on hearing it were too violent for her reason, and she continued for many hours in a high Delirium. She is still extremely ill, and her Physicians are greatly afraid of her going into a Decline. We are therefore preparing for Bristol, where we mean to be in the course of the next week. And now my dear Margaret let me talk a little of your affairs; and in the first place I must inform you that it is confidently reported, your Father is going to be married; I am very unwilling to beleive so unpleasing a report, and at the same time cannot wholly discredit it. I have written to my friend Susan Fitzgerald, for information concerning it, which as she is at present in Town, she will be very able to give me. I know not who is the Lady. I think your Brother is extremely right in the resolution he has taken of travelling, as it will perhaps contribute to obliterate from his remembrance, those disagreable Events, which have lately so much afflicted him— I am happy to find that tho' secluded from all the World, neither you nor Matilda are dull or unhappy —that you may never know what it is to, be either is the wish of your sincerely affectionate

C.L.

P. S. I have this instant received an answer from my friend Susan, which I enclose to you, and on which you will make your own reflections.

The enclosed *letter*

My dear CHARLOTTE

You could not have applied for information concerning the report of Sir George Lesleys Marriage, to any one better able to give it you than I am. Sir George is certainly married; I was myself present at the Ceremony, which you will not be surprised at when I subscribe myself your Affectionate

SUSAN LESLEY

LETTER THE THIRD is from Miss *Margaret Lesley* to Miss *C. Lutterell*

Lesley Castle   February the 16th

I have made my own reflections on the letter you enclosed to me, my Dear Charlotte and I will now tell you what those reflections were. I reflected that if by this second Marriage Sir George should have a second family, our fortunes must be considerably diminushed—

that if his Wife should be of an extravagant turn, she would encourage him to persevere in that gay and Dissipated way of Life to which little encouragement would be necessary, and which has I fear already proved but too detrimental to his health and fortune—that she would now become Mistress of those Jewels which once adorned our Mother, and which Sir George had always promised us—that if they did not come into Perthshire I should not be able to gratify my curiosity of beholding my Mother-in-law and that if they did, Matilda would no longer sit at the head of her Father's table—. These my dear Charlotte were the melancholy reflections which crowded into my imagination after perusing Susan's letter to you, and which instantly occurred to Matilda when she had perused it likewise. The same ideas, the same fears, immediately occupied her Mind, and I know not which reflection distressed her most, whether the probable Diminution of our Fortunes, or her own Consequence. We both wish very much to know whether Lady Lesley is handsome and what is your opinion of her; as you honour her with the appellation of your friend, we flatter ourselves that she must be amiable. My Brother is already in Paris. He intends to quit it in a few Days, and to begin his route to Italy. He writes in a most chearfull manner, says that the air of France has greatly recovered both his Health and Spirits; that he has now entirely ceased to think of Louisa with any degree either of Pity or Affection, that he even feels himself obliged to her for her Elopement, as he thinks it very good fun to be single again. By this, you may perceive that he has entirely regained that chearful Gaiety, and sprightly Wit, for which he was once so remarkable. When he first became acquainted with Louisa which was little more than three years ago, he was one of the most lively, the most agreable young Men of the age—. I beleive you never yet heard the particulars of his first acquaintance with her. It commenced at our cousin Colonel Drummond's; at whose house in Cumberland he spent the Christmas, in which he attained the age of two and twenty. Louisa Burton was the Daughter of a distant Relation of Mrs. Drummond, who dieing a few Months before in extreme poverty, left his only Child then about eighteen to the protection of any of his Relations who would protect her. Mrs. Drummond was the only one who found herself so disposed—Louisa was therefore removed from a miserable Cottage in Yorkshire to an elegant Mansion in Cumberland, and from every pecuniary Distress that Poverty could inflict, to every elegant Enjoyment that Money could purchase—. Louisa was naturally ill-tempered and Cunning; but she had been taught to disguise her real Disposition, under the appearance of insinuating Sweetness, by a father who but too well knew, that to be married, would be the only chance she would have of not being starved, and who flattered himself that with such an extroidinary share of personal beauty, joined to a gentleness of Manners, and an engaging address, she might stand a good chance of pleasing some young Man who might afford to marry a girl without a Shilling. Louisa perfectly entered into her father's schemes and was determined to forward them with all her care and attention. By dint of Perseverance and Application, she had at length so thoroughly disguised her natural disposition under the mask of Innocence, and Softness, as to impose upon every one who had not by a long and constant intimacy with her discovered her real Character. Such was Louisa when the hapless Lesley first beheld her at Drummond-house. His heart which (to use your favourite comparison) was as delicate as sweet and as tender as a Whipt- syllabub, could not resist her attractions. In a very few Days, he was falling in love, shortly after actually fell, and before he had known her a Month, he had married her. My Father was at first highly displeased at so hasty and imprudent a connection; but when he found that they did not mind it, he soon became perfectly reconciled to the match. The Estate near Aberdeen which my brother possesses by the bounty of his great Uncle independant of Sir George, was entirely sufficient to support him and my Sister in Elegance and Ease. For the first twelvemonth, no one could be happier than Lesley, and no one more amiable to appearance than Louisa, and so plausibly did she act and so cautiously behave that tho' Matilda and I often spent several weeks together with them, yet we neither of us had any suspicion of her real Disposition. After the birth of Louisa however, which one would have thought would have strengthened her regard for Lesley, the mask she had so long supported was by degrees thrown aside, and as probably she then thought herself secure in the affection of her Husband (which did indeed appear if possible augmented by the birth of his Child) she seemed to take no pains to prevent that affection from ever diminishing. Our visits therefore to Dunbeath, were now less frequent and by far less agreable than they used to be. Our absence was however never either mentioned or lamented by Louisa who in the society of young Danvers with whom she became acquainted at Aberdeen (he was at one of the Universities there,) felt infinitely happier than in that of Matilda and your friend, tho' there certainly never were pleasanter girls than we are. You know the sad end of all Lesleys connubial happiness; I will not repeat it—. Adeiu my dear Charlotte; although I have not yet mentioned anything of the matter, I hope you will do me the justice to beleive that I *think* and *feel*, a great deal for your Sisters affliction. I do not doubt but that the healthy air of the Bristol downs will intirely remove it, by erasing from her Mind the remembrance of Henry. I am my dear Charlotte yrs ever

M. L.

LETTER THE FOURTH is from Miss *C. Lutterell* to Miss *M. Lesley*

Bristol   February 27th

MY DEAR PEGGY

I have but just received your letter, which being directed to Sussex while I was at Bristol was obliged to be forwarded to me here, and from some unaccountable Delay, has but this instant reached me—. I return you many thanks for the account it contains of Lesley's acquaintance, Love and Marriage with Louisa, which has not the less entertained me for having often been repeated to me before.

I have the satisfaction of informing you that we have every reason to imagine our pantry is by this time nearly cleared, as we left Particular orders with the servants to eat as hard as they possibly could, and to call in a couple of Chairwomen to assist them. We brought a cold Pigeon pye, a cold turkey, a cold tongue, and half a dozen Jellies with us, which we were lucky enough with the help of our Landlady, her husband, and their three children, to get rid of, in less than two days after our arrival. Poor Eloisa is still so very indifferent both in Health and Spirits, that I very much fear, the air of the Bristol downs, healthy as it is, has not been able to drive poor Henry from her remembrance.

You ask me whether your new Mother in law is handsome and amiable—I will now give you an exact description of her bodily and mental charms. She is short, and extremely well made; is naturally pale, but rouges a good deal; has fine eyes, and fine teeth, as she will take care to let you know as soon as she sees you, and is altogether very pretty. She is remarkably good- tempered when she has her own way, and very lively when she is not out of humour. She is naturally extravagant and not very affected; she never reads anything but the letters she receives from me, and never writes anything but her answers to them. She plays, sings and Dances, but has no taste for either, and excells in none, tho' she says she is passionately fond of all. Perhaps you may flatter me so far as to be surprised that one of whom I speak with so little affection should be my particular friend; but to tell you the truth, our friendship arose rather from Caprice on her side than Esteem on mine. We spent two or three days together with a Lady in Berkshire with whom we both happened to be connected—. During our visit, the Weather being remarkably bad, and our party particularly stupid, she was so good as to conceive a violent partiality for me, which very soon settled in a downright Friendship and ended in an established correspondence. She is probably by this time as tired of me, as I am of her; but as she is too

Polite and I am too civil to say so, our letters are still as frequent and affectionate as ever, and our Attachment as firm and sincere as when it first commenced. As she had a great taste for the pleasures of London, and of Brighthelmstone, she will I dare say find some difficulty in prevailing on herself even to satisfy the curiosity I dare say she feels of beholding you, at the expence of quitting those favourite haunts of Dissipation, for the melancholy tho' venerable gloom of the castle you inhabit. Perhaps however if she finds her health impaired by too much amusement, she may acquire fortitude sufficient to undertake a Journey to Scotland in the hope of its Proving at least beneficial to her health, if not conducive to her happiness. Your fears I am sorry to say, concerning your father's extravagance, your own fortunes, your Mothers Jewels and your Sister's consequence, I should suppose are but too well founded. My friend herself has four thousand pounds, and will probably spend nearly as much every year in Dress and Public places, if she can get it—she will certainly not endeavour to reclaim Sir George from the manner of living to which he has been so long accustomed, and there is therefore some reason to fear that you will be very well off, if you get any fortune at all. The Jewels I should imagine too will undoubtedly be hers, and there is too much reason to think that she will preside at her Husbands table in preference to his Daughter. But as so melancholy a subject must necessarily extremely distress you, I will no longer dwell on it—.

Eloisa's indisposition has brought us to Bristol at so unfashionable a season of the year, that we have actually seen but one genteel family since we came. Mr and Mrs Marlowe are very agreable people; the ill health of

their little boy occasioned their arrival here; you may imagine that being the only family with whom we can converse, we are of course on a footing of intimacy with them; we see them indeed almost every day, and dined with them yesterday. We spent a very pleasant Day, and had a very good Dinner, tho' to be sure the Veal was terribly underdone, and the Curry had no seasoning. I could not help wishing all dinner-time that I had been at the dressing it—. A brother of Mrs Marlowe, Mr Cleveland is with them at present; he is a good-looking young Man, and seems to have a good deal to say for himself. I tell Eloisa that she should set her cap at him, but she does not at all seem to relish the proposal. I should like to see the girl married and Cleveland has a very good estate. Perhaps you may wonder that I do not consider myself as well as my Sister in my matrimonial Projects; but to tell you the truth I never wish to act a more principal part at a Wedding than the superintending and directing the Dinner, and therefore while I can get any of my acquaintance to marry for me, I shall never think of doing it myself, as I very much suspect that I should not have so much time for dressing my own Wedding- dinner, as for dressing that of my friends. Yours sincerely
C. L.

LETTER THE FIFTH is from Miss *Margaret Lesley* to Miss *Charlotte Lutterell*
Lesley-Castle   March 18th

On the same day that I received your last kind letter, Matilda received one from Sir George which was dated from Edinburgh, and informed us that he should do himself the pleasure of introducing Lady Lesley to us on the following evening. This as you may suppose considerably surprised us, particularly as your account of her Ladyship had given us reason to imagine there was little chance of her visiting Scotland at a time that London must be so gay. As it was our business however to be delighted at such a mark of condescension as a visit from Sir George and Lady Lesley, we prepared to return them an answer expressive of the happiness we enjoyed in expectation of such a Blessing, when luckily recollecting that as they were to reach the Castle the next Evening, it would be impossible for my father to receive it before he left Edinburgh, we contented ourselves with leaving them to suppose that we were as happy as we ought to be. At nine in the Evening on the following day, they came, accompanied by one of Lady Lesleys brothers. Her Ladyship perfectly answers the description you sent me of her, except that I do not think her so pretty as you seem to consider her. She has not a bad face, but there is something so extremely unmajestic in her little diminutive figure, as to render her in comparison with the elegant height of Matilda and Myself, an insignificant Dwarf. Her curiosity to see us (which must have been great to bring her more than four hundred miles) being now perfectly gratified, she already begins to mention their return to town, and has desired us to accompany her. We cannot refuse her request since it is seconded by the commands of our Father, and thirded by the entreaties of Mr. Fitzgerald who is certainly one of the most pleasing young Men, I ever beheld. It is not yet determined when we are to go, but when ever we do we shall certainly take our little Louisa with us. Adeiu my dear Charlotte;

Matilda unites in best wishes to you, and Eloisa, with yours ever
M. L.

LETTER THE SIXTH is from *Lady Lesley* to Miss *Charlotte Lutterell*
Lesley-Castle   March 20th

We arrived here my sweet Friend about a fortnight ago, and I already heartily repent that I ever left our charming House in Portman-square for such a dismal old weather-beaten Castle as this. You can form no idea sufficiently hideous, of its dungeon- like form. It is actually perched upon a Rock to appearance so totally inaccessible, that I expected to have been pulled up by a rope; and sincerely repented having gratified my curiosity to behold my Daughters at the expence of being obliged to enter their prison in so dangerous and ridiculous a manner. But as soon as I once found myself safely arrived in the inside of this tremendous building, I comforted myself with the hope of having my spirits revived, by the sight of two beautifull girls, such as the Miss Lesleys had been represented to me, at Edinburgh. But here again, I met with nothing but Disappointment and Surprise. Matilda and Margaret Lesley are two great, tall, out of the way, over-grown, girls, just of a proper size to inhabit a Castle almost as large in comparison as themselves. I wish my dear Charlotte that you could but behold these Scotch giants; I am sure they would frighten you out of your wits. They will do very well as foils to myself, so I have invited them to accompany me to London where I hope to be in the course of a fortnight. Besides these two fair Damsels, I found a little humoured Brat here who I beleive is some relation to them, they told me who she was, and gave me a long rigmerole story of her father and a Miss *Somebody* which I have entirely forgot. I hate scandal and detest Children. I have been plagued ever since I came here with tiresome visits from a parcel of Scotch wretches, with terrible hardnames; they were so civil, gave me so many invitations, and talked of coming again so soon, that I could not help affronting them. I suppose I shall not see them any more, and yet as a family party we are so stupid, that I do not know what to do with myself. These girls have no Music, but Scotch airs, no Drawings but Scotch Mountains, and no Books but Scotch Poems—and I hate everything Scotch. In general I can spend half the Day at my toilett with a great deal of pleasure, but why should I dress here, since there is not a creature in the House whom I have any wish to please. I have just had a conversation with my Brother in which he has greatly offended me, and which as I have nothing more entertaining to send you I will gave you the particulars of. You must know that I have for these 4 or 5 Days past strongly suspected William of entertaining a partiality to my eldest Daughter. I own indeed that had I been inclined to fall in love with any woman, I should not have made choice of Matilda Lesley for the object of my passion; for there is nothing I hate so much as a tall Woman: but however there is no accounting for some men's taste and as William is himself nearly six feet high, it is not wonderful that he should be partial to that height. Now as I have a very great affection for my Brother and should be extremely sorry to see him unhappy, which I suppose he means to be if he cannot marry Matilda, as moreover I know that his circumstances will not allow him to marry any one without a fortune, and that Matilda's is entirely dependant on her Father, who will neither have his own inclination nor my permission to give her anything at present, I thought it would be doing a good- natured action by my Brother to let him know as much, in order that he might choose for himself, whether to conquer his passion, or Love and Despair. Accordingly finding myself this Morning alone with him in one of the horrid old rooms of this Castle, I opened the cause to him in the following Manner.

"Well my dear William what do you think of these girls? for my part, I do not find them so plain as I expected: but perhaps you may think me partial to the Daughters of my Husband and perhaps you are right— They are indeed so very like Sir George that it is natural to think"—

"My Dear Susan (cried he in a tone of the greatest amazement) You do not really think they bear the least resemblance to their Father! He is so very plain!—but I beg your pardon—I had entirely forgotten to whom I was speaking—"

"Oh! pray dont mind me; (replied I) every one knows Sir George is horribly ugly, and I assure you I always thought him a fright."

"You surprise me extremely (answered William) by what you say both with respect to Sir George and his Daughters. You cannot think your Husband so deficient in personal Charms as you speak of, nor can you surely see any resemblance between him and the Miss Lesleys who are in my opinion perfectly unlike him and perfectly Handsome."

"If that is your opinion with regard to the girls it certainly is no proof of their Fathers beauty, for if they are perfectly unlike him and very handsome at the same time, it is natural to suppose that he is very plain."

"By no means, (said he) for what may be pretty in a Woman, may be very unpleasing in a Man."

"But you yourself (replied I) but a few minutes ago allowed him to be very plain."

"Men are no Judges of Beauty in their own Sex." (said he).

"Neither Men nor Women can think Sir George tolerable."

"Well, well, (said he) we will not dispute about *his* Beauty, but your opinion of his *daughters* is surely very singular, for if I understood you right, you said you did not find them so plain as you expected to do!"

"Why, do *you* find them plainer then?" (said I).

"I can scarcely beleive you to be serious (returned he) when you speak of their persons in so extroidinary a Manner. Do not you think the Miss Lesleys are two very handsome young Women?"

"Lord! No! (cried I) I think them terribly plain!"

"Plain! (replied He) My dear Susan, you cannot really think so! Why what single Feature in the face of either of them, can you possibly find fault with?"

"Oh! trust me for that; (replied I). Come I will begin with the eldest—with Matilda. Shall I, William?" (I looked as cunning as I could when I said it, in order to shame him).

"They are so much alike (said he) that I should suppose the faults of one, would be the faults of both."

"Well, then, in the first place; they are both so horribly tall!"

"They are *taller* than you are indeed." (said he with a saucy smile.)

"Nay, (said I), I know nothing of that."

"Well, but (he continued) tho' they may be above the common size, their figures are perfectly elegant; and as to their faces, their Eyes are beautifull."

"I never can think such tremendous, knock-me-down figures in the least degree elegant, and as for their eyes, they are so tall that I never could strain my neck enough to look at them."

"Nay, (replied he) I know not whether you may not be in the right in not attempting it, for perhaps they might dazzle you with their Lustre."

"Oh! Certainly. (said I, with the greatest complacency, for I assure you my dearest Charlotte I was not in the least offended tho' by what followed, one would suppose that William was conscious of having given me just cause to be so, for coming up to me and taking my hand, he said) "You must not look so grave Susan; you will make me fear I have offended you!"

"Offended me! Dear Brother, how came such a thought in your head! (returned I) No really! I assure you that I am not in the least surprised at your being so warm an advocate for the Beauty of these girls "—

"Well, but (interrupted William) remember that we have not yet concluded our dispute concerning them. What fault do you find with their complexion?"

"They are so horridly pale."

"They have always a little colour, and after any exercise it is considerably heightened."

"Yes, but if there should ever happen to be any rain in this part of the world, they will never be able raise more than their common stock—except indeed they amuse themselves with running up and Down these horrid old galleries and Antichambers."

"Well, (replied my Brother in a tone of vexation, and glancing an impertinent look at me) if they *have* but little colour, at least, it is all their own."

This was too much my dear Charlotte, for I am certain that he had the impudence by that look, of pretending to suspect the reality of mine. But you I am sure will vindicate my character whenever you may hear it so cruelly aspersed, for you can witness how often I have protested against wearing Rouge, and how much I always told you I disliked it. And I assure you that my opinions are still the same.—. Well, not bearing to be so suspected by my Brother, I left the room immediately, and have been ever since in my own Dressing-room writing to you. What a long letter have I made of it! But you must not expect to receive such from me when I get to Town; for it is only at Lesley castle, that one has time to write even to a Charlotte Lutterell.—. I was so much vexed by William's glance, that I could not summon Patience enough, to stay and give him that advice respecting his attachment to Matilda which had first induced me from pure Love to him to begin the conversation; and I am now so thoroughly convinced by it, of his violent passion for her, that I am certain he would never hear reason on the subject, and I shall there fore give myself no more trouble either about him or his favourite. Adeiu my dear girl—

Yrs affectionately

SUSAN L.

LETTER THE SEVENTH is from Miss C. *Lutterell* to Miss *M. Lesley*

Bristol the 27th of March

I have received Letters from you and your Mother-in-law within this week which have greatly entertained me, as I find by them that you are both downright jealous of each others Beauty. It is very odd that two pretty Women tho' actually Mother and Daughter cannot be in the same House without falling out about their faces. Do be convinced that you are both perfectly handsome and say no more of the Matter. I suppose this letter must be directed to Portman Square where probably (great as is your affection for Lesley Castle) you will not be sorry to find yourself. In spite of all that people may say about Green fields and the Country I was always of opinion that London and its amusements must be very agreable for a while, and should be very happy could my Mother's income allow her to jockey us into its Public-places, during Winter. I always longed particularly to go to Vaux-hall, to see whether the cold Beef there is cut so thin as it is reported, for I have a sly suspicion that few people understand the art of cutting a slice of cold Beef so well as I do: nay it would be hard if I did not know something of the Matter, for it was a part of my Education that I took by far the most pains with. Mama always found me *her* best scholar, tho' when Papa was alive Eloisa was *his*. Never to be sure were there two more different Dispositions in the World. We both loved Reading. *She* preferred Histories, and I Receipts. She loved drawing, Pictures, and I drawing Pullets. No one could sing a better song than she, and no one make a better Pye than I.— And so it has always continued since we have been no longer children. The only difference is that all disputes on the superior excellence of our Employments *then* so frequent are now no more. We have for many years entered into an agreement always to admire each other's works; I never fail listening to *her* Music, and she is as constant in eating my pies. Such at least was the case till Henry Hervey made his appearance in Sussex. Before the arrival of his Aunt in our neighbourhood where she established herself you know about a twelvemonth ago, his visits to her had been at stated times, and of equal and settled Duration; but on her removal to the Hall which is within a walk from our House, they became both more frequent and longer. This as you may suppose could not be pleasing to Mrs Diana who is a professed enemy to everything which is not directed by Decorum and Formality, or which bears the least resemblance to Ease and Good- breeding. Nay so great was her aversion to her Nephews behaviour that I have often heard her give such hints of it before his face that had not Henry at such times been engaged in conversation with Eloisa, they must have caught his Attention and have very much distressed him. The alteration in my Sisters behaviour which I have before hinted at, now took place. The Agreement we had entered into of admiring each others productions she no longer seemed to regard, and tho' I constantly applauded even every Country-dance, she played, yet not even a pidgeon-pye of my making could obtain from her a single word of approbation. This was certainly enough to put any one in a Passion; however, I was as cool as a cream-cheese and having formed my plan and concerted a scheme of Revenge, I was determined to let her have her own way and not even to make her a single reproach. My scheme was to treat her as she treated me, and tho' she might even draw my own Picture or play Malbrook (which is the only tune I ever really liked) not to say so much as "Thank you Eloisa;" tho' I had for many years constantly hollowed whenever she played, B*ravo, bravissimo, encore, da capo, allegretto, con expressione,* and *poco presto* with many other such outlandish words, all of them as Eloisa told me expressive of my Admiration; and so indeed I suppose they are, as I see some of them in every Page of every Music book, being the sentiments I imagine of the composer.

I executed my Plan with great Punctuality. I can not say success, for alas! my silence while she played seemed not in the least to displease her; on the contrary she actually said to me one day " Well Charlotte, I am very glad to find that you have at last left off that ridiculous custom of applauding my Execution on the Harpsichord till you made my head ake, and yourself hoarse. I feel very much obliged to you for keeping your admiration to yourself." I never shall forget the very witty answer I made to this speech. "Eloisa (said I) I beg you would be quite at your Ease with respect to all such fears in future, for be assured that I shall always keep my admiration to myself and my own pursuits and never extend it to yours." This was the only very severe thing I ever said in my Life; not but that I have often felt myself extremely satirical but it was the only time I ever made my feelings public.

I suppose there never were two Young people who had a greater affection for each other than Henry and Eloisa; no, the Love of your Brother for Miss Burton could not be so strong tho' it might be more violent.

You may imagine therefore how provoked my Sister must have been to have him play her such a trick. Poor girl! she still laments his Death with undiminished constancy, notwithstanding he has been dead more than six weeks; but some People mind such things more than others. The ill state of Health into which his loss has thrown her makes her so weak, and so unable to support the least exertion, that she has been in tears all this Morning merely from having taken leave of Mrs. Marlowe who with her Husband, Brother and Child are to leave Bristol this morning. I am sorry to have them go because they are the only family with whom we have here any acquaintance, but I never thought of crying; to be sure Eloisa and Mrs Marlowe have always been more together than with me, and have therefore contracted a kind of affection for each other, which does not make Tears so inexcusable in them as they would be in me. The Marlowes are going to Town; Cliveland accompanies them; as neither Eloisa nor I could catch him I hope you or Matilda may have better Luck. I know not when we shall leave Bristol, Eloisa's spirits are so low that she is very averse to moving, and yet is certainly by no means mended by her residence here. A week or two will I hope determine our Measures—in the mean time believe me and etc—and etc—

CHARLOTTE LUTTERELL.

LETTER THE EIGHTH is from Miss *Lutterell* to Mrs *Marlowe*

Bristol April 4th

I feel myself greatly obliged to you my dear Emma for such a mark of your affection as I flatter myself was conveyed in the proposal you made me of our Corresponding; I assure you that it will be a great releif to me to write to you and as long as my Health and Spirits will allow me, you will find me a very constant correspondent; I will not say an entertaining one, for you know my situation suffciently not to be ignorant that in me Mirth would be improper and I know my own Heart too well not to be sensible that it would be unnatural. You must not expect news for we see no one with whom we are in the least acquainted, or in whose proceedings we have any Interest. You must not expect scandal for by the same rule we are equally debarred either from hearing or inventing it.—You must expect from me nothing but the melancholy effusions of a broken Heart which is ever reverting to the Happiness it once enjoyed and which ill supports its present wretchedness. The Possibility of being able to write, to speak, to you of my lost Henry will be a luxury to me, and your goodness will not I know refuse to read what it will so much releive my Heart to write. I once thought that to have what is in general called a Friend (I mean one of my own sex to whom I might speak with less reserve than to any other person) independant of my sister would never be an object of my wishes, but how much was I mistaken! Charlotte is too much engrossed by two confidential correspondents of that sort, to supply the place of one to me, and I hope you will not think me girlishly romantic, when I say that to have some kind and compassionate Friend who might listen to my sorrows without endeavouring to console me was what I had for some time wished for, when our acquaintance with you, the intimacy which followed it and the particular affectionate attention you paid me almost from the first, caused me to entertain the flattering Idea of those attentions being improved on a closer acquaintance into a Friendship which, if you were what my wishes formed you would be the greatest Happiness I could be capable of enjoying. To find that such Hopes are realised is a satisfaction indeed, a satisfaction which is now almost the only one I can ever experience.—I feel myself so languid that I am sure were you with me you would oblige me to leave off writing, and I cannot give you a greater proof of my affection for you than by acting, as I know you would wish me to do, whether Absent or Present. I am my dear Emmas sincere friend

E. L.

LETTER THE NINTH is from Mrs *Marlowe* to Miss *Lutterell*

Grosvenor Street, April 10th

Need I say my dear Eloisa how wellcome your letter was to me I cannot give a greater proof of the pleasure I received from it, or of the Desire I feel that our Correspondence may be regular and frequent than by setting you so good an example as I now do in answering it before the end of the week—. But do not imagine that I claim any merit in being so punctual; on the contrary I assure you, that it is a far greater Gratification to me to write to you, than to spend the Evening either at a Concert or a Ball. Mr Marlowe is so desirous of my appearing at some of the Public places every evening that I do not like to refuse him, but at the same time so much wish to remain at Home, that independant of the Pleasure I experience in devoting any portion of my Time to my Dear Eloisa, yet the Liberty I claim from having a letter to write of spending an Evening at home with my little Boy, you know me well enough to be sensible, will of itself be a sufficient Inducement (if one is necessary) to my maintaining with Pleasure a Correspondence with you. As to the subject of your letters to me, whether grave or merry, if they concern you they must be equally interesting to me; not but that I think the melancholy Indulgence of your own sorrows by repeating them and dwelling on them to me, will only encourage and increase them, and that it will be more prudent in you to avoid so sad a subject; but yet knowing as I do what a soothing and melancholy Pleasure it must afford you, I cannot prevail on myself to deny you so great an Indulgence, and will only insist on your not expecting me to encourage you in it, by my own letters; on the contrary I intend to fill them with such lively Wit and enlivening Humour as shall even provoke a smile in the sweet but sorrowfull countenance of my Eloisa.

In the first place you are to learn that I have met your sisters three friends Lady Lesley and her Daughters, twice in Public since I have been here. I know you will be impatient to hear my opinion of the Beauty of three Ladies of whom you have heard so much. Now, as you are too ill and too unhappy to be vain, I think I may venture to inform you that I like none of their faces so well as I do your own. Yet they are all handsome—Lady Lesley indeed I have seen before; her Daughters I beleive would in general be said to have a finer face than her Ladyship, and yet what with the charms of a Blooming complexion, a little Affectation and a great deal of small-talk, (in each of which she is superior to the young Ladies) she will I dare say gain herself as many admirers as the more regular features of Matilda, and Margaret. I am sure you will agree with me in saying that they can none of them be of a proper size for real Beauty, when you know that two of them are taller and the other shorter than ourselves. In spite of this Defect (or rather by reason of it) there is something very noble and majestic in the figures of the Miss Lesleys, and something agreably lively in the appearance of their pretty little Mother-in-law. But tho' one may be majestic and the other lively, yet the faces of neither possess that Bewitching sweetness of my Eloisas, which her present languor is so far from diminushing. What would my Husband and Brother say of us, if they knew all the fine things I have been saying to you in this letter. It is very hard that a pretty woman is never to be told she is so by any one of her own sex without that person's being suspected to be either her determined Enemy, or her professed Toad-eater. How much more amiable are women in that particular! One man may say forty civil things to another without our supposing that he is ever paid for it, and provided he does his Duty by our sex, we care not how Polite he is to his own.

Mrs Lutterell will be so good as to accept my compliments, Charlotte, my Love, and Eloisa the best wishes for the recovery of her Health and Spirits that can be offered by her affectionate Friend

E. MARLOWE.

I am afraid this letter will be but a poor specimen of my Powers in the witty way; and your opinion of them will not be greatly increased when I assure you that I have been as entertaining as I possibly could.

LETTER THE TENTH is from Miss *Margaret Lesley* to
Miss Charlotte Lutterell
Portman Square April 13th
MY DEAR CHARLOTTE

We left Lesley-Castle on the 28th of last Month, and
arrived safely in London after a Journey of seven Days;
I had the pleasure of finding your Letter here waiting
my Arrival, for which you have my grateful Thanks.
Ah! my dear Friend I every day more regret the serene
and tranquil Pleasures of the Castle we have left, in
exchange for the uncertain and unequal Amusements
of this vaunted City. Not that I will pretend to assert
that these uncertain and unequal Amusements are in
the least Degree unpleasing to me; on the contrary
I enjoy them extremely and should enjoy them even
more, were I not certain that every appearance I make in
Public but rivetts the Chains of those unhappy Beings
whose Passion it is impossible not to pity, tho' it is out
of my power to return. In short my Dear Charlotte it
is my sensibility for the sufferings of so many amiable
young Men, my Dislike of the extreme admiration
I meet with, and my aversion to being so celebrated
both in Public, in Private, in Papers, and in Printshops,
that are the reasons why I cannot more fully enjoy, the
Amusements so various and pleasing of London. How
often have I wished that I possessed as little Personal
Beauty as you do; that my figure were as inelegant; my
face as unlovely; and my appearance as unpleasing as
yours! But ah! what little chance is there of so desirable
an Event; I have had the small-pox, and must therefore
submit to my unhappy fate.

I am now going to intrust you my dear Charlotte

with a secret which has long disturbed the tranquility of my days, and which is of a kind to require the most inviolable Secrecy from you. Last Monday se'night Matilda and I accompanied Lady Lesley to a Rout at the Honourable Mrs Kickabout's; we were escorted by Mr Fitzgerald who is a very amiable young Man in the main, tho' perhaps a little singular in his Taste—He is in love with Matilda—. We had scarcely paid our Compliments to the Lady of the House and curtseyed to half a score different people when my Attention was attracted by the appearance of a Young Man the most lovely of his Sex, who at that moment entered the Room with another Gentleman and Lady. From the first moment I beheld him, I was certain that on him depended the future Happiness of my Life. Imagine my surprise when he was introduced to me by the name of Cleveland—I instantly recognised him as the Brother of Mrs Marlowe, and the acquaintance of my Charlotte at Bristol. Mr and Mrs M. were the gentleman and Lady who accompanied him. (You do not think Mrs Marlowe handsome?) The elegant address of Mr Cleveland, his polished Manners and Delightful Bow, at once confirmed my attachment. He did not speak; but I can imagine everything he would have said, had he opened his Mouth. I can picture to myself the cultivated Understanding, the Noble sentiments, and elegant Language which would have shone so conspicuous in the conversation of Mr Cleveland. The approach of Sir James Gower (one of my too numerous admirers) prevented the Discovery of any such Powers, by putting an end to a Conversation we had never commenced, and by attracting my attention to himself. But oh! how inferior are the accomplishments of Sir James to those of his so greatly envied Rival! Sir James is one of the most frequent of our Visitors, and is almost always of our Parties. We have since often met Mr and Mrs Marlowe but no Cleveland—he is always engaged some where else. Mrs Marlowe fatigues me to Death every time I see her by her tiresome Conversations about you and Eloisa. She is so stupid! I live in the hope of seeing her irrisistable Brother to night, as we are going to Lady Flambeaus, who is I know intimate with the Marlowes. Our party will be Lady Lesley, Matilda, Fitzgerald, Sir James Gower, and myself. We see little of Sir George, who is almost always at the gaming-table. Ah! my poor Fortune where art thou by this time? We see more of Lady L. who always makes her appearance (highly rouged) at Dinner-time. Alas! what Delightful Jewels will she be decked in this evening at Lady Flambeau's! Yet I wonder how she can herself delight in wearing them; surely she must be sensible of the ridiculous impropriety of loading her little diminutive figure with such superfluous ornaments; is it possible that she can not know how greatly superior an elegant simplicity is to the most studied apparel? Would she but Present them to Matilda and me, how greatly should we be obliged to her, How becoming would Diamonds be on our fine majestic figures! And how surprising it is that such an Idea should never have occurred to HER. I am sure if I have reflected in this manner once, I have fifty times. Whenever I see Lady Lesley dressed in them such reflections immediately come across me. My own Mother's Jewels too! But I will say no more on so melancholy a subject —let me entertain you with something more pleasing—Matilda had a letter this morning from Lesley, by which we have the pleasure of finding that he is at Naples has turned Roman-Catholic, obtained one of the Pope's Bulls for annulling his 1st Marriage and has since actually married a Neapolitan Lady of great Rank and Fortune. He tells us moreover that much the same sort of affair has befallen his first wife the worthless Louisa who is likewise at Naples had turned Roman-catholic, and is soon to be married to a Neapolitan Nobleman of great and Distinguished merit. He says, that they are at present very good Friends, have quite forgiven all past errors and intend in future to be very good Neighbours. He invites Matilda and me to pay him a visit to Italy and to bring him his little Louisa whom both her Mother, Step-mother, and himself are equally desirous of beholding. As to our accepting his invitation, it is at Present very uncertain; Lady Lesley advises us to go without loss of time; Fitzgerald offers to escort us there, but Matilda has some doubts of the Propriety of such a scheme—she owns it would be very agreable. I am certain she likes the Fellow. My Father desires us not to be in a hurry, as perhaps if we wait a few months both he and Lady Lesley will do themselves the pleasure of attending us. Lady Lesley says no, that nothing will ever tempt her to forego the Amusements of Brighthelmstone for a Journey to Italy merely to see our Brother. "No (says the disagreable Woman) I have once in my life been fool enough to travel I dont know how many hundred Miles to see two of the Family, and I found it did not answer, so Deuce take me, if ever I am so foolish again." So says her Ladyship, but Sir George still Perseveres in saying that perhaps in a month or two, they may accompany us. Adeiu my Dear Charlotte Yrs faithful

MARGARET LESLEY.

*

THE HISTORY OF ENGLAND

FROM THE REIGN OF HENRY THE 4TH TO THE DEATH OF CHARLES THE 1ST BY A PARTIAL, PREJUDICED, AND IGNORANT HISTORIAN.

*

To Miss Austen, eldest daughter of the Rev. George Austen, this work is inscribed with all due respect by THE AUTHOR.

N.B. There will be very few Dates in this History.

THE HISTORY OF ENGLAND

HENRY the 4th

Henry the 4th ascended the throne of England much to his own satisfaction in the year 1399, after having prevailed on his cousin and predecessor Richard the 2nd, to resign it to him, and to retire for the rest of his life to Pomfret Castle, where he happened to be murdered. It is to be supposed that Henry was married, since he had certainly four sons, but it is not in my power to inform the Reader who was his wife. Be this as it may, he did not live for ever, but falling ill, his son the Prince of Wales came and took away the crown; whereupon the King made a long speech, for which I must refer the Reader to Shakespear's Plays, and the Prince made a still longer. Things being thus settled between them the King died, and was succeeded by his son Henry who had previously beat Sir William Gascoigne.

HENRY *the 5th*

This Prince after he succeeded to the throne grew quite reformed and amiable, forsaking all his dissipated companions, and never thrashing Sir William again. During his reign, Lord Cobham was burnt alive, but I forget what for. His Majesty then turned his thoughts to France, where he went and fought the famous Battle of Agincourt. He afterwards married the King's daughter Catherine, a very agreeable woman by Shakespear's account. In spite of all this however he died, and was succeeded by his son Henry.

HENRY *the 6th*

I cannot say much for this Monarch's sense. Nor would I if I could, for he was a Lancastrian. I suppose you know all about the Wars between him and the Duke of York who was of the right side; if you do not, you had better read some other History, for I shall not be very diffuse in this, meaning by it only to vent my spleen *against*, and shew my Hatred *to* all those people whose parties or principles do not suit with mine, and not to give information. This King married Margaret of Anjou, a Woman whose distresses and misfortunes were so great as almost to make me who hate her, pity her. It was in this reign that Joan of Arc lived and made such a ROW among the English. They should not have burnt her —but they did. There were several Battles between the Yorkists and Lancastrians, in which the former (as they ought) usually conquered. At length they were entirely overcome; The King was murdered—The Queen was sent home—and Edward the 4th ascended the Throne.

EDWARD *the 4th*

This Monarch was famous only for his Beauty and his Courage, of which the Picture we have here given of him, and his undaunted Behaviour in marrying one Woman while he was engaged to another, are sufficient proofs. His Wife was Elizabeth Woodville, a Widow who, poor Woman! was afterwards confined in a Convent by that Monster of Iniquity and Avarice Henry the 7th. One of Edward's Mistresses was Jane Shore, who has had a play written about her, but it is a tragedy and therefore not worth reading. Having performed all these noble actions, his Majesty died, and was succeeded by his son.

EDWARD *the 5th*

This unfortunate Prince lived so little a while that nobody had him to draw his picture. He was murdered by his Uncle's Contrivance, whose name was Richard the 3rd.

RICHARD *the 3rd*

The Character of this Prince has been in general very severely treated by Historians, but as he was a *York*, I am rather inclined to suppose him a very respectable Man. It has indeed been confidently asserted that he killed his two Nephews and his Wife, but it has also been declared that he did not kill his two Nephews, which I am inclined to beleive true; and if this is the case, it may also be affirmed that he did not kill his Wife, for if Perkin Warbeck was really the Duke of York, why might not Lambert Simnel be the Widow of Richard. Whether innocent or guilty, he did not reign long in peace, for Henry Tudor E. of Richmond as great a villain as ever lived, made a great fuss about getting the Crown and having killed the King at the battle of Bosworth, he succeeded to it.

HENRY the 7th

This Monarch soon after his accession married the Princess Elizabeth of York, by which alliance he plainly proved that he thought his own right inferior to hers, tho' he pretended to the contrary. By this Marriage he had two sons and two daughters, the elder of which Daughters was married to the King of Scotland and had the happiness of being grandmother to one of the first Characters in the World. But of *her*, I shall have occasion to speak more at large in future. The youngest, Mary, married first the King of France and secondly the D. of Suffolk, by whom she had one daughter, afterwards the Mother of Lady Jane Grey, who tho' inferior to her lovely Cousin the Queen of Scots, was yet an amiable young woman and famous for reading Greek while other people were hunting. It was in the reign of Henry the 7th that Perkin Warbeck and Lambert Simnel before mentioned made their appearance, the former of whom was set in the stocks, took shelter in Beaulieu Abbey, and was beheaded with the Earl of Warwick, and the latter was taken into the Kings kitchen. His Majesty died and was succeeded by his son Henry whose only merit was his not being quite so bad as his daughter Elizabeth.

HENRY the 8th

It would be an affront to my Readers were I to suppose that they were not as well acquainted with the particulars of this King's reign as I am myself. It will therefore be saving *them* the task of reading again what they have read before, and *myself* the trouble of writing what I do not perfectly recollect, by giving only a slight sketch of the principal Events which marked his reign. Among these may be ranked Cardinal Wolsey's telling the father Abbott of Leicester Abbey that "he was come to lay his bones among them," the reformation in Religion and the King's riding through the streets of London with Anna Bullen. It is however but Justice, and my Duty to declare that this amiable Woman was entirely innocent of the Crimes with which she was accused, and of which her Beauty, her Elegance, and her Sprightliness were sufficient proofs, not to mention her solemn Protestations of Innocence, the weakness of the Charges against her, and the King's Character; all of which add some confirmation, tho' perhaps but slight ones when in comparison with those before alledged in her favour. Tho' I do not profess giving many dates, yet as I think it proper to give some and shall of course make choice of those which it is most necessary for the Reader to know, I think it right to inform him that her letter to the King was dated on the 6th of May. The Crimes and Cruelties of this Prince, were too numerous to be mentioned, (as this history I trust has fully shown;) and nothing can be said in his vindication, but that his abolishing Religious Houses and leaving them to the ruinous depredations of time has been of infinite use to the landscape of England in general, which probably was a principal motive for his doing it, since otherwise why should a Man who was of no Religion himself be at so much trouble to abolish one which had for ages been established in the Kingdom. His Majesty's 5th Wife was the Duke of Norfolk's Neice who, tho' universally acquitted of the crimes for which she was beheaded, has been by many people supposed to have led an abandoned life before her Marriage—of this however I have many doubts, since she was a relation of that noble Duke of Norfolk who was so warm in the Queen of Scotland's cause, and who at last fell a victim to it. The Kings last wife contrived to survive him, but with difficulty effected it. He was succeeded by his only son Edward.

EDWARD *the 6th*

As this prince was only nine years old at the time of his Father's death, he was considered by many people as too young to govern, and the late King happening to be of the same opinion, his mother's Brother the Duke of Somerset was chosen Protector of the realm during his minority. This Man was on the whole of a very amiable Character, and is somewhat of a favourite with me, tho' I would by no means pretend to affirm that he was equal to those first of Men Robert Earl of Essex, Delamere, or Gilpin. He was beheaded, of which he might with reason have been proud, had he known that such was the death of Mary Queen of Scotland; but as it was impossible that he should be conscious of what had never happened, it does not appear that he felt particularly delighted with the manner of it. After his decease the Duke of Northumberland had the care of the King and the Kingdom, and performed his trust of both so well that the King died and the Kingdom was left to his daughter in law the Lady Jane Grey, who has been already mentioned as reading Greek. Whether she really understood that language or whether such a study proceeded only from an excess of vanity for which I beleive she was always rather remarkable, is uncertain. Whatever might be the cause, she preserved the same appearance of knowledge, and contempt of what was generally esteemed pleasure, during the whole of her life, for she declared herself displeased with being appointed Queen, and while conducting to the scaffold, she wrote a sentence in Latin and another in Greek on seeing the dead Body of her Husband accidentally passing that way.

MARY

This woman had the good luck of being advanced to the throne of England, in spite of the superior pretensions, Merit, and Beauty of her Cousins Mary Queen of Scotland and Jane Grey. Nor can I pity the Kingdom for the misfortunes they experienced during her Reign, since they fully deserved them, for having allowed her to succeed her Brother—which was a double peice of folly, since they might have foreseen that as she died without children, she would be succeeded by that disgrace to humanity, that pest of society, Elizabeth. Many were the people who fell martyrs to the protestant Religion during her reign; I suppose not fewer than a dozen. She married Philip King of Spain who in her sister's reign was famous for building Armadas. She died without issue, and then the dreadful moment came in which the destroyer of all comfort, the deceitful Betrayer of trust reposed in her, and the Murderess of her Cousin succeeded to the Throne.——

ELIZABETH

It was the peculiar misfortune of this Woman to have bad Ministers——Since wicked as she herself was, she could not have committed such extensive mischeif, had not these vile and abandoned Men connived at, and encouraged her in her Crimes. I know that it has by many people been asserted and beleived that Lord Burleigh, Sir Francis Walsingham, and the rest of those who filled the cheif offices of State were deserving, experienced, and able Ministers. But oh! how blinded such writers and such Readers must be to true Merit, to Merit despised, neglected and defamed, if they can persist in such opinions when they reflect that these men, these boasted men were such scandals to their Country and their sex as to allow and assist their Queen in confining for the space of nineteen years, a *woman* who if the claims of Relationship and Merit were of no avail, yet as a Queen and as one who condescended to place confidence in her, had every reason to expect assistance and protection; and at length in allowing Elizabeth to bring this amiable Woman to an untimely, unmerited, and scandalous Death. Can any one if he reflects but for a moment on this blot, this everlasting blot upon their

understanding and their Character, allow any praise to
Lord Burleigh or Sir Francis Walsingham? Oh! what
must this bewitching Princess whose only friend was
then the Duke of Norfolk, and whose only ones now Mr
Whitaker, Mrs Lefroy, Mrs Knight and myself, who was
abandoned by her son, confined by her Cousin, abused,
reproached and vilified by all, what must not her most
noble mind have suffered when informed that Elizabeth
had given orders for her Death! Yet she bore it with a
most unshaken fortitude, firm in her mind; constant in
her Religion; and prepared herself to meet the cruel fate
to which she was doomed, with a magnanimity that
would alone proceed from conscious Innocence. And
yet could you Reader have beleived it possible that some
hardened and zealous Protestants have even abused her
for that steadfastness in the Catholic Religion which
reflected on her so much credit? But this is a striking
proof of *their* narrow souls and prejudiced Judgements
who accuse her. She was executed in the Great Hall at
Fortheringay Castle (sacred Place!) on Wednesday the
8th of February 1586—to the everlasting Reproach of
Elizabeth, her Ministers, and of England in general. It
may not be unnecessary before I entirely conclude my
account of this ill-fated Queen, to observe that she had
been accused of several crimes during the time of her
reigning in Scotland, of which I now most seriously do
assure my Reader that she was entirely innocent; having never been guilty of anything more than Impru-
dencies into which she was betrayed by the openness
of her Heart, her Youth, and her Education. Having I
trust by this assurance entirely done away every Suspicion and every doubt which might have arisen in the
Reader's mind, from what other Historians have writ-

ten of her, I shall proceed to mention the remaining Events that marked Elizabeth's reign. It was about this time that Sir Francis Drake the first English Navigator who sailed round the World, lived, to be the ornament of his Country and his profession. Yet great as he was, and justly celebrated as a sailor, I cannot help foreseeing that he will be equalled in this or the next Century by one who tho' now but young, already promises to answer all the ardent and sanguine expectations of his Relations and Friends, amongst whom I may class the amiable Lady to whom this work is dedicated, and my no less amiable self.

Though of a different profession, and shining in a different sphere of Life, yet equally conspicuous in the Character of an Earl, as Drake was in that of a Sailor, was Robert Devereux Lord Essex. This unfortunate young Man was not unlike in character to that equally unfortunate one *Frederic Delamere*. The simile may be carried still farther, and Elizabeth the torment of Essex may be compared to the Emmeline of Delamere. It would be endless to recount the misfortunes of this noble and gallant Earl. It is sufficient to say that he was beheaded on the 25th of Feb, after having been Lord Lieutenant of Ireland, after having clapped his hand on his sword, and after performing many other services to his Country. Elizabeth did not long survive his loss, and died so miserable that were it not an injury to the memory of Mary I should pity her.

JAMES *the 1st*

Though this King had some faults, among which and as the most principal, was his allowing his Mother's death, yet considered on the whole I cannot help liking him. He married Anne of Denmark, and had several Children; fortunately for him his eldest son Prince Henry died before his father or he might have experienced the evils which befell his unfortunate Brother.

As I am myself partial to the roman catholic religion, it is with infinite regret that I am obliged to blame the Behaviour of any Member of it: yet Truth being I think very excusable in an Historian, I am necessitated to say that in this reign the roman Catholics of England did not behave like Gentlemen to the protestants. Their Behaviour indeed to the Royal Family and both Houses of Parliament might justly be considered by them as very uncivil, and even Sir Henry Percy tho' certainly the best bred man of the party, had none of that general politeness which is so universally pleasing, as his attentions were entirely confined to Lord Mounteagle.

Sir Walter Raleigh flourished in this and the preceeding reign, and is by many people held in great veneration and respect—But as he was an enemy of the noble Essex, I have nothing to say in praise of him, and must refer all those who may wish to be acquainted with the particulars of his life, to Mr Sheridan's play of the Critic, where they will find many interesting anecdotes as well of him as of his friend Sir Christopher Hatton.—His Majesty was of that amiable disposition which inclines to Friendship, and in such points was possessed of a keener penetration in discovering Merit than many other people. I once heard an excellent Sharade on a Carpet, of which the subject I am now on reminds me, and as I think it may afford my Readers some amusement to *find it out*, I shall here take the liberty of presenting it to them.

SHARADE

My first is what my second was to King James the 1st, and you tread on my whole.

The principal favourites of his Majesty were Car, who was afterwards created Earl of Somerset and whose name perhaps may have some share in the above mentioned Sharade, and George Villiers afterwards Duke of Buckingham. On his Majesty's death he was succeeded by his son Charles.

CHARLES the 1st

This amiable Monarch seems born to have suffered misfortunes equal to those of his lovely Grandmother; misfortunes which he could not deserve since he was her descendant. Never certainly were there before so many detestable Characters at one time in England as in this Period of its History; never were amiable men so scarce. The number of them throughout the whole Kingdom amounting only to *five*, besides the inhabitants of Oxford who were always loyal to their King and faithful to his interests. The names of this noble five who never forgot the duty of the subject, or swerved from their attachment to his Majesty, were as follows—The King himself, ever stedfast in his own support —Archbishop Laud, Earl of Strafford, Viscount Faulkland and Duke of Ormond, who were scarcely less strenuous or zealous in the cause. While the *villians* of the time would make too long a list to be written or read; I shall therefore content myself with mentioning the leaders of the Gang. Cromwell, Fairfax, Hampden, and Pym may be considered as the original Causers of all the disturbances, Distresses, and Civil Wars in which

England for many years was embroiled. In this reign as well as in that of Elizabeth, I am obliged in spite of my attachment to the Scotch, to consider them as equally guilty with the generality of the English, since they dared to think differently from their Sovereign, to forget the Adoration which as *Stuarts* it was their Duty to pay them, to rebel against, dethrone and imprison the unfortunate Mary; to oppose, to deceive, and to sell the no less unfortunate Charles. The Events of this Monarch's reign are too numerous for my pen, and indeed the recital of any Events (except what I make myself) is uninteresting to me; my principal reason for undertaking the History of England being to Prove the innocence of the Queen of Scotland, which I flatter myself with having effectually done, and to abuse Elizabeth, tho' I am rather fearful of having fallen short in the latter part of my scheme. —As therefore it is not my intention to give any particular account of the distresses into which this King was involved through the misconduct and Cruelty of his Parliament, I shall satisfy myself with vindicating him from the Reproach of Arbitrary and tyrannical Government with which he has often been charged. This, I feel, is not difficult to be done, for with one argument I am certain of satisfying every sensible and well disposed person whose opinions have been properly guided by a good Education—and this Argument is that he was a *Stuart*.

FINIS
Saturday Nov: 26th 1791.
*

A COLLECTION OF LETTERS

To Miss Cooper

Cousin Conscious of the Charming Character which in every Country, and every Clime in Christendom is Cried, Concerning you, with Caution and Care I Commend to your Charitable Criticism this Clever Collection of Curious Comments, which have been Carefully Culled, Collected and Classed by your Comical Cousin

The Author.

*

A COLLECTION OF LETTERS

Letter the First
From A Mother to Her Friend.

My Children begin now to claim all my attention in different Manner from that in which they have been used to receive it, as they are now arrived at that age when it is necessary for them in some measure to become conversant with the World, My Augusta is 17 and her sister scarcely a twelvemonth younger. I flatter myself that their education has been such as will not disgrace their appearance in the World, and that *they* will not disgrace their Education I have every reason to beleive. Indeed they are sweet Girls—. Sensible yet unaffected—Accomplished yet Easy—. Lively yet Gentle—. As their progress in every thing they have learnt has been always the same, I am willing to forget the difference of age, and to introduce them together into Public. This very Evening is fixed on as their first *entrée* into Life, as we are to drink tea with Mrs Cope and her Daughter. I am glad that we are to meet no one, for my Girls sake, as it would be awkward for them to enter too wide a Circle on the very first day. But we shall proceed by degrees.—Tomorrow Mr Stanly's family will drink tea with us, and perhaps the Miss Phillips's will meet them. On Tuesday we shall pay Morning Visits—On Wednesday we are to dine at Westbrook. On Thursday we have Company at home. On Friday we are to be at a Private Concert at Sir John Wynna's—and on Saturday we expect Miss Dawson to call in the Morning—which will complete my Daughters Introduction into Life. How they will bear so much dissipation I cannot imagine; of their spirits I have no fear, I only dread their health.

This mighty affair is now happily over, and my Girls are *out*. As the moment approached for our departure, you can have no idea how the sweet Creatures trembled with fear and expectation. Before the Carriage drove to the door, I called them into my dressing- room, and as soon as they were seated thus addressed them. "My dear Girls the moment is now arrived when I am to reap the rewards of all my Anxieties and Labours to-wards you during your Education. You are this Evening to enter a World in which you will meet with many wonderfull Things; Yet let me warn you against suffering yourselves to be meanly swayed by the Follies and Vices of others, for beleive me my beloved Children that if you do—I shall be very sorry for it." They both assured me that they would ever remember my advice with Gratitude, and follow it with attention; That they were prepared to find a World full of things to amaze and to shock them: but that they trusted their behaviour would never give me reason to repent the Watchful Care with which I had presided over their infancy and formed their Minds— "With such expectations and such intentions (cried I) I can have nothing to fear from you—and can chearfully conduct you to Mrs Cope's without a fear of your being seduced by her Example, or contaminated by her Follies. Come, then my Children (added I) the Carriage is driving to the door, and I will not a moment delay the happiness you are so impatient to enjoy." When we arrived at Warleigh, poor Augusta could scarcely breathe, while Margaret was all Life and Rapture. "The long-expected Moment is now arrived (said she) and we shall soon be in the World."—In a few Moments we were in Mrs Cope's parlour, where with her daughter she sate ready to receive us. I observed with delight the impression my Children made on them—. They were indeed two sweet, elegant-looking Girls, and tho' somewhat abashed from the peculiarity of their situation, yet there was an ease in their Manners and address which could not fail of pleasing—. Imagine my dear Madam how delighted I must have been in beholding as I did, how attentively they observed every object they saw, how disgusted with some Things, how enchanted with others, how astonished at all! On the whole however they returned in raptures with the World, its Inhabitants, and Manners.

Yrs Ever—A. F.

LETTER THE SECOND
From a Young Lady crossed in Love to her friend

Why should this last disappointment hang so heavily on my spirits? Why should I feel it more, why should it wound me deeper than those I have experienced before? Can it be that I have a greater affection for Willoughby than I had for his amiable predecessors? Or is it that our feelings become more acute from being often wounded? I must suppose my dear Belle that this is the Case, since I am not conscious of being more sincerely attached to Willoughby than I was to Neville, Fitzowen, or either of the Crawfords, for all of whom I once felt the most lasting affection that ever warmed a Woman's heart. Tell me then dear Belle why I still sigh when I think of the faithless Edward, or why I weep when I behold his Bride, for too surely this is the case—. My Friends are all alarmed for me; They fear my declining health; they lament my want of spirits; they dread the effects of both. In hopes of releiving my melancholy, by directing my thoughts to other objects, they have invited several of their friends to spend the Christmas with us. Lady Bridget Darkwood and her sister-in-law, Miss Jane are expected on Friday; and Colonel Seaton's family will be with us next week. This is all most kindly meant by my Uncle and Cousins; but what can the presence of a dozen indefferent people do to me, but weary and distress me—. I will not finish my Letter till some of our Visitors are arrived.

Friday Evening

Lady Bridget came this morning, and with her, her sweet sister Miss Jane—. Although I have been acquainted with this charming Woman above fifteen Years, yet I never before observed how lovely she is. She is now about 35, and in spite of sickness, sorrow and Time is more blooming than I ever saw a Girl of 17. I was delighted with her, the moment she entered the house, and she appeared equally pleased with me, attaching herself to me during the remainder of the day. There is something so sweet, so mild in her Countenance, that she seems more than Mortal. Her Conversation is as bewitching as her appearance; I could not help telling her how much she engaged my admiration—. "Oh! Miss Jane (said I)—and stopped from an inability at the moment of expressing myself as I could wish— Oh! Miss Jane—(I repeated) —I could not think of words to suit my feelings— She seemed waiting for my speech—. I was confused— distressed—my thoughts were bewildered—and I could only add—"How do you do?" She saw and felt for my Embarrassment and with admirable presence of mind releived me from it by saying—"My dear Sophia be not uneasy at having exposed yourself—I will turn the Conversation without appearing to notice it. "Oh! how I loved her for her kindness!" Do you ride as much as you used to do?" said she—. "I am advised to ride by my Physician. We have delightful Rides round us, I have a Charming horse, am uncommonly fond of the Amusement, replied I quite recovered from my Confusion, and in short I ride a great deal." "You are in the right my Love," said she. Then repeating the following line which was an extempore and equally adapted to recommend both Riding and Candour—

"Ride where you may, Be Candid where you can," she added," I rode once, but it is many years ago—She spoke this in so low and tremulous a Voice, that I was silent—. Struck with her Manner of speaking I could make no reply. "I have not ridden, continued she fixing her Eyes on my face, since I was married." I was never so surprised—"Married, Ma'am!" I repeated. "You may well wear that look of astonishment, said she, since what I have said must appear improbable to you—Yet nothing is more true than that I once was married."

"Then why are you called Miss Jane?"

"I married, my Sophia without the consent or knowledge of my father the late Admiral Annesley. It was therefore necessary to keep the secret from him and from every one, till some fortunate opportunity might offer of revealing it—. Such an opportunity alas! was but too soon given in the death of my dear Capt. Dashwood—Pardon these tears, continued Miss Jane wiping her Eyes, I owe them to my Husband's memory. He fell my Sophia, while fighting for his Country in America after a most happy Union of seven years—. My Children, two sweet Boys and a Girl, who had constantly resided with my Father and me, passing with him and with every one as the Children of a Brother (tho' I had ever been an only Child) had as yet been the comforts of my Life. But no sooner had I lossed my Henry, than these sweet Creatures fell sick and died—. Conceive dear Sophia what my feelings must have been when as an Aunt I attended my Children to their early Grave—. My Father did not survive them many weeks—He died, poor Good old man, happily ignorant to his last hour of my Marriage.'

"But did not you own it, and assume his name at your husband's death?"

"No; I could not bring myself to do it; more especially

when in my Children I lost all inducement for doing it. Lady Bridget, and yourself are the only persons who are in the knowledge of my having ever been either Wife or Mother. As I could not Prevail on myself to take the name of Dashwood (a name which after my Henry's death I could never hear without emotion) and as I was conscious of having no right to that of Annesley, I dropt all thoughts of either, and have made it a point of bearing only my Christian one since my Father's death." She paused—"Oh! my dear Miss Jane (said I) how infinitely am I obliged to you for so entertaining a story! You cannot think how it has diverted me! But have you quite done?"

"I have only to add my dear Sophia, that my Henry's elder Brother dieing about the same time, Lady Bridget became a Widow like myself, and as we had always loved each other in idea from the high Character in which we had ever been spoken of, though we had never met, we determined to live together. We wrote to one another on the same subject by the same post, so exactly did our feeling and our actions coincide! We both eagerly embraced the proposals we gave and received of becoming one family, and have from that time lived together in the greatest affection."

"And is this all? said I, I hope you have not done."

"Indeed I have; and did you ever hear a story more pathetic?"

"I never did—and it is for that reason it pleases me so much, for when one is unhappy nothing is so delightful to one's sensations as to hear of equal misery."

"Ah! but my Sophia why are *you* unhappy?"

"Have you not heard Madam of Willoughby's Marriage?"

"But my love why lament *his* perfidy, when you bore so well that of many young Men before?"

"Ah! Madam, I was used to it then, but when Willoughby broke his Engagements I had not been dissapointed for half a year."

"Poor Girl!" said Miss Jane.

Letter the Third
From a Young Lady in distressed Circumstances to her friend

A few days ago I was at a private Ball given by Mr Ashburnham. As my Mother never goes out she entrusted me to the care of Lady Greville who did me the honour of calling for me in her way and of allowing me to sit forwards, which is a favour about which I am very indifferent especially as I know it is considered as confering a great obligation on me "So Miss Maria (said her Ladyship as she saw me advancing to the door of the Carriage) you seem very smart to night— *my* poor Girls will appear quite to disadvantage by *you*— I only hope your Mother may not have distressed herself to set *you* off. Have you got a new Gown on?"

"Yes Ma'am." replied I with as much indifference as I could assume.

"Aye, and a fine one too I think—(feeling it, as by her permission I seated myself by her) I dare say it is all very smart—But I must own, for you know I always speak my mind, that I think it was quite a needless piece of expence—Why could not you have worn your old striped one? It is not my way to find fault with People because they are poor, for I always think that they are more to be despised and pitied than blamed for it, especially if they cannot help it, but at the same time I must say that in my opinion your old striped Gown would have been quite fine enough for its Wearer—for to tell you the truth (I always speak my mind) I am very much afraid that one half of the people in the room will not know whether you have a Gown on or not—But I suppose you intend to make your fortune to night—. Well, the sooner the better; and I wish you success."

"Indeed Ma'am I have no such intention—"

"Who ever heard a young Lady own that she was a Fortune-hunter?" Miss Greville laughed but I am sure Ellen felt for me.

"Was your Mother gone to bed before you left her?" said her Ladyship.

"Dear Ma'am, said Ellen it is but nine o'clock."

"True Ellen, but Candles cost money, and Mrs Williams is too wise to be extravagant."

"She was just sitting down to supper Ma'am."

"And what had she got for supper?" "I did not observe." "Bread and Cheese I suppose." "I should never wish for a better supper." said Ellen. "You have never any reason replied her Mother, as a better is always provided for you." Miss Greville laughed excessively, as she constantly does at her Mother's wit.

Such is the humiliating Situation in which I am forced to appear while riding in her Ladyship's Coach—I dare not be impertinent, as my Mother is always admonishing me to be humble and patient if I wish to make my way in the world. She insists on my accepting every invitation of Lady Greville, or you may be certain that I would never enter either her House, or her Coach with the disagreable certainty I always have of being

abused for my Poverty while I am in them.—When
we arrived at Ashburnham, it was nearly ten o'clock,
which was an hour and a half later than we were desired to be there; but Lady Greville is too fashionable
(or fancies herself to be so) to be punctual. The Dancing however was not begun as they waited for Miss
Greville. I had not been long in the room before I was
engaged to dance by Mr Bernard, but just as we were
going to stand up, he recollected that his Servant had
got his white Gloves, and immediately ran out to fetch
them. In the mean time the Dancing began and Lady
Greville in passing to another room went exactly before me—She saw me and instantly stopping, said to
me though there were several people close to us,

"Hey day, Miss Maria! What cannot you get a partner? Poor Young Lady! I am afraid your new Gown was
put on for nothing. But do not despair; perhaps you
may get a hop before the Evening is over." So saying,
she passed on without hearing my repeated assurance of
being engaged, and leaving me very much provoked at
being so exposed before every one—Mr Bernard however soon returned and by coming to me the moment
he entered the room, and leading me to the Dancers
my Character I hope was cleared from the imputation
Lady Greville had thrown on it, in the eyes of all the old
Ladies who had heard her speech. I soon forgot all my
vexations in the pleasure of dancing and of having the
most agreable partner in the room. As he is moreover
heir to a very large Estate I could see that Lady Greville
did not look very well pleased when she found who had
been his Choice—She was determined to mortify me,
and accordingly when we were sitting down between
the dances, she came to me with more than her usual

insulting importance attended by Miss Mason and said loud enough to be heard by half the people in the room, "Pray Miss Maria in what way of business was your Grandfather? for Miss Mason and I cannot agree whether he was a Grocer or a Bookbinder." I saw that she wanted to mortify me, and was resolved if I possibly could to Prevent her seeing that her scheme succeeded. "Neither Madam; he was a Wine Merchant." "Aye, I knew he was in some such low way— He broke did not he?" "I beleive not Ma'am." "Did not he abscond?" "I never heard that he did." "At least he died insolvent?" "I was never told so before." "Why, was not your *father* as poor as a Rat" "I fancy not." "Was not he in the Kings Bench once?" "I never saw him there." She gave me *such* a look, and turned away in a great passion; while I was half delighted with myself for my impertinence, and half afraid of being thought too saucy. As Lady Greville was extremely angry with me, she took no further notice of me all the Evening, and indeed had I been in favour I should have been equally neglected, as she was got into a Party of great folks and she never speaks to me when she can to anyone else. Miss Greville was with her Mother's party at supper, but Ellen preferred staying with the Bernards and me. We had a very pleasant Dance and as Lady G— slept all the way home, I had a very comfortable ride.

The next day while we were at dinner Lady Greville's Coach stopped at the door, for that is the time of day she generally contrives it should. She sent in a message by the servant to say that "she should not get out but that Miss Maria must come to the Coach-door, as she wanted to speak to her, and that she must make haste and come immediately—" "What an impertinent Message Mama!" said I—"Go Maria—" replied she—Accordingly I went and was obliged to stand there at her Ladyships pleasure though the Wind was extremely high and very cold.

"Why I think Miss Maria you are not quite so smart as you were last night—But I did not come to examine your dress, but to tell you that you may dine with us the day after tomorrow—Not tomorrow, remember, do not come tomorrow, for we expect Lord and Lady Clermont and Sir Thomas Stanley's family—There will be no occasion for your being very fine for I shant send the Carriage— If it rains you may take an umbrella—" I could hardly help laughing at hearing her give me leave to keep myself dry—"And pray remember to be in time, for I shant wait—I hate my Victuals overdone—But you need not come before the time—How does your Mother do? She is at dinner is not she?" "Yes Ma'am we were in the middle of dinner when your Ladyship came." "I am afraid you find it very cold Maria." said Ellen. "Yes, it is an horrible East wind —said her Mother—I assure you I can hardly bear the window down—But you are used to be blown about by the wind Miss Maria and that is what has made your Complexion so rudely and coarse. You young Ladies who cannot often ride in a Carriage never mind what weather you trudge in, or how the wind shews your legs. I would not have my Girls stand out of doors as you do in such a day as this. But some sort of people have no feelings either of cold or Delicacy—Well, remember that we shall expect you on Thursday at 5 o'clock—You must tell your Maid to come for you at night—There will be no Moon—and you will have an horrid walk home—My compts to Your Mother—I

am afraid your dinner will be cold—Drive on—" And
away she went, leaving me in a great passion with her
as she always does.

Maria Williams.

LETTER THE FOURTH
From a Young Lady rather impertinent to her friend.

We dined yesterday with Mr Evelyn where we were
introduced to a very agreable looking Girl his Cousin.
I was extremely pleased with her appearance, for added
to the charms of an engaging face, her manner and
voice had something peculiarly interesting in them. So
much so, that they inspired me with a great curiosity
to know the history of her Life, who were her Parents,
where she came from, and what had befallen her, for
it was then only known that she was a relation of Mr
Evelyn, and that her name was Grenville. In the evening
a favourable opportunity offered to me of attempting
at least to know what I wished to know, for every
one played at Cards but Mrs Evelyn, My Mother, Dr
Drayton, Miss Grenville and myself, and as the two
former were engaged in a whispering Conversation,
and the Doctor fell asleep, we were of necessity obliged
to entertain each other. This was what I wished and
being determined not to remain in ignorance for want
of asking, I began the Conversation in the following
Manner.

"Have you been long in Essex, Ma'am?"

"I arrived on Tuesday."

"You came from Derbyshire?"

"No, Ma'am! appearing surprised at my question,
from Suffolk." You will think this a good dash of mine

my dear Mary, but you know that I am not wanting for Impudence when I have any end in veiw. "Are you pleased with the Country Miss Grenville? Do you find it equal to the one you have left?"

"Much superior Ma'am in point of Beauty." She sighed. I longed to know for why.

"But the face of any Country however beautiful said I, can be but a poor consolation for the loss of one's dearest Friends." She shook her head, as if she felt the truth of what I said. My Curiosity was so much raised, that I was resolved at any rate to satisfy it.

"You regret having left Suffolk then Miss Grenville?" "Indeed I do." "You were born there I suppose?" "Yes Ma'am I was and passed many happy years there—"

"That is a great comfort—said I—I hope Ma'am that you never spent any unhappy one's there."

"Perfect Felicity is not the property of Mortals, and no one has a right to expect uninterrupted Happiness.—Some Misfortunes I have certainly met with."

"*What* Misfortunes dear Ma'am?" replied I, burning with impatience to know every thing. "*None* Ma'am I hope that have been the effect of any wilfull fault in me." " I dare say not Ma'am, and have no doubt but that any sufferings you may have experienced could arise only from the cruelties of Relations or the Errors of Friends." She sighed—"You seem unhappy my dear Miss Grenville —Is it in my power to soften your Misfortunes?" "*Your* power Ma'am replied she extremely surprised; it is in *no one's* power to make me happy." She pronounced these words in so mournfull and solemn an accent, that for some time I had not courage to reply. I was actually silenced. I recovered myself however in a few moments and looking at her with all the affection I could, "My dear

Miss Grenville said I, you appear extremely young—and may probably stand in need of some one's advice whose regard for you, joined to superior Age, perhaps superior Judgement might authorise her to give it. I am that person, and I now challenge you to accept the offer I make you of my Confidence and Friendship, in return to which I shall only ask for yours—"

"You are extremely obliging Ma'am—said she—and I am highly flattered by your attention to me—But I am in no difficulty, no doubt, no uncertainty of situation in which any advice can be wanted. Whenever I am however continued she brightening into a complaisant smile, I shall know where to apply."

I bowed, but felt a good deal mortified by such a repulse; still however I had not given up my point. I found that by the appearance of sentiment and Friendship nothing was to be gained and determined therefore to renew my attacks by Questions and suppositions. "Do you intend staying long in this part of England Miss Grenville?"

"Yes Ma'am, some time I beleive."

"But how will Mr and Mrs Grenville bear your absence?"

"They are neither of them alive Ma'am." This was an answer I did not expect—I was quite silenced, and never felt so awkward in my Life—-.

LETTER THE FIFTH
From a Young Lady very much in love to her Friend

My Uncle gets more stingy, my Aunt more particular, and I more in love every day. What shall we all be at this rate by the end of the year! I had this morning the happiness of receiving the following Letter from my dear Musgrove.

Sackville St: Janry 7th

It is a month to day since I first beheld my lovely Henrietta, and the sacred anniversary must and shall be kept in a manner becoming the day—by writing to her. Never shall I forget the moment when her Beauties first broke on my sight—No time as you well know can erase it from my Memory. It was at Lady Scudamores. Happy Lady Scudamore to live within a mile of the divine Henrietta! When the lovely Creature first entered the room, oh! what were my sensations? The sight of you was like the sight ofa wonderful fine Thing. I started—I gazed at her with admiration —She appeared every moment more Charming, and the unfortunate Musgrove became a captive to your Charms before I had time to look about me. Yes Madam, I had the happiness of adoring you, an happiness for which I cannot be too grateful. "What said he to himself is Musgrove allowed to die for Henrietta? Enviable Mortal! and may he pine for her who is the object of universal admiration, who is adored by a Colonel, and toasted by a Baronet! Adorable Henrietta how beautiful you are! I declare you are quite divine! You are more than Mortal. You are an Angel. You are Venus herself. In short Madam you are the prettiest Girl I ever saw in my Life—and her Beauty is encreased in her Musgroves Eyes, by permitting him to love her and allowing me to hope. And ah! Angelic Miss Henrietta Heaven is my witness how ardently I do hope for the death of your villanous Uncle and his abandoned Wife, since my fair one will not consent to be mine till their decease has placed her in affluence above what my fortune can procure—. Though it is an improvable Estate—. Cruel Henrietta to persist in such a resolution! I am at Present with my sister where I mean to continue till my own house which tho' an excellent one is at Present somewhat out of repair, is ready to receive me. Amiable princess of my Heart farewell—Of that Heart which trembles while it signs itself Your most ardent Admirer and devoted humble servt.

T. MUSGROVE.

There is a pattern for a Love-letter Matilda! Did you ever read such a master-piece of Writing? Such sense, such sentiment, such purity of Thought, such flow of Language and such unfeigned Love in one sheet? No, never I can answer for it, since a Musgrove is not to be met with by every Girl. Oh! how I long to be with him! I intend to send him the following in answer to his Letter tomorrow.

MY DEAREST MUSGROVE—. Words cannot express how happy your Letter made me; I thought I should have cried for joy, for I love you better than any body in the World. I think you the most amiable, and the handsomest Man in England, and so to be sure you are. I never read so sweet a Letter in my Life. Do write me another just like it, and tell me you are in love with me in every other line. I quite die to see you. How shall we manage to see one another? for we are so much in love that we cannot live asunder. Oh! my dear Musgrove you cannot think how impatiently I wait for the death of my Uncle and Aunt—If they will not Die soon, I beleive I shall run mad, for I get more in love with you every day of my Life.

How happy your Sister is to enjoy the pleasure of your Company in her house, and how happy every body in London must be because you are there. I hope you will be so kind as to write to me again soon, for I never read such sweet Letters as yours. I am my dearest Musgrove most truly and faithfully yours for ever and ever

HENRIETTA HALTON.

I hope he will like my answer; it is as good a one as I can write though nothing to his; Indeed I had always heard what a dab he was at a Love-letter. I saw him you know for the first time at Lady Scudamores—And when I saw her Ladyship afterwards she asked me how I liked her Cousin Musgrove?

"Why upon my word said I, I think he is a very handsome young Man."

"I am glad you think so replied she, for he is distractedly in love with you."

"Law! Lady Scudamore said I, how can you talk so ridiculously?"

"Nay, t'is very true answered she, I assure you, for he was in love with you from the first moment he beheld you."

"I wish it may be true said I, for that is the only kind of love I would give a farthing for—There is some sense in being in love at first sight."

"Well, I give you Joy of your conquest, replied Lady Scudamore, and I beleive it to have been a very complete one; I am sure it is not a contemptible one, for my Cousin is a charming young fellow, has seen a great deal of the World, and writes the best Love-letters I ever read."

This made me very happy, and I was excessively pleased with my conquest. However, I thought it was proper to give myself a few Airs—so I said to her—

"This is all very pretty Lady Scudamore, but you know that we young Ladies who are Heiresses must not throw ourselves away upon Men who have no fortune at all."

"My dear Miss Halton said she, I am as much convinced of that as you can be, and I do assure you that I should be the last person to encourage your marrying anyone who had not some pretensions to expect a fortune with you. Mr Musgrove is so far from being poor that he has an estate of several hundreds an year which is capable of great Improvement, and an excellent House, though at Present it is not quite in repair."

"If that is the case replied I, I have nothing more to say against him, and if as you say he is an informed young Man and can write a good Love-letter, I am sure I have no reason to find fault with him for admiring me, tho' perhaps I may not marry him for all that Lady Scudamore."

"You are certainly under no obligation to marry him answered her Ladyship, except that which love himself will dictate to you, for if I am not greatly mistaken you are at this very moment unknown to yourself, cherishing a most tender affection for him."

"Law, Lady Scudamore replied I blushing how can you think of such a thing?"

"Because every look, every word betrays it, answered she; Come my dear Henrietta, consider me as a friend, and be sincere with me —Do not you prefer Mr Musgrove to any man of your acquaintance?"

"Pray do not ask me such questions Lady Scuda-more, said I turning away my head, for it is not fit for me to answer them."

"Nay my Love replied she, now you confirm my suspicions. But why Henrietta should you be ashamed to own a well-placed Love, or why refuse to confide in me?"

"I am not ashamed to own it; said I taking Courage. I do not refuse to confide in you or blush to say that I do love your cousin Mr Musgrove, that I am sincerely attached to him, for it is no disgrace to love a handsome Man. If he were plain indeed I might have had reason to be ashamed of a passion which must have been mean since the object would have been unworthy. But with such a figure and face, and such beautiful hair as your Cousin has, why should I blush to own that such superior merit has made an impression on me."

"My sweet Girl (said Lady Scudamore embracing me with great affection) what a delicate way of thinking you have in these matters, and what a quick discernment for one of your years! Oh! how I honour you for such Noble Sentiments!"

"Do you Ma'am said I; You are vastly obliging. But pray Lady Scudamore did your Cousin himself tell you of his affection for me I shall like him the better if he did, for what is a Lover without a Confidante?"

"Oh! my Love replied she, you were born for each other. Every word you say more deeply convinces me that your Minds are actuated by the invisible power of simpathy, for your opinions and sentiments so exactly coincide. Nay, the colour of your Hair is not very different. Yes my dear Girl, the poor despairing Musgrove did reveal to me the story of his Love—. Nor was I surprised at it—I know not how it was, but I had a kind of presentiment that he would be in love with you."

"Well, but how did he break it to you?"

"It was not till after supper. We were sitting round the fire together talking on indifferent subjects, though to say the truth the Conversation was cheifly on my side for he was thoughtful and silent, when on a sudden he interrupted me in the midst of something I was saying, by exclaiming in a most Theatrical tone—

Yes I'm in love I feel it now And Henrietta Halton has undone me.

"Oh! What a sweet way replied I, of declaring his Passion! To make such a couple of charming lines about me! What a pity it is that they are not in rhime!"

"I am very glad you like it answered she; To be sure there was a great deal of Taste in it. And are you in love with her, Cousin? said I. I am very sorry for it, for unexceptionable as you are in every respect, with a pretty Estate capable of Great improvements, and an excellent House tho' somewhat out of repair, yet who can hope to aspire with success to the adorable Henrietta who has had an offer from a Colonel and been toasted by a Baronet"—"*That* I have—" cried I. Lady Scudamore continued. "Ah dear Cousin replied he, I am so well convinced of the little Chance I can have of winning her who is adored by thousands, that I need no assurances of yours to make me more thoroughly so. Yet surely neither you or the fair Henrietta herself will deny me the exquisite Gratification of dieing for her, of falling a victim to her Charms. And when I am dead"—continued her—

"Oh Lady Scudamore, said I wiping my eyes, that

such a sweet Creature should talk of dieing!"

"It is an affecting Circumstance indeed, replied Lady Scudamore." "When I am dead said he, let me be carried and lain at her feet, and perhaps she may not disdain to drop a pitying tear on my poor remains."

"Dear Lady Scudamore interrupted I, say no more on this affecting subject. I cannot bear it."

"Oh! how I admire the sweet sensibility of your Soul, and as I would not for Worlds wound it too deeply, I will be silent."

"Pray go on." said I. She did so.

"And then added he, Ah! Cousin imagine what my transports will be when I feel the dear precious drops trickle on my face! Who would not die to haste such extacy! And when I am interred, may the divine Henrietta bless some happier Youth with her affection, May he be as tenderly attached to her as the hapless Musgrove and while HE crumbles to dust, May they live an example of Felicity in the Conjugal state!"

Did you ever hear any thing so pathetic? What a charming wish, to be lain at my feet when he was dead! Oh! what an exalted mind he must have to be capable of such a wish! Lady Scudamore went on.

"Ah! my dear Cousin replied I to him, such noble behaviour as this, must melt the heart of any woman however obdurate it may naturally be; and could the divine Henrietta but hear your generous wishes for her happiness, all gentle as is her mind, I have not a doubt but that she would pity your affection and endeavour to return it." "Oh! Cousin answered he, do not endeavour to raise my hopes by such flattering assurances. No, I cannot hope to please this angel of a Woman, and the only thing which remains for me to do, is to die." "True

Love is ever desponding replied I, but I my dear Tom will give you even greater hopes of conquering this fair one's heart, than I have yet given you, by assuring you that I watched her with the strictest attention during the whole day, and could plainly discover that she cherishes in her bosom though unknown to herself, a most tender affection for you."

"Dear Lady Scudamore cried I, This is more than I ever knew!"

"Did not I say that it was unknown to yourself? I did not, continued I to him, encourage you by saying this at first, that surprise might render the pleasure still Greater." "No Cousin replied he in a languid voice, nothing will convince me that I can have touched the heart of Henrietta Halton, and if you are deceived yourself, do not attempt deceiving me." "In short my Love it was the work of some hours for me to Persuade the poor despairing Youth that you had really a preference for him; but when at last he could no longer deny the force of my arguments, or discredit what I told him, his transports, his Raptures, his Extacies are beyond my power to describe."

"Oh! the dear Creature, cried I, how passionately he loves me! But dear Lady Scudamore did you tell him that I was totally dependant on my Uncle and Aunt?"

"Yes, I told him every thing."

"And what did he say."

"He exclaimed with virulence against Uncles and Aunts; Accused the laws of England for allowing them to Possess their Estates when wanted by their Nephews or Neices, and wished *he* were in the House of Commons, that he might reform the Legislature, and rectify all its abuses."

"Oh! the sweet Man! What a spirit he has!" said I.

"He could not flatter himself he added, that the adorable Henrietta would condescend for his sake to resign those Luxuries and that splendor to which she had been used, and accept only in exchange the Comforts and Elegancies which his limited Income could afford her, even supposing that his house were in Readiness to receive her. I told him that it could not be expected that she would; it would be doing her an injustice to suppose her capable of giving up the power she now possesses and so nobly uses of doing such extensive Good to the poorer part of her fellow Creatures, merely for the gratification of you and herself."

"To be sure said I, I *am* very Charitable every now and then. And what did Mr Musgrove say to this?"

"He replied that he was under a melancholy necessity of owning the truth of what I said, and that therefore if he should be the happy Creature destined to be the Husband of the Beautiful Henrietta he must bring himself to wait, however impatiently, for the fortunate day, when she might be freed from the power of worthless Relations and able to bestow herself on him."

What a noble Creature he is! Oh! Matilda what a fortunate one I am, who am to be his Wife! My Aunt is calling me to come and make the pies, so adeiu my dear friend, and beleive me yours etc—

H. HALTON.

Finis.

SCRAPS

To Miss FANNY CATHERINE AUSTEN
MY DEAR NEICE
As I am prevented by the great distance between
Rowling and Steventon from superintending your Education myself, the care of which will probably on that
account devolve on your Father and Mother, I think it
is my particular Duty to Prevent your feeling as much
as possible the want of my personal instructions, by
addressing to you on paper my Opinions and Admoni-
tions on the conduct of Young Women, which you will
find expressed in the following pages.—
I am my dear Neice
Your affectionate Aunt
THE AUTHOR.

THE FEMALE PHILOSOPHER
A LETTER

MY DEAR LOUISA
Your friend Mr Millar called upon us yesterday in
his way to Bath, whither he is going for his health; two
of his daughters were with him, but the eldest and the
three Boys are with their Mother in Sussex. Though
you have often told me that Miss Millar was remarkably handsome, you never mentioned anything of her
Sisters' beauty; yet they are certainly extremely pretty.
I'll give you their description.—Julia is eighteen; with

a countenance in which Modesty, Sense and Dignity are happily blended, she has a form which at once presents you with Grace, Elegance and Symmetry. Charlotte who is just sixteen is shorter than her Sister, and though her figure cannot boast the easy dignity of Julia's, yet it has a pleasing plumpness which is in a different way as estimable. She is fair and her face is expressive sometimes of softness the most bewitching, and at others of Vivacity the most striking. She appears to have infinite Wit and a good humour unalterable; her conversation during the half hour they set with us, was replete with humourous sallies, Bonmots and repartees; while the sensible, the amiable Julia uttered sentiments of Morality worthy of a heart like her own. Mr Millar appeared to answer the character I had always received of him. My Father met him with that look of Love, that social Shake, and cordial kiss which marked his gladness at beholding an old and valued friend from whom thro' various circumstances he had been separated nearly twenty years. Mr Millar observed (and very justly too) that many events had befallen each during that interval of time, which gave occasion to the lovely Julia for making most sensible reflections on the many changes in their situation which so long a period had occasioned, on the advantages of some, and the disadvantages of others. From this subject she made a short digression to the instability of human pleasures and the uncertainty of their duration, which led her to observe that all earthly Joys must be imperfect. She was proceeding to illustrate this doctrine by examples from the Lives of great Men when the Carriage came to the Door and the amiable Moralist with her Father and Sister was obliged to depart; but not without a promise of spending five or six months with us on their return. We of course mentioned you, and I assure you that ample Justice was done to your Merits by all. "Louisa Clarke (said I) is in general a very pleasant Girl, yet sometimes her good humour is clouded by Peevishness, Envy and Spite. She neither wants Understanding or is without some pretensions to Beauty, but these are so very trifling, that the value she sets on her personal charms, and the adoration she expects them to be offered are at once a striking example of her vanity, her pride, and her folly." So said I, and to my opinion everyone added weight by the concurrence of their own.

Your affectionate
ARABELLA SMYTHE.

THE FIRST ACT OF A COMEDY

CHARACTERS

Popgun	Maria
Charles	Pistolletta
Postilion	Hostess
Chorus of ploughboys	Cook
and	and
Strephon	Chloe

SCENE—AN INN
Enter Hostess, Charles, Maria, and Cook.

HOSTESS TO MARIA) If the gentry in the Lion should want beds, shew them number 9.

MARIA) Yes Mistress.— *Exit* Maria

HOSTESS TO COOK) If their Honours in the Moon

ask for the bill of fare, give it them.

COOK) I wull, I wull. *Exit* Cook.

HOSTESS TO CHARLES) If their Ladyships in the Sun ring their Bell—answer it.

CHARLES) Yes Madam. EXEUNT Severally.

Scene Changes to the Moon, and discovers Popgun and Pistoletta.

PISTOLETTA) Pray papa how far is it to London?

POPGUN) My Girl, my Darling, my favourite of all my Children, who art the picture of thy poor Mother who died two months ago, with whom I am going to Town to marry to Strephon, and to whom I mean to bequeath my whole Estate, it wants seven Miles.

Scene Changes to the Sun—

Enter Chloe and a chorus of ploughboys.

CHLOE) Where am I? At Hounslow.—Where go I? To London—. What to do? To be married—. Unto whom? Unto Strephon. Who is he? A Youth. Then I will sing a song.

Song

I go to Town And when I come down, I shall be married to Streephon* [*Note the two e's] And that to me will be fun.

CHORUS) Be fun, be fun, be fun,

And that to me will be fun.

Enter Cook—

COOK) Here is the bill of fare.

CHLOE READS) 2 Ducks, a leg of beef, a stinking partridge, and a tart.—I will have the leg of beef and the partridge. *Exit* Cook

And now I will sing another song.

Song—

I am going to have my dinner,

After which I shan't be thinner,
I wish I had here Strephon
For he would carve the partridge if it should
be a tough one.
CHORUS) Tough one, tough one, tough one
For he would carve the partridge if it
Should be a tough one.
Exit Chloe and Chorus.—
Scene Changes to the Inside of The Lion.
Enter Strephon and Postilion.
STREPH:) You drove me from Staines to this place, from whence I mean to go to Town to marry Chloe. How much is your due?
POST:) Eighteen pence.
STREPH:) Alas, my friend, I have but a bad guinea with which I mean to support myself in Town. But I will pawn to you an undirected Letter that I received from Chloe.
POST:) Sir, I accept your offer.
End of the First Act.

A LETTER from a YOUNG LADY, whose feelings being too strong for her Judgement led her into the commission of Errors which her Heart disapproved.

Many have been the cares and vicissitudes of my past life, my beloved Ellinor, and the only consolation I feel for their bitterness is that on a close examination of my conduct, I am convinced that I have strictly deserved them. I murdered my father at a very early period of my Life, I have since murdered my Mother, and I am now going to murder my Sister. I have changed my religion so often that at present I have not an idea of any left. I have been a perjured witness in every public tryal for these last twelve years; and I have forged my own Will. In short there is scarcely a crime that I have not committed—But I am now going to reform. Colonel Martin of the Horse guards has paid his Addresses to me, and we are to be married in a few days. As there is something singular in our Courtship, I will give you an account of it. Colonel Martin is the second son of the late Sir John Martin who died immensely rich, but bequeathing only one hundred thousand pound apeice to his three younger Children, left the bulk of his fortune, about eight Million to the present Sir Thomas. Upon his small pittance the Colonel lived tolerably contented for nearly four months when he took it into his head to determine on getting the whole of his eldest Brother's Estate. A new will was forged and the Colonel produced it in Court—but nobody would swear to it's being the right will except himself, and he had sworn so much that Nobody beleived him. At that moment I happened to be passing by the door of the Court, and was beckoned in by the Judge who told the Colonel that I was a Lady ready to witness anything for the cause of Justice, and advised him to apply to me. In short the Affair was soon adjusted. The Colonel and I swore to its' being the right will, and Sir Thomas has been obliged to resign all his illgotten wealth. The Colonel in gratitude waited on me the next day with an offer of his hand —. I am now going to murder my Sister.

Yours Ever,
ANNA PARKER.

A TOUR THROUGH WALES—
in a LETTER from a YOUNG LADY—

MY DEAR CLARA

I have been so long on the ramble that I have not till now had it in my power to thank you for your Letter—. We left our dear home on last Monday month; and proceeded on our tour through Wales, which is a principality contiguous to England and gives the title to the Prince of Wales. We travelled on horseback by preference. My Mother rode upon our little poney and Fanny and I walked by her side or rather ran, for my Mother is so fond of riding fast that she galloped all the way. You may be sure that we were in a fine perspiration when we came to our place of resting. Fanny has taken a great many Drawings of the Country, which are very beautiful, tho' perhaps not such exact resemblances as might be wished, from their being taken as she ran along. It would astonish you to see all the Shoes we wore out in our Tour. We determined to take a good Stock with us and therefore each took a pair of our own besides those we set off in. However we were obliged to have them both capped and heelpeiced at Carmarthen, and at last when they were quite gone, Mama was so kind as to lend us a pair of blue Sattin Slippers, of which we each took one and hopped home from Hereford delightfully—

I am your ever affectionate
ELIZABETH JOHNSON.

A TALE.
A Gentleman whose family name I shall conceal, bought a small Cottage in Pembrokeshire about two

years ago. This daring Action was suggested to him by his elder Brother who promised to furnish two rooms and a Closet for him, provided he would take a small house near the borders of an extensive Forest, and about three Miles from the Sea. Wilhelminus gladly accepted the offer and continued for some time searching after such a retreat when he was one morning agreably releived from his suspence by reading this advertisement in a Newspaper.

TO BE LETT
A Neat Cottage on the borders of an extensive forest and about three Miles from the Sea. It is ready furnished except two rooms and a Closet.

The delighted Wilhelminus posted away immediately to his brother, and shewed him the advertisement. Robertus congratulated him and sent him in his Carriage to take possession of the Cottage. After travelling for three days and six nights without stopping, they arrived at the Forest and following a track which led by it's side down a steep Hill over which ten Rivulets meandered, they reached the Cottage in half an hour. Wilhelminus alighted, and after knocking for some time without receiving any answer or hearing any one stir within, he opened the door which was fastened only by a wooden latch and entered a small room, which he immediately perceived to be one of the two that were unfurnished—From thence he proceeded into a Closet equally bare. A pair of stairs that went out of it led him into a room above, no less destitute, and these apartments he found composed the whole of the House. He was by no means displeased with this discovery, as he had the comfort of reflecting that he should not be obliged to lay out anything on furniture himself—. He returned immediately to his Brother, who took him the next day to every Shop in Town, and bought what ever was requisite to furnish the two rooms and the Closet, In a few days everything was completed, and Wilhelminus returned to take possession of his Cottage. Robertus accompanied him, with his Lady the amiable Cecilia and her two lovely Sisters Arabella and Marina to whom Wilhelminus was tenderly attached, and a large number of Attendants.—An ordinary Genius might probably have been embarrassed, in endeavouring to accomodate so large a party, but Wilhelminus with admirable presence of mind gave orders for the immediate erection of two noble Tents in an open spot in the Forest adjoining to the house. Their Construction was both simple and elegant—A couple of old blankets, each supported by four sticks, gave a striking proof of that taste for architecture and that happy ease in overcoming difficulties which were some of Wilhelminus's most striking Virtues.

We hope that you have enjoyed reading this book from The Large Print Book Company.

If you are interested in other titles we publish, please get in touch with us and we will be happy to send you our latest catalogue.

You can write to us at P.O. Box 970, Sanbornville, NH 03872-0970.

Or you can visit our website at www.largeprintbookco.com.

Our website contains a copy of our latest catalogue.

THE LARGE PRINT BOOK COMPANY

READINGS ON

EMILY DICKINSON

OTHER TITLES IN THE GREENHAVEN PRESS
LITERARY COMPANION SERIES:

AMERICAN AUTHORS

Maya Angelou
Nathaniel Hawthorne
Ernest Hemingway
Herman Melville
Arthur Miller
John Steinbeck
Mark Twain

BRITISH AUTHORS

Jane Austen

WORLD AUTHORS

Sophocles

BRITISH LITERATURE

The Canterbury Tales
Lord of the Flies
Shakespeare: The Comedies
Shakespeare: The Sonnets
Shakespeare: The Tragedies
A Tale of Two Cities

THE GREENHAVEN PRESS
Literary Companion
TO AMERICAN AUTHORS

READINGS ON

EMILY DICKINSON

David Bender, *Publisher*
Bruno Leone, *Executive Editor*
Scott Barbour, *Managing Editor*
Bonnie Szumski, *Series Editor*
Tamara Johnson, *Book Editor*

Greenhaven Press, San Diego, CA

Library of Congress Cataloging-in-Publication Data

Readings on Emily Dickinson / Tamara Johnson, book editor.
     p.   cm. — (The Greenhaven Press literary com-
panion to American authors)
   Includes bibliographical references and index.
   ISBN 1-56510-634-2 (pbk. : alk. paper). —
ISBN 1-56510-635-0 (lib. : alk. paper)
   1. Dickinson, Emily, 1830–1886—Criticism and
interpretation. 2. Women and literature—Massachusetts
—History—19th century. I. Johnson, Tamara. II. Series.
PS1541.Z5R43   1997
811'.4—dc20
                                                        96-44979
                                                           CIP

Cover photo: Amherst College Library

Copyright ©1997 by Greenhaven Press, Inc.
PO Box 289009
San Diego, CA 92198-9009
Printed in the U.S.A.

> **When much in the Woods as a little Girl, I was told that the snake would bite me, that I might pick a poisonous flower, or Goblins kidnap me, but I went along and met no one but Angels, who were far shyer of me than I could be of them, so I haven't that confidence in fraud in which many exercise.**

Emily Dickinson

Contents

Chapter 3: Dickinson's Poetic Themes

FOREWORD

*"'Tis the good reader that
makes the good book."*

Ralph Waldo Emerson

The story's bare facts are simple: The captain, an old and scarred seafarer, walks with a peg leg made of whale ivory. He relentlessly drives his crew to hunt the world's oceans for the great white whale that crippled him. After a long search, the ship encounters the whale and a fierce battle ensues. Finally the captain drives his harpoon into the whale, but the harpoon line catches the captain about the neck and drags him to his death.

A simple story, a straightforward plot—yet, since the 1851 publication of Herman Melville's *Moby-Dick*, readers and critics have found many meanings in the struggle between Captain Ahab and the whale. To some, the novel is a cautionary tale that depicts how Ahab's obsession with revenge leads to his insanity and death. Others believe that the whale represents the unknowable secrets of the universe and that Ahab is a tragic hero who dares to challenge fate by attempting to discover this knowledge. Perhaps Melville intended Ahab as a criticism of Americans' tendency to become involved in well-intentioned but irrational causes. Or did Melville model Ahab after himself, letting his fictional character express his anger at what he perceived as a cruel and distant god?

Although literary critics disagree over the meaning of *Moby-Dick*, readers do not need to choose one particular interpretation in order to gain an understanding of Melville's novel. Instead, by examining various analyses, they can gain numerous insights into the issues that lie under the surface of the basic plot. Studying the writings of literary critics can also aid readers in making their own assessments of *Moby-Dick* and other literary works and in developing analytical thinking skills.

The Greenhaven Literary Companion Series was created with these goals in mind. Designed for young adults, this unique anthology series provides an engaging and comprehensive introduction to literary analysis and criticism. The essays included in the Literary Companion Series are chosen for their accessibility to a young adult audience and are expertly edited in consideration of both the reading and comprehension levels of this audience. In addition, each essay is introduced by a concise summation that presents the contributing writer's main themes and insights. Every anthology in the Literary Companion Series contains a varied selection of critical essays that cover a wide time span and express diverse views. Wherever possible, primary sources are represented through excerpts from authors' notebooks, letters, and journals and through contemporary criticism.

Each title in the Literary Companion Series pays careful consideration to the historical context of the particular author or literary work. In-depth biographies and detailed chronologies reveal important aspects of authors' lives and emphasize the historical events and social milieu that influenced their writings. To facilitate further research, every anthology includes primary and secondary source bibliographies of articles and/or books selected for their suitability for young adults. These engaging features make the Greenhaven Literary Companion series ideal for introducing students to literary analysis in the classroom or as a library resource for young adults researching the world's great authors and literature.

Exceptional in its focus on young adults, the Greenhaven Literary Companion Series strives to present literary criticism in a compelling and accessible format. Every title in the series is intended to spark readers' interest in leading American and world authors, to help them broaden their understanding of literature, and to encourage them to formulate their own analyses of the literary works that they read. It is the editors' hope that young adult readers will find these anthologies to be true companions in their study of literature.

INTRODUCTION

Much beloved throughout the world, Emily Dickinson was the first American poet to successfully bridge the gap between nineteenth-century lyric verse—in the tradition of Edgar Allan Poe, Herman Melville, and Ralph Waldo Emerson—and the modern free verse championed by Walt Whitman. Unlike Whitman, who simply discarded popular assumptions about rhyme, meter, and rhythm in order to pursue his own rambling muse, Dickinson pushed the limits of traditional form. In her quiet reflections on home and nature, rhyme is stretched to its furthest capabilities, with jarring results. Her meditations on death, desire, and spiritual confusion are delicate yet bold in their honesty. More than a hundred years after her death her poetry continues to influence the way readers look at literature.

A number of the essays included in the Greenhaven Literary Companion to Emily Dickinson are written by poets. Occasionally the essays are accompanied by poetic tributes to Dickinson, who continues to inspire poets and critics alike. As a whole, the writers and scholars represented in this collection provide teachers and students with a range of opinion on Dickinson—who has not always been well received. The varied viewpoints reflect alternative methods scholars use for better understanding a work of poetry, including cultural, historical, and biographical analyses. These varied approaches allow students to discover diverse materials from which to generate topics for research papers, group studies, and oral presentations.

The essays in this companion are selected and organized for students encountering Emily Dickinson for the first time. Collectively they demonstrate a range of possibilities for the beginning scholar. Some essays offer insight into the poet's life and its influence on her work. Some select specific poems for line-by-line analysis. Others evaluate Dickinson's body of work and rank her among other poets. The essays serve not only as models but represent the large numbers of studies that continue to be published. Additional listings at the end of this book point students toward various publications that are recommended for further research.

The brief biography is designed to provide students with a basic sketch of Dickinson's life: when and where she was born, the cultural climate and educational opportunities of her time, some difficulties she encountered in writing and publishing her poetry, and the events that led to the posthumous discovery of her work. Because details of Dickinson's life are sketchy, several excerpts from letters by people who knew the poet are included. Although Dickinson's poetry does have some autobiographical elements, care has been taken not to confuse the speaker of the poems with Emily Dickinson herself.

This collection has several important features. Most of the essays concern a single, focused topic, either a single idea or a unique approach to a particular work. Introductions clarify and summarize the main point so that the reader will know what to expect. Interspersed within the essays, the reader will find inserts that add authenticity, supplementary information, or illustrative anecdotes. Inserts are drawn from sources such as original letters by Dickinson and poems by the authors. *Readings on Emily Dickinson* gives students a wide selection of critical essays to explore a unique and complex poet.

EMILY DICKINSON: A BIOGRAPHY

Emily Dickinson lived and died in the small Massachusetts farming village of Amherst. Her New England ancestors had endured tough times in the town, stressing the values of hard work, religious fervor, and frugality. Among her Puritan fore-fathers, even words were chosen carefully so as not to waste them, a trait that Emily seems to have instinctively incorpo-rated in her highly unusual poems. With the exception of a year at Mount Holyoke Seminary for Girls, a nearby boarding school, and several short trips to Boston, Washington, and Philadelphia, Emily always lived under the same roof as her parents and sister, Lavinia. Even after marrying, her brother, Austin, moved just next door, where the three siblings could continue to spend many hours together in conversation.

An intensely private woman, Emily grew to avoid contact with all but her immediate family. She ordered her personal letters burned upon her death. Her poetry, which Lavinia found in bundles inside her desk, survives today only be-cause her sister did not see fit to burn it. Not all the poems were saved, however. Some were destroyed with the letters. Others were altered so as not to reveal too much about the life of the woman many knew only as the "Myth of Amherst."

THE IMPORTANCE OF HOME AND FAMILY

Emily Dickinson's childhood seems relatively uneventful. She was born on December 10, 1830, the middle child of Ed-ward Dickinson and Emily Norcross, two of Amherst's most respected citizens. Edward was a lawyer, a politician, and the treasurer of Amherst College. Emily's father placed a high value on education, writing often while on business trips to remind his children to study. Emily Norcross, daugh-ter of a prosperous family, saw her marriage to Edward as a practical decision rather than the result of a romantic courtship. Edward looked upon his engagement to Miss Norcross rather dispassionately as well, having found, as he wrote shortly before the marriage, a woman with whom he could live out his vision of the perfect married couple:

> May we be virtuous, intelligent, industrious and by the exercise of every virtue, & the cultivation of every excellence, be esteemed and respected & beloved by all—We must be determined to do our duty to each other, & to all our friends, and let others do as they may.

To the Dickinsons, the Homestead, as they called their large brick house, was "the real world." The day began with Edward Dickinson's deep voice reading from the Bible or, when Mr. Dickinson was on one of his frequent business trips, in quiet study and contemplation. Though the Dickinsons had servants, nineteenth-century domestic duties were a big part of Emily's day as well. Mrs. Dickinson taught her daughters to bake bread, wash clothes, sew, and clean house, jobs Emily often complained about in letters to friends and relatives. Lavinia (or Vinnie as Emily's sister was called), seems to have found household tasks more agreeable than Emily did.

It is clear that despite their many chores, both girls loved the Homestead. Their letters reveal homesickness not only when they were away from home themselves, but also when a family member was missing from the household. When Austin was away at law school, for example, Emily wrote to him at Harvard in October 1851:

> You had a windy evening going back to Boston, and we thought of you many times and hoped you would not be cold. Our fire burned so cheerfully I couldn't help thinking of how many were *here* and how many were *away*, and I wished so many times during that long evening that the door would open and you come walking in. Home is holy—nothing of doubt or distrust can enter its blessed portals. I feel it more and more as the great world goes on and one another forsake, in whom you place your trust—here seems indeed to be a bit of Eden.

Though all the siblings were close, the bond between Austin and Emily was special. Outwardly shy, Emily enjoyed her brother's irreverent humor and they both shared a deep appreciation for nature. When Austin married, it was to Susan Gilbert, one of Emily's closest friends. Susan shared Emily's sharp wit and love of poetry, an interest Austin had developed as well. On at least one occasion, Austin asked Emily for her opinion of some poems he had written. Though he clearly respected Emily's judgment, he had no idea what brilliance Emily possessed. Nor did Susan, who received close to a hundred poems from Emily throughout her life.

EDUCATION AND A SOCIAL LIFE

Though Emily was known throughout Amherst as a poet, the extent of her talent was hidden from nearly everyone. As a child, she was never singled out by teachers as particularly gifted. In fact, her school years seem oddly unremarkable. She studied such subjects as mathematics, geography, ancient history, and English grammar. After a year at Mount Holyoke in 1847, Emily dropped out, citing illness. Though she did in fact miss some school due to a bad cough, it seems unlikely that this was reason enough for her to return home.

She was often homesick; a longing for her family and for Amherst weighed heavily on her mind. It is possible that the curriculum at Mount Holyoke did not provide the intellectual challenge that she had expected. Emily was a voracious reader, and there was always a variety of books and newspapers at the Homestead. Though her father frowned on certain reading materials, afraid they would "joggle the mind," Emily was still able to read from a wide spectrum of books including Shakespeare and her contemporaries George Eliot and Charlotte and Emily Brontë.

Of course, the Bible was a constant and powerful influence, as well. By the time Emily entered her teens, religious revivals were taking place all over New England. Revivals, gatherings led by itinerant charismatic preachers, or circuit riders, were often attended by crowds so large no building could hold them. There was tremendous pressure at such meetings for spectators to commit to Christianity or to a specific Christian congregation, and in the excitement of the moment many did.

Similar pressure was in evidence at Mount Holyoke, where students were openly encouraged to publicly declare their devotion to Christ. Emily, though deeply interested in spiritual matters, was afraid of being "easily deceived," and when the girls were asked one by one to declare their faith Emily was unable to do so. This perceived failing distressed her deeply, as she wanted to count herself among the converted as her roommate and cousin Emily Lavinia Norcross did. Long discussions on this subject with her friend Abiah Root continued by letter for many years. The continued pressure on Emily to declare what she could not feel in her heart probably played a role in Emily's decision to leave Mount Holyoke. Certainly the question of faith became a constant theme in her poetry.

Back in Amherst, Emily resumed the interests of a normal teenager. There were lots of parties to attend, as well as taffy pulls and carriage rides. Social calls were common etiquette and both Vinnie and Emily either went calling or received visitors almost every day. Some of the visitors were young lawyers from Mr. Dickinson's law office. Others were university students. Exchanging valentines was a popular custom: Emily wrote a Valentine's Day poem, possibly to a young man named George Howland, that was printed in the *Springfield Republican* in 1852.

Emily Dickinson did not start writing poetry seriously, however, until about 1858, when she was in her late twenties. She was admired by then for her piano playing, her singing voice, and her sense of humor. She was considered well liked and attractive if not beautiful. Suddenly, she withdrew from nearly all social activity and began writing furiously. She stashed poems in her sewing basket, wrote ideas on the back of grocery lists. Some poems she recopied carefully, then bound with thread and hid in her dresser drawers.

People began to call her "the myth" because she was so rarely seen in public. Rumors began to circulate about her delicate mind, and there was speculation that she had fallen in love and had been rejected, possibly by a married man. While it is unclear whether a single event or circumstance was responsible for such a sudden and irrepressible flash of inspiration coupled with reclusiveness, several events no doubt had tremendous impact on Emily's life.

AUSTIN'S MARRIAGE

One event that certainly affected Emily deeply was her brother's marriage to Susan. Emily and Susan were such close friends that several biographers have concluded that it was Emily rather than Austin who was in love with Susan. Certainly the elder Mr. Dickinson was charmed early on by the bright and energetic girl his son was courting, often escorting Susan home after her visits to the Homestead. In anticipation of Austin's marriage, Edward built the couple a home next to his own. It was hoped that the Evergreens, as they called the new house, would represent a new generation of Dickinsons. With father and son now legal partners as well, the prestige of the Dickinson name could only have been seen as a move up for Susan, a barkeeper's daughter whose childhood was marred by her father's alcoholism.

Austin and Sue's marriage was not a happy one. Though at first he kept his unhappiness from the family—perhaps he was afraid to disappoint Edward—Austin would later describe his July 1856 wedding as "going to his execution." Sue's high-spirited nature began to take on a cruel edge and what she said in anger Austin would beg her to take back. When two orphaned cousins, Anna and Clara Newman, came to live at the Evergreens in 1858, Sue, according to family friends, enjoyed treating them like poor relations. Visitors to the Evergreens observed "chaotic behavior" and "bursts of temper." Even before the wedding, letters from Emily to Sue point to some sort of falling out between the women:

> Sue—you can go or stay—There is but one alternative—We differ often lately and this must be the last.

> You need not fear to leave me lest I should be alone, for I often part with things I fancy I have loved,—sometimes to the grave and sometimes to an oblivion rather bitterer than death— thus my heart bleeds so frequently I shant mind the hemorrhage, and I only add an agony to previous ones.

The sisters-in-law made up, however, and for two years after the wedding Emily spent a lot of time at the Evergreens. Because of Austin's prestige in the community and, following his father, his position as treasurer of Amherst College, guests at the Evergreens often included prominent intellectuals. Sue's preference for a more bohemian crowd brought artists and professionals together, a mix Emily enjoyed. Her father apparently did not: On one occasion Edward Dickinson, thinking it indecent for Emily to be out so late, showed up at midnight to escort his daughter home from the Evergreens, an incident that was surely embarrassing for her.

As Austin became less and less comfortable opening his house to the odd array of characters his wife attracted, he began taking solitary night walks while his houseguests carried on in what he referred to as "my wife's tavern." Occasionally his oldest sister would accompany him. Emily too was tiring of the merrymaking. When the Austin Dickinsons entertained celebrated poet and philosopher Ralph Waldo Emerson in December of 1857, Emily did not attend the gathering. Whether another rift had occurred is unclear, but, in any case, as the atmosphere at the Evergreens became ever more erratic, life at the Homestead assumed its opposite character. Austin began to see the Homestead as a haven from Susan, whose temper had become so explosive she had taken to throwing knives.

Austin's despair in his relationship with Susan culminated in an affair with Mabel Loomis Todd, beginning in 1882. Todd was a family friend and frequent visitor at the Evergreens; tensions between Susan and Austin thereafter were at times nearly unbearable.

Susan felt, perhaps correctly, that the Dickinson sisters sided with their brother in his decision to openly pursue his romance with Mabel (who was also married, to David Peck Todd, a professor of astronomy at Amherst College and a friend of Austin's in spite of the affair). The atmosphere between the Evergreens and the Homestead turned from icy to outwardly hostile. Susan's acid tongue wounded Emily so deeply at times that Vinnie claimed Susan's meanness shortened Emily's life by ten years. At the least, the close relationship between Sue and Emily dissolved.

Mrs. Dickinson's Convalescence

While the hostility between the Evergreens and the Homestead was hard on Emily, another situation predating the feud with Susan was not only emotionally taxing for Emily, but physically exhausting as well. When Mrs. Dickinson fell ill with an undiagnosed malady (some suspect hypochondria) in November 1855, responsibility for her care fell to her daughters. Though Mrs. Dickinson survived her husband by eight years, she was bedridden much of her later life and needed constant attention until her death in November 1882.

Emily, who was not particularly close to her mother, felt this nearly thirty-year burden acutely. Clearly the most brilliant of the Dickinson children, she was offered no financial or emotional encouragement to pursue her intellectual or literary interests as was the Harvard-educated Austin. Though in childhood the Dickinson girls were schooled in nearly the same manner as their brother, and though in theory Edward Dickinson wanted his girls to receive a well-rounded education, Edward Dickinson did not like his grown daughters to appear too literary. In an essay he wrote for the *New England Inquirer* in 1827, Emily's father had this to say about women's role in society:

> What duties were females designed to perform? Were they intended for Rulers, or Legislators, or Soldiers? Were they intended for the learned professions;—to engage in those branches of business, which require the exertion of great strength, or the exercise of great skill?...
>
> Modesty and sweetness of disposition, and patience and forbearance and fortitude, are the cardinal virtues of the female sex.... These will atone for the want of brilliant talents, or great attainment.

With her mother's illness, Emily, who had always known there was more to life than drudgery, and who had always hurried through her housework, her sewing, and her cleaning in order to take long walks in the garden with her dog Carlo, now had additional demands on her free time. Increasingly, she viewed such interests as fashion as time-consuming and trivial distractions, and as she looked for ways to simplify her life, she adopted a wardrobe made up almost entirely of white dresses, which did not have to be matched or color coordinated and which required no special laundering beyond the bleaching already given to the sheets and towels.

This costume added an air of mystery to the woman who now rarely left her house. With no interest in Susan's gatherings, and with the shopping and visiting left to the more sociable Vinnie, Emily's contact with the outside world was conducted primarily through the mail. Nevertheless, the letters she wrote to friends and neighbors were extraordinary, often taking on the cadence of poetry themselves.

A TIME OF MANY PARTINGS

As childhood friends married and began to leave Amherst with their husbands, Emily and Vinnie shared the additional isolation of being labeled spinsters in the community. By 1858, the most eligible of Amherst's citizens had stopped thinking of Emily as a suitable wife. Abiah Root and other girlfriends Emily had once held in close confidence wrote rarely once they were married.

In addition, as many as thirty-three young acquaintances of Emily's died between 1851 and 1854, including Emily Lavinia Norcross, with whom Emily had stayed in close contact since Mount Holyoke. These losses deeply affected

Emily, whose poetry almost obsessively focuses on death. In November 1858 she wrote to some family friends, Dr. and Mrs. Josiah Gilbert:

> I can't stay any longer in a world of death. Austin is ill of scarlet fever. I buried my garden last week—our man Dick, lost a little girl through the scarlet fever. I thought perhaps that *you* were dead, and not knowing the sexton's address, interrogated the daisies. Ah! dainty—dainty Death! Ah! democratic Death! Grasping the proudest zinnia from my purple garden.

ONLY SEVEN POEMS PUBLISHED

Despite the numerous losses and disappointments Emily suffered, a theme of hope persisted in her poetry and in her life. Frustrated in her few attempts to seek guidance from other writers, she continued writing even more seriously in isolation, but with a determination that must have come from a deep inner confidence in her own abilities.

After answering a call for submissions in the *Atlantic Monthly* in 1862, for example, Emily received a polite reply from Colonel Thomas Wentworth Higginson, a distinguished man of letters who was serving as editor for the magazine's younger writers. Higginson did not submit Emily's work for publication, and even wrote to the *Atlantic* senior editor, James T. Fields, the day after receiving Emily's poems: "I foresee that 'Young Contributor' will send me worse things than ever now. Two such specimens came yesterday & day before—fortunately *not* to be forwarded for publication!" Still, Emily continued to seek Higginson's advice, sending him numerous poems during a twenty-year correspondence. Not until long after her death was Higginson forced to recognize his student's genius.

Two writers who had more confidence in Emily's writing were Helen Hunt Jackson, a poet and novelist who had herself grown up in Amherst and who urged Emily to send her poetry out for publication, and Mabel Loomis Todd, who was instrumental in getting the poems published after Emily's death. Emily was successful in publishing only seven of her poems during her lifetime. All of the poems were published anonymously and were so edited that Emily was hesitant to entrust further work to the whims of editors who clearly misunderstood it.

When widespread publication of her work began to seem less and less likely, Emily began to bind her poems into several homemade books, or fascicles. In 1864 her writing was interrupted when she was forced to travel to Boston for eye treatment. She remained there for seven months and on her return had difficulty resuming her regular chores and, presumably, her writing.

When her father died suddenly in 1874, Emily's grief was deep. She continued to write, although not with the frequency of previous years, and her isolation became so deep that she refused to meet visitors face to face, preferring to talk to them from behind a screen or door. Eventually she watered her garden in the dark so as not to be seen. Yet, she continued her many correspondences, writing draft after draft of her letters before sending them out. Often she would include a poem, which a few friends might circulate among themselves. Many of Amherst's citizens were curious to meet her. One eager for the opportunity was Mabel Loomis Todd, who wrote in her journal:

> [Austin's] sister Emily is called in Amherst "the myth." She has not been out of her house for fifteen years. One inevitably thinks of [Dickens's eccentric] Miss Havisham in speaking of her. She writes the strangest poems, & very remarkable ones. She is in many respects a genius. She wears always white, & has her hair arranged as was the fashion fifteen years ago when she went into retirement. She wanted me to come and sing to her, but she would not see me. She has frequently sent me flowers and poems, & we have a very pleasant friendship in that way. So last Sunday I went over there with Mr. Dickinson. . . . It was odd to think, as my voice rang out through the big silent house that Miss Emily in her weird white dress was outside in the shadow hearing every word, & the mother, bed-ridden for years was listening up the stairs. When I stopped Emily sent me in a glass of rich sherry & a poem written as I sang. I know I shall yet see her. No one has seen her in all those years except her own family. She is very brilliant and strong, but has become disgusted with society & declared she would leave it when she was quite young.

Mabel never did see Emily, who died of a kidney disease in 1886. But she did get to read the over eighteen hundred poems or fragments of poems hidden among her belongings, and she was ultimately responsible for their publication.

A Sister's Persistence Leads to Recognition

Vinnie was the one who found the poems and, immediately recognizing their quality, who was determined to have Emily's talent acknowledged. Though she and Susan were still barely speaking, she knew of her sister-in-law's interest in poetry and asked if Susan would edit a few of the poems for her. Seeing neither public interest nor profit in Emily's work, Susan refused. Vinnie then turned to Mabel, who was well liked in Amherst and well connected in literary circles. Mabel agreed not only to edit Emily's poetry, but to try to persuade Colonel Higginson to change his opinion of its worth.

Higginson advised against a book, finding the poems "too crude in form," but Mabel persisted, sending her select favorites until he finally admitted there were many that were "passable." When he insisted on giving the poems titles, however, they were occasionally so lacking in a basic understanding of the poems that Mabel had to intervene. But Higginson's approval was crucial. Even with it, Mabel had a difficult time finding a publisher to accept the poems. After several rejections, Vinnie offered to pay for the initial costs, afraid that with any further delays in publication, Emily's friends and acquaintances would grow old and die, leaving no one to appreciate her poems.

She need not have worried. *Poems*, published in 1890, created such a stir that a second series of Emily's poetry was released in 1891, followed by *Letters* in 1894 and a third series of *Poems* in 1896. Sales were so high there was a court battle over the royalties, ending with Vinnie awarded copyright ownership. In 1914, Susan and Austin's daughter Mattie (Martha Dickinson Bianchi) edited two more books: *The Life and Letters of Emily Dickinson* and *The Complete Poems of Emily Dickinson*.

Despite enormous public interest, some early critics responded unfavorably to Dickinson's poems because she did not adhere to the strict conventions of rhyme and meter of the day. Unlike her contemporary Walt Whitman, who did away with rhyme and meter altogether, Dickinson stretched the limits of traditional form by making use of near or slant rhymes, using the dash for emphasis, and employing capitalization for effect. Her innovations preceded those of some experimental or postmodern poets by as much as one hundred years.

Like her rhymes, the messages of her poems are often just within the reach of understanding. "Tell all the Truth but tell it slant," begins one, showing that the heart of understanding is usually not in what seems most obvious to us, but in what lies just under the surface. Like riddles, her definitions of such concepts as love, faith, and honesty stretch our mental faculties so that the reader begins to question definitions once taken for granted. Then, just as knowledge gets most slippery, Dickinson gives the reader a concrete image to hold on to:

> This World is not Conclusion.
> A Species stands beyond—
> Invisible, as Music—
> But positive, as Sound—
> It beckons, and it baffles—
> Philosophy—don't know—
> And through a Riddle, at the last—
> Sagacity, must go—
> To guess it, puzzles scholars—
> To gain it, Men have borne
> Contempt of Generations
> And Crucifixion, shown—
> Faith slips—and laughs, and rallies—
> Blushes, if any see—
> Plucks at a Twig of Evidence—
> And asks a Vane, the way—
> Much Gesture, from the Pulpit—
> Strong Hallelujahs roll—
> Narcotics cannot still the Tooth
> That nibbles at the soul—
>   (501)

Each poem on hope, or nature, or God, shows that there is not a single all-encompassing truth, but many delicate truths that change from person to person, day to day, poem to poem.

Today, Dickinson's place in American poetry is secure. Poets such as Hart Crane, Adrienne Rich, and Amy Lowell have expressed their gratitude for Dickinson's work in their own poetry. Her poems have been read all over the world and have been translated into many languages. In examining the essays contained in this volume, readers may gain a deeper appreciation of Emily Dickinson's work.

CHAPTER 1

Emily Dickinson: The Woman and the Poet

Dickinson Constructed Her Own Elusive Image

Joyce Carol Oates

A prolific fiction writer and respected literary critic, Joyce Carol Oates won the National Book Award in 1970 for her novel *them*. The following excerpt is from a 1986 lecture in which Oates states that "writing is invariably an act of rebellion" and suggests that the question of Dickinson's true identity remains unanswerable at least in part because the persona, or poetic identity, Dickinson created is difficult to distinguish from her true inner nature—a nature that even the poet herself described largely through contradiction.

Emily Dickinson is the most paradoxical of poets: the very poet of paradox. By way of voluminous biographical material, not to mention the extraordinary intimacy of her poetry, it would seem that we know everything about her: yet the common experience of reading her work, particularly if the poems are read sequentially, is that we come away seeming to know nothing. We would recognize her inimitable voice anywhere—in the "prose" of her letters no less than in her poetry—yet it is a voice of the most deliberate, the most teasing anonymity. "I'm Nobody!" is a proclamation to be interpreted in the most literal of ways. Like no other poet before her and like very few after her—Rilke comes most readily to mind, and, perhaps, Yeats and Lawrence—Dickinson exposes her heart's most subtle secrets; she confesses the very sentiments that, in society, would have embarrassed her dog (to paraphrase a remark of Dickinson's to Thomas Wentworth Higginson, explaining her aversion for the company of most people, whose prattle of "Hallowed things" offended her). Yet who is this "I" at the center of experience? In her astonishing body of 1,775 poems Dickinson records what is

From Joyce Carol Oates, "'Soul at the White Heat': The Romance of Emily Dickinson's Poetry," in *(Woman) Writer: Occasions and Opportunities* (New York: Dutton, 1988). Copyright The Ontario Review, Inc. Reprinted by permission of the author.

surely one of the most meticulous examinations of the phenomenon of human "consciousness" ever undertaken. The poet's persona—the tantalizing "I"—seems, in nearly every poem, to be addressing us directly with perceptions that are ours as well as hers. (Or his: these "Representatives of the Verse," though speaking in Dickinson's voice, are not restricted to the female gender.) The poems' refusal to be rhetorical, their daunting intimacy, suggests the self-evident in the way that certain Zen koans and riddles suggest the self-evident while being indecipherable. But what is challenged is, perhaps, "meaning" itself:

> Wonder—is not precisely Knowing
> And not precisely Knowing not—
> A beautiful but bleak condition
> He has not lived who has not felt—
>
> Suspense—is his maturer Sister—
> Whether Adult Delight is Pain
> Or of itself a new misgiving—
> This is the Gnat that mangles men—

In this wonder there is a tone of the purest anonymity, as if the poet, speaking out of her "beautiful but bleak condition," were speaking of our condition as well. Dickinson's idiom has the startling ring of contemporaneity, like much of Shakespeare's; she speaks from the interior of a life as we might imagine ourselves speaking, gifted with genius's audacity and shorn of the merely local and time-bound. If anonymity is the soul's essential voice—its seductive, mesmerizing, fatal voice—then Emily Dickinson is our poet of the soul: our most endlessly fascinating American poet. As Whitman so powerfully addresses the exterior of American life, so Dickinson addresses—or has she helped create?—its unknowable interior.

No one who has read even a few of Dickinson's extraordinary poems can fail to sense the heroic nature of this poet's quest. It is riddlesome, obsessive, haunting, very often frustrating (to the poet no less than to the reader), but above all heroic; a romance of epic proportions. For the "poetic enterprise" is nothing less than the attempt to realize the soul. And the attempt to realize the soul (in its muteness, its perfection) is nothing less than the attempt to create a poetry of transcendence—the kind that outlives its human habitation and its name.

Dare you see a Soul *at the White Heat?*

Then crouch within the door—
Red—is the Fire's common tint—
But when the vivid Ore
Has vanquished Flame's conditions,
It quivers from the Forge
Without a color, but the light
Of unanointed Blaze.
Least Village has its Blacksmith
Whose Anvil's even ring
Stands symbol for the finger Forge
That soundless tugs—within—
Refining these impatient Ores
With Hammer, and with Blaze
Until the Designated Light
Repudiate the Forge—

Only the soul "at the white heat" achieves the light of
"unanointed Blaze"—colorless, soundless, transcendent.
This is the triumph of art as well as the triumph of personality, but it is not readily achieved.

TWO SELVES IN CONFLICT

Very often the "self" is set in opposition to the soul. The personality is mysteriously split, warring: "Of Consciousness,
her awful Mate / The Soul cannot be rid—" And: "Me from
Myself—to banish— / Had I Art—" A successful work of art
is a consequence of the integration of conscious and unconscious elements; a balance of what is known and not quite
known held in an exquisite tension. Art *is* tension, and poetry of the kind Emily Dickinson wrote is an art of strain, of
nerves strung brilliantly tight. It is compact, dense, coiled in
upon itself very nearly to the point of pain: like one of those
stellar bodies whose gravity is so condensed it is on the point
of disappearing altogether. How tight, how violent, this syntax!—making the reader's heart beat quickly, at times, in
sympathy with the poet's heart. By way of Dickinson's radically experimental verse—and, not least, her employment of
dashes as punctuation—the drama of the split self is made
palpable. One is not merely told of it, one is made to experience it.

Anything less demanding would not be poetry, but prose—
the kind of prose written by other people. Though Dickinson
was an assured writer of prose herself, "prose" for her assumes a pejorative tone: see the famously rebellious poem in
which the predicament of the female (artist? or simply "female"?) is dramatized—

They shut me up in Prose—
As when a little Girl
They put me in the Closet—
Because they liked me "still"—

Still! Could themself have peeped—
And seen my Brain—go round—
They might as wise have lodged a Bird
For Treason—in the Pound—

Himself has but to will
And easy as a Star
Abolish his Captivity—
And laugh—No more have I—

Prose—it might be speculated—is discourse; poetry ellipsis. Prose is spoken aloud; poetry overheard. The one is presumably articulate and social, a shared language, the voice of "communication"; the other is private, allusive, teasing, sly, idiosyncratic as the spider's delicate web, a kind of witchcraft unfathomable to ordinary minds. Poetry, paraphrased, is something other than poetry, while prose *is* paraphrase. Consequently the difficulty of much of Dickinson's poetry, its necessary strategies, for the act of writing is invariably an act of rebellion, a way of (secretly, subversively) "abolishing" captivity:

Tell all the Truth but tell it slant—
Success in Circuit lies
Too bright for our infirm Delight
The Truth's superb surprise
As Lightning to the Children eased
With explanation kind
The Truth must dazzle gradually
Or every man be blind—

Surely there is a witty irony behind the notion that lightning can be domesticated by way of "kind explanations" told to children; that the dazzle of Truth might be gradual and not blinding. The "superb surprise" of which the poet speaks is too much for mankind to bear head-on—like the Medusa it can be glimpsed only indirectly, through the subtly distorting mirror of art.

Elsewhere, in a later poem, the poet suggests a radical distinction between two species of consciousness. Two species of human being?—

Best Witchcraft is Geometry
To the magician's mind—
His ordinary acts are feats
To thinking of mankind.

The "witchcraft" of art is (mere) geometry to the practitioner: by which is meant that it is orderly, natural, obedient to its own rules of logic; an ordinary event. What constitutes the "feat" is the relative ignorance of others—nonmagicians. It is a measure of the poet's modesty that, in this poem and in others, she excludes herself from the practice of witchcraft, even as she brilliantly practices it. Dickinson is most herself when she stands, like us, in awe of her remarkable powers as if sensing how little she controls them; how little, finally, the mute and unknowable Soul has to do with the restless, ever-improvising voice. "Silence," says the poet, "is all we dread. / There's Ransom in a Voice—/ But Silence is Infinity. / Himself have not a face."

A DISTINCTIVE VOICE

If one were obliged to say what Emily Dickinson's poems as a whole are about, the answer must be ambiguous. The poems are in one sense about the creation of the self capable of creating in turn this very body of poetry. For poetry does not "write itself"—the mind may feed on the heart, but the heart is mute, and requires not only being fed upon but being scrupulously tamed. Like virtually all poets of genius, Emily Dickinson worked hard at her craft. Passion comes unbidden—poetry's flashes of great good luck come unbidden—but the structures into which such flashes are put must be intellectually interesting. For the wisdom of the heart is after all ahistorical—it is always the same wisdom, one might say, across centuries. But human beings live in time, not simply in Time. The historical evolution of one's craft cannot be ignored: in creating art one is always, in a sense, vying for space with preexisting art. Emily Dickinson is perhaps our greatest American poet not because she felt more deeply and more profoundly than other people, or even that she "distilled amazing sense from ordinary Meanings," but that she wrote so well.

Dickinson discovered, early on, her distinctive voice—it is evident in letters written when she was a girl—and worked all her life to make it ever more distinctive. She was the spider, sometimes working at night in the secrecy of her room, unwinding a "Yarn of Pearl" unperceived by others and plying "from Nought to Nought / In unsubstantial Trade—" but she was far more than merely the spider: she is the presence, never directly cited, or even hinted at, who intends to dazzle the world with her genius. Literary fame is not precisely a goal, but it *is* a subject to which the poet has given some thought: "Some—Work for Immortality— / the Chiefer part, for Time— / "He—Compensates—immediately— / The former—Checks—on Fame—" And, more eloquently in these late, undated poems that might have been written by an elder poet who had in fact enjoyed public acclaim:

Fame is a bee.
　　It has a song—
It has a sting—
　　Ah, too, it has a
wing.

And:

Fame is a fickle food
Upon a shifting plate
Whose table once a
Guest but not
The second time is set.

Whose crumbs the crows inspect
And with ironic caw
Flap past it to the
Farmer's Corn—
Men eat of it and die.

Dickinson's specific practice as a writer might strike most people as haphazard, if not wasteful, but clearly it was the practice most suited to her temperament and her domestic situation. During the day, while working at household tasks, she jotted down sentences or fragments of sentences as they occurred to her, scribbling on any handy scrap of paper (which suggests the improvised, unplanned nature of the process). Later, in her room, she added these scraps to her scrapbasket collection of phrases, to be "used" when she wrote poetry or letters. Both Dickinson's poetry and prose, reading as if they were quickly—breathlessly—imagined, are the consequence of any number of drafts and revisions. As biographers have noted, a word or a phrase or a striking image might be worked into a poem or a letter years after it was first written down: the motive even in the private correspondence is to create a persona, not to speak spontaneously. And surely, after a point, it was not possible for Dickinson to speak except by way of a persona.

A Difficult Poet to Know

Helen McNeil

When confronted by a truly unusual poet such as
Dickinson, critics must often reexamine their ideas
of what makes a poem great or even good. With no
standard by which to make comparisons, Dickinson's work was often misinterpreted and misunderstood by early readers who simply were not sophisticated enough to transcend the conventions of the
day. In the following article, Helen McNeil attempts
to define Dickinson on her own terms.

McNeil, who received her Ph.D. from Yale, wrote
her study *Emily Dickinson* while lecturer at the University of East Anglia, not far from her subject's
birthplace. It was written in the centenary year of
Emily Dickinson's death.

Emily Dickinson (1830–86) was one of the indispensable
poets in English; one of the very greatest English poets. Her
accomplishment is so radically original that the entire
model of what poetry can know (and write) changes when
her work is taken into account. And when our sense of writing changes, our entire model of knowledge shifts. Emily
Dickinson was a woman; she wrote consciously and with
profound insight about her womanly life. If we who read her
are women, her accomplishment enlarges our recognition
of ourselves.

The poetry of Emily Dickinson was virtually unknown
during her lifetime, although she wrote almost 1,800 poems
and fragments. Since then, Dickinson has gradually gained
acceptance as an important lyric poet, though her range has
often been considered limited. Some of her more cheerful
lyrics have been standard anthology poems in the United
States for many years, thus inadvertently disguising her clarity and fierceness. A collected *Poems* finally appeared in
1955, and her rich and demanding letters were published in

1958. Dickinson's poetry is now readily available in paperback, and specialist studies have begun to flood from the presses. One recent study begins by describing Dickinson as the finest American woman poet.

Emily Dickinson was indeed American, and proudly so; she was a middle-class New England woman, well educated in terms of the prevailing cultural norms. In 'The Robin's my Criterion for Tune—' she wrote that 'Because I see—New Englandly', even a queen in one of her poems 'discerns like me—/Provincially—'. There is some irony in the way Dickinson is using 'provincial' in that last line. Dickinson did not consider American literature to be provincial. Also, anyone who writes accurately must write from experience, from their own province. Dickinson's poetry is set in that immediate moment of existence, with little nostalgia for a more overtly poetic medieval past.

Dickinson's kind of excellence, her kind of womanliness and the kind of poet she was are all, however, much less self-evident. One function of Dickinson's accomplishment is to force us to reconsider what we understand by greatness, gender and poetic knowledge. By coming to know her, we come to know them in a different way. . . .

CHANGES ASSUMPTIONS OF GREATNESS

It is, in fact, easy not to know Emily Dickinson. Because she is such an original writer, she has tended to be described according to what she is not: not a man, not like Walt Whitman, not 'professional', not normal, and not married. A writer who is described as different from what we know is bound to seem difficult. A writer who is said to come from a group whose limitations we think we know—an old maid American Victorian recluse poet, for example—is going to look limited.

It is easy not to know Dickinson because the type she manifests—the great woman poet—is still in the root sense not known by our culture. And whenever there is ignorance, there are reasons why ignorance has settled in that particular spot. I also do not know Dickinson fully. Whenever I open her *Complete Poems* I find her describing some new state or arguing some new premise or pioneering some new use of language. I have also had to find my way out of assuming that because I am a woman I would know automatically what Dickinson would think, and accept instead the surprise of what she truly thinks. Emily Dickinson has a lot to teach us, not least when she offers her awesomely accurate inside pictures of taboo subjects such as fear, hopeless longing, dread, death and loss.

FROM A LETTER TO T.W. HIGGINSON

Published after Dickinson's death in Letters of Emily Dickinson, *this letter to T.W. Higginson responds to the editor's criticism of her work. Though she acknowledges Higginson's opinion of her unconventional style, Dickinson is clearly aware of her own potential for greatness.*

If fame belonged to me, I could not escape her; if she did not, the longest day would pass me on the chase, and the approbation of my dog would forsake me then. My barefoot rank is better.

You think my gait "spasmodic." I am in danger, sir. You think me "uncontrolled." I have no tribunal.

Would you have time to be the "friend" you should think I need? I have a little shape: it would not crowd your desk, nor make much racket as the mouse that dents your galleries.

For the non-academic reader, the many points where Dickinson diverges from literary tradition have little importance. Dickinson is a very direct writer, and the emotional tenor and major themes of her poems reveal themselves easily. Typically, she begins a poem with a powerful recognition:

It was not Death, for I stood up,
And all the Dead, lie down—
It was not Night, for all the Bells
Put out their Tongues, for Noon.

This imagery is complex and quick-changing, with a surreal image of church bells sticking out their tongues coming hard upon the eerie picture of the speaker as perhaps a vertical corpse. Yet the tone is unmistakeable—a nightmarish, fixed terror mixed with a curiously calm investigatory interest.

Even though her works have only gradually filtered through to a large public, there is a genuinely popular element to Dickinson. It is those trained in critical theory who find Dickinson 'different', because she doesn't fit a received model for literary greatness. I believe Dickinson's poetry changes literary theory. To think about how Dickinson wrote is to experience gaps and silences in the existing models. Reading her fully means redefining those models. It is an exhilarating sensation.

Dickinson's Need for Seclusion

Adrienne Rich

Critic, essayist, and feminist, Adrienne Rich is best known as a poet. In 1974 Rich shared the National Book Award with poet Allen Ginsberg. Her poems "Aunt Jennifer's Tigers" and "Diving into the Wreck" are among the most widely anthologized poems of our time. This excerpt from her essay "Vesuvius at Home: The Power of Emily Dickinson" is a meditation on the life and work of a poet Rich calls a genius. It begins in the first person with the author making a drive to Dickinson's old homestead.

I am travelling at the speed of time, along the Massachusetts Turnpike. For months, for years, for most of my life, I have been hovering like an insect against the screens of an existence which inhabited Amherst, Massachusetts, between 1831 and 1884. The methods, the exclusions, of Emily Dickinson's existence could not have been my own; yet more and more, as a woman poet finding my own methods, I have come to understand her necessities, could have been witness in her defense.

"Home is not where the heart is," she wrote in a letter, "but the house and the adjacent buildings." A statement of New England realism, a directive to be followed. Probably no poet ever lived so much and so purposefully in one house; even, in one room. Her niece Martha told of visiting her in her corner bedroom on the second floor at 280 Main Street, Amherst, and of how Emily Dickinson made as if to lock the door with an imaginary key, turned and said: "Matty: here's freedom."

I am travelling at the speed of time, in the direction of the house and buildings.

Western Massachusetts: the Connecticut Valley: a coun-

Excerpted from "Vesuvius at Home: The Power of Emily Dickinson," in *On Lies, Secrets, and Silence: Selected Prose, 1966–1978* by Adrienne Rich. Copyright ©1979 by W.W. Norton & Company, Inc. Reprinted by permission of the author and W.W. Norton & Company, Inc.

tryside still full of reverberations: scene of Indian uprisings, religious revivals, spiritual confrontations, the blazing-up of the lunatic fringe of the Puritan coal. How peaceful and how threatened it looks from Route 91, hills gently curled above the plain, the tobacco-barns standing in fields sheltered with white gauze from the sun, and the sudden urban sprawl: ARCO, McDonald's, shopping plazas. The country that broke the heart of Jonathan Edwards, that enclosed the genius of Emily Dickinson. It lies calmly in the light of May, cloudy skies breaking into warm sunshine, light-green spring softening the hills, dogwood and wild fruit-trees blossoming in the hollows.

From Northhampton bypass there's a 4-mile stretch of road to Amherst—Route 9—between fruit farms, steakhouses, supermarkets. The new University of Massachusetts rears its skyscrapers up from the plain against the Pelham Hills. There is new money here, real estate, motels. Amherst succeeds on Hadley almost without notice. Amherst is green, rich-looking, secure; we're suddenly in the center of town, the crossroads of the campus, old New England college buildings spread around two village greens, a scene I remember as almost exactly the same in the dim past of my undergraduate years when I used to come there for college weekends.

Left on Seelye Street, right on Main; driveway at the end of a yellow picket fence. I recognize the high hedge of cedars screening the house, because twenty-five years ago I walked there, even then drawn toward the spot, trying to peer over. I pull into the driveway behind a generous 19th-century brick mansion with wings and porches, old trees and green lawns. I ring at the back door—the door through which Dickinson's coffin was carried to the cemetery a block away.

A JUSTIFICATION FOR SECLUSION

For years I have been not so much envisioning Emily Dickinson as trying to visit, to enter her mind, through her poems and letters, and through my own intimations of what it could have meant to be one of the two mid–19th-century American geniuses, and a woman, living in Amherst, Massachusetts. Of the other genius, Walt Whitman, Dickinson wrote that she had heard his poems were "disgraceful." She knew her own were unacceptable by her world's standards of poetic convention, and of what was appropriate, in partic-

"E."

*Though Dickinson was seen by some, including her editor
T.W. Higginson, as slightly crazy, poet Adrienne Rich views
Dickinson's life choices as not only deliberate but necessary to
the creation of her work. In this poem, found in Albert Gelpi's*
Emily Dickinson: The Mind of a Poet, *Rich portrays Dickinson's solitary life as its own response to Higginson and others
who were unable to appreciate Dickinson on her own terms.*

'Halfcracked' to Higginson, living,
afterward famous in garbled versions–
your hoard of dazzling scraps a battlefield–
now your old snood

mothballed at Harvard
and you in your variorum monument
equivocal to the end–
who are you?

Gardening the day-lily,
wiping the wine-glass stems,
your thought pulsed on behind
a forehead battered paper-thin,

you, woman, masculine
in singlemindedness,
for whom the word was more
than a symptom–

a condition of being.
Till the air buzzing with spoiled language
sang in your ears
of Perjury

and in your halfcracked way you chose
silence for entertainment,
chose to have it out at last
on your own premises.

ular, for a woman poet. Seven were published in her lifetime,
all edited by other hands; more than a thousand were laid
away in her bedroom chest, to be discovered after her death.
When her sister discovered them, there were decades of
struggle over the manuscripts, the manner of their presentation to the world, their suitability for publication, the poet's
own final intentions. Narrowed-down by her early editors
and anthologists, reduced to quaintness or spinsterish odd-

ity by many of her commentators, sentimentalized, fallen-in-love with like some gnomic Garbo, still unread in the breadth and depth of her full range of work, she was, and is, a wonder to me when I try to imagine myself into that mind.

I have a notion that genius knows itself; that Dickinson chose her seclusion, knowing she was exceptional and knowing what she needed. It was, moreover, no hermetic retreat, but a seclusion which included a wide range of people, of reading and correspondence. Her sister Vinnie said, "Emily is always looking for the rewarding person." And she found, at various periods, both women and men: her sister-in-law Susan Gilbert, Amherst visitors and family friends such as Benjamin Newton, Charles Wadsworth, Samuel Bowles, editor of the Springfield *Republican* and his wife; her friends Kate Anthon and Helen Hunt Jackson, the distant but significant figures of Elizabeth Barrett, the Brontës, George Eliot. But she carefully selected her society and controlled the disposal of her time. Not only the "gentlewoman in plush" of Amherst were excluded; Emerson visited next door but she did not go to meet him; she did not travel or receive routine visits; she avoided strangers. Given her vocation, she was neither eccentric nor quaint; she was determined to survive, to use her powers, to practice necessary economies. . . .

Upstairs at last: I stand in the room which for Emily Dickinson was "freedom." The best bedroom in the house, a corner room, sunny, overlooking the main street of Amherst in front, the way to her brother Austin's house on the side. Here, at a small table with one drawer, she wrote most of her poems. Here she read Elizabeth Barrett's "Aurora Leigh," a woman poet's narrative poem of a woman poet's life; also George Eliot; Emerson; Carlyle; Shakespeare; Charlotte and Emily Brontë. Here I become, again, an insect, vibrating at the frames of windows, clinging to panes of glass, trying to connect. The scent here is very powerful. Here in this white-curtained, high-ceilinged room, a redhaired woman with hazel eyes and a contralto voice wrote poems about volcanoes, deserts, eternity, suicide, physical passion, wild beasts, rape, power, madness, separation, the daemon, the grave. Here, with a darning-needle, she bound these poems—heavily emended and often in variant versions—into booklets, secured with darning-thread, to be found and read after her death. Here she knew "freedom," listening from above-stairs to a visitor's piano-playing, escaping from the pantry where she was mistress of the household bread and puddings, watching, you feel, watching ceaselessly, the life of sober Main Street below. From this room she glided downstairs, her hand on the polished bannister, to meet the complacent magazine editor, Thomas Higginson, unnerve him while claiming she herself was unnerved. "Your scholar," she signed herself in letters to him. But she was an independent scholar, used his criticism selectively, saw him rarely and always on *her* premises. It was a life deliberately organized on her terms. The terms she had been handed by society— Calvinist Protestantism, Romanticism, the 19th-century corseting of women's bodies, choices, and sexuality—could spell insanity to a woman genius. What this one had to do was retranslate into a dialect called metaphor: her native language. "Tell all the Truth—but tell it Slant—." It is always what is under pressure in us, especially under pressure of concealment—that explodes in poetry.

Dickinson Was Misunderstood by Those Closest to Her

Amy Lowell

Amy Lowell was an American poet, critic, and biographer who became a leader of the Imagist movement of the early 1900s. The Imagists sought to break poetry out of the restrictive meter and stiff diction pioneered by English writers such as William Wordsworth. The poetry of the Imagists tended to be short, written in free verse, and constructed around a single, spectacular metaphor. Their influence is still apparent in contemporary poetry.

Lowell, who was known as much for her cigar smoking and outspoken nature as for her writing, lived a very different life than her subject. In this excerpt she laments Dickinson's isolation and obscurity as much as she praises the highly original vision of her predecessor.

I wonder what made Emily Dickinson as she was. She cannot be accounted for by any trick of ancestry or early influence. She was the daughter of a long line of worthy people; her father, who was the leading lawyer of Amherst, Massachusetts, and the treasurer of Amherst College, is typical of the aims and accomplishments of the race. Into this well-ordered, high-minded, average, and rather sombre milieu, swept Emily Dickinson like a beautiful, stray butterfly, 'beating in the void her luminous wings in vain.' She knew no different life; and yet she certainly did not belong to the one in which she found herself. She may have felt this in some obscure fashion; for, little by little, she withdrew from the world about her, and shut herself up in a cocoon of her own spinning. She had no heart to fight; she never knew that a battle was on and that she had been selected for a place in the vanguard; all she could do was to retire, to hide her wounds, to carry out her little skirmishings and advances in byways and side-tracks, slowly winning a territory which the enemy took no trouble to dispute. What she did seemed insignificant and individual, but thirty years after her death the flag under which she fought had become a great banner, the symbol of a militant revolt. It is an odd story, this history of Imagism, and perhaps the oddest and saddest moment in it is comprised in the struggle of this one brave, fearful, and unflinching woman.

There is very little to tell about Emily Dickinson's life. In a sense, she had no life except that of the imagination. Born in Amherst in December, 1830, she died there in May, 1886. Her travels consisted of occasional trips to Boston, and one short sojourn in Washington during her father's term in Congress. As the years went on, she could scarcely be induced to leave her own threshold; what she saw from her window, what she read in her books, were her only external *stimuli*. Those few people whom she admitted to her friendship were loved with the terrible and morbid exaggeration of the profoundly lonely. In this isolation, all resilience to the blows of illness and death was atrophied. She could not take up her life again because there was no life to take. Her thoughts came to be more and more preoccupied with the grave. Her letters were painful reading indeed to the normal-minded. Here was a woman with a nice wit, a sparkling sense of humour, sinking under the weight of an introverted imagination to a state bordering upon neurasthenia; for her horror of publicity would not certainly be classed as a 'phobia.' The ignorance and unwisdom of her friends confused illness with genius, and, reversing the usual experience in such cases, they saw in the morbidness of hysteria, the sensitiveness of a peculiarly artistic nature. In the introduction to the collection of her letters, the editor, Mrs. Mabel Loomis Todd, says, 'In her later years, Emily Dickinson rarely addressed the envelopes; it seemed as if her sensitive nature shrank from the publicity which even her handwriting would undergo, in the observation of indifferent eyes. Various expedients were resorted to—obliging friends frequently performed this office for her; sometimes a printed newspaper label was pasted upon the envelope; but the actual strokes of her own pencil were, so far as possible, reserved exclusively for friendly eyes.'

That is no matter for laughter, but for weeping. What loneliness, disappointment, misunderstanding must have preceded it! What unwise protection against the clear, buffeting winds of life must have been exerted to shut the poor

"THE SISTERS"

Originally published in 1925, Amy Lowell's poem "The Sisters" asks why Lowell and women like her write poetry. In this excerpt, which appears in The Complete Poetical Works of Amy Lowell, *Lowell praises Dickinson over such famous poets as Sappho and Elizabeth Barrett Browning.*

. . . I go dreaming on,
In love with these my spiritual relations.
I rather think I see myself walk up
A flight of wooden steps and ring a bell
And send a card in to Miss Dickinson.
Yet that's a very silly way to do.
I should have taken the dream twist-ends about
And climbed over the fence and found her deep
Engrossed in the doing of a hummingbird
Among nasturtiums. Not having expected strangers,
She might forget to think me one, and holding up
A finger say quite casually: "Take care.
Don't frighten him, he's only just begun."
"Now this," I well believe I should have thought,
"Is even better than Sappho. With Emily
You're really here, or never anywhere at all
In range of mind." Wherefore, having begun
In the strict centre, we could slowly progress
To various circumferences, as we pleased.
We could, but should we? That would quite depend
On Emily. I think she'd be exacting,
Without intention possibly, and ask
A thousand tight-rope tricks of understanding.
But, bless you, I would somersault all day
If by so doing I might stay with her.
I hardly think that we should mention souls
Although they might just round the corner from us
In some half-quizzical, half-wistful metaphor.
I'm very sure that I should never seek
To turn her parables to stated fact.
Sappho would speak, I think, quite openly,
And Mrs. Browning guard a careful silence,
But Emily would set doors ajar and slam them
And love you for your speed of observation.

soul into her stifling hot-house! The times were out of joint
for Emily Dickinson. Her circle loved her, but utterly failed
to comprehend. Her daring utterances shocked; her whim-
sicality dazed. The account of this narrow life is heart-
rending. Think of Charles Lamb joking a New England dea-
con; imagine Keats's letters read aloud to a Dorcas Society;
conceive of William Blake sending the 'Songs of Experience'
to the 'Springfield Republican'! Emily Dickinson lived in an
atmosphere of sermons, church sociables, and county newspapers. It is ghastly, the terrible, inexorable waste of Nature,
but it is a fact. The direct descendant of Blake (although she
probably never heard of him) lived in this surrounding. The
marvel is that her mind did not give way. It did not; except
in so far as her increasing shrinking from society and her
preoccupation with death may be considered giving way.
She lived on; she never ceased to write; and the torture
which she suffered must have been exquisite indeed.

SMALL ATTEMPTS AT RECOGNITION THWARTED

Whenever a little door opened, some kind friend immediately slammed it to. Her old school companion Mrs. Jackson,
better known as H.H., the author of 'Ramona,' repeatedly
begged her to write for the 'No Name Series,' then just starting. And the poet whom everybody deemed so retiring was
half inclined to accept. She needed to be pushed into the
healthy arena of publicity, a little assistance over the bump
of her own shyness and a new, bright, and vigorous life
would have lain before her. In an evil moment she asked the
advice of Mr. Thomas Wentworth Higginson. The very words
of her letter show her half pleading to be urged on:

> Dear Friend:
>   Are you willing to tell me what is right? Mrs. Jackson, of
> Colorado, was with me a few moments this week, and wished
> me to write for this. I told her I was unwilling, and she asked
> me why? I said I was incapable, and she seemed not to be-
> lieve me and asked me not to decide for a few days. Meantime
> she would write to me. . . . I would regret to estrange her, and
> if you would be willing to give me a note saying you disap-
> proved it and thought me unfit, she would believe you.

The disapproval was cordially given; the door shut again
upon the prisoner, who thanks her jailor with the least hint
of regret between the lines:

> Dear Friend:
>   . . . I am glad I did as you would like. The degradation to

displease you, I hope I may never incur.

Mild, sweet-tempered, sympathetic, and stupid Mr. Higginson! It was an evil moment when Emily chose him for the arbiter of her fate. And yet who, at the time, would have done better? Certainly not Longfellow, nor Lowell, nor Emerson. Poe? But Emily could not write to a man like Poe. Whitman? She herself says in another letter to her mentor, 'You speak of Mr. Whitman. I never read his book, but was told that it was disgraceful.'

No, there was no hope. All her friends were in the conspiracy of silence. They could not believe that the public was made up of many people as sensitive as themselves. Mrs. Gordon L. Ford has related an interesting anecdote illustrative of this point of view. I will give it in her own words:

> Dr. Holland once said to me, 'Her poems are too ethereal for publication.' I replied. 'They are beautiful—so concentrated——but they remind me of air-plants that have no roots in earth.' 'That is true,' he said, 'a perfect description;' and I think these lyrical ejaculations, these breathed-out projectiles, sharp as lances, would at that time have fallen into idle ears.

And yet when her first volume was published posthumously, it went through six editions in as many months.

The truth is that, as someone once said to me, the average man is a good deal above the average. A fact which the newly awakened interest in poetry is proving every day. This same first edition was published in 1890, more than twenty years before Imagism as a distinct school was heard of, but its reception shows that the soil was already ripe for sowing.

Why Emily Dickinson Wore White

Kathryn Whitford

The responsibility of housework in the nineteenth century was a tremendous burden to Emily Dickinson, who wrote about her chores in letters to friends and family. Clothing of various colors and patterns was difficult to clean and sew and took a certain amount of mental energy to coordinate, update, and keep seasonal. Dickinson scholar Kathryn Whitford believes that to Emily Dickinson, who had little use for fashion, these chores were distractions from her writing. Whitford speculates that Dickinson's mysterious white dresses were nothing more than a practical convenience.

In classrooms and in discussion with readers of Emily Dickinson's poetry, one hears not only that she withdrew from the world, but that in response to an unrequited love she wore only "bridal white" during the last decades of her life. Her choice of white has served as the capstone to arguments setting forth her mental or emotional frailties. The time has come to recognize that although she chose to wear white she almost certainly did not think of it as "bridal."

Millicent Todd Bingham prefaced her book *Emily Dickinson's Home* with the hope that the work would "replace queerness with reasonableness as an explanation of Emily Dickinson's conduct." Her argument that keeping a large house without central heating, without gas or electricity and without running water, so occupied Emily's time that she was forced to retire from the social life of the community in order to find time for her poetry has gradually been accepted by the academic community; but the myth of "bridal white" persists. In the hope of once again replacing "queerness with reasonableness" this paper will place Emily's

Kathryn Whitford, "Why Emily Dickinson Wore White," *Dickinson Studies*, no. 55, 1985. Reprinted by permission of the author.

white dresses in their proper nineteenth-century context.

Emily Dickinson and her friends would not have associated white exclusively with "bridal" because congregational weddings of her day were usually simpler affairs than they have since become. A wedding gown was not then a costume for a single day, but a dress that could be worn for other events. It might be white, but it might also be gray or mauve, or, for a winter wedding, even brown or navy. Moreover, white was a common color for summer dresses for girls and young women. The chief argument against Emily's "bridal white," however, lies not in the marriage customs of the day but in the rigors of nineteenth-century housekeeping and laundry.

THE EXPECTATION OF LABOR

About January of 1856, after the family had moved into the Dickinson homestead, Mrs. Dickinson was in ill health and as Emily wrote to Mrs. J.G. Holland, "Vinnie and I 'regulated' and Vinnie and I 'got settled' and still we keep our father's house and mother lies upon the lounge." Mrs. Dickinson's invalidism continued for several years, throwing the burden of housekeeping upon her daughters. The house was large and the family, although they employed an ironing woman and a washerwoman by the day, did not keep live-in household help until the early sixties when the Irish housegirl named Margaret O'Brien was hired. Even with the addition of a maid-of-all-work, household tasks probably consumed more of Dickinson's time than has been recognized by anyone except Mrs. Bingham. Thomas Johnson wrote that "like her mother and unlike her sister, Lavinia was willing to undertake responsibility for routine domestic affairs." Careful reading of Emily's letters supports Mrs. Bingham's argument that Emily was actively involved in the domestic duties of the household.

Three times in the 1850s Dickinson wrote that she had made up the fires and prepared breakfast and then, because the rest of the family was not yet awake, she was seizing the brief quiet time to write her letter. In 1864, when Margaret O'Brien left the household and Margaret Maher had not yet been hired, Dickinson wrote Mrs. Holland that "Besides wiping the dishes for Margaret, I wash them now, while she becomes Mrs. Lawler." Other references to dishes suggest that wiping dishes was one of Dickinson's tasks even when domestic help was present. No housemaid remained long in the Dickinson service during the four years after Margaret O'Brien's marriage, so it seems probable that Emily washed and wiped the dishes from many meals. The Dickinson women had their dresses cut and sometimes made by professional sewingwomen of the town, but they were clearly responsible for making their own intimate garments such as petticoats, nightgowns, robes, etc. In 1859 Emily wrote, "I am sewing for Vinnie." In December, 1861, a letter notes, "Took up my work hemming strings for mother's gown." In 1863, "I finished mama's saque, all but the overcasting." Thomas Wentworth Higginson's letter to his wife (Aug. 16, 1870) states that Emily "makes all the bread for her father likes only hers," a statement confirmed by Ellen E. Dickinson, the wife of Emily's cousin Willie, who wrote in 1890 that Emily "was a past mistress of cookery and housekeeping. She made desserts for the household dinners; delicious confections and bread." One begins to wonder how she had time to be a poet.

It is against this background that one must see not only her withdrawal from society but her adoption of white dresses. Millicent Todd Bingham says that Dickinson's retirement came not because she shunned people but because "she wanted time" and that she made no decision to withdraw but was "drawn into an inch-by-inch retirement quite apart from any hypothetical heartbreak." Thomas Johnson characterizes Dickinson's rejection of society as "her kind of economy, a frugality she sought in order to make the most of her world."

The white dresses were probably also an "inch-by-inch" approach to her frugality with time. It is unlikely that a serviceable dress was discarded in such a household. But at some point Dickinson must have made a deliberate decision to replace her dresses only with white ones. In a letter of about 1860 she wrote Lavinia Norcross, "My sphere is doubtless calicoes, nevertheless I thought it meet to sport a little wool. The mirth it has occasioned will deter me from further exhibitions." The letter suggests that Dickinson is already wearing chiefly cotton dresses appropriate for housework and baking. She would need her plain brown wool less and less as she ceased to leave the house and grounds. It was the calicoes and ginghams that gave place to white dresses.

There is no hint of a washerwoman after the advent of the first of the housegirls to the Dickinson household; on the

other hand there are indications that the washing and ironing were now household functions. Although the heavy
wash, household linens, etc., was undoubtedly performed by
the domestic, the care of their own dresses would ordinarily
have been the responsibility of the women of the household,
if only because the caution required in washing colored fabrics and calicoes could not be entrusted safely to a maid-of-
all-work. Dickinson's letter to Louise and Fanny Norcross
suggests, however, that she as well as Maggie was busy on
washday. The family was expecting a visit from Edward
Dickinson's formidable sister Elizabeth, and Emily wrote, "I
hoped she'd come while you were here to help me with the
starch," apparently for the pillowcases.

A PRACTICAL DECISION

The problems and extra work connected with washing colored cottons, and particularly calicoes, stemmed from the
fact that few nineteenth-century dyes were stable. Old veg-
etable dyes had given a genuinely fast turkey red and log-
wood black, but neither color was suitable for the Dickinson
women. Other dyes were sunfast but not waterfast, or the
other way around. The tan, brown and olive colors in general use were so fugitive that Catherine Beecher in her *Trea-
tise on Domestic Economy* recommended washing dresses of
those colors in a hay infusion to preserve the colors, or, in
truth, to restore the color lost in washing. It was not until the
introduction of modern vat colors, after 1914, that commer-
cially dyed fabrics could be expected to hold their colors.
Even then, as Charles E. Pellew comments in his volume
Dyes and Dyeing,

> The extra cost of the dyestuffs and the difficulty of dyeing to
> shade, furnish an excuse for increasing the price of the goods.
> And the perhaps not unnatural disinclination of shopkeepers
> to push the sale of materials which, in their opinion, are quite
> unnecessarily fast, has combined to delay the general adop-
> tion of these remarkably valuable coloring agents.

Earlier he had fulminated that "a calico dress which keeps
its color so that it can be worn for a second summer, is an
abomination not to be endured" by greedy merchants.
Pellew's comment goes far toward explaining the succession
of poor heroines in "faded calico" marching across the pages
of nineteenth-century fiction. It also explains Catherine
Beecher's elaborate instructions for washing calico or other

colored cottons.

Such fabrics were never to be boiled or washed in very warm water. They were never to be "left long in the water" or permitted to remain crumpled or folded while wet as it "injures the colors." Translated that means that the dyes would run. For the same reason the water in which they were washed was to be changed "whenever it appears dingy, or the light parts will look dirty." They must not be rubbed with soap, but grease should be removed with "French chalk, starch, magnesia or Wilmington clay." Colored dresses were to be dried, inside out, in the shade and never allowed to freeze. Catherine Beecher further suggested that the starch for calicoes be made with coffee water because ordinary white starch would leave a faint bloom on the dark colors. The alternative was to starch calicoes with glue dissolved in an appropriate quantity of water.

Miss Beecher comments that some people washed calicoes without soap, in bran water, "four quarts of wheat-bran to two pails of water," and followed by rinsing in bran water. How they then got the bran out of the clothes she doesn't say, but a more extended rule for the same method was still being printed in 1903. As an afterthought Miss Beecher adds that potato water is equally good, "take eight peeled and grated potatoes to one gallon of water."

By comparison, washing white items was easy. The wash was sorted into coarse whites and fine whites, or one assumes, the equivalent of household linens and family undergarments. Both classes were soaked overnight and then boiled (two hours for coarse whites, half an hour for fine whites), washed with potash soap, rinsed, starched and hung out to dry in the sun. Potash soap was a mild bleaching agent, the forerunner of the washing soda still on the market. Chlorine bleaching powder had been invented before 1800 and was available by the middle of the nineteenth century, but Miss Beecher does not mention it, preferring the potash soap for which she supplies a recipe, adding that since the soap improves with age it would be well to make "two barrels at once." She also recommends mild lye solutions for bleaching natural linen, and salt, lemon juice, and buttermilk for removing stains resistant to boiling.

It is against this background of housekeeping practices that one must examine what is recorded about the poet's dresses after she began staying home. Her dressmaker and her neighbors were unanimous in testifying that Emily wore only white. Yet as late as 1870 white seems to have had no esoteric significance for her. When T.W. Higginson called upon her, she was obviously keyed up and determined to make her best impression. She entered the room in her customary white gown, but with Lavinia's blue net shawl about her shoulders. In other words, she did not categorically wear only white; she wore only white dresses. Higginson described her gown as piqué, immaculately clean. Later Eugene Field, who had been a neighbor of the Dickinsons in his youth, described her white dresses as simple almost to severity.

Looking closely at the scraps of evidence available after nearly one hundred years, it becomes clear that because the withdrawal and the white gowns were both efforts to gain time for herself, Emily's choice of white was clear-headed and practical. Her dresses were the farthest removed from bridal finery. They were in fact, more nearly a uniform. The uniform was white for the same reason that the uniforms of doctors, nurses, cooks and butchers were white, which in turn was the same reason that nineteenth-century sheets and towels, pillowcases and table linen were uncompromisingly white. White linen and cotton were the easiest fabrics to wash. So long as Dickinson wore white dresses she did not have to cope with the special demands of calico or other colored fabrics. Even better, her white dresses, like her petticoats, could be added to the household wash of "fine whites" to be soaked and boiled by the maid-of-all-work and starched in the same tub with petticoats and pillowcases. The simplicity of the dresses insured that there would be small need of fluting irons whether used by herself or Maggie, of whom she wrote in 1870, "Maggie is ironing, and a cotton and linen and ruffle heat make the [girl's] cheeks red."

The authors of *The American Woman's Home* proposed to solve the problems of washing and ironing by the establishment of neighborhood laundries where "one or two women could do in fine style what now is very indifferently done by the disturbance and disarrangement of all other domestic processes in these families. Whoever set neighborhood-laundries on foot will do much to solve the American housekeeper's hardest problem." By wearing white dresses Emily Dickinson solved the problem for herself. She simplified her living and gained time for poetry and her intense inner life.

Dickinson Found Significance in Minor Events

Ella Gilbert Ives

In this excerpt from a 1907 essay first published in the *Boston Transcript*, poet and teacher Ella Gilbert Ives responds to early critics of Dickinson with wit and sensitivity. While she concedes that Dickinson's rhymes are often imperfect, her rhythms jolting, Ives makes the case that Dickinson forged a new style in measuring a voice so unique she compares it to "the first bullet."

In an attempt to appropriately evaluate Dickinson's poetic sensibility, Ives turns to the life of the poet: her family, her surroundings, and her literary influences. She also looks at Dickinson's relationship with Thomas W. Higginson, who coedited Dickinson's *Poems* after her death.

"If fame belonged to me, I could not escape her."

Emily Dickinson long eluded her pursuer; but no sooner had she left her chrysalis than Fame, also a winged elf, flew by her side, became her unescapable companion. In life she was arrogantly shy of a public that now shares her innermost confidence, and touches with rude or hallowed finger the flesh of her sensitive poetry; the soul of it, happily only the sympathetic can reach.

Many obvious, many contradictory things, have been said about this profound thinker and virile writer on a few great themes. Those who cling to the old order and regard perfect form essential to greatness, have had their fling at her eccentricities, her blemishes, her crudities; they place her with the purveyors of raw material to the artistic producers of the race. They deny her rank with the creators of permanent

From Ella Gilbert Ives, "Emily Dickinson: Her Poetry, Prose, and Personality," *Boston Transcript*, October 5, 1907.

beauty and value. Others such as hail a Wagner, a Whitman, or a Turner, as an originator of new types and a contributor of fresh streams of life blood to art or literature, accept Emily Dickinson as another proof of Nature's fecundity, versatility and daring. All acknowledge in her elements of power and originality; but especially a certain probing quality that penetrates and discloses like an X-ray.

By long-accepted standards, doubtless, she does not measure up to greatness. The first bullet was an innovation to one who drew the long bow. He did not know what to make of hot shot without the whiz and the grace of the arrow—least of all when it struck home and shattered his pet notions. Emily Dickinson's power of condensation, the rhythmic hammer of her thoughts, whether in prose or verse, is so phenomenal that it calls for a new system of weights and measures. Perhaps there is nothing essentially new here. Franklin merely identified an acquaintance of Noah's when he flew his kite; Newton, had he talked the apple over with Eve, might have found her intelligent on the fall; but both philosophers drew as near to originality as mortal is ever permitted to draw by the jealous gods. Emily Dickinson, whatever her size, is of nobody's kind but her own....

No art can be adequately understood apart from the artist. Emily Dickinson is the best commentary upon her verse. I have recently visited "the house behind the hedge," where she was born and died. I have stood in the old-fashioned garden where she strolled, and grew intimate with bird and bee, butterfly and flower. I have listened to her bluebird, who

> Shouts for joy to nobody
> But his seraphic self,

and seen her robin brood its young. I have looked across her landscape on a June day at the Pelham range and repeated:

> The skies can't keep their secret,
> They tell it to the hills.

And letting thought and feeling slip in her accustomed grooves, I have ceased to wonder that Emily Dickinson shut herself in behind that austere but tonic hemlock hedge, and made her house a nunnery. I seemed to hear her voice saying:

> The soul selects her own society
> Then shuts the door;
> On her divine majority
> Obtrude no more.

The events of Emily Dickinson's life are singularly few,

but she invests each with significance. Her perception is at times as vivid as if, called to die, she were taking a last look. Deep and powerful are the strokes with which she limns an emotion, as if she were standing at a judgment bar. If the adjective "intense" were not so overworked, I should employ it. Had Emily Dickinson written novels they would have had the Brontëan quality—flame. A friend tells me that during the later years of her life the poet was accustomed to keep a candle burning in her window at night for the belated traveller. It is symbolic of her genius.

It is the brevity and searching quality (in inverse ratio) of Emily Dickinson's poetry that render it unique, and augur permanence, not so much that it lights the pathway, as that it explores the heart and touches the quick of experience. Her verse is never didactic, yet always earnest; too serious for wit, yet having the very kernel of wit—surprise—to an extraordinary degree. This dressing up of the primal emotions in strange, often outlandish garb, or exhibiting them naked yet not ashamed, has a singular effect, and throws the mind back with questioning upon the writer herself, and the influences that made her what she was—the loneliest figure in the world of letters.

They are not far to seek. There was the mother, whom "Noah would have liked," and the father, who stepped "like Cromwell, when he gets the kindlings." She sketches both saliently: "Mother drives with Tim to carry pears to settlers. Sugar pears with hips like hams, and the flesh of bonbons. ... Father is growing better, though physically reluctant. ... You know he never played, and the straightest engine has its leaning hour." To [her friend and mentor Colonel Thomas W.] Higginson she wrote: "My mother does not care for thought, and father, too busy with his briefs to notice what we do. He buys me many books, and begs me not to read them, because he fears they joggle the mind." To another friend she wrote: "Mother is very fond of flowers and of recollection, that sweetest flower."

To Colonel Higginson she talked much about her father— a man who "read on Sunday lonely and rigorous books"; and so inspired her with awe that she did not learn to tell time until fifteen years old, because he had tried to explain it to her when a little child, and she was afraid to tell him she did not understand; also afraid to ask anyone else lest he should hear of it. He did not wish his children when young to read anything but the Bible. But at least two books early ran the blockade: *Kavanagh*, brought home by her brother, was hidden under the piano cover; and Lydia Maria Child's *Letters from New York*, sent by a friend, found refuge in a box beside the doorstep. . . .

She had earlier written to Colonel Higginson: "You inquire my books? For poets, I have Keats and Mr. and Mrs. Browning. For prose, Mr. Ruskin, Sir Thomas Browne, and the *Revelations*. . . . My companions: hills, sir, and the sundown, and a dog as large as myself that my father bought me. They are better than kings, because they know, but do not tell.". . .

Six years later, when her nature was flowering under the sunshine of his appreciation, and the pruning of his criticism, she wrote to him—her "master": "Of our greatest acts we are ignorant. You were not aware that you saved my life. To thank you in person has been since then one of my few requests."

This was granted, and in 1870 occurred Higginson's first interview with the poet. She met her own description: "Small like the wren; and my hair is bold, like the chestnut burr; and my eyes like the sherry in the glass that the guest leaves." Another friend has said of her: "She was not beautiful, yet had many beauties"—a word that suits, too, her intellect.

I have not dwelt upon Emily Dickinson's faults; they speak for themselves, and sometimes with such a din that the virtues cannot be heard. Granted that her poetry is uneven, so rugged of rhyme and rhythm that it jolts the mind like a corduroy road—I prefer it to a flowery bed of ease. Many can lull, but few can awake.

Emily Dickinson's Puritan Heritage

John Robinson

Emily Dickinson's poems seem to exist outside of a historical context, refusing to answer such questions as Why here? and Why now? John Robinson, author of the study *Emily Dickinson: Looking to Canaan*, attempts to answer for her by locating the poet in her native New England town, in a different time—the time of the Salem witch trials.

In this new context, he proposes that Dickinson's reaction to the hysteria of the 1690s would likely be similar to her reaction to the American Civil War, which, although it was certainly the obsession of her time, hardly enters her poetry at all. He suggests to readers that her focus on what was timeless would not have allowed her to be blindly overtaken by any cause that she herself could not scrutinize honestly and carefully. To further his point, Robinson analyzes one short stanza that reveals much about Dickinson's view of time and history and compares his findings with those of previous critics.

'Tell it slant,' Emily Dickinson once advised. I want to begin, not with the nineteenth-century Amherst, Massachusetts, where she was born, but—though still in New England—some miles and years away in seventeenth-century Salem.

Notoriously, in 1692 her Puritan forebears were hanging witches there. Curious to know the future, young girls had made means to find out, amongst other things, about their likely marriages. The signs that they saw in the process frightened them and, in turn, their own disturbed behaviour alarmed their families who quickly regarded them as victims. Accusations were made. Trials were held. Enemies were executed.

But there were still more accusations, more trials, more executions, till the judicial process itself seemed to be out of control. Piercing glances, touches, tetchiness might be interpreted as the public signs of private connection with malign power—and the interpretation might be lethal. There was judgement in the eye of the beholder and, however reluctant they might be to convict on 'spectral testimony', the tendency of the courts was to make the insubstantial real. Fear and mistrust produced their own map of what, in reflections published the following year, the Reverend Cotton Mather called *The Wonders of the Invisible World.*

History was being made out of belief; and those crucial, investigative questions, why *now*? why *here*?, were not allowed their proper weight. History was accounted for in terms which left time and place out of the reckoning. There was an incompleteness in the human response, a failure of intelligence which was scarcely distinguishable from a failure of that confidence which we call love.

It is hardly likely that Emily Dickinson would have been guilty of such failure. So lightly ironic was she about received opinion, so independent of the rigidities of dogma, that it is difficult to see her being possessed by the destructive vigour of the judges of Salem. She was not so narrowly purposeful, yet her inheritance was that tradition which celebrated the timeless wonders of the invisible world, and, in manifold ways, she, too, tended to lock history out of her imagination. An obvious example is that, although there are soldiers, battlefields, and martial imagery in her poems, the American Civil War, which came in the middle of her life, is missing from them. More generally, many of her poems resist the reader's enquiries about the where and when of location, and so resist, too, the attendant why here? and why now? which are part of the attempt to form a judgement. She does not help us to see how she might have changed or developed as a poet. Her poems are often reluctant to locate us in the circumstances of their generation. . . .

If we turn from the historians' Salem to Emily Dickinson we can see in the following slight stanza the ways in which her interest in timelessness is intimately connected with, effectively, a withdrawal from participation and a submission to the control of circumstances.

Witchcraft was hung, in History,
But History and I

Find all the Witchcraft that we need
Around us, every Day—

When? Where? Out of what process, and with what consequences? Her mind does not work with such questions, so
time is telescoped and made inaccessible to us as 'in History'.
(There is no special significance in her capitals; generally
she used them, as in German, for nouns.) It is possible to
hang only witches, not witchcraft, so the first line is figurative and it is this figurativeness which facilitates one of the
two slippages in the poem. When it first appears 'witchcraft'
means the malefic working of pins stuck into poppets, of cer-
emonies to deploy the powers of darkness to cause suffering
or death; but 'Witchcraft' in the third line means the magic
of the wonderful, the marvellous, the extraordinary, the be-
nign. The poem turns on this pun. The other slippage is from
'History' meaning 'what is over and done with' to 'History'
meaning 'the sum of all pasts, presents and futures'. The
whole poem pivots on 'But': 'Witchcraft' is supposed to have
survived the assault made on it in the past and 'History' to be
truly shaped by what is innate in nature and not by something done long ago, once upon a time. We can have History
without historical events. History does not change: around
us, 'every Day', there is always 'Witchcraft'.

This stanza is one of those bright notes where she writes
with the air of someone who has pulled out a plum, and in
this it is not at all representative of her great poetry; but the
position she takes in it is characteristic of her thought and
indicates one of the reasons that some of her poems are difficult of approach. She wants to make human process (here,
of hanging in the past but not hanging now) unimportant
and a misperception. The witchcraft that is 'Around us,
every Day' is so persistent and undefined that it would obviously be futile to try to do anything to it. It is beyond human
power. Although its source is not located for us in the poem,
plainly it is not witches. In the past there was (repellent)
hanging, whereas there is now desirable magic. But the opposition in the poem is not really between now and then; it
is between then and always. It is not that we now know better, having learned from experience. It is that the past provides clear evidence of the way that human history is superfluous and in contrast there is another sort of history which
is real. The Olympian manner of 'History and I' marks not
transcendental arrogance but her sense of the secondariness

and the foreignness and the inertness of time when measured against the things which really matter.

What is this History which is untouched by history and which is the same every day?

DICKINSON IN THE PRESENT DAY

Emily Dickinson spent her life seeking to live in its dimensions—though she used other names and frames for it than the one in the poem above ('history' is a rare word in her vocabulary). It is as though she came to a conviction about the way her life should be oriented and then began to explore the implications of that orientation. Her thought was not progressive. It was not nourished by and dependent on thoughts that she had had before. In this sense it stayed still to dilate the moment and [*Looking to Canaan*] follows her in this by tracing her work not as a development but as an amplification. She had no project for her work. She did not carry through a purpose.

The effect of this has been to make her poems seem more than usually subject to the contingencies of circumstance—a chance meeting with a snake, or a hummingbird, a storm, some thoughts on a sunset. But when those poems are of great depth and turbulence and when, repeatedly, they revert to the same areas of disturbance, they encourage the view that there is an essential biographical pattern. Often commentators have felt that there is a story here if only they could find it, a novel of her life which would give them the generative springs.

Others have been less sanguine. She left behind nearly eighteen hundred lyrics—too many and too varied to be taken whole, and, though a tribute to the nomadic movement of her imagination, very uneven. Sometimes her poems are stringent, taut, fiercely alert; sometimes they are sentimental. Some show depths of insight and subtlety which set a reader's expectations high only for them to be betrayed by other work which, though it uses the same form and may set similar difficulties of approach, covers over the commonplace. Sometimes her tone is ironic, sometimes wistful; sometimes it is clamorous, sometimes plaintive, sometimes fulsome.

Faced with such multiplicity, R.P. Blackmur resorted to the desperate expedient of patronizing her thus:

She was a private poet who wrote indefatigably as some

women cook or knit. Her gift for words and the cultural predicament of her time drove her to poetry instead of anti-macassars.

This is to make her a poet of scraps, some of which are accidentally brilliant; but Adrienne Rich is struggling with the same essential difficulty when she says that Emily Dickinson was many poets, and so is David Porter in his campaigning: 'We find, no matter with what ingenuity we look, no solar system into whose gravitational field all her experiences were attracted.' Given the challenge of her multiplicity, we can see why Allen Tate's view that she was caught up in Emerson's war on Calvin has proved so durable. When we have an individual poet whose own work seems to fragment, an analogical claim is very persuasive. (R.P. Blackmur scoffed at him: 'When he has got his image all made he proceeds to sort out its component parts.')

It is apparent that we have to cope with a number of absences. Emily Dickinson is open to the making of theses because she never prepared her poems for publication, and to this editorial absence must be added the ambiguity and tentativeness of the dashes which she generally used in preference to firmer, conventional punctuation, and the lack of guidance which results from her poems being untitled. Nor did she leave, in either letter or essay, any extended prose discussion of the way she thought about her art. We are denied even secure texts or an unshakeable order of composition, and the man who has done most to give them to us observes of her poems: 'The dating of them is conjectural and for the most part will always remain so.'

The consequence is that inconvenient poems—there may be a number, for one mood contradicts another—may be neglected because any study of her work must necessarily be so very selective. Yet a piece of little merit on its own may receive much prominence because it illuminates some aspect of her thought, whereas a wonderful poem may be stubborn enough and opaque enough and so concentratedly itself as to make a reader doubt the illumination after all. We feel we need some secure centre which will enable us to determine what counts, and that seems to take us back to the story of her life.

I do not think that we should entirely relinquish this sense just because we cannot satisfy our curiosity. So figurative is Emily Dickinson's thought and so attracted by the riddle and the parable that it is difficult to believe that knowledge of, for example, the configurations of a frustrated love affair would not modify the contexts of some poems. So from her life-story we might receive significant help.

However, I think that underlying the biographical hope there has been a wish to provide what the verse does not provide and thus subtly to change its character by supplying its absences. We have little difficulty with time and place when she is writing about nature. The problems come with the space and span of poems which evoke states of feeling. We want to bring them under control by containing them under causes, yet I think that this shows an—understand-able—reluctance to cross their imaginative threshold and occupy them on their own terms. It is as if we wanted to think of the poems themselves as acts of management and to derive some control-system from them.

We can see that our own acts of naming are acts of man-agement which are achieved at the cost of severance. We refer, for example, to cedars, streams, birds' eggs and cloud formations as 'nature' and exclude from that word any pos-sible reference to smoke-stacks. But why should we divide the world so as to form a grouping which will bring together worms and sunshine, or connect the rainbow and the scor-pion? The word 'nature' makes a choice for us. In doing this it both releases and inhibits by giving us the resources but also putting on us the limitations of certain inherited ways of dividing up our experience with words. If we see Emily Dickinson as a poet of revelations we can see that in some sense she must be a poet of those moments when the words run out. Her very practice is a contradiction: using words to evoke the wordless, using words made in history to point be-yond history. If we see words as names and names as forms of control we can see that she is at a difficult intersection. . . .

In approaching her work we face, then, the contradiction that few have been less interested in temporal circumstances than she and that, at her finest, she prized those nameless moments when she seemed, with awe, to be at the edge of the eternal, yet we know about them only because she en-tered history, used the communal language, and was not simply a receptor but one who took initiatives as a creator. The kind of retreat we have from agency in the passive 'was hanged' of her witchcraft stanza sometimes carries through to the extent of her using uninflected verbs as if she could make an art of the infinitive. 'Be seen', 'arise', 'remit' are examples (from 'Further in Summer than the Birds'). In context are they past, present, or future? Are they first, second, or third person? They seem to wish to escape from time. Yet she could not. We have her work because of a series of interventions in history of which hers was the first and to which, in selecting and appraising as readers, we add another.

Emily Dickinson Ranks Among the World's Greatest Poets

Allen Tate

Author of numerous books of poetry, Allen Tate is perhaps best known for his poem "Ode to the Confederate Dead." His novel *The Fathers* was first published in 1928. Distinguished also as a critic, his collections of essays include *Reactionary Essays on Poetry and Ideas* and *Reason and Madness.* Tate was editor of such literary journals as the *Sewanee Review* and *Hound and Horn.* In this much-anthologized essay, Tate puts Dickinson in the company of the most famous poets of the Western world—John Donne, Alfred, Lord Tennyson, and William Shakespeare.

Personal revelation of the kind that [poets John] Donne and [Emily] Dickinson strove for, in the effort to understand their relation to the world, is a feature of all great poetry; it is probably the hidden motive for writing. It is the effort of the individual to live apart from a cultural tradition that no longer sustains him. But this culture, which I now wish to discuss a little, is indispensable: there is a great deal of shallow nonsense in modern criticism which holds that poetry—and this is a half-truth that is worse than false—is essentially revolutionary. It is only indirectly revolutionary: the intellectual and religious background of an age no longer contains the whole spirit, and the poet proceeds to examine that background in terms of immediate experience. But the background is necessary: otherwise all the arts (not only poetry) would have to rise in a vacuum. Poetry does not dispense with tradition; it probes the deficiencies of a tradition. But it must have a tradition to probe. It is too bad that [poet and critic Matthew] Arnold did not explain his doctrine, that poetry is a criticism of life, from the viewpoint of its back-

From "Emily Dickinson," in *Reactionary Essays on Poetry and Ideas* by Allen Tate (New York: Scribner, 1936). Reprinted by permission of Mrs. Allen Tate.

ground: we should have been spared an era of academic misconception, in which criticism of life meant a diluted pragmatism, the criterion of which was respectability. The poet in the true sense "criticizes" his tradition, either as such, or indirectly by comparing it with something that is about to replace it; he does what the root-meaning of the verb implies—he *discerns* its real elements and thus establishes its value, by putting it to the test of experience.

What is the nature of a poet's culture? Or, to put the question properly, what is the meaning of culture for poetry? All the great poets become the material of what we popularly call culture: we study them to acquire it. It is clear that [Joseph] Addison was more cultivated than [William] Shakespeare; nevertheless Shakespeare is a finer source of culture than Addison. What is the meaning of this? Plainly it is that learning has never had anything to do with culture except instrumentally: the poet must be exactly literate enough to write down fully and precisely what he has to say, but no more. The source of a poet's true culture lies back of the paraphernalia of culture, and not all the historical activity of an enlightened age can create it.

A culture cannot be consciously created. It is an available source of ideas that are imbedded in a complete and homogeneous society. The poet finds himself balanced upon the moment when such a world is about to fall, when it threatens to run out into looser and less self-sufficient impulses. This world order is assimilated, in Miss Dickinson, as medievalism was in Shakespeare, to the poetic vision; it is brought down from abstraction to personal sensibility.

BETWEEN THOUGHT AND FEELING

In this connection it may be said that the prior conditions for great poetry, given a great talent, may be reduced to two: the thoroughness of the poet's discipline in an objective system of truth, and his lack of consciousness of such a discipline. For this discipline is a number of fundamental ideas the origin of which the poet does not know; they give form and stability to his fresh perceptions of the world; and he cannot shake them off. This is his culture, and, like Tennyson's God, it is nearer than hands and feet. With reasonable certainty we unearth the elements of Shakespeare's culture, and yet it is equally certain—so innocent was he of his own resources— that he would not know what our discussion is about. He appeared at the collapse of the medieval system as a rigid pattern of life, but that pattern remained in Shakespeare what Shelley called a "fixed point of reference" for his sensibility. Miss Dickinson, as we have seen, was born into the equilibrium of an old and a new order. Puritanism could not be to her what it had been to the generation of Cotton Mather—a body of absolute truths: it was an unconscious discipline timed to the pulse of her life.

TO EMILY DICKINSON

Hart Crane was one of many poets of substance to be profoundly influenced by the work of Emily Dickinson. In this poem, from his Complete Poems and Selected Letters, *Crane laments the fact that Dickinson was fully appreciated only after her death.*

You who desired so much—in vain to ask—
Yet fed your hunger like an endless task,
Dared dignify the labor, bless the quest—
Achieved that stillness ultimately best,

Being, of all, least sought for: Emily, hear!
O sweet, dead Silencer, most suddenly clear
When singing that Eternity possessed
And plundered momently in every breast;

—Truly no flower yet withers in your hand,
The harvest you descried and understand
Needs more than wit to gather, love to bind.
Some reconcilement of remotest mind—

Leaves Ormus rubyless, and Ophir chill.
Else tears heap all within one clay-cold hill.

The perfect literary situation: it produces, because it is rare, a special and perhaps the most distinguished kind of poet. I am not trying to invent a new critical category. Such poets are never very much alike on the surface; they show us all the varieties of poetic feeling; and, like other poets, they resist all classification but that of temporary convenience. But, I believe, Miss Dickinson and John Donne would have this in common: their sense of the natural world is not blunted by a too-rigid system of ideas: yet the ideas, the abstractions, their education or their intellectual heritage, are not so weak as to let their immersion in nature, or their purely personal quality, get out of control. The two poles of the mind are not separately visible; we infer them from the lucid tension that may be most readily illustrated by polar activity. There is no thought as such at all: nor is there feeling: there is that unique focus of experience which is at once neither and both.

Like Miss Dickinson, Shakespeare is without opinions: his peculiar merit is also deeply involved in his failure to think about anything; his meaning is not in the content of his expression: it is in the tension of the dramatic relations of his characters. This kind of poetry is at the opposite of intellectualism. (Miss Dickinson is obscure and difficult, but that is not intellectualism.) To T.W. Higginson, the editor of the *Atlantic Monthly*, who tried to advise her, she wrote that she had no education. In any sense that Higginson could understand, it was quite true. His kind of education was the conscious cultivation of abstractions. She did not reason about the world she saw: she merely saw it. The "ideas" implicit in the world within her rose up, concentrated in her immediate perception.

That kind of world at present has for us something of the fascination of a buried city. There is none like it. When such worlds exist, when such cultures flourish, they support not only the poet but all members of society. For, from these, the poet differs only in his gift for exhibiting the structure, the internal lineaments, of his culture by threatening to tear them apart: a process that concentrates the symbolic emotions of society while it seems to attack them. The poet may hate his age; he may be an outcast like Villon; but this world is always there as the background to what he has to say. It is the lens through which he brings nature to focus and control—the clarifying medium that concentrates his personal feeling. It is ready-made; he cannot make it; with it, his poetry has a spontaneity and a certainty of direction that, without it, it would lack. No poet could have invented the ideas of "The Chariot," only a great poet could have found their imaginative equivalents. Miss Dickinson was a deep mind writing from a deep culture, and when she came to poetry, she came infallibly.

DICKINSON'S CRITICISM DESERVES ATTENTION

Infallibly, at her best; for no poet has ever been perfect, nor is Emily Dickinson. Her precision of statement is due to the directness with which the abstract framework of her thought acts upon its unorganized material. The two elements of her style, considered as point of view, are immortality, or the idea of permanence, and the physical process of death or decay. Her diction has two corresponding features: words of Latin or Greek origin and, sharply opposed to these, the concrete Saxon element. It is this verbal conflict that gives her verse its high tension; it is not a device deliberately seized upon, but a feeling for language that senses out the two fundamental components of English and their metaphysical relation: the Latin for ideas and the Saxon for perceptions—the peculiar virtue of English as a poetic language.

Like most poets Miss Dickinson often writes out of habit: the style that emerged from some deep exploration of an idea is carried on as verbal habit when she has nothing to say. She indulges herself:

> There's something quieter than sleep
> Within this inner room!
> It wears a sprig upon its breast,
> And will not tell its name.
>
> Some touch it and some kiss it,
> Some chafe its idle hand:
> It has a simple gravity
> I do not understand!
>
> While simple hearted neighbors
> Chat of the "early dead,"
> We, prone to periphrasis,
> Remark that birds have fled!

It is only a pert remark; at best a superior kind of punning—one of the worst specimens of her occasional interest in herself. But she never had the slightest interest in the public. Were four poems or five published in her lifetime? She never felt the temptation to round off a poem for public exhibition. Higginson's kindly offer to make her verse "correct" was an invitation to throw her work into the public ring—the ring of Lowell and Longfellow. He could not see that he was tampering with one of the rarest literary integrities of all time. Here was a poet who had no use for the supports of authorship—flattery and fame; she never needed money.

She had all the elements of a culture that has broken up, a culture that on the religious side takes its place in the museum of spiritual antiquities. Puritanism, as a unified version of the world, is dead; only a remnant of it in trade may be said to survive. In the history of puritanism she comes between Hawthorne and Emerson. She has Hawthorne's matter, which a too irresponsible personality tends to dilute into a form like Emerson's; she is often betrayed by words. But she is not the poet of personal sentiment; she has more to say than she can put down in any one poem. Like Hardy and Whitman, she must be read entire; like Shakespeare, she never gives up her meaning in a single line.

She is therefore a perfect subject for the kind of criticism which is chiefly concerned with general ideas. She exhibits one of the permanent relations between personality and objective truth, and she deserves the special attention of our time, which lacks that kind of truth.

She has Hawthorne's intellectual toughness, a hard, definite sense of the physical world. The highest flights to God, the most extravagant metaphors of the strange and the remote, come back to a point of casuistry, to a moral dilemma of the experienced world. There is, in spite of the homiletic vein of utterance, no abstract speculation, nor is there a message to society; she speaks wholly to the individual experience. She offers to the unimaginative no riot of vicarious sensation; she has no useful maxims for men of action. Up to this point her resemblance to Emerson is slight: poetry is a sufficient form of utterance, and her devotion to it is pure. But in Emily Dickinson the puritan world is no longer self-contained; it is no longer complete; her sensibility exceeds its dimensions. She has trimmed down its supernatural proportions; it has become a morality; instead of the tragedy of the spirit there is a commentary upon it. Her poetry is a magnificent personal confession, blasphemous and, in its self-revelation, its honesty, almost obscene. It comes out of an intellectual life toward which it feels no moral responsibility. Cotton Mather would have burnt her for a witch.

CHAPTER 2

Poetic Analysis

READINGS ON
EMILY DICKINSON

Two Explications

Nancy Lenz Harvey and Thomas H. Johnson

An explication is a line-by-line prose interpretation of a poem. Because poetry often employs such techniques as word ambiguity, paradox, and compression, explication is usually much less simple than it would appear by definition. Similarly, the explication itself is open to interpretive readings since the way a reader views a text has everything to do with education, associations, and personal biases.

What follows are two of Dickinson's poems as they are explicated by some of the finest scholars in the field. The first explication, Nancy Lenz Harvey's "What Soft Cherubic Creatures," appeared in a 1969–1970 volume of the *Explicator*, a journal devoted to poetic interpretation. The second explication is from Thomas H. Johnson's book-length study *Emily Dickinson: An Interpretive Biography*, first published in 1955.

"WHAT SOFT CHERUBIC CREATURES"

What Soft—Cherubic Creatures—
These Gentlewomen are—
One would as soon assault a Plush—
Or violate a Star—

Such Dimity Convictions—
A Horror so refined
Of freckled Human Nature—
Of Deity—ashamed—

It's such a common—Glory—
A Fisherman's—Degree—
Redemption—Brittle Lady—
Be so—ashamed of Thee—

Emily Dickinson's "What Soft Cherubic Creatures" is a sting-

Part I, Nancy Lenz Harvey, "Dickinson's 'What Soft Cherubic Creatures,'" *Explicator*, vol. 28 (1970). Reprinted with permission of the Helen Dwight Reid Educational Foundation. Published by Heldref Publications, 1319 18th St. NW, Washington, DC 20036-1802. Copyright ©1970. Part II, from *Emily Dickinson: An Interpretive Biography* by Thomas H. Johnson (Cambridge, MA: Harvard University Press); ©1955 by the President and Fellows of Harvard College. Reprinted by permission of the publisher.

ing denunciation of the hypocrisy embodied in gentlewomen. Although they appear delicate and remote—"One would as soon assault a Plush / Or violate a Star" (lines 3-4)—these ladies are neither soft nor cherubic. Their very label is a misnomer; their invective against humankind and the Godhead is anything but gentle. This first stanza is then both caustic and satirical.

BEAUTY LIES IN HUMAN IMPERFECTIONS

The second stanza explicates reasons for the poet's tone. These ladies with their dainty, delicate, "dimity" convictions and their "refined" horror are abashed by "freckled Human Nature" (lines 5-7). Human nature, besmirched by original sin, contains within it all the *ugliness* of the flesh, sin and sex—ideas abhorrent to the *gentler* sort. Yet as the ladies shame the flesh, they inadvertently shame the Deity, for man is made in God's image.

These first two stanzas seem to be clear and straightforward, while the third and final stanza becomes curiously ambiguous, and the punctuation of stanzas 2 and 3 increases this ambiguity. If the lines "It's such a common—glory— / A Fisherman's—Degree—" (lines 9-10) are read as part of those "Dimity Convictions," the flesh is condemned once more because it is a *common* glory—a second-rate glory. It is thus of low estate, that level of society known only to the laborer, the "fisherman's degree." The words *common* and *degree* are often spouted by those who feel themselves remote from the herd, who fail to see a humanity basic to all men.

If, however, these lines begin another thought, then the poem moves progressively to a theological note, and the diction—"common glory," "fisherman's degree," and "redemption"—reinforces this note. Not only are the ladies in horror of human nature, made in the image of God, but they have also failed to realize that human nature is the common or shared glory of God and man. This is the nature chosen by God as He becomes the man Jesus— the man who is a fisher of men. Since the purpose of Christ's life and passion is solely for the redemption of human nature, the closing lines are closely related to the poem as a whole. The ladies are now rightly called: they are "brittle" ladies capable of meanness and sharp cruelty; for they have not only denied the humanity of others and of themselves, but they have also denied their God. Redemption, if now, would "be ashamed" of them.

The rich ambiguity of this last stanza tightens the unity of the poem. The theological reading strengthens the tie of the last two lines to the poem as a whole and combines with the other reading to underscore the superciliousness of the ladies. The cherubic ladies of the opening line become nothing less than alienated creatures who have so distanced themselves from both God and man that they are more *mineral* than *human*—they are brittle creatures. . . .

"BECAUSE I COULD NOT STOP FOR DEATH"

In 1863 Death came into full stature as a person. "Because I could not stop for Death" is a superlative achievement wherein Death becomes one of the great characters of literature.

It is almost impossible in any critique to define exactly the kind of reality which her character Death attains, simply because the protean shifts of form are intended to forestall definition. A poem can convey the nuances of exultation, agony, compassion, or any mystical mood. But no one can successfully define mysticism because the logic of language has no place for it. One must therefore assume that the reality of Death, as Emily Dickinson conceived him, is to be perceived by the reader in the poems themselves. Any analysis can do no more than suggest what may be looked for.

In "Because I could not stop for Death" Emily Dickinson envisions Death as a person she knew and trusted, or believed that she could trust. He might be any Amherst gentleman . . . who at one time or another had acted as her squire.

> Because I could not stop for Death—
> He kindly stopped for me—
> The Carriage held but just Ourselves—
> And Immortality.

The carriage holds but the two of them, yet the ride, as she states with quiet emphasis, is a last ride together. Clearly there has been no deception on his part. They drive in a leisurely manner, and she feels completely at ease. Since she understands it to be a last ride, she of course expects it to be unhurried. Indeed, his graciousness in taking time to stop for her at that point and on that day in her life when she was so busy she could not possibly have taken time to stop for him, is a mark of special politeness. She is therefore quite willing to put aside her work. And again, since it is to be her last ride, she can dispense with her spare moments as well as her active ones.

> We slowly drove—He knew no haste
> And I had put away
> My labor and my leisure too
> For His Civility—

She notes the daily routine of the life she is passing from. Children playing games during a school recess catch her eye at the last. And now the sense of motion is quickened. Or perhaps more exactly one should say that the sense of time comes to an end as they pass the cycles of the day and the seasons of the year, at a period of both ripeness and decline.

> We passed the School, where Children strove
> At Recess—in the Ring—
> We passed the Fields of Gazing Grain—
> We passed the Setting Sun—

How insistently "passed" echoes through the stanza! She now conveys her feeling of being outside time and change, for she corrects herself to say that the sun passed them, as it of course does all who are in the grave. She is aware of dampness and cold, and becomes suddenly conscious of the sheerness of the dress and scarf which she now discovers that she wears.

> Or rather—He passed Us—
> The Dews drew quivering and chill—
> For only Gossamer, my Gown—
> My Tippet—only Tulle—

The two concluding stanzas, with progressively decreasing concreteness, hasten the final identification of her "House." It is the slightly rounded surface "of the Ground," with a scarcely visible roof and a cornice "in the Ground." To time and seasonal change, which have already ceased, is now added motion. Cessation of all activity and creativeness is absolute. At the end, in a final instantaneous flash of memory, she recalls the last objects before her eyes during the journey: the heads of the horses that bore her, as she had surmised they were doing from the beginning, toward—it is the last word—"Eternity."

> We paused before a House that seemed
> A Swelling of the Ground—
> The Roof was scarcely visible—
> The Cornice—in the Ground—
>
> Since then—'tis Centuries—and yet
> Feels shorter than the Day
> I first surmised the Horses Heads
> Were toward Eternity—

Gradually, too, one realizes that Death as a person has re-
ceded into the background, mentioned last only imperson-
ally in the opening words "We paused" of the fifth stanza,
where his services as squire and companion are over. In this
poem concrete realism melds into "awe and circumference"
with matchless economy.

Diverging Viewpoints on a Classic Poem

Gerhard Friedrich, John Ciardi, and Caroline Hogue

Three critics discuss one of Dickinson's most popular poems, "I Heard a Fly buzz—when I died—." The discussion begins with an analysis by Gerhard Friedrich which appeared in the *Explicator*—a scholarly journal devoted entirely to interpreting single poems—in 1955. In this essay, Friedrich states that to understand this much-discussed poem, a reader first needs to answer two questions: What is the significance of the fly buzzing? and what does the repetition of the word *see* in the last line mean?

While Friedrich's response to the second question seems to have stirred little controversy, his answers to the first drew a quick reaction from John Ciardi in the *Explicator* some months later. Then in 1961, Caroline Hogue responded to Ciardi's analysis by offering some historical facts that contradict both critics' interpretations. It is interesting to note that Ciardi was no longer sure he agreed with all he said in his essay, although he remained convinced of his main point.

I heard a Fly buzz—when I died—
The Stillness in the Room
Was like the Stillness in the Air—
Between the Heaves of Storm—

The Eyes around—had wrung them dry—
And Breaths were gathering firm
For that last Onset—when the King
Be witnessed—in the Room—

I willed my Keepsakes—Signed away
What portion of me be
Assignable—and then it was
There interposed a Fly—

Gerhard Friedrich, "Dickinson's 'I Heard a Fly Buzz When I Died,'" *Explicator*, vol. 13, April 1955; John Ciardi, a response to Friedrich in the January 1956 issue of the *Explicator*, and Caroline Hogue's response to both Friedrich and Ciardi in the November 1961 *Explicator*. Reprinted with permission of the Helen Dwight Reid Educational Foundation. Published by Heldref Publications, 1319 18th St. NW, Washington, DC 20036-1802; ©1955, 1956, 1961.

With Blue—uncertain stumbling Buzz—
Between the light—and me—
And then the Windows failed—and then
I could not see to see—
                    (#465)

Gerhard Friedrich

This poem seems to present two major problems to the interpreter. First, what is the significance of the buzzing fly in relation to the dying person, and second, what is the meaning of the double use of "see" in the last line? An analysis of the context helps to clear up these apparent obscurities, and a close parallel found in another Dickinson poem reinforces such interpretation.

In an atmosphere of outward quiet and inner calm, the dying person collectedly proceeds to bequeath his or her worldly possessions, and while engaged in this activity of "willing," finds his attention withdrawn by a fly's buzzing. The fly is introduced in intimate connection with "my keepsakes" and "what portion of me be assignable"; it follows—and is the culmination of—the dying person's preoccupation with cherished material things no longer of use to the departing owner. In the face of death, and even more of a possible spiritual life beyond death, one's concern with a few earthly belongings is but a triviality, and indeed a distraction from a momentous issue. The obtrusiveness of the inferior, physical aspects of existence, and the busybody activity associated with them, is poignantly illustrated by the intervening insect (cf. the line "Buzz the dull flies on the chamber window," in the poem beginning "How many times these low feet staggered"). Even so small a demonstrative, demonstrable creature is sufficient to separate the dying person from "the light," i.e. to blur the vision, to short-circuit mental concentration, so that spiritual awareness is lost. The last line of the poem may then be paraphrased to read: "Waylaid by irrelevant, tangible, finite objects of little importance, I was no longer capable of that deeper perception which would clearly reveal to me the infinite spiritual reality." As Emily Dickinson herself expressed it, in another Second Series poem beginning "Their height in heaven comforts not":

I'm finite, I can't see.

This timid life of evidence
Keeps pleading, "I don't know."

The dying person does in fact not merely suffer an unwelcome external interruption of an otherwise resolute expectancy, but falls from a higher consciousness, from liberating insight, from faith, into an intensely skeptical mood. The fly's buzz is characterized as "blue, uncertain, stumbling," and emphasis on the finite physical reality goes hand in hand with a frustrating lack of absolute assurance. The only portion of a man not properly "assignable" may be that which dies and decomposes! To the dying person, the buzzing fly would thus become a timely, untimely reminder of man's final, cadaverous condition and putrefaction.

The sudden fall of the dying person into the captivity of an earth-heavy skepticism demonstrates of course the inadequacy of the earlier pseudo-stoicism. What seemed then like composure, was after all only a pause "between the heaves of storm"; the "firmness" of the second stanza proved to be less than veritable peace of mind and soul; and so we have a profoundly tragic human situation, namely the perennial conflict between two concepts of reality, most carefully delineated.

The poem should be compared with its illuminating counterpart of the Second Series, "Their height in heaven comforts not," and may be contrasted with "Death is a dialogue between," "I heard as if I had no ear," and the well-known "I never saw a moor."

JOHN CIARDI

I read Mr. Gerhard Friedrich's explication . . . of Emily Dickinson's poem with great interest, but I find myself preferring a different explication.

Mr. Friedrich says of the fly: "Even so small a demonstrative, demonstrable creature is sufficient to separate the dying person from 'the light,' i.e. to blur the vision, to short-circuit mental concentration, so that spiritual awareness is lost. The last line of the poem may then be paraphrased to read: 'Waylaid by irrelevant, tangible, finite objects of little importance, I was no longer capable of that deeper perception which would clearly reveal to me the infinite spiritual reality.'"

Mr. Friedrich's argument is coherent and respectable, but I feel it tends to make Emily more purely mystical than I sense her to be. I understand that fly to be the last kiss of the world, the last buzz from life. Certainly Emily's tremendous attachment to the physical world, and her especial delight both in minute creatures for their own sake, and in minute actions for the sake of the dramatic implications that can be loaded into them, hardly needs to be documented. Any number of poems illustrate her delight in the special significance of tiny living things. "Elysium is as Far" will do as a single example of her delight in packing a total-life significance into the slightest actions:

> What fortitude the Soul contains,
> That it can so endure
> The accent of a coming Foot—
> The opening of a Door—

I find myself better persuaded, therefore, to think of the fly not as a distraction taking Emily's thoughts from glory and blocking the divine light (When did Emily ever think of living things as a distraction?), but as a last dear sound from the world as the light of consciousness sank from her, i.e. "the windows failed." And so I take the last line to mean simply: "And then there was no more of me, and nothing to see with."

In writing her best poems [Emily Dickinson] was never at the mercy of her emotions or of the official rhetoric. She mastered her themes by controlling her language. She could achieve a novel significance, for example, by starting with a death scene that implies the orthodox questions and then turning the meaning against itself by the strategy of surprise answers. . . . ["I heard a Fly buzz—when I died"] operates in terms of all the standard religious assumptions of her New England, but with a difference. They are explicitly gathered up in one phrase for the moment of death, with distinct Biblical overtones, "that last Onset—when the King / Be witnessed—in the Room." But how is he witnessed?

As the poet dramatizes herself in a deathbed scene, with family and friends gathered round, her heightened senses report the crisis in flat domestic terms that bring to the reader's mind each of the traditional questions only to deny them without even asking them. Her last words were squandered in distributing her "Keepsakes," trivial tokens of this life rather than messages from the other. The only sound of heavenly music, or of wings taking flight, was the "Blue—uncertain stumbling Buzz" of a fly that filled her dying ear. Instead of a final vision of the hereafter, this world simply faded from her eyes: the light in the windows failed and then she "could not see to see." The King witnessed in this power is physical death, not God. To take this poem literally as an attempted inside view of the gradual extinction of consciousness and the beginning of the soul's flight into eternity would be to distort its meaning, for this is not an imaginative projection of her own death. In structure, in language, in imagery it is simply an ironic reversal of the conventional attitudes of her time and place toward the significance of the moment of death. Yet mystery is evoked by a single word, that extraordinarily interposed color "Blue."

To misread such a poem would be to misunderstand the whole cast of Dickinson's mind. Few poets saw more clearly the boundary between what can and what cannot be comprehended, and so held the mind within its proper limitations. . . .

CAROLINE HOGUE

Emily Dickinson's "I Heard A Fly Buzz When I Died" should be read, I think, with a particular setting in mind—a nineteenth-century deathbed scene. Before the age of powerful anodynes death was met in full consciousness, and the way of meeting it tended to be stereotype. It was affected with a public interest and concern, and was witnessed by family and friends. They crowded the death chamber to await expectantly a burst of dying energy to bring on the grand act of passing. Commonly it began with last-minute bequests, the wayward were called to repentance, the backslider to reform, gospel hymns were sung, and finally as climax the dying one gave witness in words to the Redeemer's presence in the room, how He hovered, transplendent in the upper air, with open arms outstretched to receive the departing soul. This was death's great moment. Variants there were, of course, in case of repentant and unrepentant sinners. Here in this poem the central figure of the drama is expected to make a glorious exit. The build-up is just right for it, but at the moment of climax "There interposed a fly." And what kind of a fly? A fly "with blue, uncertain stumbling buzz"—a blowfly.

How right is Mr. Gerhard Friedrich in his explication . . . to associate the fly with putrefaction and decay. And how wrong, I think, is Mr. John Ciardi . . . in calling the fly "the last kiss of the world," and speaking of it as one of the small creatures Emily Dickinson so delighted in. She could not possibly have entertained any such view of a blowfly. She was a practical housewife, and every housewife abhors a blowfly. It pollutes everything it touches. Its eggs are maggots. It is as carrion as a buzzard.

What we know of Emily Dickinson gives us assurance that just as she would abhor the blowfly she would abhor the deathbed scene. How devastatingly she disposes of the projected one in the poem. "They talk of hallowed things and embarrass my dog" she writes in 1862 in a letter to [her friend and mentor Thomas W.] Higginson.

An Explication of "The first Day's Night had come"

Constance Rooke

Canadian scholar Constance Rooke conducts a line-by-line examination of one of Dickinson's more complex poems. Rooke reveals meaning in the poem by analyzing such aspects as plot, tone, and metaphor and derives the multiple meanings that are evident in all good poems.

> The first Day's Night had come—
> And grateful that a thing
> So terrible—had been endured—
> I told my Soul to sing—
>
> She said her Strings were snapt—
> Her Bow—to Atoms blown—
> And so to mend her—gave me work
> Until another Morn—
>
> And then—a Day as huge
> As Yesterdays in pairs,
> Unrolled its horror in my face—
> Until it blocked my eyes—
>
> My Brain—begun to laugh—
> I mumbled—like a fool—
> And tho' 'tis Years ago—that Day—
> My Brain keeps giggling—still.
>
> And Something's odd—within—
> That person that I was—
> And this One—do not feel the same—
> Could it be Madness—this?
>   (#410)

"The first Day's Night had come" is a lyric projected as drama. Its time begins on the first day of the speaker's new life: a life wholly formed as the aftermath of "a thing / So terrible" that it has created a radical discontinuity in the life and

Constance Rooke, "'The First Day's Night Had Come': An Explication of J.410," *Emily Dickinson Bulletin*, vol. 24 (1973). Reprinted by permission of the author.

personality of its endurer. Characters are born within the speaker, characters whose job it is to piece out the future of pain in dialogue and protective, ironic gesture. The tone which arises in the poem is crucially ironic and naked at the same time; all disguises reveal, and are created by, the lacerated passions beneath. From this tension, if at all, the speaker must summon continuance and its doubtful blessing.

The poem begins:

> The first Day's Night had come—
> And grateful that a thing
> So terrible—had been endured—
> I told my Soul to sing—

We need not speculate on the identity of that thing so terrible, which almost inevitably presents itself to our imaginations as the loss of a lover, or a possible psychosis. With this first speech there are other questions more problematic. Is it likely that she should be grateful for only this brief and bare endurance? And out of what mood, given this situation, does one tell one's soul to sing? On the one hand, she may indeed be grateful, astonished that she has in any fashion survived so far. Then the injuction to her soul may be delirious and earnest. On the other hand, this talking to one's soul may be to begin a mad game. Souls, furthermore, do not ordinarily need to be commanded into song; they are supposed to do that spontaneously. Her gratitude may be a mocking of her own deprivation, and her order to the soul a grim recognition that free song is past.

> She said her Strings were snapt—
> Her bow—to Atoms blown—
> And so to mend her—gave me work
> Until another Morn—

The personified soul's reply extends the metaphor with unpleasant, deadly restraint. The metaphor is the poet's toy, her effort to stay despair. Within the terms of the metaphor, the soul-mending is similarly busy-work. One questions whether the soul were put together again by that next morning. It is a tidy little image for such an ultimate task, its limitations suggesting a patchwork job at best.

> And then—a Day as huge
> As Yesterdays in pairs,
> Unrolled its horror in my face—
> Until it blocked my eyes—

If she had thought her night work effective, she rose to find

it far otherwise. She had tried to manage her pain in minia-
ture compass, within the play world established between
herself and a doll soul. But daylight brought monstrous
twins to threaten the dollmaker. There is no possessive
apostrophe in "Yesterdays," which helps us to see the day in
pairs. Perhaps as malicious footmen, giants who unroll their
horror as if at the start of a carpet which will only be un-
wound at her life's end. Most of their horror is in the dupli-
cation of her pain; each day will it be twice as bad as the day
before? This horizontal nightmare leaves only the alternative of the barren, vertical self out of time. She is so appalled
by the vision of her anguished situation that her eyes are
blocked and she turns inward.

> My Brain—begun to laugh—
> I mumbled—like a fool—
> And tho' 'tis Years ago—that Day—
> My Brain keeps giggling—still.

Reality cannot be endured, but there is nowhere else to live.
In the vacuum, after the shock of withdrawal, laughter
sounds. It must be someone else who laughs so cruelly as if
to reveal the prison and the foolishness of struggle. The sick-
ened brain, bereft of intellectual power by this departure
from reality, diverges from the speaker to become a separate
character. Marvellous, covert syntax suggests this confusion
of identity. The speaker is reduced to mumbling in the face
of the brain's superior laughter; but she also "mumbled" the
brain to begin with, foolishly, and so created her own half-
witted tormentor. Thus, "like a fool" applies to both the
laughter and the mumbling, and ultimately to the schizo-
phrenic retreat which deprives her of reality and the faint
hope of renewal. Years later, the laughter has subsided to
giggles but the hideous joke persists. The extent of this defeat is queried in the final stanza.

> And Something's odd—within—
> That person that I was—
> And this One—do not feel the same—
> Could it be Madness—this?

"That person" is remote. The vague remarking of the fact
that "Something's odd—within," the pause before "—
within" like a fearful admission of her residence there or shy
pretense of a distinction no longer valid, suggest the seriousness of her discontinuity. And there is a childishness in
her expression of the sense that these two persons do not

feel the same. The speaker is docile now, fading out—as good a definition of madness, perhaps, as any. Certainly the reader's horror is greater here than in that other country where the speaker still wrestled with her demons.

Editorial Decisions Affect Dickinson Collections

Marta L. Werner

When Emily Dickinson died in 1886, she left behind several bound books, or "fascicles," that have since been published in various forms and under several titles. In addition to the fascicles she left many separate poems, scraps, and ideas behind, some completed, some in various states of development. It is impossible to know how Dickinson intended her work to be collected—if in fact she meant her work to be collected at all.

Essayist Marta L. Werner asserts that because any act of editing, including changing Dickinson's distinctive handwriting into typed letters, necessarily changes the way we read the poems, editing Dickinson's poems today "paradoxically involves unediting them." When we return the slashes, variant word choices, even the writing in the margins, we not only see intended messages more clearly, we see Dickinson as a forerunner to many postmodern writers who have just recently begun experimenting with unconventional methods of presentation similar to Dickinson's self-edited works. Werner is the author of *Emily Dickinson's Open Folios: Scenes of Reading, Surfaces of Writing*, from which this article is excerpted.

In 1858 or 1859 Emily Dickinson began binding her work into the small packets that her first editors, Mabel Loomis Todd and Thomas Wentworth Higginson, called *fascicles*: a cluster of flowers, the leaves of a book. To assemble a packet Dickinson first copied her poems in ink onto uniform sheets of stationery, then stacked several copied sheets together, stabbed two holes in the set, at last threading them through

From the Introduction to *Emily Dickinson's Open Folios: Scenes of Reading, Surfaces of Writing* by Marta L. Werner (Ann Arbor: University of Michigan Press, 1995). Copyright ©1995 by Marta L. Werner. Reprinted by permission of the author and publisher.

with string tied once in the front. In the earliest packets poems are fitted into blank spaces on the page, few alternate word choices appear to complicate readings, and ambiguities are neatly ~~struck out~~. Later, however, in the creatively charged 1860s, a significant change takes place inside of the fascicles, a change almost certainly reflecting a change in Dickinson's attitude toward "final authorial intention." At this juncture the packets take on the character of a workshop: variant word choices appear in abundance, and the almost habitual quatrain of the early work is ruptured and transformed under the pressures of a new vision.

In 1981 Ralph W. Franklin completed his vast facsimile edition of *The Manuscript Books of Emily Dickinson.* In his edition Franklin restores, as far as is currently possible, the original order and internal sequence of the forty fascicles, revises the dating schema of the [Thomas H.] Johnson variorum, and charts Dickinson's poetic activity up until approximately 1864, when she ceased attempts at fine, handcrafted bookmaking. The focus of Franklin's edition, then, is those poems that, though never authorized by Dickinson for circulation in the realm of public discourse, may be understood as [what Franklin calls in his introduction] "a personal enactment of the public act that, for reasons unexplained, she denied herself."

On the one hand, the immense erudition and scholarly authority of Franklin's edition confirm the gigantic authority of Dickinson's poetry. On the other hand, the source of Franklin's authority as editor of Dickinson's work may be fundamentally different, even antithetical, to the authority of the writing itself, and to Dickinson's art—her rigor—of "choosing not choosing." [To borrow the title of Sharon Cameron's book on Dickinson's fascicles.] By the very act of entering the loved work of an author into the social and economic networks of distribution, an editor necessarily chooses to choose; the creation of what Jonathan Arac calls an "authoritative critical identity" for Emily Dickinson requires that there be omissions and exclusions: *of* fragments, scraps, lost events. *The Manuscript Books of Emily Dickinson,* edited by Franklin in two volumes, offers a portrait of the artist as bookmaker: what is central—that is, canonical—is what was/is bound in a book.

Yet what if, as Cameron wonders, "Dickinson is looking for her own language and finding it in the margins"?

"SUNDAY—SECOND OF MARCH"

Leaving Dickinson's poems and fragments as close to the original as possible allows interpretations impossible under previous editors. This fragment, collected in Marta Werner's Open Folios, *was originally written in pencil, the left and right margins in a lighter hand. The date of the fragment is March 2, 1884.*

```
Of                    Sunday —

         Second        of        March ,

         and      the       Crow ,              when
injury
         and     Snow         high

                                                passed
         as       the      Spire ,

         and          scarlet         it

too   Expectations            of

         things      that      never

         come  ,      because          know it
innocent
         forever        here —

      "  The       Twilight      says

         to     the       Turret

         if    you      want

         an      Existence            To
```

Emily Dickinson did not stop writing in 1864; rather, she stopped writing *books*. In the final decade of her life, sometimes called the "late prolific period," Dickinson abandoned even the minimal bibliographical apparatus of the fascicles, along with their dialectical structure, to explore a language as free in practice as in theory and to induce the unbinding of the scriptural economy. "Strange," as Rilke wrote in *The*

Duino Elegies, "to see meanings that clung together once, floating away / in every direction." In the 1870s and 1880s the leaves of the folios lie scattered: the end of linearity is signaled not in their apparent disorder but, rather, in their apprehension of multiple or contingent orders. No longer marking a place in a book, the loose leaves of stationery and scraps of paper are risked to still wilder forms of circulation: "Joy and Gravitation have their own ways."

As Susan Howe and others have pointed out, the signs of a fundamental ambivalence toward synthesis and closure that culminated in the scattering of manuscript leaves in the last decade of Dickinson's life are present in her work almost from its inception. Around 1860 the first variant word lists appear along the fringes of Dickinson's poems like an alien voicing, disturbing set borders and summoning into the work [again quoting Cameron] the "spell of difference." Here "the desire for limit" gives way before "the difficulty in enforcing it." Thus, Emily Dickinson's manuscript books— and here I refer not to Franklin's twentieth-century reconstructions but to the packets themselves—define a boundary that is also a threshold at "the austere reach of the book." [See Susan Howe's *The Birth-mark.*] Beyond this threshold, itself an unstable one, lie the rough and fair copy drafts of poems composed after Dickinson ceased binding her work into volumes, the letters she wrote over the course of a lifetime, and, most problematically of all, a large number of extrageneric materials—now generally labeled prose fragments and drafts—written after 1870 and left in various stages of composition and crisis at the time of her death. These writings belong to a forgotten canon. . . .

There can never be an authorized edition of Dickinson's writings. The gold imprimatur—emblem or face of Harvard's authority stamped across the blue binding of Johnson's *Letters* (1958)—is a false witness: like displaced enunciations, the drafts and fragments escape from the plot of "pure scholarship" to reappear always outside the *texte propre* and the law of the censor. . . . Today editing Emily Dickinson's late writings paradoxically involves unediting them, constellating these works not as still points of meaning or as incorruptible texts but, rather, as *events* and phenomena of freedom.

CHAPTER 3

Dickinson's Poetic Themes

READINGS ON
EMILY DICKINSON

Dickinson's Poems Lack Essential Elements

R.P. Blackmur

R.P. Blackmur is considered one of the twentieth century's leading literary critics. In this excerpt from his 1937 essay "Emily Dickinson: Notes on Prejudice and Fact," Blackmur explains why he considers some of Dickinson's poems good but few, if any, great.

Like T.S. Eliot, Ezra Pound, and others associated with New Criticism (a still-influential literary movement that attempts to isolate individual works of literature from a writer's personal, cultural, or historical influences), Blackmur evaluates Dickinson's poems largely on the basis of the poet's adherence to certain formal conventions. Examples of such conventions are consistent use of imagery and metaphor, a logical progression of ideas toward one main theme, and precision of language, including word order.

Though Blackmur finds Dickinson's poems lacking in the essential classic elements, he does find them rich in insight, honesty, and originality, a series of happy "accidents" that helps explain the poet's appeal.

Over two-thirds of Emily Dickinson's nine hundred odd printed poems are exercises, and no more, some in the direction of poetry, and some not. The object is usually in view, though some of the poems are but exercises in pursuit of an unknown object, but the means of attainment are variously absent, used in error, or ill-chosen. The only weapon constantly in use is . . . the natural aptitude for language; and it is hardly surprising to find that that weapon, used alone and against great odds, should occasionally produce an air of frantic strain instead of strength, of conspicuous

From R.P. Blackmur, "Emily Dickinson: Notes on Prejudice and Fact," in *Language as Gesture* by R.P. Blackmur (New York: Harcourt Brace Jovanovich, 1952). Reprinted by permission of the Estate of R.P. Blackmur.

oddity instead of indubitable rightness.

Let us take for a first example a reasonably serious poem on one of the dominant Dickinson themes, the obituary theme of the great dead—a theme to which [American novelists Nathaniel] Hawthorne and Henry James were equally addicted—and determine if we can where its failure lies.

> More life went out, when He went
> Than ordinary breath,
> Lit with a finer phosphor
> Requiring in the quench
>
> A power of renownéd cold—
> The climate of the grave
> A temperature just adequate
> So anthracite to live.
>
> For some an ampler zero,
> A frost more needle keen
> Is necessary to reduce
> The Ethiop within.
>
> Others extinguish easier—
> A gnat's minutest fan
> Sufficient to obliterate
> A tract of citizen.

The first thing to notice—a thing characteristic of exercises—is that the order or plot of the elements of the poem is not that of a complete poem; the movement of the parts is downward and toward a disintegration of the effect wanted. A good poem so constitutes its parts as at once to contain them and to deliver or release by the psychological force of their sequence the full effect only when the poem is done. Here the last quatrain is obviously wrongly placed; it comes like an afterthought, put in to explain why the third stanza was good. It should have preceded the third stanza, and perhaps with the third stanza—both of course in revised form—might have come at the very beginning, or perhaps in suspension between the first and second stanzas. Such suggestions throw the poem into disorder; actually the disorder is already there. It is not the mere arrangement of stanzas that is at fault; the units in disorder are deeper in the material, perhaps in the compositional elements of the conception, perhaps in the executive elements of the image-words used to afford circulation to the poem, perhaps elsewhere in the devices not used but wanted. The point for emphasis is that it is hard to believe that a conscientious poet could have failed to see that no amount of correction and polish could raise this exercise to the condition of a mature poem. The material is all there—the inspiration and the language; what it requires is a thorough revision—a re-seeing calculated to compose in objective form the immediacy and singleness of effect which the poet no doubt herself felt.

Perhaps we may say—though the poem is not near so bad an example as many—that the uncomposed disorder is accepted by the poet because the poem was itself written automatically. To the sensitive hand and expectant ear words will arrange themselves, however gotten hold of, and seem to breed by mere contact. The brood is the meaning we catch up to. Is not this really automatic writing *tout court*? Most of the Dickinson poems seem to have been initially as near automatic writing as may be. The bulk remained automatic, subject to correction and multiplication of detail. Others, which reach intrinsic being, have been patterned, inscaped, injected one way or another with the elan or elixir of the poet's dominant attitudes. The poem presently examined remains too much in the automatic choir; the elan is there, which is why we examine it at all, but without the additional advantage of craft it fails to carry everything before it.

WORD CHOICES UNINTELLIGIBLE

The second stanza of the poem is either an example of automatic writing unrelieved, or is an example of bad editing, or both. Its only meaning is in the frantic strain toward meaning—a strain so frantic that all responsibility toward the shapes and primary significance of words was ignored. "A temperature just adequate / So Anthracite to live" even if it were intelligible, which it is not, would be beyond bearing awkward to read. It is not bad grammar alone that works ill; words sometimes make their own grammar good on the principle of ineluctable association—when the association forces the words into meaning. Here we have [an arbitrary word choice]. The word *anthracite* is the crux of the trouble. Anthracite is coal; is hard, is black, gives heat, and has a rushing crisp sound; it has a connection with carbuncle and with a fly-borne disease of which one symptom resembles a carbuncle; it is stratified in the earth, is formed of organic matter as a consequence of enormous pressure through geologic time; etc., etc. One or several of these senses may contribute to the poem; but because the context does not denominate it, it does not appear which. My own guess is that Emily Dickinson wanted the effect of something hard and cold and perhaps black and took *anthracite* off the edge of her vocabulary largely because she liked the sound. This is another way of saying that *anthracite* is an irresponsible product of her aptitude for language. . . .

Another nice question is involved in the effect of the *order* of the verbs used to represent the point of death: *quench, reduce, extinguish, obliterate.* The question is, are not these verbs pretty nearly interchangeable? Would not any other verb of destructive action do just as well? In short, is there any word in this poem which either fits or contributes to the association at all exactly? I think not—with the single exception of "phosphor."

The burden of these observations on words will I hope have made itself plain; it is exactly the burden of the observations on the form of the whole poem. The poem is an exercise whichever way you take it: an approach to the organization of its material but by no means a complete organization. It is almost a rehearsal—a doing over of something not done—and a variation of stock intellectual elements in an effort to accomplish an adventure in feeling. The reader can determine for himself—if he can swallow . . . the anthracite . . .—how concrete and actual the adventure was made. . . .

Let us present two more examples and stop. We have the word *plush* in different poems as follows. "One would as soon assault a plush or violate a star . . . Time's consummate plush . . . A dog's belated feet like intermittent plush . . . We step like plush, we stand like snow . . . Sentences of plush." The word is on the verge of bursting with wrong meaning, and on account of the bursting, the stress with which the poet employed it, we are all prepared to accept it, and indeed do accept it, when suddenly we realize the wrongness, that "plush" was not what was meant at all, but was a substitute for it. The word has been distorted but not transformed on the page; which is to say it is not in substantial control. Yet it is impossible not to believe that to Emily Dickinson's ear it meant what it said and what could not otherwise be said.

The use of the word *purple* is another example of a word's getting out of control through the poet's failure to maintain an objective feeling of responsibility toward language. We have, in different poems, a "purple host" meaning "soldiers";

"purple territories," associated with salvation in terms of "Pizarro's shores"; "purple" meaning "dawn"; a "purple finger" probably meaning "shadow"; a purple raveling of cloud at sunset; ships of purple on seas of daffodil; the sun quenching in purple; a purple brook; purple traffic; a peacock's purple train, purple none can avoid—meaning death; no suitable purple to put on the hills; a purple tar wrecked in peace, the purple well of eternity; the purple or royal state of a corpse; the Purple of Ages; a sowing of purple seed which is inexplicable; the purple of the summer; the purple wheel of faith; day's petticoat of purple; etc., etc. Taken cumulatively, this is neither a distortion nor a transformation of sense; it is very near an obliteration of everything but a favorite sound, meaning something desirable, universal, distant, and immediate. I choose the word as an example not because it is particularly bad—it is not, it is relatively harmless—but because it is typical and happens to be easy to follow in unexpanded quotation. It is thoroughly representative of Emily Dickinson's habit of so employing certain favorite words that their discriminated meanings tend to melt into the single sentiment of self-expression. We can feel the sentiment but we have lost the meaning. The willing reader can see for himself the analogous process taking place—with slightly different final flavors—in word after word: for example in the words *dateless, pattern, compass, circumference, ecstasy, immortality, white, ruby, crescent, peninsula,* and *spice.* The meanings become the conventions of meanings, the asserted agreement that meaning is there. That is the end toward which Emily Dickinson worked, willy-nilly, in her words. If you can accept the assertion for the sake of the knack—not the craft—with which it is made you will be able to read much more of her work than if you insist on actual work done.

THREE SAVING ACCIDENTS

But there were, to repeat and to conclude, three saving accidents at work in the body of Emily Dickinson's work sufficient to redeem in fact a good many poems to the state of their original intention. There was the accident of cultural crisis, the skeptical faith and desperately experimental mood, which both released and drove the poet's sensibility to express the crisis personally. There was the accident that the poet had so great an aptitude for language that it could seldom be completely lost in the conventional formulas toward which her meditating mind ran. And there was the third accident that the merest self-expression, or the merest statement of recognition or discrimination or vision, may sometimes also be, by the rule of unanimity and a common tongue, its best objective expression.

When two or more of the accidents occur simultaneously a poem or a fragment of a poem may be contrived. . . .

> Presentiment is that long shadow on the lawn
> Indicative that suns go down;
> The notice to the startled grass
> That darkness is about to pass.

If the reader compares this poem with Andrew Marvell's classic poem "To His Coy Mistress," he will see what can be gotten out of the same theme when fully expanded. The difference is of magnitude; the magnitude depends on craft; the Dickinson poem stops, Marvell's is completed. What happens when the poem does not stop may be shown in the following example of technical and moral confusion.

> I got so I could hear his name
> Without—
> Tremendous gain!
> That stop-sensation in my soul,
> And thunder in the room.
>
> I got so l could walk across
> That angle in the floor
> Where he turned—so—and I turned how—
> And all our sinew tore.
>
> I got so I could stir the box
> In which his letters grew—
> Without that forcing in my breath
> As staples driven through.
>
> Could dimly recollect a Grace—
> I think they called it "God,"
> Renowned to ease extremity
> When formula had failed—
>
> And shape my hands petition's way—
> Tho' ignorant of word
> That Ordination utters—
> My business with the cloud.
>
> If any Power behind it be
> Not subject to despair,
> To care in some remoter way
> For so minute affair
> As misery—

Itself too vast for interrupting more,
Supremer than—
Superior to—

Nothing is more remarkable than the variety of inconsistency this effort displays. The first three stanzas are at one level of sensibility and of language and are as good verse as Emily Dickinson ever wrote. The next two stanzas are on a different and fatigued level of sensibility, are bad verse and flat language, and have only a serial connection with the first three. The last stanza, if it is a stanza, is on a still different level of sensibility and not on a recognizable level of language at all: the level of desperate inarticulateness to which no complete response can be articulated in return. One knows from the strength of the first three stanzas what might have been meant to come after and one feels like writing the poem oneself—the basest of all critical temptations. We feel that Emily Dickinson let herself go. The accidents that provided her ability here made a contrivance which was not a poem but a private mixture of first-rate verse, bad verse, and something that is not verse at all. Yet—and this is the point—this contrivance represents in epitome the whole of her work; and whatever judgment you bring upon the epitome you will, I think, be compelled to bring upon the whole.

No judgment is so persuasive as when it is disguised as a statement of facts. I think it is a fact that the failure and success of Emily Dickinson's poetry were uniformly accidental largely because of the private and eccentric nature of her relation to the business of poetry. She was neither a professional poet nor an amateur; she was a private poet who wrote indefatigably as some women cook or knit. Her gift for words and the cultural predicament of her time drove her to poetry instead of antimacassars. Neither her personal education nor the habit of her society as she knew it ever gave her the least inkling that poetry is a rational and objective art and most so when the theme is self-expression. She came, as critic Allen Tate says, at the right time for one kind of poetry: the poetry of sophisticated, eccentric vision. That is what makes her good—in a few poems and many passages representatively great. But she never undertook the great profession of controlling the means of objective expression. That is why the bulk of her verse is not representative but mere fragmentary indicative notation. The pity of it is that the document her whole work makes shows noth-

ing so much as that she had the themes, the insight, the observation, and the capacity for honesty, which had she only
known how—or only known why—would have made the
major instead of the minor fraction of her verse genuine poetry. But her dying society had no tradition by which to teach
her the one lesson she did not know by instinct.

Emily Dickinson's Vision of "Circumference"

Jane Langton

Writer Jane Langton has collaborated with artist Nancy Ekholm Burkert in an attempt to see Dickinson's poetry as part of a larger artistic circle and asserts that Dickinson's "odd" lifestyle was essential to her message as a poet.

The word *circumference*, as Dickinson used it, represented not only a philosophy of the poet's art, but a state of her "well-roundedness," a result of bold experimentation she conducted in the language of her poetry and letters. This well-roundedness may seem ironic to those who look only on the surface of Dickinson's isolated life. Though she avoided attending lectures or meetings with others, she carefully scrutinized the details of her inner life and those of the world immediately around her.

Throughout her life Emily Dickinson was conscious of gaps—between childhood and maturity, girlhood and the "translation" of marriage, the lover and the loved, "no hope" and "hope," the living and the dead, time and eternity. In her poetry there is a perpetual sense of separation, of reaching across an impassable gulf, of crossing a shaking bridge, of hammering at a door that is locked and sealed. One feels that if she could only stretch her hand across the abyss, totter to the other side of the bridge, and fling open the door, then somehow she could unite the two separated things. If only by the main strength of her two fists she could pull them together, then she could achieve her object, "circumference," a rapturous state of suspended fulfillment and perfection.

She staked her Feathers—Gained an Arc—
Debated—Rose again—

From commentary by Jane Langton in *Acts of Light: Poems by Emily Dickinson* (Boston: New York Graphic Society, 1980). Reprinted by permission of the author and Little, Brown & Company.

This time—beyond the estimate
Of Envy, or of Men—

And now, among Circumference—
Her steady Boat be seen—
At home—among the Billows—As
The Bough where she was born—

Like a bird she has described a daring arc upon the air, and this time she has completed the circle. She exists at last (whether by exaltation, or by resurrection after death) in a state of bliss called circumference. With the same reverence she uses the word "sum" as another precious totality, in which the random cluttered parts of life, as unlike as apples and oranges, as impossible as an incorruptible soul in a corruptible body, could be added together into a single whole.

But how? How to close the circle, find the sum? In spite of abysses, Alps, doors with "hasps of steel," there was a kind of circumference that was always available to her, one sum that could be achieved at will: the closed circle of a finished poem, the sum of a few perfect stanzas. In the practice of her art there was a kind of seamless perfection like that of the eternal note of the bird's song. . . .

Toward a Rounded Perfection

It was as an artist seeking this kind of rounded perfection that Emily Dickinson withdrew from society. Her solitude was imperative, but to her contemporaries it looked curious and queerly unconventional.

Thomas Wentworth Higginson first encountered it in 1869, when he sent her a bland invitation to hear him speak at the Boston Woman's Club on the Greek goddesses. "You must come down to Boston sometimes? All ladies do."

Emily must have smiled. She issued a counter-invitation, "Could it please your convenience to come so far as Amherst I should be very glad," and wrapped her remoteness about her: "I do not cross my Father's ground to any House or town."

Emily Dickinson was not like "all ladies." Lectures on the goddesses did not interest her. There was too much to do at home, too much of first importance, too much that could not be delayed. Her priorities were like those of Thoreau, who thought it not worth his while to go around the world "to count the cats in Zanzibar," who urged his readers to explore "the private sea, the Atlantic and Pacific Ocean of one's being alone." Emily Dickinson had no need to go to Boston.

There were her own interior spaces to examine:

> Soto! Explore thyself!
> Therein thyself shalt find
> The "Undiscovered Continent"
> No Settler had the Mind.

Her chamber was not a refuge of timid hiding, but a pioneering frontier, a place of adventure. Often the floor of that upstairs room became a watery deep on which she was swept out to sea—

Among the children to whom Emily Dickinson was a presence rather than an absence was [her niece] Matty, who was treated to this vivid explanation of her Aunt Emily's runaway escapes to the privacy of her own room: "She would stand looking down, one hand raised, thumb and forefinger closed on an imaginary key, and say, with a quick turn of her wrist, 'It's just a turn—and freedom, Matty!'"

HER OWN STANDARD OF MEASURE

In her lifetime Emily Dickinson's poems were generally thought too odd for public print. Odd they remain, but with the singularity of genius. Her distortions of the language are an example of her uniqueness. Her English is her own invention, a curious dialect in which parts of speech are wrenched and forced into outlandish shapes to fit a higher grammar that is hers alone. Adjectives are driven to dizzy extremes: "Admirabler Show," "The Birds jocoser sung." Almost any word can become an exotic negative: "Swerveless Tune," "Perturbless Plan." Words that don't fit are simply omitted:

> How dare I therefore, stint a faith
> On which so [much that is] vast depends—

And where common usage might call for the declarative mood, Emily Dickinson's poems often riot in a rampaging, giddy, transubstantiated subjunctive:

> Without the Snow's Tableau
> Winter, were lie—to me—
> Because I see—New Englandly—

We can see the method in her skewed syntax in a poem about the sound of the wind:

> Inheritance, it is, to us—
> Beyond the Art to Earn—
> Beyond the trait to take away
> By Robber, since the Gain
> Is gotten not of fingers—
> And inner than the Bone—

The simple adjective "inner" has been pushed into a corner where, by the lucky accident that it happens to end in "er," it seems to mean "more inner," like a comparative. Thus her use of "than" has a bizarre correctness. The phrase succeeds and the reader feels a twinge in the marrow.

A Letter to Dr. and Mrs. J.G. Holland

Dickinson's perception of life and its events as evolving in a circular manner is illustrated in this excerpt from a letter the poet sent to Dr. and Mrs. J.G. Holland in 1853. As Dickinson describes herself returning, circlelike, to the same events over and over again, the world itself begins to appear fuller and more circular to Dickinson as well. The complete letter can be found in Mabel Loomis Todd's collection Letters of Emily Dickinson.

If it wasn't for broad daylight, and cooking-stoves, and roosters, I'm afraid you would have occasion to smile at my letters often, but so sure as "this mortal" essays immortality, a crow from a neighboring farm-yard dissipates the illusion, and I am here again.

And what I mean is this—that I thought of you all last week, until the world grew rounder than it sometimes is, and I broke several dishes.

Monday, I solemnly resolved I would be *sensible*, so I wore thick shoes, and thought of Dr. Humphrey, and the Moral Law. One glimpse of *The Republican* makes me break things again—I read in it every night.

Her meter too is distinctive. At first glance it looks simple. Over and over again, three and four beats alternate in four-line quatrains:

This is my letter to the World
That never wrote to Me—
The simple News that Nature told—
With tender Majesty

In many poems two lines of three beats are followed by a line of four beats and a final line of three:

I stepped from Plank to Plank
A slow and cautious way
The Stars about my Head I felt
About my Feet the Sea.

These homely rhythms have been traced to the meters of the hymns Emily Dickinson must have sung in church, hymns like this one by Isaac Watts:

> Come, sound his Praise abroad,
> And hymns of Glory sing:
> Jehovah is the Sovereign God,
> The universal King.

She may also have studied hymn meters more carefully in her father's copy of Watts's *Christian Psalmody*. But Emily Dickinson was too original to be content for long with anyone else's rules. Sometimes she took daring liberties with the pat rhythms of the hymns, breaking the singsong meters to suit her meaning:

> Just lost, when I was saved!
> Just felt the world go by!
> Just girt me for the onset with Eternity,
> When breath blew back,
> And on the other side
> I heard recede the disappointed tide!

To Thomas Wentworth Higginson this sort of dramatic irregularity was "uncontrolled," and he reproved her "spasmodic" gait. Nor was he the only one to be put off by her lopsided rhythms and bold ways with rhyme, by lines that matched "pearl" with "bowl," "blood" with "dead," "plucking" with "morning." In her lifetime only a handful of poems by Emily Dickinson was published (all anonymously), although the newspapers and popular journals of her day regularly printed hosts of sentimental verses by less talented women. Perhaps it was because Lizzie Lincoln and Fanny Fern and Grace Greenwood and Minnie Myrtle could be trusted to make pretty twins of all their rhymes and jingle their meters more dependably. Even so august a poet as Oliver Wendell Holmes was grateful to the friend who altered his rhyming at the last minute before going to press, changing his careless matching of "gone" with "forlorn" to a tidier "gone" and "wan."

Reading the doggerel that appeared day after day, year in and year out, in the newspaper edited by Samuel Bowles, Emily must have wondered at it. Jokingly she complained to Higginson of being "the only Kangaroo among the Beauty, Sir."

She was not to be a beauty to Higginson until after her death. His lack of perception has been explained by Dickinson scholar Thomas Johnson: "He was trying to measure a cube by the rules of plane geometry."

Dickinson Acquired a Unique Understanding of Faith

Richard Wilbur

When Emily Dickinson, at age seventeen, refused to stand at a Mount Holyoke revival meeting and declare herself a Christian, she was the only one among her classmates to so refuse. Yet her poems and letters have always revealed a deeply religious nature. Distinguished poet Richard Wilbur, winner of both the Pulitzer Prize and the National Book Award, uncovers a logic to the unorthodox beliefs of a writer who wrote much about both faith and hypocrisy.

The poems of Emily Dickinson are a continual appeal to experience, motivated by an arrogant passion for the truth. "Truth is so rare a thing," she once said, "it is delightful to tell." And, sending some poems to Colonel Higginson, she wrote, "Excuse them, if they are untrue." And again, to the same correspondent, she observed, "Candor is the only wile"—meaning that the writer's bag of tricks need contain one trick only, the trick of being honest. That her taste for truth involved a regard for objective fact need not be argued: we have her poem on the snake, and that on the hummingbird, and they are small masterpieces of exact description. She liked accuracy; she liked solid and homely detail; and even in her most exalted poems we are surprised and reassured by buckets, shawls, or buzzing flies.

But her chief truthfulness lay in her insistence on discovering the facts of her inner experience. She was a Linnaeus to the phenomena of her own consciousness, describing and distinguishing the states and motions of her soul. The results of this "psychic reconnaissance," as [critic George F.] Whicher called it, were several. For one thing, it made her articulate about inward matters which poetry had never so

Excerpted from "Sumptuous Destitution" by Richard Wilbur, in *Emily Dickinson: Three Views* (Amherst, MA: Amherst College Press, 1960). Reprinted by permission of Amherst College Press.

sharply defined; specifically, it made her capable of writing two such lines as these:

A perfect, paralyzing bliss
Contented as despair.

We often assent to the shock of a paradox before we understand it, but those lines are so just and so concentrated as to explode their meaning instantly in the mind. They did not come so easily, I think, to Emily Dickinson. Unless I guess wrongly as to chronology, such lines were the fruit of long poetic research; the poet had worked toward them through much study of the way certain emotions can usurp consciousness entirely, annulling our sense of past and future, cancelling near and far, converting all time and space to a joyous or grievous here and now. It is in their ways of annihilating time and space that bliss and despair are comparable.

Which leads me to a second consequence of Emily Dickinson's self-analysis. It is one thing to assert as pious doctrine that the soul has power, with God's grace, to master circumstance. It is another thing to find out personally, as Emily Dickinson did in writing her psychological poems, that the aspect of the world is in no way constant, that the power of external things depends on our state of mind, that the soul selects its own society and may, if granted strength to do so, select a superior order and scope of consciousness which will render it finally invulnerable. She learned these things by witnessing her own courageous spirit.

THREE MAIN PRIVATIONS

Another result of Emily Dickinson's introspection was that she discovered some grounds, in the nature of her soul and its affections, for a personal conception of such ideas as Heaven and Immortality, and so managed a precarious convergence between her inner experience and her religious inheritance. What I want to attempt now is a rough sketch of the imaginative logic by which she did this. I had better say before I start that I shall often seem demonstrably wrong, because Emily Dickinson, like many poets, was consistent in her concerns but inconsistent in her attitudes. The following, therefore, is merely an opinion as to her main drift.

Emily Dickinson never lets us forget for very long that in some respects life gave her short measure; and indeed it is possible to see the greater part of her poetry as an effort to cope with her sense of privation. I think that for her there

were three major privations: she was deprived of an orthodox and steady religious faith; she was deprived of love; she
was deprived of literary recognition.

At the age of 17, after a series of revival meetings at Mount
Holyoke Seminary, Emily Dickinson found that she must
refuse to become a professing Christian. To some modern
minds this may seem to have been a sensible and necessary
step; and surely it was a step toward becoming such a poet
as she became. But for her, no pleasure in her own integrity
could then eradicate the feeling that she had betrayed a deficiency, a want of grace. In her letters to Abiah Root she
tells of the enhancing effect of conversion on her fellow-
students, and says of herself in a famous passage:

> *I* am one of the lingering bad ones, and so do I slink away,
> and pause and ponder, and ponder and pause, and do work
> without knowing why, not surely, for this brief world, and
> more sure it is not for heaven, and I ask what this message
> *means* that they ask for so very eagerly: *you* know of this
> depth and fulness, will you try to tell me about it?

There is humor in that, and stubbornness, and a bit of
characteristic lurking pride: but there is also an anguished
sense of having separated herself, through some dry inca-
pacity, from spiritual community, from purpose, and from
magnitude of life. As a child of evangelical Amherst, she inevitably thought of purposive, heroic life as requiring a vigorous faith. Out of such a thought she later wrote:

> The abdication of Belief
> Makes the Behavior small—
> Better an ignis fatuus
> Than no illume at all—

That hers was a species of religious personality goes
without saying; but by her refusal of such ideas as original
sin, redemption, hell, and election, she made it impossible
for herself—as Whicher observed—"to share the religious
life of her generation." She became an unsteady congregation of one.

Her second privation, the privation of love, is one with
which her poems and her biographies have made us exceedingly familiar, though some biographical facts remain
conjectural. She had the good fortune, at least once, to bestow her heart on another; but she seems to have found her
life, in great part, a history of loneliness, separation, and
bereavement.

As for literary fame, some will deny that Emily Dickinson ever greatly desired it, and certainly there is evidence mostly from her latter years, to support such a view. She *did* write that "Publication is the auction/ Of the mind of man." And she *did* say to Helen Hunt Jackson, "How can you print a piece of your soul?" But earlier, in 1861, she had frankly expressed to Sue Dickinson the hope that "sometime" she might make her kinfolk proud of her. The truth is, I think, that Emily Dickinson knew she was good, and began her career with a normal appetite for recognition. I think that she later came, with some reason, to despair of being understood or properly valued, and so directed against her hopes of fame what was by then a well-developed disposition to renounce. That she wrote a good number of poems about fame supports my view: the subjects to which a poet returns are those which vex him.

DISTANT DESIRES CREATE INTENSE LONGINGS

What did Emily Dickinson do, as a poet, with her sense of privation? . . .

[She] elected the economy of desire, and called her privation good, rendering it positive by renunciation. And so she came to live in a huge world of delectable distances. Far-off words like "Brazil" or "Circassian" appear continually in her poems as symbols or things distanced by loss or renunciation, yet infinitely prized and yearned-for. So identified in her mind are distance and delight that, when ravished by the sight of a hummingbird in her garden, she calls it "the mail from Tunis." And not only are the objects of her desire distant; they are also very often moving away, their sweetness increasing in proportion to their remoteness. "To disappear enhances," one of the poems begins, and another closes with these lines:

> The Mountain—at a given distance—
> In Amber—lies—
> Approached—the Amber flits—a little—
> And That's—the Skies—

To the eye of desire, all things are seen in a profound perspective, either moving or gesturing toward the vanishing-point. Or to use a figure which may be closer to Miss Dickinson's thought, to the eye of desire the world is a centrifuge, in which all things are straining or flying toward the occult circumference. In some such way, Emily Dickinson conceived her world, and it was in a spatial metaphor that she gave her personal definition of Heaven. "Heaven," she said, "is what I cannot reach."

At times it seems that there is nothing in her world but her own soul, with its attendant abstraction, and, at a vast remove, the inscrutable Heaven. On most of what might intervene she has closed the valves of her attention, and what mortal objects she does acknowledge are riddled by desire to the point of transparency. Here is a sentence from her correspondence: "Enough is of so vast a sweetness, I suppose it never occurs, only pathetic counterfeits." The writer of that sentence could not invest her longings in any finite object. Again she wrote, "Emblem is immeasurable—that is why it is better than fulfillment, which can be drained." For such a sensibility, it was natural and necessary that things be touched with infinity. Therefore her nature poetry, when most serious, does not play descriptively with birds or flowers but presents us repeatedly with dawn, noon, and sunset, those grand ceremonial moments of the day which argue the splendor of Paradise. Or it shows us the ordinary landscape transformed by the electric brilliance of a storm; or it shows us the fields succumbing to the annual mystery of death. In her love-poems, Emily Dickinson was at first covetous of the [unnamed] beloved himself; indeed, she could be idolatrous, going so far as to say that his face, should she see it again in Heaven, would eclipse the face of Jesus. But in what I take to be her later work the beloved's lineaments, which were never very distinct, vanish entirely; he becomes pure emblem, a symbol of remote spiritual joy, and so is all but absorbed into the idea of Heaven. The lost beloved is, as one poem declares, "infinite when gone," and in such lines as the following we are aware of him mainly as an instrument in the poet's commerce with the beyond.

Of all the Souls that stand create—
I have elected—One—
When Sense from Spirit—flies away—
And Subterfuge—is done—
When that which is—and that which was—
Apart—intrinsic—stand—
And this brief Tragedy of Flesh—
Is shifted—like a Sand—
When Figures show their royal Front—
And Mists—are carved away,
Behold the Atom—I preferred—
To all the lists of Clay!

RENUNCIATION LEADS TO DIVINE HAPPINESS

... One psychic experience which she interpreted as beatitude was "glee," or as some would call it, euphoria. Now a notable thing about glee or euphoria is its gratuitousness. It seems to come from nowhere, and it was this apparent sourcelessness of the emotion from which Emily Dickinson made her inference. "The 'happiness' without a cause," she said, "is the best happiness, for glee intuitive and lasting is the gift of God." Having foregone all earthly causes of happiness, she could only explain her glee, when it came, as a divine gift—a compensation in joy for what she had renounced in satisfaction, and a foretaste of the mood of Heaven. The experience of glee, as she records it, is boundless: all distances collapse, and the soul expands to the very circumference of things. Here is how she put it in one of her letters: "Abroad is close tonight and I have but to lift my hands to touch the 'Hights of Abraham.'" And one of her gleeful poems begins,

'Tis little—I could care for Pearls—
Who own the ample sea—

How often she felt that way we cannot know, and it hardly matters. As Robert Frost has pointed out, happiness can make up in height for what it lacks in length; and the important thing for us, as for her, is that she construed the experience as a divine gift. So also she thought of the power to write poetry, a power which, as we know, came to her often; and poetry must have been the chief source of her sense of blessedness. The poetic impulses which visited her seemed "bulletins from Immortality," and by their means she converted all her losses into gains, and all the pains of her life to that clarity and repose which were to her the qualities of Heaven.

Emily Dickinson's Feminist Humor

Suzanne Juhasz, Christanne Miller,
and Martha Nell Smith

Her humor often underestimated by critics and biographers, Emily Dickinson is usually portrayed as a tragic figure haunted by personal demons. But though her poems deal with serious personal issues, they show a public awareness that is often displayed with humor.

In her animal poems, for example, nonhuman characters amplify various social roles, a technique that not only precedes that of American poet Ogden Nash by nearly a hundred years but shows that she is deeply aware of her own limited social role, as well.

In their book *The Comic Power in Emily Dickinson,* from which this excerpt is taken, Suzanne Juhasz, Christanne Miller, and Martha Nell Smith argue that Dickinson's political humor is best appreciated in light of her perspective as a white, middle-class woman keenly aware of the expectations placed on a woman writer in her era.

Although Emily Dickinson was a noted wit in her circle of friends and family, and although her poetry is surely clever, frequently downright funny, and, as we shall argue, throughout possessed of a significant comic vision, criticism has paid little attention to her humor. Dickinson's profound scrutiny of life-and-death matters has usually taken precedence in the analysis and evaluation of her work. Yet comedy is a part of that profundity, and this volume brings the comic aspects of her vision to center stage for the first time. It is no coincidence that feminist critics have chosen this subject, for comedy is aligned with subversive and disruptive modes that offer alternative perspectives on culture. But even as it is a cliché in American social politics that "feminists have no sense of humor," so the comedy specifically associated with women's critique of patriarchy is often overlooked.

A feminist critical approach to Dickinson's comedy reveals a poet whose topic and audience are larger than herself. It shows how Dickinson critiques the established culture through language forms that stress their status as performance and demand the participation of an audience. In particular, focusing on comedy highlights her responses as a nineteenth-century upper-middle-class woman to situations in which she is both attracted to and angered by patriarchal power, situations in which she critiques contemporary institutions, and situations in which she feels suffocated by social conventions. Through formal elements of voice, image, and narrative, Dickinson teases, mocks, even outrages her audience in ways that are akin both to the gestures of traditional comedy and to specifically feminist humor. In short, Dickinson's comedy is not contained by poems that are obviously funny but pervades her writing to offer a transforming vision of the world.

Dickinson the tragedienne, however, has by now received so much press that this role has become a norm in critical representations of her, in feminist as well as traditional readings. George Whicher, setting the tone for contemporary receptions of Dickinson, writes in 1938, "by mastery of her suffering she won a sanity that could make even grief a plaything." Thus, this critical story goes, Dickinson is a heroine *because* she suffered so, and because she gave us great poetry out of this suffering. Not all subsequent critics have been so charitable about the triumph of her fragile sanity, but most agree that her despair and desolation are the crucible in which her poetry is forged. Whicher proposes a compensatory, even therapeutic theory for Dickinson's poetry:

> In projecting her intensest feelings on paper she was finding a form of relief in action; she was, in Emerson's phrase, "grinding into paint" her burden of despair. So she was enabled to fulfill the prescript of her generation for utter rectitude of conduct, which for her meant the stifling of hopes, and yet keep the bitter waters from stagnating in her breast. Though her mental balance was unsteady for some years to come, she achieved and held it.

Such an approach makes the relation of art to biography a closed circuit. There is no audience; or, more properly, the poet's audience is herself. Life experiences govern the experience that is the poem, mediated only in that the poem is seen not simply to describe but to offer a degree of control over them. Without reference, then, to the performance aspect of the literary act, that is, to the complex function of any poem, such critics end by simplifying not only the affective purpose of the poem but its content as well.

ONE READER'S COMIC RESPONSE

This anonymous limerick was found in an old publication and reprinted in Dickinson Studies #78: Emily Dickinson in Public.

> There once was a poet named Emily
> who lived in the heart of her family.
> She never went out
> but lived without doubt
> on metaphor, symbol and simile.

As we might expect, critics who focus on the direct link between biography and poetry are especially prone to emphasize the tragic elements of Dickinson's art. To take three important examples in more recent criticism, John Cody, Paula Bennett, and Vivian Pollak—for all of their ideological differences and notwithstanding the forty-years' span their works cover—have reinforced a sense of Dickinson as tragic heroine. . . .

ROLE OF THE AUDIENCE DIMINISHED

We do not argue here that there are no tragic elements in Dickinson's life or art. We take issue, however, with the totality or one-dimensionality of the position. It edits out the wry, the witty, the playful, the tough, the challenging, the successful Dickinson. Moreover, it takes Dickinson all too literally, ignoring her own directives about reading and writing: "Tell all the Truth but tell it slant—/ Success in Circuit lies." Telling it slant implies the participation in the poetic act of voice, gesture, posture, attitude, and style. It implies, in other words, the necessity of performance, so that the poem cannot be seen as *simply* the compulsive outpouring of powerful feelings. Life experience—all the Truth—has been crafted and shaped for some purpose, and a corollary to the fact that the words are performed is that some audience is anticipated. The poem's affective purpose has to do with a reader as well as with the poet herself.

Comedy becomes possible in a poetics of this kind. To begin with, comedy stresses the role of the audience and its response to the joke. Additionally, comedy implies commentary: the comedienne's art is always slant, never wholly caught up in a feeling or a situation. From this perspective we can see how Dickinson critiques her subject as much as she embodies it. Comedy implies, as well, winning rather than losing, the affirmation of life rather than its destruction. These elements do exist in Dickinson's poetry, and taking her slant, or allowing for her comic perspective, enables us to experience them. . . .

The extent to which one *finds* Dickinson funny, or feminist, depends on several factors. First, because much of Dickinson's comic vision stems from her gender consciousness, it is difficult to separate that consciousness, or her feminism, from her humor. To appreciate the full range of Dickinson's humor, one must be able to conceive of her as a sharp critic of her world, as a self-conscious writer identifying with (at least white middle-class) women's experience as a basis for social criticism, and as a crafter of multiple levels of intention in her poems. In contrast, to the extent that one envisions this poet as unconscious of her self and her craft, or as a victim suffering under tyrannical parents, patriarchy generally, or her own neuroses, one will not find humor in her poems. . . .

POEMS SHOW AWARENESS IN EXAGGERATION

In "I'm Nobody! Who are you?" for example, the speaker coyly introduces herself as charmingly unimportant. Here the poet mocks the pretensions of the public world by imagining public figures as loud bullfrogs and herself as someone unrecognizable to the crowd

> I'm Nobody! Who are you?
> Are you—Nobody—Too?
> Then there's a pair of us!
> Don't tell! they'd advertise—you know!
>
> How dreary—to be—Somebody!
> How public—like a Frog—
> To tell one's name—the livelong June—
> To an admiring Bog!

The audience who would appreciate one's announcement of

self-importance has the character of a swamp, something one sinks in, not something with an opinion to be respected. Similarly, being "Somebody" in the terms of this poem constitutes self-advertisement (telling one's own name) or allowing others to "advertise" for you—that is, identity in this context is a result of staged marketing rather than of production or worth. Any person of reasonable modesty, the poet implies, would rather be hiding out with her, another "Nobody," free from the "Bog." The apparent lack of guile in the speaker's opening playfully conspiratorial tone slides into pointed—but still apparently playful—social observation, as she rhymes "Frog" with "Bog" to describe the "Somebod[ies]" and the audience she scorns. Cuteness allows the speaker to satirize her subject sharply yet keep her charm.

"She sights a Bird—she chuckles—" contains similarly accessible comedy with the light ironic twist familiar in Dickinson's simplest comic poems.

> She sights a Bird—she chuckles—
> She flattens—then she crawls—
> She runs without the look of feet—
> Her eyes increase to Balls—
>
> Her Jaws stir—twitching—hungry—
> Her Teeth can hardly stand—
> She leaps, but Robin leaped the first—
> Ah, Pussy, of the Sand,
>
> The Hopes so juicy ripening—
> You almost bathed your Tongue—
> When Bliss disclosed a hundred Toes—
> And fled with every one—

In the first two stanzas, this marvelous portrait of the pouncing cat has the structure of comic suspense. The cat's motions, while described realistically enough to be immediately recognizable, exaggerate each of her movements so that the "Pussy" is cartoon-like, a figure that epitomizes hungry cat-ness. Then, with "Ah, Pussy, of the Sand," the narrative turns to provide a second and more speculative type of humor. The poet here redescribes the event in more abstract and metaphorical terms, thereby making it a kind of parable of the failed attempt to gain a prize. Rather than moralizing, however, Dickinson maintains the comic tone through her continued exaggeration, and by animating Hopes and Bliss. Just as you "almost bathe" your panting, salivating "Tongue"—the ultimate sign of animal desire—

"Bliss" reveals its extraordinary mobility: it "disclose[s] a hundred Toes," "every one" carrying it safely away. Here is a comic primal scene for all failure to procure "Bliss."

As both poems above indicate, animals play major roles in Dickinson's funny poems, which often function as fables that comment on human foibles by means of the poems' furred or winged subjects. The clever jingly rhymes of many of these ditties proclaim them true forerunners of Ogden Nash.

> The butterfly obtains
> But little sympathy
> Though favorably mentioned
> In Etymology—
>
> Because he travels freely
> And wears a proper coat
> The circumspect are certain
> That he is dissolute—
>
> Had he the homely scutcheon
> Of modest Industry
> 'Twere fitter certifying
> For Immortality—

This poem opposes the New England Protestant work ethic with the sly notion that nature has more liberal values for its denizens. The butterfly, a kind of playboy of the Western skies, not only has fun but looks good—both qualities destined to make him the subject of much headshaking from the good citizens of the kind of town that Dickinson knew all too well. However, in this poem, the butterfly emerges triumphant—a candidate for Immortality by means of Etymology if not Industry. The play with all those multisyllabic rhyme words—*sympathy* with *Etymology, coat* with *dissolute,* and *Industry* with *Immortality*—points both to the highminded seriousness of the town's morality and also to a means by which others outside of the system might mock it.

Dickinson writes about despised as well as admired creatures:

> A Rat surrendered here
> A brief career of Cheer
> And Fraud and Fear.
>
> Of Ignominy's due
> Let all addicted to
> Beware.
>
> The most obliging Trap
> It's tendency to snap
> Cannot resist—

Temptation is the Friend
Repugnantly resigned
At last.

If the butterfly poem questions a too-simplistic morality, this
one takes an alternative stance, interrogating an equally
prevalent tendency to admire the charming rogue. Not, however, because crime doesn't pay, but because, more profoundly, the excessive egotism it engenders is in the end
self-defeating. The Rat, although quite properly caught, is a
comic character throughout his drama because of his anar-
chic bravado. The jaunty meter and playful rhymes charac-
terize him as a cocky blend of Cheer and Fraud and Fear. His
problem, however, is in thinking himself bigger than his
(nonexistent) britches. There is more to the world than oneself. Rats may swagger, but traps will snap. So be it.

Naming as a Strategy in Dickinson's Poems

Sharon Cameron

Dickinson defines internal emotions as well as she describes external events. Through use of metaphor and imagistic language, the poet gives name to a specific feeling—a particular pain, for instance—as the word is experienced not in a variety of circumstances and with varying levels of intensity, but as a feeling that is specific, recognizable: "Pain—has an Element of Blank—".

Often complex, Dickinson's methods of definition present some problems for author Sharon Cameron. Because Dickinson's poems often begin with the definition rather than end with it, Cameron argues that the naming lacks the finality of the last word and leaves the reader to question its exactness. This excerpt is from Cameron's influential study *Lyric Time: Dickinson and the Limits of Genre.*

For Emily Dickinson, perhaps no more so than for the rest of us, there was a powerful discrepancy between what was "inner than the Bone—" and what could be acknowledged. To the extent that her poems are a response to that discrepancy—are, on the one hand, a defiant attempt to deny that the discrepancy poses a problem and, on the other, an admission of defeat at the problem's enormity—they have much to teach us about the way in which language articulates our life. There is indeed a sense in which these poems test the limits of what we might reveal if we tried, and also of what, despite our exertions, will not give itself over to utterance. The question of the visibility of interior experience is one that will concern me in this chapter, for it lies at the heart of what Dickinson makes present to us. In "The Dream of Communication," Geoffrey Hartman writes, "Art 'repre-

Excerpted from *Lyric Time: Dickinson and the Limits of Genre* by Sharon Cameron. Copyright ©1979 by The Johns Hopkins University Press. Reprinted by permission of The Johns Hopkins University Press.

sents' a self which is either insufficiently 'present' or feels it-self as not 'presentable.'" On both counts one thinks of Dickinson, for her poems disassemble the body in order to penetrate to the places where feelings lie, as if hidden, and they tell us that bodies are not barriers the way we sometimes think they are. Despite the staggering sophistication with which we discuss complex issues, like Dickinson, we have few words, if any, for what happens inside us. Perhaps this is because we have been taught to conceive of ourselves as perfectly inexplicable or, if explicable, then requiring the aid of someone else to scrutinize what we are explicating, to validate it. We have been taught that we cannot see for ourselves—this despite the current emphasis on [self-analysis]. But Dickinson tells us that we can see. More important, she tells us how to name what we see. . . .

Naming Pain

The most excruciating interior experience, and perhaps the most inherently nameless, is that of pain. If we leave aside for a moment, though it is hardly an irrelevant consideration, the fact that pain is private, not sharable, we see that Dickinson also insists its torture is a consequence of the ways in which it distorts perception. Again and again, she tells us that pain is atemporal and hence dislocating. It jars one's ordinary sense of oneself and the relation of that self to the world:

> Pain—expands the Time—
> Ages coil within
> The minute Circumference
> Of a single Brain—
> . . . .

And it is dogged:

> It struck me—every Day—
> The Lightning was as new
> As if the Cloud that instant slit
> And let the Fire through—
>
> It burned Me—in the Night—
> It Blistered to My Dream—
> It sickened fresh upon my sight—
> With every Morn that came—
>
> I thought that Storm—was brief—
> The Maddest—quickest by—
> But Nature lost the Date of This—
> And left it in the Sky—

In consequence, the self suffers separation from its own experience:

> . . . .
> And Something's odd—within—
> The person that I was—
> And this One—do not feel the same—
> Could it be Madness—this?

The experience of the self perceived as other is a central occurrence in Dickinson's poetry, a kind of ritual enactment her speakers survive to tell about. She had called madness "The yawning Consciousness" and spoke of "a Cleaving in my Mind—/As if my Brain had split—". . .

What she needed to survive such experiences was "Pyramidal Nerve," for she knew: "Power is only Pain—/Stranded, thro' Discipline." This discipline had naming at its heart, for names specify relationships that have been lost, forgotten, or hitherto unperceived. Dickinson knew, moreover, that the power of names was in part a consequence of their ability to effect a reconciliation between a self and that aspect of it which had been rendered alien. Names were a way of remembering and accepting ownership of something that, by forgetting or refusing to know, one had previously repudiated. Metaphor, then, is a response to pain in that it closes the gap between feeling and one's identification of it. Metaphoric names are restorative in nature in that they bring one back to one's senses by acknowledging that what has been perceived by them can be familiarized through language.

But names are social as well as personal strategies. As Kenneth Burke suggests, a work of art "singles out a pattern of experience that is sufficiently representative of our social structure, that recurs sufficiently . . . for people to 'need a word for it' and to adopt an attitude toward it. Each work of art is the addition of a word to an informal dictionary." While in some respects metaphor and analogy are a last resort, they are also often all we have. In lieu of direct names we improvise or we do without. Such improvisation of course has rules, since language is in the public domain and what we have to work with is a vocabulary that is, more than one might suspect, "given." Thus, finding new names for interior experience is an ambivalent process, for on the one hand by the very insistence upon its necessity, the invention of a new name defies the social matrix. On the other hand, since articulation is a matter of social coherence, it must make reference to that matrix. Hence, naming is in need of precisely that thing which it deems inadequate.

SOME PROBLEMS WITH DICKINSON'S POETRY OF DEFINITION

Up to this point I have spoken about naming as an act that performs a function both social and personal, and I have gone so far as to make hyperbolic claims for its efficacy. But there are problems with naming in Dickinson's poetry. The names Dickinson gives us for experiences are frequently the most striking aspect of her poetry, and they occur often, as one might expect, in poems of definition. The problem they ask us to consider is precisely their relationship to the context in which they occur. Definitions in Dickinson's poems take two forms. The first group of statements contain the copula as the main verb, and their linguistic structure is some variation of the nominative plus the verb "to be" plus the rest of the predicate. The characteristics of the predicate are transferred to the nominative, and this transference becomes a fundamental aspect of the figurative language, as the following examples indicate:

> God is a distant—stately Lover—
> Mirth is the Mail of Anguish—
> Crisis is a Hair/Toward which forces creep
> The Lightning is a yellow Fork/From Tables in the sky
> Safe Despair it is that raves—/Agony is frugal.
> Water, is taught by thirst.
> Utmost is relative—/Have not or Have/Adjacent sums
> Faith—is the Pierless Bridge
> Drama's Vitallest Expression is the Common Day

The previous assertions are global in nature, encapsulating the totality or whole of the subject under scrutiny. The following group of assertions attempt to establish a single aspect or identic property of the thing being defined:

> A South Wind—has a pathos/Of individual Voice—
> Pain—has an Element of Blank—
> Remembrance has a Rear and Front—

Or they personify characteristic actions and attributes of the subject under consideration, distinguishing and so defining them:

> The Heart asks Pleasure—first—
> Absence disembodies—so does Death
> The Admirations—and Contempts—of time—/Show justest—
>   through an Open Tomb—

Many of these assertions are frankly aphoristic:

> A Charm invests a face/Imperfectly beheld—
> Perception of an object costs/Precise the Object's loss—

for in both groups, feeling and experience are abstracted from the context that prompted them, and from temporal considerations; the words are uttered in the third person present tense and may lack definite and indefinite articles, all of these strategies contributing to the speaker's authority, as they make a claim to experiential truth that transcends the limitations of personal experience. The distinctions between the two groups may seem to exist more in formulation than in function. Nonetheless, given a range of utterance, the former assertions lie at the epigrammatic extreme and occur with more frequency in the poems (it is thus with them that I shall be most concerned); the latter assertions, which appear with increased frequency in the letters, by their very admission of partiality, come closer to confessing their evolution from a particular incident or context.

The function of a successful formulation, one that says reality is one way and not another, is that it have no qualification; that it be the last word. The problem in many of Dickinson's poems is that it is the first word. It was Emerson who called proverbs "the literature of reason, or the statements of an absolute truth without qualification," and there is a sense in which statements like "Capacity to Terminate/Is a Specific Grace" or "Not 'Revelation'—'tis that waits/But our unfurnished eyes" preclude further statement because any statement will qualify them.

Hobbes, in *The Leviathan*, makes the following observation about names and definitions:

> Seeing then that truth consists in the right ordering of names in our affirmations, a man that seeketh precise truth had need to remember what every name he useth stands for ... or else he will find himself entangled in words, as a bird in lime-twigs.... And therefore in geometry (which is the only science which it hath pleased God hitherto to bestow on mankind), men begin at settling the significations of their words; which settling of significations they call *definitions*, and place them in the beginning of their reckoning. (part I, chapter IV)

Geometric constructions are not, however, metaphoric ones, and it is important to note that in poems such definitional knowledge is credited best when it occurs at the end of a speaker's reckoning. Perhaps this is because, unlike Hobbes, we believe that, at least in poems, definitions are neither arbitrary nor conventionally agreed-upon assignations. Wrested from experience, they imply a choice whose nature is only made manifest by its context.

But Dickinson's names and definitions not only posit themselves at the beginning of poems, they also shrug off the need for further context, for it is difficult to acknowledge the complexity of a situation while stressing its formulaic qualities—unless the point of the formulation is to reveal complexity. In fact, definitions are often predicated on the assumption that experience can be expressed summarily as one thing. The detachable quality of some of Dickinson's lines receives comment as early as 1892 when Mabel Loomis Todd writes:

> How does the idea of an "Emily Dickinson Yearbook" strike you?... My thought is that with isolated lines from the already published poems, many of which are perfect comets of thought, and some of those wonderful epigrams from the *Letters*, together with a mass of *unpublished* lines which I should take from poems which could never be used entire, I could make the most brilliant year-book ever issued.... If I do not do it, some one else will want to, because ED abounds so in epigrams—.

One of her first biographers, George Whicher, comments: "Her states of mind were not progressive but approximately simultaneous." R.P. Blackmur summarizes the situation less charitably when he speaks of Dickinson's poems as "mere fragmentary indicative notation," and in a statement cited only in part in the Introduction, he explains himself: "The first thing to notice—a thing characteristic of exercises—is that the order or plot of the elements of the poem is not that of a complete poem; the movement of the parts is downwards and towards a disintegration of the effect wanted. A good poem so constitutes its parts as at once to contain them and to deliver or release by the psychological force of their sequence the full effect only when the poem is done." For how a poem tells the time of the experience it narrates directly determines the crucial relationship between what we might distinguish as the mechanism of that poem's closure and its true completion, which would be perceived as a "natural" end even were the utterance to continue beyond. We have different modes of reference to the movement that leads to the coincidence of closure and internal completion within a given poem. We speak of a poem's progressions, of emotions if not of actions, of its building. We are thus presuming that a poem has development, a sense of its own temporal structure. When a poem remains innocent of the knowledge of an ordering temporality, the poem and its meaning are problematic.

These problems are notable at the simplest level of relationship. In essays dealing with aspects of aphasia, or language disturbance, Roman Jakobson makes a distinction between the two opposite tropes of metaphor and metonymy. Assuming that language is predicated upon modes of relation, he distinguishes between the internal relation of similarity (and contrast), which underlies metaphor, and the external relation of contiguity (and remoteness), which determines metonymy. Jakobson concludes that any verbal style shows a marked preference for either the metaphoric or metonymic device. Now Dickinson's predilection for the metonymic device is clear. That preference becomes significant when we note that Jakobson's description of a contiguity disorder (the language impairment that affects the perception of context) offers a fairly accurate picture of many of Dickinson's problematic poems. "First," he writes, "the relational words are omitted." Then:

> The syntactical rules organizing words into higher units are lost; this loss, called agrammatism, causes the degeneration of the sentence into a mere "word heap.". . . Word order becomes chaotic; the ties of grammatical coordination and subordination . . . are dissolved. As might be expected, words endowed with purely grammatical functions, like conjunctions, prepositions, pronouns, and articles, disappear first, giving rise to the so-called "telegraphic style."

Jakobson's description resonates against a similar, albeit less technical, comment on Dickinson's poems made by Louis Untermeyer: "The few lines become telegraphic and these telegrams seem not only self-addressed but written in a code." When Jakobson further explains that the type of aphasia affecting contexture tends to give rise to one-sentence utterances and one-word sentences, we recall how many of Dickinson's poems are single sentences. Again, in a less clinical assertion, Donald Thackery writes of Dickinson's "shorthand vocabulary": "One notices how many of her poems seem less concerned with a total conception than with expressing a series of staccato inspirations occurring to her in the form of individual words." In addition, Jakobson asserts that aphasics of this type make frequent use of quasi-metaphors which are based on inexact identification, and his description of that identification is reminiscent of the definitional poems about which I have been speaking. Jakobson concludes: "Since the hierarchy of linguistic units is a superposition of ever larger contexts, the contiguity disorder which affects the construction of contexts destroys this hierarchy." We recall [Dickinson critic Albert] Gelpi's words: "The very confusion of the syntax . . . forces the reader to concentrate on the basic verbal units and derive the strength and meaning largely from the circumference of words."

I have mentioned the Jakobson studies with hesitation, for it would be a mistake to assume that we could diagnose such a disorder from Dickinson's poems. Perhaps the primary reason for citing Jakobson is not to make a brash connection between disease and poetic style, but rather to query the curiosity of relationship between statements so essentially alien: literary criticism of a particular poet, and the description of a linguistic disorder. For one is obliged to note that the predilection for definitional statements, many of which are of a quasi-metaphoric nature, the frequent omission of words that perform grammatical functions, and the absence of contextual clarity bear a striking relationship to Jakobson's description of a contiguity disorder, and that his description brings together and clarifies many of the earlier critical assertions about the poems. Insofar as poetic speech is a violation of the linguistic status quo, it should come as no surprise that such speech deviates from the ordinary configurations that bear our meanings out. That the deviations take these particular forms, however, is a fact that invites interpretation even as it mystifies any summary conclusions.

Dickinson's Tone of Voice Lends Credibility to Difficult Subjects

Archibald MacLeish

Emily Dickinson wrote about death, despair, and God with great skill. As three-time Pulitzer Prize–winning poet and playwright Archibald MacLeish points out, she does so without becoming pretentious or overly sentimental. MacLeish admires the person-to-person nature of her poetry and the restraint that seems the natural voice of a New England woman.

By comparing Dickinson's poems to those of Donne, Rilke, Yeats, and Pound, MacLeish offers evidence of Dickinson's greatness and argues that, in some cases, Dickinson's achievements surpass those of the other poets.

No one can read these poems ... without perceiving that he is not so much reading as being spoken to. There is a curious energy in the words and a tone like no other most of us have ever heard. Indeed, it is the tone rather than the words that one remembers afterwards. Which is why one comes to a poem of Emily's one has never read before as to an old friend.

But what then is the tone? How does this unforgettable voice speak to us? For one thing, and most obviously, it is a wholly spontaneous tone. There is no literary assumption of posture or pose in advance. There is no sense that a subject has been chosen—that a theme is about to be developed. Occasionally, in the nature pieces, the sunset scenes, which are so numerous in the early poems, one feels the presence of the pad of water-color paper and the mixing of the tints, but when she began to write as poet, which she did, miraculously, within a few months of her beginnings as a writer, all that awkwardness disappears. Breath is drawn and there are words that will not leave you time to watch her coming to-

Archibald MacLeish, "The Private World," in *Emily Dickinson: Three Views* (Amherst, MA: Amherst College Press, 1960). Reprinted by permission of Amherst College Press.

ward you. Poem after poem—more than a hundred and fifty of them—begins with the word "I," the talker's word. She is already in the poem before she begins it, as a child is already in the adventure before he finds a word to speak of it. To put it in other terms, few poets and they among the most valued—Donne comes again to mind—have written more *dramatically* than Emily Dickinson, more in the live locutions of dramatic speech, words born living on the tongue, written as though spoken. It is almost impossible to begin one of her successful poems without finishing it. The punctuation may bewilder you. The density of the thing said may defeat your understanding. But you will read on nevertheless because you will not be able to stop. Something is being *said* to *you* and you have no choice but hear.

And this is a second characteristic of the voice—that it not only speaks but speaks to *you.* We are accustomed in our time—unhappily accustomed, I think—to the poetry of the overheard soliloquy, the poetry written by the poet to himself or to a little group of the likeminded who can be counted on in advance to "understand." Poetry of this kind can create universes when the poet is Rilke but even in Rilke there is something sealed and unventilated about the creation which sooner or later stifles the birds. The subject of poetry is the human experience and its object must therefore be humanity even in a time like ours when humanity seems to prefer to limit its knowledge of the experience of life to the life the advertisers offer it. It is no excuse to a poet that humanity will not listen. It never has listened unless it was made to— and least of all, perhaps, in those two decades of the Civil War and after in which Emily Dickinson wrote.

The materialism and vulgarity of those years were not as flagrant as the materialism and vulgarity in which we live but the indifference was greater. America was immeasurably farther from Paris, and Amherst was incomparably farther from the rest of America, and in and near Amherst there were less than a dozen people to whom Emily felt she could show her poems—and only certain poems at that. But her poems, notwithstanding, were never written to herself. The voice is never a voice over-heard. It is a voice that speaks to us almost a hundred years later with such an urgency, such an immediacy, that most of us are half in love with this girl we call by her first name, and read with scorn Colonel Higginson's description of her as a "plain, shy little person

... without a single good feature." We prefer to remember her own voice describing her eyes—"like the sherry the guest leaves in the glass."

There is nothing more paradoxical in the whole history of poetry, to my way of thinking, than Emily Dickinson's commitment of that live voice to a private box full of pages and snippets tied together with little loops of thread. Other poets have published to the general world poems capable of speaking only to themselves or to one or two beside. Emily locked away in a chest a voice which cries to all of us of our common life and love and death and fear and wonder.

A LACK OF SELF-PITY

Or rather, does *not* cry. For that is a third characteristic of this unforgettable tone: that it does not clamor at us even when its words are the words of passion or of agony. This is a New England voice—it belongs to a woman who "sees New Englandly"—and it has that New England restraint which is really a self-respect which also respects others. There is a poem of Emily's which none of us can read unmoved—which moves me, I confess, so deeply that I cannot always read it. It is a poem which, in another voice, might indeed have cried aloud, but in hers is quiet. I think it is the quietness which moves me most. It begins with these six lines:

> I can wade Grief—
> Whole Pools of it—
> I'm used to that—
> But the least push of Joy
> Breaks up my feet—
> And I tip—drunken

One has only to consider what this might have been, written otherwise by another hand—for it would have had to be another hand. Why is it not maudlin with self-pity here? Why does it truly touch the heart and the more the more it is read? Because it is impersonal? It could scarcely be more personal. Because it is oblique?—Ironic? It is as candid as agony itself. No, because there *IS* no self-pity. Because the tone which can contain "But the least push of Joy/Breaks up my feet" is incapable of self-pity. Emily is not only the actor in this poem, she is the removed observer of the action also. When we drown in self-pity we throw ourselves into ourselves and go down. But the writer of this poem is both in it and out of it: both suffers it and sees. Which is to say that she is poet.

There is another famous poem which makes the same
point:

> She bore it till the simple veins
> Traced azure on her hand—
> Till pleading, round her quiet eyes
> The purple Crayons stand.
>
> Till Daffodils had come and gone
> I cannot tell the sum,
> And then she ceased to bear it
> And with the Saints sat down.

Here again, as so often in her poems of death—and death is,
of course, her constant theme—the margin between mawk-
ishness and emotion is thin, so thin that another woman, living, as she lived, in constant contemplation of herself, might
easily have stumbled through. But here again what saves
her, and saves the poem, is the tone: "She bore it till . . ."
"And then she ceased to bear it/And with the Saints sat
down." If you have shaped your mouth to say "And with the
Saints sat down" you cannot very well weep for yourself or
for anyone else, veins purple on the hand or not.

LETTERS AND POEMS SHARE SIMILAR THEMES

*As do her poems, Dickinson's personal letters, including
many she wrote to Dr. and Mrs. J.G. Holland, reveal an intimate world that includes insects and birds and a heaven that
would be incomplete without neighbors. This excerpt can be
found in* Letters of Emily Dickinson.

I'd love to be a bird or bee, that whether hum or sing, still
might be near. . . .

Heaven is large—is it not? Life is short too, isn't it? Then
when one is done, is there not another, and—and—then if
God is willing, we are neighbors then.

Anyone who will read Emily's poems straight through in
their chronological order in Thomas H. Johnson's magnificent Harvard edition will feel, I think, as I do, that without
her extraordinary mastery of tone her achievement would
have been impossible. To write constantly of death, of grief,
of despair, of agony, of fear is almost to insure the failure of
art, for these emotions overwhelm the mind and art must
surmount experience to master it. A morbid art is an imperfect art. Poets must learn Yeats's lesson that life is tragedy but

if the tragedy turns tragic for them they will be crippled poets. Like the ancient Chinese in *Lapis Lazuli*, like our own beloved Robert Frost who has looked as long and deeply into the darkness of the world as a man well can, "their eyes, their ancient glittering eyes" must be *gay*. Emily's eyes, color of the sherry the guests leave in the glass, had that light in them:

> Dust is the only Secret—
> Death, the only One
> You cannot find out all about
> In his "native town."
>
> Nobody knew "his Father"—
> Never was a Boy—
> Hadn't any playmates,
> Or "Early history"—
>
> Industrious! Laconic!
> Punctual! Sedate!
> Bold as a Brigand!
> Stiller than a Fleet!
>
> Builds, like a Bird, too!
> Christ robs the Nest—
> Robin after Robin
> Smuggled to Rest!

Ezra Pound, in his translation of *The Women of Trachis*, has used a curiously compounded colloquialism which depends on just such locutions to make the long agony of Herakles supportable. Emily had learned the secret almost a century before.

But it is not only agony she is able to put in a supportable light by her mastery of tone. She can do the same thing with those two opposing subjects which betray so many poets: herself and God. She sees herself as small and lost and doubtless doomed—but she sees herself always, or almost always, with a saving smile which is not entirely tender:

> Two full Autumns for the Squirrel
> Bounteous prepared—
> Nature, Hads't thou not a Berry
> For thy wandering Bird?

and

> I was a Phebe—nothing more—
> A Phebe—nothing less—
> The little note that others dropt
> I fitted into place—
>
> I dwelt too low that any seek—
> Too shy, that any blame—

> A Phebe makes a little print
> Upon the Floors of Fame—

and

> A Drunkard cannot meet a Cork
> Without a Revery—
> And so encountering a Fly
> This January Day
> Jamaicas of Remembrance stir
> That send me reeling in—
> The moderate drinker of Delight
> Does not deserve the spring—

I suppose there was never a more delicate dancing on the crumbling edge of the abyss of self-pity—that suicidal temptation of the lonely—than Emily's, but she rarely tumbles in. She sees herself in the awkward stumbling attitude and laughs.

THE SUBJECT OF GOD

As she laughs too, but with a child's air of innocence, at her father's Puritan God, that Neighbor over the fence of the next life in the hymnal:

> Abraham to kill him
> Was distinctly told—
> Isaac was an Urchin—
> Abraham was old—
>
> Not a hesitation—
> Abraham complied—
> Flattered by Obeisance
> Tyranny demurred—
>
> Isaac—to his children
> Lived to tell the tale—
> Moral—with a Mastiff
> Manners may prevail.

It is a little mocking sermon which would undoubtedly have shocked Edward Dickinson with his "pure and terrible" heart, but it brings the god of Abraham closer to New England than he had been for the two centuries preceding—brings him, indeed, as close as the roaring lion in the yard: so close that he can be addressed politely by that child who always walked with Emily hand in hand:

> Lightly stepped a yellow star
> To its lofty place
> Loosed the Moon her silver hat
> From her lustral Face
> All of the Evening softly lit

As an Astral Hall
Father I observed to Heaven
You are punctual—

But more important than the confiding smile which makes
it possible to speak familiarly to the God of Elder Brewster is
the hot and fearless and wholly human anger with which
she is able to face him at the end. Other poets have confronted God in anger but few have been able to manage it
without rhetoric and posture. There is something about that
ultimate face to face which excites and embarrassing self-
consciousness in which the smaller of the two opponents
seems to strut and "beat it out even to the edge of doom." Not
so with Emily. She speaks with the laconic restraint appropriate to her country, which is New England, and herself,
which is a small, shy gentlewoman who has suffered much:

Of God we ask one favor,
That we may be forgiven—
For what, he is presumed to know—
The Crime, from us, is hidden—
Immured the whole of Life
Within a magic Prison

It is a remarkable poem and its power, indeed its possibility,
lies almost altogether in its voice, its tone. The figure of the
magic prison is beautiful in itself, but it is effective in the
poem because of the level at which the poem is spoken—the
level established by that "he is presumed to know." At another
level even the magic prison might well become pretentious.

But it is not my contention here that Emily Dickinson's
mastery of tone is merely a negative accomplishment, a kind
of lime which prepares the loam for clover. On the contrary
I should like to submit that her tone is the root itself of her
greatness. The source of poetry, as Emily knew more positively than most, is a particular awareness of the world. "It is
that," she says, meaning by "that" a poet, which "Distills
amazing sense / From ordinary Meanings," and the distilla-
tion is accomplished not by necromancy but by perception—
by the particularity of the perception—which makes what is
"ordinary meaning" to the ordinary, "amazing sense" to the
poet. The key to the poetry of any poem, therefore, is its particularity—the uniqueness of its vision of the world it sees.
In some poems the particularity can be found in the images
into which the vision is translated. In others it seems to exist
in the rhythm which carries the vision "alive into the heart."

In still others it is found in a play of mind which breaks the light of the perception like a prism. The particularity has as many forms almost as there are poets capable of the loneliness in which uniqueness is obliged to live. With Emily Dickinson it is the tone and timbre of the speaking voice. When she first wrote Colonel Higginson to send him copies of her verses she asked him to tell her if they "breathed" and the word, like all her words, was deliberately chosen. She knew, I think, what her verses were, for she knew everything that concerned her.

I should like to test my case, if I can call it that, on a short poem of four lines written probably on the third anniversary of her father's death. It is one of her greatest poems and perhaps the only poem she ever wrote which carries the curious and solemn weight of perfection. I should like you to consider wherein this perfection lies:

Lay this Laurel on the One
Too intrinsic for Renown—
Laurel—vail your deathless tree—
Him you chasten, that is He!

Play as a Theme in Dickinson's Poems

Anand Rao Thota

A native of India, Anand Rao Thota became espe-
cially interested in Emily Dickinson after hearing
Archibald MacLeish deliver a lecture on the poet at
Harvard. In his book *Emily Dickinson's Poetry*, Thota
makes comparisons between Dickinson's work and
Indian classics such as *Rig Veda.*

Though, as Thota says in his preface to his book,
he has "read all other critical studies or biographies"
of Dickinson, he tries to keep his arguments free
from their influence and to discuss his findings in
clear, everyday language.

In this essay, previously published in *Dickinson
Studies*, a scholarly journal limited to the study of
Emily Dickinson, Thota notices how often the sub-
ject of play is raised in her work.

One of the recurring words in Emily Dickinson's poems and
letters is "play," which has critical significance. Poetry, as
she affirms to Higginson, was her only "playmate": "you
asked me if I wrote now? I have no other playmate—."

Dickinson records in a playful tone scenes from nature
which were a constant source of ecstasy for her:

The Bird did prance—the Bee did play—
The Sun ran miles away

One of the most amusing compositions of Dickinson is on
the play of seasons around a mountain. The ideas and experiences are orchestrated through words that literally portray
a scene of "play" in nature:

The Mountain sat upon the Plain

Dickinson is unique in describing the play of seasons with
such an enchantment that she equates the experience with
that of a contact with "Eternity":

Indifferent Seasons doubtless play

Anand Rao Thota, "Play in Dickinson," *Dickinson Studies*, no. 46, bonus issue, 1983.

PLAY AND NATURE

Even fearful scenes of nature have their moments of play—
Dickinsonian version of DISCORDIA CONCORS, a technique which is very remote to the romantic mode and akin
to that of the metaphysicals. She succeeds through her poetry in projecting a playful mood in spite of the fact she describes an awful scene.

The Clouds their Backs together laid

This playful attitude that Dickinson succeeds in projecting through her poems is very significant because the subject described in a few poems is relegated to the background
and quite another message is conveyed. For instance, the following lines of the poem are palpably a description of "The
Lightning"; but, ultimately, they project the puritan conception of God.

The Lightning playeth—all the while—

PLAY AS A STRATEGY

This complex use of the word play by Dickinson is neither
casual nor accidental. In fact, it is a deliberate strategy
evolved to withdraw from experience in order to portray it
objectively. This is what makes Dickinson's poetry typically
unromantic. The personality that is revealed is that of a poet
who could write to her cousins just before her death a two-
word message "Called Back." She not only distanced herself
from her experiences throughout her life but also there is
factual evidence through this letter that she could withdraw
herself from the experience of her own impending death,
and make a playful comment upon it.

Quite early in her career as a poet, Dickinson cultivated
her sensibility which is replete with playful stances:
"Blessed are they that play, for theirs is the Kingdom of
Heaven." It is a remarkable way of coming to terms with life
and perhaps a "cunning" strategy to convert its experience
into art, echoing, as it does, the Bible: "cunning in playing"
(I Samuel 16:18). Dickinson acknowledges this aspect of her
life and art when she writes . . .

It is easy to work when the soul is at play—

When the experiences in life tease her "Like a Panther in the
Glove," she counters the situation by adopting a pose of play.

I play at Riches—to appease

Dickinson applies the strategy of play to reveal complex implications that her poems embody. She refers to the confrontation between God and Moses in the poem 597. The Biblical episode is introduced by playing with the idea of Moses himself, who is called "Old Moses." While dealing with the incident of the Bible, she plays down the Bible itself: "And tho' in soberer moments—/No Moses there can be/I'm satisfied—." Because, to her, it is just a "Romance." But further still in the poem the historical event of the meeting between God and Moses is stated as "tantalizing play" between two boys, tho' not of equal strength:

While God's adroiter will

On Moses—seemed to fasten
With tantalizing Play
As Boy—should deal with lesser Boy—
To prove ability.

The stark reality of "tomb" is also not outside her playful poetic grasp even in the later phase of her poetic career:

Sweet hours have perished here;
    This is a mighty room;
Within its precincts hopes have played,—
    Now shadows in the tomb.

PLAY AND MEMORY

There are scores of poems by Dickinson which center around the idea of play. The source of this play is recollection: "When Memory rings her Bell, let all Thoughts run in." Recollection does not, as in Wordsworth, flash on the "inward eye" and result, as it were, in a mystic stance: "bliss of the solitude." In Dickinson, recollection "plays" and re-enacts the life experiences with all their sound and fury, signifying not only the past experiences but also that are in store after this earthly existence.

Over and over, like a Tune—

While describing the play of recollection, Dickinson indulges in striking psychological speculation annihilating the concepts of time—of past, of present and of future. The play of recollection unites the past with the present and also anticipates the future in the present, by affording an imaginative glimpse through "Cornets of Paradise." Thus "Phantom Battlements" become the melting pot for the three aspects of time.

Studying the conditions of her life with "a Hum," Dickinson strives to present playfully her experiences through her poems that reveal all the liveliness of the situation that is being poetically worked out. She makes the process significant through a playful scrutiny of the issues that confronted her times. Dickinson was conditioned, esthetically speaking, to develop a counter-point to puritan culture which engulfed her socially. Deprived of the avenues for revolt against a superficially monolithic but internally disintegrating culture, which frowned on deviation, she withdrew herself from the culture to rise above it to record her amused observations in her letters and poems.

Dickinson's Style Broke with Convention

Cheryl Walker

While other women were publishing long, flowery reflections on love, faith, and beauty, Dickinson's poems fit the writer's complex ideas into short, tight sentences, with a vocabulary hardly considered appropriate to the feminine sensibility of her time. Aware of public expectations, Dickinson continued to write about "feminine" subjects such as unattainable love, but in a complex manner that called certain conventions into question.

In the following excerpt, scholar Cheryl Walker uses four passages by Dickinson to illustrate the genius of a woman she compares to a more compressed, more obscure Shakespeare. Walker is the author of *The Nightingale's Burden: Women Poets and American Culture Before 1900.*

[What] distinguishes Emily Dickinson from other women poets is her skill with words, her use of language. She retained her compression despite pressure from her closest friends and critics, people like Samuel Bowles and T.W. Higginson, who would have made her more discursive. She introduced unusual vocabulary into women's poetry—vocabulary borrowed from various professions mainly closed to women, like law, medicine, the military, and merchandising. I agree with critic Adrienne Rich that she knew she was a genius. Nothing else could explain her peculiar invulnerability to contemporary criticism of her work.

Dickinson wrote many poems about violation. The integrity of some poems was literally violated by editors who made unauthorized changes before printing them. But the poet triumphed in the end. She created a unique voice in American poetry and would not modulate it, even for Higginson who directed her to writers like Maria Lowell and Helen Hunt Jackson as models.

Like Lowell and Jackson, Dickinson did not look down on the female poetic subjects of her day. She used them; but she used them in what would come to be perceived as a poetic assault on the feminine conventions from which they sprung. She was not, for instance, taken in by the propaganda of "true womanhood." She saw behind the virtue of modesty the caricature of the double-bind.

> A Charm invests a face
> Imperfectly beheld—
> The Lady dare not lift her Vail
> For fear it be dispelled—
>
> But peers beyond her mesh—
> And wishes—and denies—
> Lest Interview—annul a want
> That Image—satisfies—

Perhaps Dickinson's ambivalent relation to the world has more to do with this lady "who dare not lift her Vail" than has previously been perceived. What this poem captures is the feelings of a woman who must obtain what she wants through deception and manipulation. Thus it does not simply represent the familiar Dickinson wisdom that hunger tantalizes where satiety cloys. This woman's feelings become part of the substance of the poem. They are fear (of male rejection), curiosity, and desire. The lady must finally deny her desires, sublimate her will to power, and assume a passive role. "A Charm" might also serve as a commentary on a poem written three years earlier.

> Our lives are Swiss—
> So still—so Cool—
> Till some odd afternoon
> The Alps neglect their Curtains
> And we look farther on!
>
> *Italy* stands the other side!
> While like a guard between—
> The solemn Alps—
> The siren Alps
> Forever intervene!

We recognize the theme of the unattained. . . . Here, however, the barriers both forbid assault and invite it. They are both awesome and enticing. Like the lady who "peers beyond her mesh," this speaker hasn't accepted the limitations on her experience. Though undemonstrative, she remains unreconciled.

The insights made available by the comparison of these two poems can help us even when we examine the particular language that made Dickinson unique. Take, for example, the following poem written during her most creative period.

I had not minded—Walls—
Were Universe—one Rock—
And far I heard his silver Call
The other side the Block—

I'd tunnel—till my Groove
Pushed sudden thro' to his—
Then my face take her Recompense—
The looking in his Eyes—

But 'tis a single Hair—
A filament—a law—
A Cobweb—wove in Adamant—
A Battlement—of Straw—

A limit like the Vail
Unto the Lady's face—
But every Mesh—a Citadel—
And Dragons—in the Crease—

This is a poem about the forbidden lover, and as such it reminds us of what Dickinson could do with conventional female subjects. Although this is not one of Dickinson's best poems, it exhibits many of her characteristic innovations and therefore makes an interesting focus for discussion. Does this poem have roots in real experience or was it merely an exercise?

In [a] letter, probably composed about this time and intended for a recipient we can no longer identify, the poet asked: "Couldn't Carlo [her dog], and you and I walk in the meadows an hour—and nobody care but the Bobolink—and *his*—a *silver* scruple? I used to think when I died—I could see you—so I died as fast as I could—but the 'Corporation' are going Heaven too so [Eternity] wont be sequestered—now [at all]—". Here we find the familiar impossible attachment forbidden by "the Corporation," the constituted powers. It is an attachment that can only be indulged in secret, in some "sequestered" place. This letter has too much unrefined feeling in it to be the product of a merely literary pose, and I suggest that the poem was also written out of felt experience, although the structural properties this experience assumed may well have been influenced by the vocabulary of secret sorrow.

Dickinson begins "I had not minded—Walls" in the sub-junctive, one of her characteristic modes. Thus, she establishes the initial grounds of the poem as those of the non-real, the if. The first two stanzas posit a set of circumstances that would allow for fulfillment, the enticement of the view. . . . The last two stanzas, in contrast, describe the limitations on fulfillment that forever intervene. . . .

Although the words themselves do not always mean what their sounds convey ("citadel" being used to suggest an obstacle instead of a possibility), there is at the levels of both meaning and sound a sense of opposition: desire vs. frustration. Dickinson's language operates on the basis of paired antitheses. Other pairings include the concrete vs. the abstract (face/recompense) the material vs. the immaterial (rock/silver call), and the hard vs. the soft (adamant/cobweb). Her code is conflict.

Thus far we might compare her use of language to Shakespeare's, which also depends upon doublings, paradoxes, contrasts. However, Dickinson, though she loved Shakespeare, chose to be more obscure, and she did this largely by breaking linguistic rules out of a commitment to compression. The first stanza, for instance, might be paraphrased: I would not have minded walls. Were the universe to have been entirely made up of rock and were I to have heard his call from afar, it would have seemed to me merely a short distance, the other side of the block. This, of course, reduces the impact of Dickinson's compression. "Block" in her poem affects one like a pun, reminding us of "rock" earlier, as well as of the geographical meaning of "block," a city street division.

Dickinson was criticized in her day for this kind of compression. It flew in the face of most contemporary poetry, which aimed at comprehensiveness through discursive exposition. Emerson was probably her closest friend here, but even he did not break rules as flagrantly as she. Her editors also grumbled at her rhymes. "His" and "eyes" did not seem like rhyming words to them. . . .

Furthermore, in the sequence filament/law, cobweb/adamant, and battlement/straw there is a reversal of terms in the final pair. The first two move from the insubstantial to the substantive, the last one from the substantive back to the insubstantial. "Adamant" is echoed in "battlement," but the "law" becomes "straw."

The structural progression from the real to the surreal is

recognizably characteristic of Dickinson. And here the lines, "A limit like the Vail / Unto the Lady's face," become significant. Like the veil, the limitations Dickinson describes are restrictive in the real world. The seemingly insubstantial "hair" is tougher than rock, and like the veil of restrictions women must accept, to pass beyond these limitations forces one to encounter terrible dragons. However, a citadel, the *Oxford English Dictionary* tells us, is a "fortress commanding a city, which it serves both to protect and to keep in subjugation." Like the prison, this image reminds us of Dickinson's Houdini-like ability to wriggle out of confining spaces, to convert limitations into creative resources. Dragons are at least interesting to contemplate. The lady's veil—the symbol of Dickinson's sense of social, legal, and literary restrictions—provided her with a certain recompense. Thus the reversal in the third stanza, where limiting law becomes insubstantial straw, works.

Ultimately, Emily Dickinson transformed her closed world into a creative space. If there is a disappointment in this poem, it comes in the second stanza where "the looking in his eyes" seems a rather weak way of describing this triumph. But whatever its limitations, this poem shows us the way an artist like Dickinson could make interesting use of motifs such as the secret sorrow and the forbidden lover. Her vision was "slant," and therefore to us thoroughly refreshing.

WORK SURPASSES TRADITIONAL EXPECTATIONS

Recently it has become fashionable to see Emily Dickinson as a woman who lived in the realm of transcendence, secure in the space she created for the exercise of her power. Although I am sympathetic with this view, I would like to add a word of caution. No one can read Dickinson's poems and letters in their entirety without a sense that the ground for security was forever shifting under her feet. She did not resort to references to fear only out of coyness. She felt it. She wrote: "In all the circumference of Expression, those guileless words of Adam and Eve never were surpassed, 'I was afraid and hid Myself.'" And elsewhere: "Your bond to your brother reminds me of mine to my sister—early, earnest, indissoluble. Without her life were fear, and Paradise a cowardice, except for her inciting voice." To rejoice that she found ways of evading the subjugation of the spirit that her society enforced upon its women should not mean ignoring her sense of vulnerability, which was real, which was tragic. In Dickinson's preoccupation with the imagery of royalty, we find her desire to exercise the full range of her talents; we find her will to power. In her preoccupation with falling, surrendering, confinement, and violation, we find her fears. Knowing what she had to give up, recognition within her lifetime, the chance to remain within the world she devoured information about through her friends and her newspaper, we can only be glad that at moments she had the perspective to write:

> The Heart is the Capital of the Mind—
> The Mind is a single State—
> The Heart and the Mind together make
> A single Continent—
>
> One is the Population—
> Numerous enough—
> This ecstatic Nation
> Seek—it is Yourself.

The puzzle of Emily Dickinson's work is finally not a question of the identity of [her mysterious love interest] or the extent of her real experience, but one of tradition and the individual talent. Although the concern with intense feeling, the ambivalence toward power, the fascination with death, the forbidden lover and secret sorrow all belong to this women's tradition, Emily Dickinson's best work so far surpasses anything that a logical extension of that tradition's codes could have produced that the only way to explain it is by the single word, genius. She was "of the Druid." That a great many poems like "I tie my Hat—I crease my Shawl" are in places not much above the women's poetry of her time is only to be expected. What Emily Dickinson did for later women poets, like Amy Lowell who wanted to write her biography, was remarkable: she gave them dignity. No other aspect of her influence was so important. After Emily Dickinson's work became known, women poets in America could take their work seriously. She redeemed the poetess for them, and made her a genuine poet.

CHRONOLOGY

1830

Emily Elizabeth Dickinson born December 10 in Amherst, Massachusetts.

1833

Sister Lavinia (Vinnie) born.

1842

Emily's father, Edward Dickinson, is elected state senator of Massachusetts.

1844

Religious revival in Amherst.

1845

Mexican-American War begins; Texas admitted to the Union.

1847

Emily attends Mount Holyoke Seminary for Girls.

1848

Seneca Falls Declaration marks beginning of women's rights movement.

1850

Edward Dickinson, Vinnie Dickinson, and Susan Gilbert join First Church of Christ during revival meeting in Amherst.

1852

Springfield Republican publishes Emily's valentine.

1853

Austin Dickinson, Emily's brother, enters Harvard Law School, becomes engaged to Susan.

1855

Edward and Austin become law partners.

1856

Austin joins First Church of Christ, marries Susan Gilbert; Austin and Susan move into the Evergreens, built by Edward Dickinson next door to the Homestead; Mrs. Dickinson's long illness begins.

1857

Emerson lectures in Amherst, stays with Austin and Sue.

1858

Orphaned cousins Clara and Anna Newman arrive as wards of Edward Dickinson, live with Austin and Susan at the Evergreens.

1859

Darwin's *Origin of the Species* is published.

1861

Civil War begins; first child, Edward (Ned), born to Austin and Sue; *Springfield Republican* publishes "I Taste a Liquor never brewed—"; "Evolution vs. Creationism" debated by Thomas Henry Huxley and Bishop Samuel Wilberforce.

1862

Springfield Republican publishes "Safe in their Alabaster Chambers"; Emily responds to letter asking for contributors to the *Atlantic Monthly*, beginning her correspondence with Colonel Thomas Higginson.

1863

Lincoln issues Emancipation Proclamation.

1864

Two more poems of Dickinson's printed; Emily in Boston for seven months for medical treatment for her eyes.

1865

General Lee surrenders; Lincoln assassinated.

1866

Daughter, Martha, born to Austin and Susan.

1869

Transcontinental railroad joined at Promontory Point, Utah.

1870

Emily receives visit by Thomas Wentworth Higginson.

1873

Austin elected treasurer of Amherst College.

1874

Edward Dickinson dies.

1875

Mrs. Dickinson becomes bedridden due to a stroke.

1880

Austin has first bout with malaria.

1881

President Garfield shot.

1882

Austin begins affair with Mabel Loomis Todd; Mabel sings for Emily behind a closed door; mother Emily Norcross Dickinson dies.

1883

Nephew Gilbert Dickinson dies.

1884

Emily has first attack of kidney disease.

1886

Emily Dickinson dies.

1890

Poems published, edited by Thomas Higginson and Mabel Loomis Todd.

1891

Second series of *Poems* published, edited by Todd and Higginson.

1894

Letters of Emily Dickinson published, edited by Mabel Loomis Todd.

1895

Austin dies.

1896

Third series of *Poems* published, edited by Todd; Vinnie successfully sues Todd for copyright ownership.

1899

Vinnie dies.

1913

Susan dies.

1914

The Single Hound published, edited by Martha Dickinson Bianchi.

FOR FURTHER RESEARCH

Millicent Todd Bingham, *Ancestors' Brocades: The Literary Debut of Emily Dickinson*. New York: Harper & Brothers, 1945.

Caesar R. Blake and Carlton F. Wells, *The Recognition of Emily Dickinson: Selected Criticism Since 1890*. Ann Arbor: University of Michigan Press, 1965.

Harold Bloom, ed., *Emily Dickinson*. New York: Chelsea House, 1985.

Carl Bode, ed., *Midcentury America: Life in the 1850s*. Carbondale and Edwardsville: Southern Illinois University Press, 1972.

Joanne Dobson, *Dickinson and the Strategies of Reticence: The Woman Writer in Nineteenth-Century America*. Bloomington: Indiana University Press, 1989.

Paul Ferlazzo, ed., *Critical Essays on Emily Dickinson*. Boston: G.K. Hall, 1984.

Albert J. Gelpi, *Emily Dickinson: The Mind of a Poet*. Cambridge, MA: Harvard University Press, 1966.

Daniel Walker Howe, ed., *Victorian America*. Philadelphia: University of Pennsylvania Press, 1976.

Suzanne Juhasz, ed., *Feminist Critics Read Emily Dickinson*. Bloomington: Indiana University Press, 1983.

Richard H. Rupp, *Critics on Emily Dickinson*. Coral Gables: University of Miami Press, 1972.

Richard B. Sewall, *The Life of Emily Dickinson*. New York: Farrar, Straus and Giroux, 1974.

William R. Sherwood, *Circumference and Circumstance: Stages in the Mind and Art of Emily Dickinson*. New York: Columbia University Press, 1968.

Judy Jo Small, *Positive as Sound: Emily Dickinson's Rhyme.* Athens: University of Georgia Press, 1990.

Barton Levi St. Armand, *Emily Dickinson and Her Culture: The Soul's Society.* Cambridge, England: Cambridge University Press, 1984.

U.S. Civil War Centennial Commission, *The United States on the Eve of the Civil War: As Described in the 1860 Census.* Washington, D.C.: U.S. Government Printing Office, 1963.

Cynthia Griffin Wolf, *Emily Dickinson.* New York: Knopf, 1986.

WORKS BY EMILY DICKINSON

Poems by Emily Dickinson (1890)
Poems by Emily Dickinson, Second Series (1891)
Letters of Emily Dickinson, 2 vols. (1894)
Poems by Emily Dickinson, Third Series (1896)
The Single Hound (1914)
Further Poems of Emily Dickinson (1929)
Unpublished Poems of Emily Dickinson (1935)
Bolts of Melody (1945)
The Poems of Emily Dickinson, 3 vols. (1955)
The Complete Poems of Emily Dickinson (1960)

INDEX